Bringing Down the Duke

EVIE DUNMORE

JOVE
New York

A JOVE BOOK
Published by Berkley
An imprint of Penguin Random House LLC
1745 Broadway, New York, NY 10019

Printed in the United States of America

Cover design and illustration by Farjana Yasmin
Cover background references courtesy of Shutterstock
Book design by Laura K. Corless

ISBN 978-1-64385-403-8

For Opa,
who taught me I could take on anything,
but don't have to put up with everything.

Chapter 1

Kent, August 1879

Absolutely not. What an utterly harebrained idea, Annabelle."
Gilbert's eyes had the rolling look of a hare that knew the hounds were upon him.

Annabelle lowered her lashes. She knew it would look demure, and demure placated her cousin best when he was all in a fluster. Of all the types of men she had learned to manage, the "ignorant yet self-important" type was not exactly the most challenging. Then again, when her very fate lay in the hands of such a man, it added insult to injury. Gilbert would snatch the chance of a lifetime from her here in his cramped little study and go straight back to admiring his freshly pinned butterflies in the display case on the desk between them.

"What would be next," he said, "joining the circus? Standing for Parliament?"

"I understand that it's unusual," she said, "but—"

"You are not going to Oxford," he bellowed, and slapped his hand down on the desk.

Her father's old desk. Left to Gilbert in her father's will rather than to her. The dignified piece of furniture did nothing for her cousin: age-worn on four carved lion paws, it would have bolstered the authority of any man throning behind it, but Gilbert was still fluffed up like a startled chicken. Well. It was understandable that he felt ambushed. She had surprised herself. After five long years as Gilbert's maid for everything, she hadn't expected to feel a yearning urge ever again. She'd kept her head down, her feet on the ground, and had accepted that the parish borders of Chorleywood were the boundaries to her dreams. And then the news that Oxford University had opened a women's college had slammed into her chest with the force of an arrow.

She had wanted to ignore it, but, after barely a week, her self-control, so laboriously acquired, had crumbled.

But surely, this was not just a case of her wanting too much. Who knew for how long Gilbert's ramshackle household would stand between her and destitution? Between her and a position where she was easy prey for a lecherous master? During the day, she went through her routines like an automaton. At night, the awareness crept in that she was forever balancing on the precipice of an abyss and there, at the bottom, lurked old age in the workhouse. In her nightmares, she fell and fell.

Her fingers felt for the slim envelope in her apron pocket. Her Oxford admission letter. A proper education could break her fall.

"This conversation is over," Gilbert said.

Her hands knotted into fists. *Calm. Stay calm.* "I didn't mean to quarrel with you," she said softly. "I thought you would be delighted." A blatant lie, that.

Gilbert's brow furrowed. "Delighted, me?" His expression slid into something like concern. "Are you quite all right?"

"Given the advantages for your family, I assumed you'd welcome the opportunity."

"Advantages—"

"I apologize, cousin. I shouldn't have wasted your precious time." She made to rise.

"Now, don't be hasty," Gilbert said, waving his hand. "Sit, sit."

She gazed at him limpidly. "I know that you have great plans for the boys," she said, "and an Oxford-certified governess would help with that."

"Indeed I have plans, sound plans," Gilbert clucked, "but you already know more Greek and Latin than is necessary, certainly more than is appropriate. And 'tis well known that too much education derails the female brain, and where's the advantage for us in that, eh?"

"I could have applied for a position as governess or companion at the manor."

This was her final shot—if mentioning Baron Ashby, lord of the manor up the hill and owner of their parish, did not move Gilbert, nothing would. Gilbert fair worshipped the ground the nobleman walked on.

Indeed, he stilled. She could almost hear his mind beginning to work, churning like the old kitchen grindstone, *old* because Gilbert never had enough coin to maintain the cottage. A logical consequence when his small salary for ringing the church bells remained the same while his family steadily grew.

"Well," Gilbert said, "that could earn a pretty penny. The master pays well."

"Indeed. But I understand. Even a fortune wouldn't justify impropriety."

"'Tis true, 'tis true, but it wouldn't be exactly improper, would it, given that it would serve a higher purpose."

"Oh," she cried, "I couldn't go, now that you've shown me all the flaws in my plan—what if my brain derailed . . ."

"Now, don't exaggerate," Gilbert said. "Your head is probably quite inured to books. However, we can't do without your hands for even a week. I'd have to hire help in your stead." He leveled an alarmingly cunning gaze at her. "The budget won't allow for that, as you know."

How unfortunate that he had to discover financial planning *now*.

No doubt he wanted her to compensate any expenses her departure would cause, since she cost him exactly . . . nothing. Unfortunately, her small scholarship would barely keep her fed and clothed.

She leaned forward in her chair. "How much would you pay a maid, cousin?"

Gilbert's eyes widened with surprise, but he recovered quickly enough.

He crossed his arms. "Two pounds."

She arched a brow. "Two pounds?"

His expression turned mulish. "Yes. Beth is, eh, in a certain way again. I'll hire additional help."

He wouldn't, but she managed to take the bite out of her voice. "Then I shall send you two pounds every month."

Gilbert frowned. "Now, how will you manage that?"

"Quite easily." *I have absolutely no idea.* "There'll be plenty of pupils in need of tutoring."

"I see."

He was not convinced, and neither was she, for even the maids at the manor wouldn't earn two pounds a month, and if she scraped together an extra two shillings, it would be a miracle.

She rose and stuck out her hand across the desk. "You have my word."

Gilbert eyed her hand as if it were an alien creature. "Tell me," he then said, "how can I be sure that those Oxford airs and graces won't rub off on you, and that you will come back here in the end?"

Her mind blanked. Odd. The entire purpose of wheedling permission out of Gilbert had been to keep her place in his household—a woman needed a place, any place. But something bristled inside her at the thought of giving her word on the matter.

"But where else would I go?" she asked.

Gilbert pursed his lips. He absently patted his belly. He took his time before he spoke again. "If you fell behind on your payments," he finally said, "I'd have to ask you to return."

Her mind turned the words over slowly. Calling her back meant he had to let her go first. He was letting her go.

"Understood," she managed.

The press of his soft fingers barely registered against her callused palm. She steadied herself against the desk, the only solid thing in a suddenly fuzzy room.

"You'll need a chaperone, of course," she heard him say.

She couldn't stifle a laugh, a throaty sound that almost startled her. "But I'm twenty-and-five years old."

"Hmph," Gilbert said. "I suppose with such an education, you'll make yourself wholly unmarriageable anyway."

"How fortunate then that I have no desire to marry."

"Yes, yes," Gilbert said. She knew he didn't approve of voluntary spinsterhood, *'twas unnatural*. But any concerns expressed over her virtue were at best a nod to protocol, and he probably suspected as much. Or, like everyone in Chorleywood, he suspected something.

As if on cue, he scowled. "There is one more thing we have to be clear about, Annabelle, quite clear indeed."

The words were already hovering between them, like buzzards readying to strike.

Have them pick at her; at this point, her sensibilities were as callused as her hands.

"Oxford, as is well known, is a place of vice," Gilbert began, "a viper pit, full of drunkards and debauchery. Should you become entangled in anything improper, if there's but a shadow of a doubt about your moral conduct, much as it pains me, you will forfeit your place in this house. A man in my position, in service of the Church of England, must stay clear of scandal."

He was, no doubt, referring to the sort of scandal involving a man. He had no reason to worry on that account. There was, however, the matter of her scholarship. Gilbert seemed to assume that it had been granted by the university, but in truth her benefactor was the National Society for Women's Suffrage, which she now had to support in their quest for a woman's right to vote. In her defense, the society had first come to her attention through a certain Lady Lucie Tedbury and her adverts for women's stipends, not because she had an interest in political activism, but it was a safe guess that on the list of moral outrages, *votes for women* would rank only marginally below *scandals of passion* in Gilbert's book.

"Fortunately, an old spinster from the country should be quite safe from any scandals," she said brightly, "even at Oxford."

Gilbert's squint returned. She tensed as he perused her. Had she overdone it? She might be past the first blush of youth, and digging up potatoes in wind, sun, and rain had penciled a few delicate lines around her eyes. But the mirror in the morning still showed the face of her early twenties, the same slanted cheekbones, the fine nose, and, a nod to her French ancestry, a mouth that always seemed on the verge of a pout. A mouth that compelled a man to go quite mad for her, or so she had been told.

She quirked her lips wryly. Whenever she met her reflection, she saw her eyes. Their green sparkle had been long dulled by an awareness no fresh debutante would possess, an awareness that shielded her far better from scandals than fading looks ever could. Truly, the last thing she wanted was to get into trouble over a man again.

Chapter 2

N ow," said Lady Lucie, "for the new members among us, there are three rules for handing a leaflet to a gentleman. One: identify a man of influence. Two: approach him firmly, but with a smile. Three: remember they can sense if you are afraid, but they are usually more afraid of you."

"Like dogs," Annabelle muttered.

The lady's sharp gray gaze shifted to her. "Why, yes."

Clearly there were good ears on this one, something to keep in mind.

Annabelle clutched the ends of her shawl against her chest in a frozen fist. The rough wool offered little protection from the chilly London fog wafting across Parliament Square, certainly not from the cutting glances of passersby. Parliament was closed for the season, but there were still plenty of gentlemen strolling around Westminster, engineering the laws that governed them all. Her stomach plunged at the thought of approaching any such man. No decent woman would talk to a stranger in the street, certainly not while brandishing pamphlets that boldly declared *The Married Women's Property Act makes a slave of every wife!*

There was of course some truth to this headline—thanks to the Property Act, a woman of means lost all her property to her husband on her wedding day . . . Still, given the disapproving glances skewering their little group, she had tried to hold her pamphlets discreetly. Her efforts had been demolished swiftly the moment Lady Lucie, secretary of the National Society for Women's Suffrage, had opened her mouth for her motivating speech. The lady was a deceptively ethereal-looking creature, dainty like a china doll with perfectly smooth pale blond hair and a delicate heart-shaped face, but her voice blared like a foghorn across the square as she charged her disciples.

How had these ladies been coerced into attendance? They were huddling like sheep in a storm, clearly wishing to be elsewhere, and she'd bet her shawl that none of them were beholden to the purse strings of a stipend committee. The red-haired girl next to her looked unassuming enough with her round brown eyes and her upturned nose, pink from the cold, but thanks to the Oxford grapevine, she knew who the young woman was: Miss Harriet Greenfield, daughter of Britain's most powerful banking tycoon. The mighty Julien Greenfield probably had no idea that his daughter was working for the cause. Gilbert certainly would have an apoplexy if he learned about any of this.

Miss Greenfield held her leaflets gingerly, as if she half expected them to try and take a bite out of her hand. "Identify, approach, smile," she murmured. "That's simple enough."

Hardly. With their collars flipped high and top hats pulled low, every man hasting past was a fortress.

The girl looked up, and their gazes caught. Best to give a cordial smile and to glance away.

"You are Miss Archer, aren't you? The student with the stipend?"

Miss Greenfield was peering up at her over her purple fur stole.

Of course. The grapevine in Oxford worked both ways.

"The very same, miss," she said, and wondered what it would be, pity or derision?

Miss Greenfield's eyes lit with curiosity instead. "You must be awfully clever to win a stipend."

"Why, thank you," Annabelle said slowly. "Awfully overeducated, rather."

Miss Greenfield giggled, sounding very young. "I'm Harriet Greenfield," she said, and extended a gloved hand. "Is this your first suffrage meeting?"

Lady Lucie seemed too absorbed by her own ongoing speech about justice and John Stuart Mill to notice them talking.

Still, Annabelle lowered her voice to a whisper. "It is my first meeting, yes."

"Oh, lovely—mine, too," Miss Greenfield said. "I so hope that this is going to be a good fit. It's certainly much harder to find one's noble cause than one would expect, isn't it?"

Annabelle frowned. "One's . . . noble cause?"

"Yes, don't you think everyone should have a noble cause? I wanted to join the Ladies' Committee for Prison Reform, but Mama would not let me. So I tried the Royal Horticulture Society, but that was a miss."

"I'm sorry to hear that."

"It's a process." Miss Greenfield was unperturbed. "I have a feeling that women's rights are a worthy cause, though I have to say the very idea of walking up to a gentleman and—"

"Is there a problem, Miss Greenfield?"

The voice cracked like a shot, making both of them flinch. Bother. Lady Lucie was glaring at them, one small fist propped on her hip.

Miss Greenfield ducked her head. "N-no."

"No? I had the impression that you were discussing something."

Miss Greenfield gave a noncommittal squeak. Lady Lucie was known to take no prisoners. There were rumors that she had single-handedly caused a diplomatic incident involving the Spanish ambassador and a silver fork . . .

"We were just a little worried, given that we are new at this," Annabelle said, and Lady Lucie's flinty gaze promptly skewered her.

Holy bother. The secretary was not a woman to mask moods with sugary smiles. Where a hundred women clamored to be domestic sun rays, this one was a thunderstorm.

Surprisingly, the lady settled for a brusque nod. "Worry not," she said. "You may work together."

Miss Greenfield perked up immediately. Annabelle bared her teeth in a smile. If they lobbied but one man of influence between the two of them, she'd be surprised.

With a confidence she did not feel, she led the girl toward the busy hackney coach stop where the air smelled of horses.

"Identify, approach, smile," Miss Greenfield hummed. "Do you think this can be done while keeping a low profile, Miss Archer? You see, my father . . . I'm not sure he is aware that working for the cause is such a public affair."

Annabelle cast a poignant glance around the square. They were in the very heart of London, in the shadow of Big Ben, surrounded by people who probably all had dealings with Miss Greenfield's father in some shape or form. Keeping a low profile would have entailed staying back in Oxford. It would have been much nicer to stay in Oxford. A gent nearing the hackneys slowed, stared, then gave her a wide berth, his lips twisting as if he had stepped into something unpleasant. Another suffragist nearby did not seem to fare much better—the men brushed her off with sneers and flicks of their gentlemanly hands. Something about these contemptuous hands made a long-suppressed emotion stir in the pit of her stomach, and it burned up her throat like acid. *Anger.*

"It's not as though my father is opposed to women's rights as such—oh," Miss Greenfield breathed. She had gone still, her attention fixing on something beyond Annabelle's shoulder.

She turned.

Near the entrance of Parliament, a group of three men materialized from the mist. They were approaching the hackneys, rapidly and purposeful like a steam train.

Uneasy awareness prickled down her spine.

The man on the left looked like a brute, with his hulking figure straining his fine clothes. The man in the middle was a gentleman, his grim face framed by large sideburns. The third man . . . The third man was what they were looking for: a man of influence. His hat was tilted low, half obscuring his face, and his well-tailored topcoat gave him the straight shoulders of an athlete rather than a genteel slouch. But he moved with that quiet, commanding certainty that said he knew he could own the ground he walked on.

As if he'd sensed her scrutiny, he looked up.

She froze.

His eyes were striking, icy clear and bright with intelligence, a cool, penetrating intelligence that would cut right to the core of things, to assess, dismiss, eviscerate.

All at once, she was as transparent and fragile as glass.

Her gaze jerked away, her heart racing. She knew his type. She had spent years resenting this kind of man, the kind who had his confidence bred into his bones, who oozed entitlement from the self-assured way he held himself to his perfectly straight aristo nose. He'd make people cower with a well-aimed glare.

It suddenly seemed important not to cower away from this man.

They wanted men of influence to hear them out? Well, she had just completed step one: *identify the gentleman.*

Two: *approach him firmly* . . . Her fingers tightened around the leaflets as her feet propelled her forward, right into his path.

His pale eyes narrowed.

Smile.

A push against her shoulder knocked her sideways. "Make way, madam!"

The brute. She had forgotten he existed; now he sent her stumbling over her own feet, and for a horrible beat the world careened around her.

A firm hand clamped around her upper arm, steadying her.

Her gaze flew up and collided with a cool glare.

Drat. It was the aristocrat himself.

And *holy hell*, this man went quite beyond what they had set out to catch. There wasn't an ounce of softness in him, not a trace of a chink in his armor. He was clean shaven, his Nordic-blond hair cropped short at the sides; in fact, everything about him was clean, straight, and efficient: the prominent nose, the slashes of his brows, the firm line of his jaw. He had the polished, impenetrable surface of a glacier.

Her stomach gave a sickening lurch.

She was face to face with the rarest of breeds: a perfectly unmanageable man.

She should run.

Her feet were rooted to the spot. She couldn't stop staring. Those eyes. A world of tightly leashed intensity shimmered in their cold depths that held her, pulled her in, until awareness sizzled between them bright and disturbing like an electric current.

The man's lips parted. His gaze dropped to her mouth. A flash of heat brightened his eyes, there and gone like lightning.

Well. No matter their position in the world, they all liked her mouth.

She forced up her hand with the pamphlets and held it right under his nose. "Amend the Married Women's Property Act, sir?"

His eyes were, impossibly, icier than before. "You play a risky game, miss."

A voice as cool and imperious as his presence.

It heated rather than calmed her blood.

"With all due respect, the risk of being pushed by a gentleman in bright daylight is usually quite low," she said. "Would you release me now, please?"

His gaze snapped to his right hand. Which was still wrapped around her arm.

His face shuttered.

The next moment, she was free.

The bustle and noise of Parliament Square reached her ears again, unnaturally loud.

The press of strong fingers round her arm lingered like the afterglow of a burn.

He was already moving past her, staring ahead, his two companions rushing after him.

She swallowed and found her mouth was dry. Her lips still tingled as if he'd brushed over them with a fingertip.

A small, gloved hand touched her sleeve, and she jumped. Miss Greenfield's brown eyes were wide with concern and . . . awe. "Miss. Are you all right?"

"Yes." *No.* Her cheeks were burning as if she had fallen nose first onto the damp cobblestones. She smoothed a trembling hand over her skirts. "Well then," she said with false cheer, "I gather the gentlemen were not interested."

From the corner of her eye, she watched the ice lord and his minions file into a large carriage. Meanwhile, Miss Greenfield was contemplating her with covert wariness, probably trying to determine politely whether she was a little unhinged. She wasn't, but there was no denying that she had acted on impulse. Lord help her. She hadn't been impulsive in so long.

"Do you know who that was?" Miss Greenfield asked.

Annabelle shook her head.

"That," the girl said, "was the Duke of Montgomery."

A duke. Of course the first man she tried to lobby turned out to be a duke, just a fraction short of a prince . . .

A pair of heels clicked rapidly behind them; Lady Lucie was approaching with the force of a small frigate. "Was that what it looked like?" she demanded. "Did you just try to lobby the Duke of Montgomery?"

Annabelle's spine straightened. "I didn't know that he was excluded from our efforts."

"He's not. Just no one has ever tried going near him before." The lady cocked her head and looked Annabelle up and down. "I can't decide whether you are one of the bravest or one of the most foolish women I've recently recruited."

"I didn't know who he was," Annabelle said. "He just looked like a man of influence."

"Well, you had that right," Lady Lucie said. "He is one of the most influential men in the country."

"Wouldn't it be worth a try, then, to speak to him?"

"Have you seen him? This is a man who divorced his wife after barely a year, kept her dowry, and made her disappear. We can safely assume that he is a lost battle where women's rights are concerned, and not squander our limited resources on him."

"A divorce?" She might be from a small place like Chorleywood, but even she knew that the aristocracy did not divorce. Still, she could not seem to let it go. "Would the duke's opinion sway other men of influence?"

Lady Lucie gave an unladylike snort. "He could sway the entire upcoming election if he wished."

"But that means that if he's against us, it hardly matters how many of the others we win for the cause, doesn't it?"

"Possibly." A frown creased Lady Lucie's brow. "But it is of no consequence. Our army is not made for attacking such a fortress."

"How about a siege, then," Annabelle said, "or a subterfuge, like a big, wooden horse."

Two pairs of eyes narrowed at her.

Oh, grand, she had thought that out loud. Being pushed by that man must've shaken her more than she'd thought.

"Well, I do like the sound of that," Lady Lucie drawled. "We should put Montgomery onto the agenda for next week's meeting." A smile curved her lips as she stuck out her hand. "Call me Lucie. You too, Miss Greenfield. And do excuse me, I believe that is Lord Chiltern over there."

They watched her plunge into the fog, her red scarf flapping behind her like a pennant. When Miss Greenfield turned back to Annabelle, her expression was serious. "You saved me from Lucie biting my head off in front of everyone earlier. Please call me Hattie."

It felt a little wrong, such familiarity first with a lady, and now an heiress. Annabelle took a deep breath. This was her new life, being a student, petitioning dukes, shaking hands with unfathomably wealthy girls in purple fur stoles. It seemed that the wisest course of action was to pretend that this was all perfectly normal.

"My pleasure," she said. "And apologies for not keeping a low profile earlier."

Hattie's laugh floated merrily across the square, attracting almost as many scandalized glances as their pamphlets.

They failed to enthuse any man of influence that afternoon. In between half-hearted attempts, Annabelle's gaze kept straying back to the direction where the coach with the duke had disappeared.

Chapter 3

When Her Majesty requested a meeting, even a duke had to comply. Even when the duke in question was notoriously occupied with running one of the oldest dukedoms in the kingdom and preferred to stay far from the madding crowds of London. One did not say no to the queen, and Sebastian Devereux, nineteenth Duke of Montgomery, knew that he was no exception to that rule. It behooved a man to know his limitations. It meant he could heed or ignore them precisely as the situation required.

He navigated the corridors of Buckingham Palace with long strides, effectively herding the royal usher before him. Secretary Lambton and Lambton's protection officer were, as usual, trotting behind somewhere.

What did she want?

The last time the queen had summoned him at such short notice, he had walked out of her apartments tasked with ending a trade war with the Ottoman Empire. It had shot his routine to hell, and he was still dealing with the backlog of paperwork. He'd prefer it to be an even greater task now—one so monumental that it would entitle him to ask for something in return.

He handed his hat and greatcoat to one of the footmen lining the hallway to the royal apartment.

"You," he said to Lambton's protection officer.

"Your Grace?"

"There was no need to push the woman."

The officer's thick brows lowered. "The one on the square?"

"Yes. Or have you accosted any others today?"

"Eh—no, Your Grace."

Sebastian nodded. "If I ever hear that you have laid a hand on a woman again, it will be the end of your employ."

The officer was not his employee. But if he wanted to see someone lose his position, Sebastian made it happen. Hectic red splotches spread on the man's throat. He bowed. "As ye wish, Yer Grace."

An East End accent, and showing so easily? Times were dire when even the palace had trouble finding decent staff.

The large wing doors swung open, revealing the usher and the gilded interior beyond.

"Your Grace. Sir Lambton." The usher dipped low as he stepped back. "Her Majesty will see you now."

The queen's stout figure rose from her armchair in a rustle of stiff black skirts.

"Montgomery." She started toward him, one bejeweled hand extended. "I am pleased to see you."

Her upturned lips said as much. She was in an appreciative mood. For now.

"Sir Lambton"—she turned to her secretary—"we trust your journey was uneventful?"

Lambton shook his head. "A near miss, ma'am. We were attacked by a feminist on Parliament Square."

The corners of her mouth pulled down sharply. "I daresay."

"She made straight for the duke."

"The gall!"

"I escaped unharmed, ma'am," Sebastian said wryly.

"This time," the queen said. "This time. Oh, they ought to be given a good whipping. Wicked, unnatural demands! And who would suffer, if they got their way? Why, these women. No gentleman in his right mind is going to be willing to protect such mannish creatures should the need arise. Tell me, Montgomery," she demanded, "did she look terribly mannish?"

Mannish? The woman had had the softest, most inviting lips he'd seen on this side of the channel. A man could easily lose himself in the pleasures to be had from a mouth like hers. But what was more remarkable was that she had looked him straight in the eye. Green eyes, slightly slanted. Her smile had not touched them.

He shook his head. "She looked female to me, ma'am."

"Hmph." The queen looked unimpressed. "You know what happens when common people have grand ideas? Chaos. Chaos happens. Just look at France." She all but whirled on her heels. "Those are tomorrow's concerns, however," she said. "Today there are more pressing matters."

Sebastian tensed. *Pressing* sounded promising. She had something that belonged to him, or her nephew did, and he would get it back only if he could offer her something she would want more. In his sixteen years as Montgomery, there had never been such a thing. He understood. It was easier to control a duke, even a dutiful one, when one held his eight-hundred-year-old family seat hostage.

The queen lowered herself back into her armchair with such gravitas one could imagine it were her throne.

"You are a rare sort of man, Montgomery," she began. "You assess, you decide, you execute, very efficiently and, remarkably . . . modestly." She fingered the diamond-encrusted crucifix that dangled from her necklace. "And I so favor modesty."

He gave a modest nod, when in fact he wasn't modest at all. He did things in moderation because it yielded results, but she was not the first to misread him on that account.

And then she said: "I want you to be the chief strategic advisor for the election campaign of the Tory party."

Ducal breeding kept his expression completely bland, but his mind screeched to a halt. "For the upcoming election?"

The queen frowned. "Yes. Something has gone awry. The Liberal party has gained a surprising lead."

Not that surprising, if one looked at the country through the sober glasses of reality instead of Disraeli's rose-tinted party ideology. But the queen had an absurd soft spot for the prime minister, upstart that he was, and now she was asking him, Sebastian, to keep the man in power?

The German cuckoo clock on the mantelpiece ticked away strategic seconds as he scanned the facts. The election was in March, little more than five months from now. Hardly enough time to turn things around, not when one had ten estates, policy work, and one unruly brother to manage. The question was, how much did she want him in particular to turn this election? Very much. He was one of her most trusted advisors at only thirty-and-five because he was good at what he did.

He locked eyes with her. "I'm honored, but I'm not a politician, ma'am."

She stiffened. "Leave us, Lambton," she commanded.

The scowl on her face deepened as soon as the door had clicked shut. "You are a politician in all but name and no one can contest your leadership," she said. "Your public endeavors have an unbroken record of success."

"I'm presently too occupied to do the task justice, ma'am."

"Regrettable," she said coolly, and, when he did not reply, "pray, is there something that would allow you to change your priorities?"

She wasn't asking as much as she was daring him to make demands on the queen of England.

His gaze didn't waver. "I spend a lot of my time convincing Hartford to sell me back Montgomery Castle," he said. "If someone convinced him to return the house, I would be free to advise the Tories."

Her eyes narrowed. "To *sell* you back the castle? And there we had been under the impression it was never properly purchased in the first place." Below her impenetrable skirts, a small foot was tapping rapidly. "Remind us, Montgomery, how did your family seat come into my nephew's possession?"

He supposed he deserved it. "My father lost it to the marquess in a card game, ma'am."

The queen's brows rose in mock surprise. "Ah. That's right. You see, one would think a castle deserves to be lost, if it is held in such low regard as to be staked in a hand of cards, would you not agree?"

"Unreservedly," he said, "but then, I am not my father."

The *tap-tap-tap* of her foot ceased. The silence that ensued was rife with an oddly personal tension. She had watched him for years as he tried to piece his family's legacy back together, never quite hindering him, never helping him, either. Except once, he suspected, when he had rid himself of his wife and the consequences had been surprisingly manageable.

"Indeed you are not," she said. "Hence, I want you to take over the campaign."

"Ma'am—"

Her hand snapped up. "Very well. Hartford will make you an offer after the election."

His muscles tensed as if he had been slammed to the ground, making his next breath difficult.

"Is the offer contingent upon the election outcome?" he managed. One needed to be clear about such things.

She scoffed. "It certainly is. The final say over the victory is of course in the hands of higher powers, but would that not be all the proof we need that the castle was truly meant to return to you?"

His mind was already steps ahead as he stood and made his way toward the doors, rearranging his schedule for the upcoming months . . .

"Duke."

He turned back slowly.

The queen was reclining in her chair, a mean gleam in her blue eyes. "If this campaign is to succeed," she said, "your comportment has to be exemplary."

He suppressed a frown. His comportment was so exemplary, all the lines so skillfully toed, that not even a divorce had managed to ruin his standing.

"Some people rumor that you are turning into an eccentric," she said, "but eccentricity is so unbecoming in a man not yet forty, agreed?"

"Agreed—"

"And yet you are hardly ever seen at parties. You do not hold dinners, you are veritably unsociable, when everyone knows politics is made over a good feast. And there was no New Year's party last year, nor the year before."

And the year before that only because there had been a duchess to manage the whole affair.

He gritted his teeth. There was no mistaking where this was going.

"The Montgomery New Year's Eve party was famous across the continent when I was a girl," the queen continued. "Your grandfather hosted the most splendid fireworks. Granted, back then it all took place at Montgomery Castle, but Claremont should do."

"You wish for me to hold a New Year's Eve party." His voice was dry as dust.

She clapped her hands together with a cheerful smack. "Why indeed. You are running late with the invitations, of course, but people will change their plans. No one will want to give the impression of not having been invited to the event of the year. So do your duty, Duke. Host a party. Make merry."

⤎⥈⤏

Make merry. The words bounced around him mockingly as the train rumbled back toward Wiltshire. Sebastian dragged his stare away from the darkening horizon.

Ramsey had just finished laying out his notebook, fountain pen, and ink blotter on the narrow table before him and made to withdraw to the servant corner of the coach.

"Ramsey, draw up a list of people needed to put together a New Year's Eve party."

Well-trained as he was, the valet couldn't stop his eyes from widening with surprise before schooling his features.

"Yes, Your Grace."

"There will have to be fireworks; expenses are of no consequence."

"Understood, Your Grace."

"And a ball," Sebastian added darkly. "I need a concept for a winter ball by next week."

"Of course, Your Grace." Ramsey reached inside his jacket and produced the slim silver case with the cigarettes. He placed it next to the ink blotter and retreated.

Sebastian took up his pen. The queen's retaliation had hit its mark. Hardly a punishment, a house party, but then, she knew how they annoyed him: the stomping crowds, the inane chatter, the stuffy air, the intrusion on his home and his work—and there was no duchess to bear the brunt of the organizing and socializing. He stilled. Was that the queen's true intention, making him feel the absence of a wife?

He put the pen down and reached for the cigarettes. He did not need reminding. A man his age should long have a duchess running his house and an entire pack of sons underfoot. And every single society matron knew that, too. They thrust their debutante daughters at him whenever he did make a show—seventeen-year-old girls, all vying to be the next Duchess of Montgomery. All of them too frightened of him to even look him in the face. His mouth curved into a sardonic smile. They would have to bear a whole lot more than look at him if they were his wife.

Unbidden, a clear green gaze flashed across his mind. The woman on the square. She had looked him straight in the eye. *She had talked back at him.* Ladies of his acquaintance had yet to dare do such a thing, but women as far below his station as her? Inconceivable. And yet Green Eyes had dared. She had split from the herd, from that faceless crowd that usually just milled at the fringes of his life, and had stepped right into his path . . . Presumptuous wench. Possibly unhinged.

He flipped open his notebook, and as he set pen to paper, all vanished but the task at hand. Castle Montgomery. Given to the first duke for services rendered during the Battle of Hastings, lost by the eighteenth duke in a hand of cards. He would get it back, even if it was the last thing he did.

Chapter 4

———❦———

"You seem distracted, Miss Archer."

A marksman-sharp gaze pinned her over the rim of metal-framed glasses, and Annabelle felt a ripple of both guilt and alarm. With his patched tweed jacket, high forehead, and impatient frown, Professor Jenkins looked every inch the brilliant academic he was. Barely forty, he was already a titan in the field of ancient Greek warfare, so if there had ever been a need to pay attention, it was during his morning tutorial.

She looked up at her father's former correspondent with contrition. "My apologies, Professor."

He leaned forward over the desk. "It's the bloody knitting, isn't it?"

"I beg your pardon?"

"The knitting," he repeated, eyeing Mrs. Forsyth balefully. "The *click-click-click* . . . it is maddening, like a furiously leaking tap."

The clicking behind Annabelle stopped abruptly, and Mrs. Forsyth's consternation filled the room. Annabelle cringed. The woman was rightfully offended—after all, Annabelle paid her sixpence an hour to sit right there, because Gilbert, confound him, had been right about one thing: she did need a chaperone. One who was approved by the warden of her college, no less. Female students were not allowed to enter the town center unescorted, nor could they be alone with a professor. Mrs. Forsyth, widowed, elderly, and smartly dressed, certainly looked the part of a respectable guardian.

But if Jenkins was vexed by the sound of knitting, she had to find another solution. He was the titan, after all. His lessons turned crumbling old pages into meaningful windows to the past; his outstanding intellect lit her own mind on fire. And in order to teach her, he took the trouble to come to the classroom the university had given to the female students: a chamber with mismatched furniture above the bakery in Little Clarendon Street.

A bakery. That was the crux of the situation. It was not the knitting that was distracting; it was the warm, yeasty scent of freshly baked bread that wafted through the cracks in the door . . .

A cart rumbled past noisily on the street below.

The professor slammed his copy of Thucydides shut with an annoyed thud.

"That is it for today," he said. "I have no doubt you will come up with an original take on this chapter by tomorrow."

Tomorrow? The warm glow following his praise faded quickly—*tomorrow* would mean another night shift at her desk. They were piling up fast here, faster than in Chorleywood.

She watched Jenkins furtively as she slid her pen and notebook back into her satchel. She'd been surprised how youthful the professor looked when, after years of dry scientific correspondence, she had finally met him in person. He was lanky, his face unlined thanks to a life spent in dimly lit archives. He was also mercurial, lost in thought one moment, sharp as a whip the next. Managing him could pose a challenge.

Downstairs in the bakery, someone began banging metal pots with great enthusiasm.

Jenkins pinched the bridge of his nose. "Come to my office in St. John's the next time," he said.

St. John's. One of the oldest, wealthiest colleges at Oxford. They said its wine collection alone could pay for the crown jewels.

"But no needles, no yarn," Jenkins said, "understood?"

⁕

Annabelle hurried down St. Giles with a still disgruntled Mrs. Forsyth in tow. She would have liked to meander and soak up the sight of the enchanting sandstone walls framing the street, but they were running late for the suffragist meeting. She could still *feel* the withered stones of the old structures, emanating centuries-old knowledge and an air of mystery. She had peeked through one of the medieval doors in the wall the other day, catching a glimpse of one of the beautiful gardens of the men's colleges that lay beyond, a little island of exotic trees and late-blooming flowers and hidden nooks, locked away like a gem in a jewelry box. Someday, she might find a way to sneak inside.

This week, the suffragists gathered at the Randolph. Hattie and her chaperoning great-aunt rented apartments in the plush hotel for the term and had kindly offered to host them all. The common room of her college, Lady Margaret Hall, would have sufficed for their small chapter, but their warden, Miss Wordsworth, didn't allow political activism on university grounds. *I shall tolerate the nature of your stipend*, she had told Annabelle during their first meeting, *but use the university's trust in you wisely*. An interesting woman, Miss Wordsworth—paying for the tutors from her own pocket to give women an education, but seeing no need whatsoever in helping women get the vote.

"Now what precisely is your group trying to achieve?" Mrs. Forsyth asked, her breath coming in audible puffs. Ah, she sounded so eerily like Aunt May when she said such things. *Now, what precisely was my nephew trying to achieve, overeducating you like this?* Aunt May had muttered something along those lines daily, during those long winter months they had spent up north together. Was that why she had chosen Mrs. Forsyth from the pool of warden-approved chaperones? She surreptitiously studied the woman from the corner of her eye. She looked a bit like Aunt May, too, with her small glasses perched on the tip of her nose . . .

"We ask that they amend the Married Women's Property Act," she said, "so that women can keep their own property after marriage."

Mrs. Forsyth frowned. "But why? Surely all the husband's worldly goods are the wife's as well?"

"But the goods would not be in her name," Annabelle said carefully. "And since only people with property to their name may vote, a woman must keep her own property if she wishes to have the vote."

Mrs. Forsyth clucked her tongue. "It is becoming clear to me why a fair girl like you has been left on the shelf. You are not only bookish but a radical political activist. All highly impractical in a wife."

"Quite," Annabelle said, because there was no way to pretend it was otherwise. She wouldn't make a convenient wife to any man she knew. It had probably been thus from the moment she had read about men like Achilles, Odysseus, Jason; demigods and men who knew how to navigate the seven seas. Men who could have taken her on an adventure. Perhaps her father should have made her read "Sleeping Beauty" instead of *The Iliad*—her life might have turned out quite differently.

At the Randolph, the meeting was about to begin: Lucie was rooting in a satchel next to a small speaker's desk. A dozen ladies had formed a chatty semicircle around Hattie's fireplace. A pink marble fireplace, with a vast, gold-framed mirror mounted above, leaf-gold, she guessed as she handed her coat to a maid.

Hattie was not here, and every seat was taken. Except one half of the French settee. The other half was occupied by a young woman wrapped in a battered old plaid. Annabelle recognized the plaid. The girl had been at Parliament Square: Lady Catriona Campbell. She

wasn't a student; she was the assistant to her father, Alastair Campbell, an Oxford professor, Scottish earl, and owner of a castle in the
Highlands. And now the lady startled her by giving her an awkward
little wave and sliding over to make more room.

A gauntlet of covert glances ensued as she moved toward the settee; yes, she was aware that her walking dress was plain and old.
Among the silky, narrow-cut modern gowns of the ladies, she must
look like a relic from a bygone era . . . *not quite as bygone as that tartan
shawl, though.*

She carefully lowered herself onto the settee's velvety seat.

"We have not yet met, I believe," she said to Lady Campbell. "I'm
Annabelle Archer."

The lady didn't look like the daughter of an earl: her face was half-
hidden behind a pair of round spectacles, and her raven hair was
pulled into an artless bun. And there was the way she wore that
shawl, quite like a turtle would wear its shell.

"I know who you are," Lady Campbell said. "You are the girl with
the stipend."

Her matter-of-factness was tempered by a soft Scottish lilt.

She seemed encouraged by Annabelle's smile, for her right hand
emerged from her plaid. "I'm Catriona. I saw you lobby the Duke of
Montgomery last week. That was very brave of you."

Annabelle absently shook the proffered hand. Montgomery. The
name brought it all back—the haughty aristocratic face, the cold
eyes, the firmness of his hand clasping her arm . . . She wasn't proud
of it, but their encounter had preoccupied her so much that she had
read up on him in the *Annals of the Aristocracy*. Like every duke worth
his salt, his ancestral line went straight to William the Conqueror,
with whom his forefathers had come over in 1066 to change the face
of Britain. His family had only amassed more land and wealth as the
centuries went by. He had become duke at nineteen. Nineteen sounded
awfully young for owning a substantial chunk of the country, but

recalling the duke's self-contained imperiousness, it seemed impossible that this man had ever been a boy. Perhaps he had sprung from somewhere fully formed, like a blond Greek demigod.

"Ladies." Lucie slapped a thick stack of papers onto her speaker's desk. Satisfied that she had everyone's attention, she gave the group a dark glance. "Our mission has just become more difficult. The Duke of Montgomery is the new advisor to the Tory election campaign."

Well, speaking of the devil.

A shocked murmur rose around Annabelle. She understood that some Tories were in favor of giving women the vote, but most were against it, whereas the opposing Liberals had a few members against women's suffrage and most in favor. The duke had thrown his weight behind the wrong party.

Lucie emerged from behind the desk with her papers. "Drastic circumstances demand drastic measures," she said as she handed out sheets, "so I propose we meet MPs in their offices from now on, and we will find out everything about them beforehand: their likes, their dislikes, and most importantly, their weaknesses. Then we tailor our approach to each man. He thinks he's an expert on justice? Use Plato to argue with him. He thinks his children will suffer should his wife get the vote? Tell him how independent women make better mothers. In short, ladies—know thy enemy."

Annabelle nodded. Strategic and manipulative—that usually worked.

The sheet Lucie had handed her was divided neatly into sections: general characteristics . . . voting record . . . notable scandals . . . *botheration*. This information was hardly common knowledge in her circles. She'd have to scour scandal sheets and public records—but when? Doing her coursework and tutoring pupils to pay Gilbert already pushed her working hours well into the night.

The door to the antechamber creaked, and Hattie crept into the room. She met Lucie's evil eye with an apologetic little smile and settled next to Annabelle in a cloud of expensive perfume.

"Good morning, Catriona, Annabelle," she chirped. "I'm late. What did I miss?"

Annabelle handed her a sheet. "We are going to spy on men of influence."

"How exciting. Oh, these would make a fabulous handbook on eligible bachelors!"

A snarl sounded from Lucie's direction. "Eligible bachelors? Have you paid any attention during our meetings?"

Hattie gave a startled huff.

"No man is eligible as long as you become his property the moment you marry him," Lucie said darkly.

"It's true, though, that the marriage-minded mamas will have a lot of this information," Lady Mabel dared to argue from the couch across.

"You may go about it by all means possible," Lucie allowed. "Just not marriage."

"And what makes you think the MPs will receive us?" Catriona asked.

"There's an election in March. Politicians like to look accessible in the months leading up to election day." Lucie turned to Annabelle, her elfin face expectant. "What do you think of this approach?"

"The idea is excellent," Annabelle said truthfully.

Lucie gave a satisfied little smile. "You inspired me. Seeing you walk up to Montgomery as if he were a mere mortal made me step back and look at our routine with a fresh eye."

"Finding information on Montgomery will be difficult," Hattie said. "He may be divorced, and we all know he wants his ancient castle back. But there's nothing ever written about him in the gossip sheets, and I read them all."

Lucie wrinkled her nose. "Because he's a favorite of the queen, so the press doesn't dare touch him. No, we need drastic measures where

Montgomery is concerned. Catriona, do you not tutor his brother? Lord Devereux?"

Catriona shook her head. "It was last term, in hieroglyphics."

"Excellent," Lucie said. "Find an excuse for your paths to cross and then you inveigle yourself . . ."

Catriona recoiled. "Me? Oh no."

Lucie's eyes narrowed. "Why ever not? You are already acquainted."

"I taught him hieroglyphs," Catriona mumbled, "that's quite different from . . ."

". . . inveigling," Hattie supplied.

"But—"

Catriona made to disappear into her plaid.

"Never mind," Lucie said brusquely. "Annabelle will do it."

Annabelle looked up, astonished and a little alarmed. "Me?"

"If you please."

"I'm afraid I cannot think of any reason to introduce myself to his lordship."

Lucie began to look strained. "You do not need a reason. You are the most beautiful of all of us. Try looking terribly impressed by whatever he says and a young man is liable to tell you all his secrets before he knows it."

"I'm not—" Annabelle began, when Hattie cut her off with a cheerful wave.

"But you are," the girl chirped, "very beautiful, such a lovely profile. I have been thinking how I'd love for you to sit for my Helen of Troy. Would you?"

Annabelle blinked. "I beg your pardon?"

Hattie wiggled her fingers at her. "I study fine arts. I paint. Thank goodness for gloves, I have the most pitiful hands in England."

No, that would be my hands, Annabelle thought. The calluses would not go away in a lifetime. "I'm honored," she said, "but I couldn't possibly fit in a sitting for a painting."

"It's due next term," Hattie said, her round eyes growing pleading.

Lucie cleared her throat. "Peregrin Devereux," she said. "Find a way to get to him."

The girls exchanged uncertain glances.

"If we want something from Lord Devereux, we need to offer him something in return," Annabelle said, starting with the obvious.

"We could pay him," Hattie suggested after a moment.

Annabelle shook her head. "He will hardly want for money."

"Young men always want for money," Hattie said, "but you are right, it may not be enough for him to tattle on his brother."

"Perhaps we have to find a way to get closer to Montgomery himself."

Hattie frowned. "But how? He's entirely unsociable."

A brooding silence fell.

"I think there is something that Lord Devereux might want," Catriona said quietly.

Hattie leaned in. "You do?"

Catriona studied her hands. "His drinking society wants the key to the wine cellar of St. John's."

Hattie gasped. "Of course he would want that."

Excitement sizzled up Annabelle's nape. Oxford's drinking societies were outrageously competitive, to a point that it had reached even the delicate ears of the female students. They said it was worth more than a first-class degree, and was as coveted as winning a tournament against Cambridge, leading the table of drunken debaucheries. Odd priorities, rich people had.

"But how do we get our hands on the key?" she asked.

Catriona looked up. "My father has it."

Indeed. As a don at St. John's, Professor Campbell would have all sorts of keys. Annabelle felt a rare grin coming on. Hattie looked like a cat about to raid the canary cage.

"Oh dear," Catriona said. "We better make this worth it."

The sun had set by the time Annabelle climbed the creaking stairs to her room in Lady Margaret Hall. There were only eight other students in her class, one of whom, namely Hattie, resided in the Randolph, so they were all easily accommodated in a modest brick house at the outskirts of town. Nothing at all like the Randolph. Still, a warm emotion filled her to the brim as she stood in the doorway to her chamber. The low light of the gas lamp cast everything in a golden glow, the narrow bed on the left, the wardrobe on the right, and, straight ahead, the rickety desk before the window. *Her* desk. Where she could sink into the myths of Greek antiquity and solve Latin puzzles. *Her* bed. Where she could sleep alone, without being kicked by a sleepy child's foot or having the blanket stolen by one of Gilbert's girls. All it took was a note on the outside of the door saying she was engaged, and the world remained outside and left her undisturbed.

She hugged her arms around herself tightly. What a gift this was, a room of her own.

She'd make the very best of it; she'd be the most diligent, appreciative student she could be.

But first . . . she groaned. First she had to help a group of suffragists infiltrate the home of the most powerful duke in England.

Chapter 5

⸺⸻❦⸻⸺

November

Sebastian skewered Peregrin with a stare over the top of the letter that had accompanied his unexpected arrival at Claremont.

"You are failing your classes."

"Yes, sir."

"You have not paid this term's tuition fee."

Peregrin raked a nervous hand through his hair, leaving it hopelessly disheveled.

"I have not."

So his attempt to train a feckless brother in financial responsibility by handing him his own account had failed.

"And this morning, Weatherly climbed up a freshly gilded rain pipe at St. John's because you were chasing him with a sword?"

"It was a foil," Peregrin muttered, "and Weatherly deserved it."

Sebastian lowered the letter onto his desk, which was already covered in neat stacks of paperwork, all of them both urgent and important. He had not time for this. Peregrin was not stupid, and he was not a young boy; there was therefore no reason for him to act like a stupid young boy, but for a year now he had been acting exactly like that, creating problems that should by any logic not even exist.

"Were you drunk?"

Peregrin shifted in his chair. "No. A Scotch, perhaps two."

If he admitted to two, one could safely double that. Drinking before noon. Well, they did say that blood will out.

"I'm disappointed." He sounded cold to his own ears.

A flush spread over Peregrin's nose and cheekbones, making him look oddly boyish. But at nearly nineteen, he was a man. Sebastian had taken over a dukedom at that age. Then again, he probably had never been as young as Peregrin.

His gaze slid past his brother to the wall. Six estate paintings to the right of the door, the one depicting Montgomery Castle still to the left. Sixteen years ago, he had ordered all paintings to be hung on the left side, the daily reminder of what his father had lost, sold, or ruined during his short reign. Granted, the foundation of the dukedom had been crumbling for decades, and his grandfather had broken most of the entails. But his father had had a choice: to fix the spreading financial rot eating away at their estates, or to surrender. He had chosen to surrender and he had done it like a Montgomery did all things—with brutal effectiveness. The recovery process had been distasteful, an endless procession of arms twisted, of favors asked and granted and traditions flouted. Sebastian almost understood why his mother had moved to France; it was easier to ignore there what he had become—a duke with a merchant's mind. Anything to get the castle back. It wasn't even that he felt a great attachment to the place. It was dark and drafty and the plumbing was terrible, and having it back would be another deadweight in his purse. But what was his was his. Duty was duty. Come March, Castle Montgomery would finally be on the right side of the door. Yes, it was a bloody inopportune time for his heir apparent to play the village idiot.

He gave Peregrin a hard look. "You spent the tuition on entertaining friends, I presume."

"Yes, sir."

He waited.

"And I . . . I played some cards."

Sebastian's jaw tensed. "Any women?"

Peregrin's flush turned splotchy. "You can hardly expect me to own it," he stammered.

Privately, Sebastian agreed; the doings of his brother behind closed doors were none of his business. But few things could trip up a wealthy, idiotic young lord more than a cunning social climber.

"You know how it is," he said. "Unless I know her parents, she is out to fleece you."

"There's no one," Peregrin said, petulant enough to indicate that there was someone.

Sebastian made a mental note to have his man comb through the demimonde and have Madam, whoever she was, informed to take her ambitions elsewhere.

He tapped his finger on the letter. "I will take compensation for the rain pipe out of your allowance."

"Understood."

"You are not coming to France with me; you will stay here and study."

A moment's hesitation, a sullen nod.

"And you will go to Penderyn for the duration of the New Year's house party."

Peregrin paled. "But—"

A glance was enough to make his brother choke his protest back down, but the tendons in Peregrin's neck were straining. Incomprehensibly, Peregrin enjoyed house parties and fireworks; in fact, the more turbulence engulfed him, the more cheerful he seemed to become, and he had been jubilant to hear about the reinstatement of the New Year's Eve party. Nothing ever happened at the estate in Wales.

"May I take a caning instead, please?" Peregrin asked.

Sebastian frowned. "At your age? No. Besides. You need more time to reflect on your idiocy than a few minutes."

Peregrin lowered his gaze to the floor.

Still, he had seen it: the flash of emotion in his brother's eyes. Had he not known better, he would have said it was hatred.

Oddly, it stung.

He leaned back in his chair. Somewhere during the sixteen years he had parented Peregrin, he must have failed him, as he was obviously not growing into the man he was meant to be. Or perhaps . . . Peregrin was growing exactly into what he was. Someone like their father.

Not while I live.

Peregrin still had his head bowed. The tops of his ears looked hot.

"You may leave me now," Sebastian said. "In fact, I do not want to see you here again until term break."

⤜⧲⤛

Peregrin Devereux was not what Annabelle had expected. With his twinkling hazel eyes and dirt-blond hair, he looked boyish, approachable . . . even likable. Everything his brother was not.

She, Hattie, and Catriona found him leaning against one of the pillars of St. John's with a half-smoked cigarette, which he politely extinguished as they approached.

He eyed their little group with faint bemusement. "Ladies, color me an optimist," he said, "but this key would put us ahead of every drinking society in Oxford, so I shudder to imagine the price. What is it going to be? A golden fleece? A head on a platter? My soul?"

He spoke with the same affected lilt as the young lordlings Annabelle knew from the dinner parties at the manor house back in the day, men who loved the sound of their own banter. It took a good ear to hear the undercurrent of alertness in Lord Devereux's voice. He was no fool, this one.

She gave him a look she hoped was coy. "Your soul is safe from us, Lord Devereux. All we ask is an invitation to your next house party at Claremont."

He blinked. "A house party," he repeated. "Just a regular house party?"

"Yes." She wondered what the irregular kind would be like.

"Now, why would you choose that, when you could have chosen anything else?" He looked genuinely taken aback.

Luckily, she had come prepared. She gave a wistful sigh. "Look at us." She gestured down the front of her old coat. "We are bluestockings. We have a reputation of being terribly unfashionable; you, however, lead the most fashionable set in Oxfordshire."

And wasn't that the truth. She couldn't afford fashion; Catriona seemed wholly uninterested; and Hattie, well, she had her very own ideas about *la mode*. Today, she had added a gargantuan turquoise plume to her hat, and it lifted the small headpiece every time the breeze picked up.

It was this bobbing feather that Lord Devereux's eyes now fixed upon. "Well," he said. "I see." His own attire spoke of money and good taste: a rakishly tilted top hat, a fine gray coat and loosely slung scarf, speckless black oxford shoes, all worn with carefully calculated carelessness to suggest that he paid fashion no mind at all.

He dragged his gaze back to Annabelle. "So you wish to become fashionable by association."

"Yes, my lord."

He nodded. "Perfectly sensible."

Still he hesitated.

She pulled the key from her coat pocket. A heavy, medieval-looking thing, it twirled around her finger once, twice, with great effect. Peregrin Devereux was no longer slouching. He focused on the key like his predatory namesake, the falcon.

"As it is," he said slowly, "there is indeed a house party planned for the week before Christmas. But it will be a more intimate, informal affair, just about a dozen gentlemen. And the duke will not be in residence." He gave an apologetic shrug.

A tension she hadn't known she'd held resolved in her chest. If the duke was not home, it might make this harebrained mission considerably easier on her friends.

"His Grace will be away?" she repeated.

Peregrin was still staring at the key. "He will be visiting Mother in France."

She turned to Hattie and Catriona, pretending to consider. "What do you think? Would this still count as a house party?"

"I believe so," Hattie squeaked. Catriona managed a hasty nod.

Heavens, both girls looked flushed and nervous. Hopefully, Lord Devereux would attribute that to the overly excitable nature of wallflowers.

"In that case, we will fulfill our end of the bargain," she said, presenting the key to the nobleman on her palm. "You have two hours to have it replicated."

"Wait," Hattie said, stilling Annabelle's hand. "Your word as a gentleman," she demanded from Lord Devereux.

A lopsided grin tilted his lips. He placed his right fist over his heart as he sketched a bow. "On my honor, Miss Greenfield. Claremont Palace awaits you."

Chapter 6

December

They had barely left the train station in Marlborough when Annabelle admitted defeat—translating Thucydides in a rumbling carriage was impossible. She lowered the book.

"There she is," Hattie cheered from the bench opposite.

Annabelle grimaced. Her stomach was roiling. Next to her, Catriona calmly kept reading while she was bounced around on her seat, and Hattie's chaperoning great-aunt seemed equally unaffected, already snoring openmouthed in the corner across.

"You look a touch pale, greenish, even," Hattie observed with her keen artistic eye. "Are you sure it is wise to read in a moving vehicle?"

"I have an essay due."

"You are on a break now," Hattie said gently.

Annabelle gave her a grave stare. "That was hardly my choice."

She was still struggling with the fact that she was en route to a ducal house party. How naïve of her to believe that securing an invitation for the ladies would suffice. Lucie had been adamant that Annabelle, too, go to the party—three wooden horses behind enemy lines were better than two—and since Lucie held the purse strings, here she was, on her way into the lion's den. She had tried a number of wholly reasonable excuses, the most reasonable being that she had nothing to wear for the occasion. Her trunk, tightly packed with Lady Mabel's walking dresses and evening gowns from seasons past, was currently thudding about on the carriage roof. Lucie herself had stayed back—she was a known radical, and the duke didn't suffer radicalism gladly.

The duke is not home.

Even if he were, it was highly unlikely that he'd remember a woman like her. Crossing paths with commoners must be a wholly unremarkable experience for him. Still. Was it truly just reading Thucydides that made her feel ill? The last time she had been inside a nobleman's house, it had been a disaster . . .

She moved the carriage curtain and peered at the landscape slipping by. Snowflakes flitted past the window, leaving the hills and sweeping ridges of Wiltshire white beneath a cloudy morning sky.

"Will it be long now?" she asked.

"Less than an hour," Hattie said. "Mind you, if it keeps snowing at this rate, we might become stranded."

Hopefully, the roads to Kent would remain clear. *Be back in Chorleywood on December twenty-second*, Gilbert had written. A little over a week from now, she would be scrubbing floors, making pies, stacking firewood, all with a fussy child strapped to her back. Hopefully, three months of scholarly life hadn't made her soft. Gilbert's wife, like her or not, needed all the help she could get.

"Say, just what made you become interested in this?" Hattie was eyeing *The History of the Peloponnesian War* in Annabelle's lap.

She studiously avoided glancing at the dancing letters. "To tell you the truth, I don't think I had a choice in the matter. My father taught me ancient Greek as soon as I could read, and the wars in Messenia were his specialty."

"Was he an Oxford man?"

"No, he went to Durham. He was a third son, so he became a clergyman. He mostly taught himself."

"If only they had educated women sooner," Hattie said, "there would be fewer books about carnage, and more about romance and beautiful things."

"But there's plenty of romance in these books. Take Helen of Troy—Menelaus launched a thousand ships to win her back."

Hattie pursed her lips. "Personally, I always found a thousand ships a little excessive. And Menelaus and Paris fought over Helen like dogs over a bone; no one asked her what she wanted. Even her obsession with Paris was compelled by a poisoned arrow—what's romantic about that?"

"Passion," Annabelle said, "Eros's arrows are infused with passion."

"Oh, passion, poison," Hattie said, "either makes people addle-brained."

She had a point. The ancient Greeks had considered passion a form of madness that infected the blood, and these days, it still inspired elopements and illegal duels and lurid novels. It could even lead a perfectly sensible vicar's daughter astray.

"Plato was romantic, though," Hattie said. "Did he not say our soul was split in two before birth, and that we spend our life searching for our other half to feel whole again?"

"Yes, he did say that."

And he had found the whole notion ridiculous, which was why his play about soulmates was a satire. Annabelle kept that to herself, for there was a dreamy glow on Hattie's face that she did not have the heart to wipe away.

"How I look forward to meeting my lost half," Hattie sighed. "Catriona, what does your soulmate look like? Catriona?"

Catriona surfaced from her book, blinking slowly like a startled owl. "My soulmate?"

"Your other half," Hattie prompted. "Your ideal husband."

Catriona blew out a breath. "Why, I'm not sure."

"But a woman must know what she desires in a man!"

"I suppose he would have to be a scholar," Catriona said, "so he would let me do my research."

"Ah." Hattie nodded. "A progressive gentleman, then."

"Indeed. How about yours?" Catriona asked quickly.

"Young," Hattie said. "He must be young, and titled, and he must be blond. That rich, dark-gold color of an old Roman coin."

"That's . . . quite specific," Catriona said.

"He will sit for my paintings," Hattie said, "and I can hardly have a grandfatherly Sir Galahad, can I? Think, have you ever seen a knight in shining armor who wasn't young and fair?"

Annabelle bit back a snort. Small village girls talked about knights and princes. Then again, for a girl like Hattie, knights and princes weren't just creatures from a fairy tale, they came to dine with her parents in St. James. And if one of them married Hattie, he would shelter and indulge her, because at the end of the day, he would have to answer to Julien Greenfield.

Even she might consider marriage under such circumstances— being well treated, with an army of staff at her command to look after the household. As it was, soulmate or not, marriage would mean an endless cycle of scrubbing, mending, and grafting for a whole family, with the added obligation of letting a man use her body for his plea- sure . . . Her fingertips dug into the velvet of the coach seat. What would be worse? Sharing a bed with a man she didn't care for, or with one who had the power to grind her heart into the dirt?

"Annabelle," Hattie said, inevitably. "Tell us about your soul- mate."

"He seems occupied elsewhere, doesn't he? It's just as well that I mean to rely on my own half."

She evaded Hattie's disapproving eyes by glancing out the win- dow again. A village was drifting past. Honey-colored stone cottages lined the street, looking edible with the snow icing roofs and chim- ney tops. A few fat pigs trundled along the pavement. The duke took care of his tenants, at least.

By the gods. "Is that Claremont?" She touched a finger to the cold windowpane.

Hattie leaned forward. "Why, it is. What a lovely house."

House and *lovely* did not describe the structure that had moved into view in the far distance. Claremont rose from the soil like an enchanted rock, huge, intricately carved, and implacable. Sprawled against a gently rising slope, it oversaw the land for miles like a ruler on a throne. It was utterly, frighteningly magnificent.

❧

The *clop-clop-clop* of the horses' hooves seemed to die away unheard in the vastness of the cobblestoned courtyard. But a lone figure was waiting at the bottom of the gray limestone stairs leading to the main house. Peregrin Devereux. He was bleary-eyed and his cravat was rumpled, but he had a firm grip when he helped them out of the carriage.

"Utterly splendid to have you here, ladies," he said, tucking a blushing Catriona's hand into the crook of his one arm and Aunty Greenfield's into the other as he led them up the stairs. "The gentlemen have eagerly awaited your arrival."

The entrance hall of Claremont rose three dizzying stories high beneath a domed glass ceiling. Statues adorned the balustrades of the upper floors. The marble slabs on the floor were arranged in black and white squares like a giant chessboard. Apt, for a man known as one of the queen's favorite strategists.

Annabelle took a deep breath and straightened her spine. *All perfectly normal.* She would make it through a weekend here. She knew how to pick up her knives and forks in the right order and how to curtsy to whom. She was proficient in French, Latin, and Greek; could sing and play the piano; and could converse about the history of Orient and Occident. Her antiquity-mad father and her maternal great-grandmother had seen to that; with Gallic determination, her petite *grand-mère* had passed on Bourbon etiquette to her descendants all the way to the vicarage. It had made Annabelle an oddity in Kent, awfully overeducated, as she had told Hattie. Who knew that it would now help her to avoid the worst pitfalls in a ducal palace?

Lord Devereux led them to a cluster of servants at the bottom of the grand staircase.

"We are about to be snowed in," he said, "so I suggest we go for a ride around the gardens within the hour."

Catriona and Hattie were enthusiastic about this plan, but then, they knew how to ride. Annabelle's experience was limited to sitting astride the old plow horse, which hardly qualified her for thoroughbreds and sidesaddles.

"I will pass," she said. "I'm of a mind to work on my translation."

"Of course," Peregrin said blandly. "Jeanne here will show you your room. Don't hesitate to ask if you need something; anything you fancy, desire, want, it will be given."

"I shall be careful what I wish for around here, then," she said.

He grinned a by-now-familiar grin.

"*Devereuuuuux.*"

The inebriated bellow reverberated off the walls, and the smile slid off Peregrin's face quick smart. "Eh. Do excuse me, miss. Ladies. It seems the gents have found the brandy."

∼⚬⚬∼

The four-poster bed in her guest chamber was almost indecently lush: oversized, the emerald green velvet drapes thick as moss, with a heap of silk cushions in brilliant jewel colors. She could not wait to stretch out on the soft, clean mattress.

Two stories below the tall windows was the courtyard, at its center a dry fountain circled by rigorously pruned yew trees. A vast snowy parkland that Peregrin called *the garden* rolled into the distance.

"Anything else, miss?"

Jeanne the maid stood waiting, her hands neatly folded in her apron.

It seemed all the splendor was going fast to her head. Why work at her translation here, when there were another two hundred rooms?

She reached for Thucydides and a notebook. "Could you please show me the library?"

"Certainly, miss. Which one?"

More than one library? "Why, the prettiest one."

Jeanne nodded as if that were a most reasonable request. "Follow me, miss."

The library was tucked away behind an arched oak door that groaned as it swung open. Through a wide stained-glass window opposite, between the two rows of dark wooden shelves, light poured in as if divided from a prism. A path of oriental rugs led to a crackling fireplace near the window, where a wing chair was waiting like a ready embrace.

Annabelle took an unsteady step over the threshold. There was an eerie tug of recognition as she surveyed the room, as if someone had peeked into her mind to see how she imagined the perfect library and had put it into stone and timber.

"It's pretty with the ceiling like this, isn't it, miss?"

Annabelle tilted back her head. The vaulted ceiling was painted a rich midnight blue and glimmered faintly with all the stars of a moonless night.

"It's beautiful." In fact . . . she was looking at a painstaking portrayal of the real sky, the winter sky, if she wasn't mistaken.

"'Tis real gold," Jeanne said proudly. "Just ring if you need anything, miss."

The door clicked softly shut behind her.

Quiet. It was so quiet here. If she held her breath, she'd hear the dust dance.

She wandered toward the fire, her fingertips trailing over leather-bound spines, the smooth curve of a globe, polished ebony wood. Textures of wealth and comfort.

The armchair was a solid, masculine thing. A padded footstool was positioned to accommodate long legs toward the grate, and a small table stood within convenient reach. The faintest hint of tobacco smoke lingered.

She hovered. It would be bold, using the chair of the master of the house.

But the master was not home.

She sank into the vast upholstery with a groan of delight.

She'd open the book in a minute. She hadn't sat down and done nothing in . . . years.

The lovely warmth from the fire began seeping into her skin. Her half-lidded gaze traced the stained-glass vignettes in the window—mystical birds and flowers, intricately entwined. Beyond, snowflakes spiraled silently, endlessly. The fire popped, softly, softly . . .

She woke with a start. There was a presence, close and looming. Her eyes snapped open, and her heart slammed against her ribs. A man stood over her. She was staring at his chest. Her pulse thudded in her ears as she forced her eyes up, and up. A black, silken cravat, perfect knotting. A stiff white collar. The hard curve of a jaw.

She already knew who he was. Still. Her stomach plunged when she finally met the pale gaze of the Duke of Montgomery.

Chapter 7

His eyes widened a fraction, and then his pupils sharpened to pinpoints.

The fine hairs on her body stood like fur on a hissing cat.

Oh, he had not forgotten her for a moment—he was staring down at her, irritation pouring off him like fog from an ice chest.

"What. Are you doing. In my house."

His voice was as compelling as she remembered, the cool precision of it slicing right into her racing thoughts. *A perfectly unmanageable man.*

Somehow, she came to her feet. "Your Grace. I thought you were in France."

Why, why would she say such a thing?

The duke's expression had changed from appalled to incredulous. "Miss Archer, is it not?" he said, almost kindly. And that was rather unnerving.

"Yes, Your Grace."

He hadn't stepped back. He stood too close, and at nearly a head taller than she. If he intended to intimidate her with his body, it was counterproductive, for intimidation roused a strong emotion in her: resistance.

He did not strike her as a man who tolerated resistance.

His fitted black coat encased remarkably straight, wide shoulders and a trim waist. His cropped, light hair looked almost white in a shaft of December sun. Austere and colorless like winter himself, the duke. And, potentially, just as capable of freezing her to death.

"You are my brother's companion, I presume," he said.

She did not like the ring he had given the word *companion*. "My Lord Devereux and I are *acquainted*, Your Grace."

She swayed forward an inch, to see if he'd do the polite thing and give her space. He didn't. She felt his gaze slide over her face, then down her throat. The disdain in his eyes said he noticed everything: the hungry hollows of her cheeks; that her earrings were not real pearls; that Lady Mabel's old walking dress had been altered by her own hand and clashed with her coloring.

Inside, she crumbled a little.

"The gall of you, to set foot under my roof," he said. "That is unusual, even for a woman such as yourself."

She blinked. A woman such as herself? "We . . . are acquainted," she repeated, her voice sounding strangely distant.

"Acquainted," Montgomery said, "if that is what you wish to call it, madam. But you picked the wrong man to be acquainted with. I hold the purse strings. Understand that your efforts with Lord Devereux will lead you nowhere."

Heat washed over her.

He wasn't displeased about finding her sleeping in his chair; he thought she was his brother's paramour.

Her and Peregrin Devereux? Ridiculous.

And yet one glance had convinced His Grace that she'd sell herself to noblemen for money.

The violent beat of her heart filled her ears. Her temper, checked for so long, uncoiled and rose like a prodded snake. It took possession, made her cock her hip and peruse him, from his angular face down to his polished shoes and up again, taking his measure as a man. She couldn't stop the regretful smirk that said he had just been found wanting.

"Your Grace," she murmured, "I'm sure your purse strings are . . . enormous. But I'm not in the market for you."

He went still as stone. "Are you suggesting that I just propositioned you?"

"Why, isn't that usually the reason why a gentleman mentions his purse strings to a woman such as I?"

A muscle in his cheek gave a twitch, and that worked like a cold shower on her hot head.

This was not good.

He was, after all, one of the most powerful men in England.

Unexpectedly, he leaned closer. "You will leave my estate as soon as the roads permit travel again," he said softly. "You will leave and you will keep away from my brother. Have I made myself clear?"

No reply came to mind. He was so close, his scent began invading her lungs, a disturbingly masculine blend of starch and shaving soap.

She managed a nod.

He stepped back, and his eyes gave an infinitesimal flick toward the door.

He was throwing her out.

Her hand twitched with the mad impulse to slap him, to see the arrogance knocked right off his noble face. Ah, but that arrogance ran to the marrow.

She remembered to snatch the Thucydides and her notebook from the side table.

His gaze pressed cold and unyielding like the muzzle of a pistol between her shoulders all the way to the door.

∽∾∾∽

The woman held her book before her like a shield as she left, every line of her slender body rigid. She closed the door very gently behind her, and somehow, that felt like a parting shot.

Sebastian flexed his fingers.

He had recognized her as soon as she had blinked up at him.

Green Eyes was in his house.

Green Eyes was his brother's bit on the side.

She had slept like an innocent in his chair, with her knees pulled to her chest and a hand tucked under her cheek, the soft pulse in her neck exposed. Her profile had been marble still, she had looked like a pre-Raphaelite muse. It had stopped even him in his tracks. She had not looked like a woman who entrapped hapless noblemen, a testimony of her skills.

Her eyes gave her away, keenly intelligent and self-possessed, and hardly innocent. Any doubts, her reactions had settled: no gently bred woman would have reacted with impertinence to his displeasure. This one had wanted to slap him; he had sensed it in his bones. *Madness.*

He stalked toward the exit.

Being ordered back from Brittany by the queen *at once* for a crisis meeting was bothersome. Finding his house teeming with drunken lordlings after traveling for twenty hours was unacceptable. But to be sniped at in his own library by this baggage—beyond the pale.

A long, anxious face awaited him when he stepped into the hallway.

"Now, Bonville."

"Your Grace." The butler he would normally describe as unflappable had a wild look about him. "I take the fullest responsibility for this . . . situation."

"I doubt there is a need for that," Sebastian said, "but do give me an account."

His housekeeper had become too flustered when he had walked through the front door without notice. She had managed to produce the guest list, and he had set off after the first name, the name of a woman he did not know.

"A dozen gentlemen arrived unannounced last night," Bonville said, "and Lord Devereux, he clapped me on the back and said, 'Bonville, be a good chap. You're already preparing the big house party, there should be plenty of food and drink.' A dozen, Your Grace! The kitchen staff . . ."

Ah, Peregrin, Peregrin. Briefly, Sebastian entertained the idea to hunt his brother down, to drag him to his study and give him a beating after all. Later. He would deal with his brother later, when anger wasn't running through his veins like a live current. And he had to play host to his uninvited guests, for to do anything else would be to admit to the world that an eighteen-year-old had just run roughshod over the Duke of Montgomery. Iron self-control kept him from grinding his teeth in front of his butler.

"And more arrived this morning." Bonville continued his harried tale. "Three young ladies and their chaperone, and we are not sure one of them is even a lady."

"She is not," Sebastian said grimly.

Wait. A chaperone?

"I thought so," Bonville said. "Why would the daughter of the Earl of Wester Ross don a ghastly plaid and stroll about like a Jacobite . . ."

Sebastian raised a hand. "Lady Catriona is here?"

"Presumably, Your Grace."

Damn. He should have heard the guest list to the end before setting out to find Madam.

"You mentioned three ladies," he said. "Who else?"

"Miss Harriet Greenfield and her aunt, Mrs. Greenfield-Carruther. We gave them the apartment with the gilded ceiling."

A Greenfield daughter and Lady Catriona. Neither of them would keep inappropriate company. So apparently Peregrin hadn't lodged his paramour under his roof. And considering how Miss Archer had attacked him, she was hardly a professional.

Sebastian frowned. Travel fatigue must have scrambled his brain to make such an error. None of it explained this woman's presence in his armchair, though.

"They are all at Oxford," he said suddenly.

"Your Grace?"

"The women," he said. "Greenfield's daughter and Lady Catriona, and I suspect the third one, too—they are bluestockings. Their manners and dress sense can be . . . atrocious."

"I see." Bonville sniffed, sounding much more like his usual self.

"Bonville, you are one of the most competent butlers in England, are you not?"

A modest flush spread over Bonville's haggard cheeks. "I aspire to be, Your Grace."

"You are. Now be competent and handle this situation. And inform kitchen staff that they will be paid double for the next two days."

He watched Bonville's back assume its usual straightness as he strode off.

That left the other issue: he had just booted a guest off his estate who, her impertinent mouth notwithstanding, had a right to his hospitality. Grand. He very, very rarely reversed a decision. He decided that the little shrew could stew awhile, and he told a footman to send for his groom. Nothing quite smoothed his temper as a long ride over the fields.

⌒⌒∾⌒⌒

You will leave my estate . . .

The words, so quietly spoken, were clanging around in Annabelle's head like a fire bell. The Duke of Montgomery had thrown her out of his house.

She had not even unpacked yet.

When she entered her chamber, she realized that her things had been unpacked for her. The bottle with jasmine perfume and Mama's old brush sat on the vanity table, her books and papers on the desk, including *Debrett's Etiquette Manual*, which she had painstakingly studied to avoid slipping up during the house party.

Her gaze narrowed at the binder with profile sheets on men of influence.

With three quick strides, she reached the desk.

General description of the gentleman's character.

She unsheathed the fountain pen like a rapier.

The Duke of M: Impossible, arrogant, high-handed, the pen scratched, *a pompous arse!*

Panting, she swiped a curl from her face. Unexpectedly, she caught her reflection in the mirror and gasped. There was a hard gleam in her eyes, and her mahogany locks were snaking in all directions: a Medusa, not Helen of Troy.

She pressed her palms to her hot cheeks. What had happened? She knew how to handle a rampant male, knew what to say and more importantly what not to say. A fool would know not to goad a peer of the realm, even if he was an arse. *Especially* not if he was an arse.

Her reflection looked back at her, chagrined. *But you do have a temper, don't you; in fact, you have just shown your true nature.*

She closed her eyes. Yes, her emotions had got the better of her before. And no, she had never really known her place. Where others were appropriately intimidated, she seemed oddly intrigued by the challenge.

She had dug deep to bury that flaw.

But the duke had known. Any gentleman would be mortified to insult an innocent woman, but he had stared right into her, and had seen something rotten.

Oh, no. Hattie and Catriona . . . what would she tell them? The bonds of friendship were so fragile, and she had only just found them.

I have to leave.

There was an inn in the gingerbread village they had passed; she could clearly picture the wrought-iron sign. How far could it be? Not more than seven miles. Seven miles was perfectly doable.

A bundle would suffice for now—jasmine bottle, brush, papers, her night rail, and the spare chemise. The books came last. Her hands were fast and meticulous, her face still afire. The duke's presence was pressing upon her; there was no evading him within these walls, where he owned every stone and creature.

She had to leave the girls something, so out came the papers again.

"How about this," she muttered. "I insulted the Duke of Montgomery to his face and he thinks I'm a strumpet, so I considered it best to take my leave." Imagine the confusion that would cause . . . She scribbled a few innocuous lines and left the note on the desk.

She laced up her boots and moved to the window. The sun had just passed the zenith; she'd have three, four hours of daylight still. Perfectly doable.

Two riders came into view in the courtyard below, dotting dark lines across the pristine white blanket.

The leading horse had sprung straight from a winter's tale, a gleaming white stallion, the play of its powerful sinews and muscles so graceful it seemed to be dancing over the snow. No doubt Hattie would have it sit for the mount of her blasted Sir Galahad.

It should have been a pitch-black beast to suit its master, though, who was no other than Montgomery himself. Her hand curled into the thick velvet curtain. His ducal posture, the adroitness with which he controlled the prancing animal . . . it made her whole body pulse with fresh anger. Would that the pretty horse tossed him on his rump.

He turned his head toward her sharply then, and she stiffened, her breath frozen in her lungs. For a moment, a rather vivid memory of his scent had brushed her nose.

She grabbed her bundle and fled.

Chapter 8

It would have been wiser to claim an indisposition and hide in her room. It certainly would have been more pragmatic—trudging through knee-deep snowdrifts made that perfectly clear. Unfortunately, both wisdom and pragmatism had abandoned her in the space of half a day. That was what happened when the past unexpectedly collided with the present: it roused the ghosts and one became erratic.

Seven years had passed since she had stood in another grand library and another aristocrat had torn her limb from limb. She would have thought that seven years was a long time, but the duke's voice, with its superior vowels and easy disdain, had gripped and shaken her like a fist.

She still shouldn't have sniped at him. Gallic pride, Aunt May had used to call it, Gallic temper . . . *rein it in, lass; you can't afford it.* Gallic pride had been silent as a snared rabbit seven years ago, when her lover's father had called her a money-grabbing harlot and she had been sent to live with Aunt May. She hadn't really been prideful since.

Panting, she paused to adjust her bundle. The path ahead was barely distinguishable from the white rolling fields on either side, but the clouds had lifted, and the wind had ceased. The trees on the ridge stood black and still like paper cuttings against the fading sky. Another five miles remaining, she knew; she was good at estimating such a thing. Shc had to be. Women such as herself went everywhere on foot.

She had barely managed another mile when the muffled thud of hoofbeats sounded behind her.

She turned.

A large brown horse was thundering along the path toward her, the rider flattened against its neck.

Her body went rigid. This was an expensive horse, one from a noble-man's stable. Her stomach was churning by the time it reached her.

"Miss. Miss Archer." The young man slid from the saddle and took off his cap, his sweat-dampened red hair sticking up. "McMahon, groom-gardener, at your service. I've been sent to retrieve you, miss."

No.

No, she would not go back there.

"I appreciate your troubles," she said, "but I'm going to the vil-lage." She pointed her thumb back over her shoulder.

Surprise flitted across his features. "To Hawthorne? But it's far still. It's cold; you'll catch the cough."

"I'm warm enough, and I walk fast."

"You've walked much farther than we expected; you must be ex-hausted," he said. "I'm to bring you back to the house."

He wasn't listening; they never did.

She gave him a wide smile, and he blinked the way men blinked when she smiled widely at them.

"McMahon, there's only one horse."

His face brightened. "Not to worry, miss, you'll have the horse."

"But it'll take us two hours walking to the house, and it will take me little more to get to Hawthorne."

McMahon assessed the situation with a deepening frown, prob-ably realizing that he could not just bundle her onto the horse if she refused to cooperate.

"His Grace will not be pleased," he finally said.

His Grace? Why did he send for her at all, when he wanted her gone?

Because he wanted it all on his own terms, the domineering autocrat.

"Tell His Grace that I refused."

McMahon's mouth fell open.

"And that I was awfully obstinate about it," she added, "a veritable shrew."

The groom slowly shook his head. "I c-can hardly tell him that, miss."

"He won't be surprised, not one bit."

"See here, miss—"

"Good afternoon, McMahon."

She did not turn her back on him, because she did have manners, excellent manners, actually.

Still McMahon looked unhappy. Would the duke take it out on the lad? She pressed her lips together; this was a matter of self-preservation.

Muttering something under his breath, McMahon finally doffed his cap, mounted, and turned the horse around, soon becoming a dark dot against the white landscape.

She pushed onward with redoubled effort, a restless urgency coursing beneath her skin. The duke wanted her back, and he was a man who got what he wanted. She needed to be faster. Also, she was coated in sweat, gluing her chemise to her back and forming crystals on her cold face. She needed to get out of the cold.

Not even half an hour had passed when there were hoofbeats again.

She turned, prepared to see a large brown horse.

The horse was gleaming white.

Hell's teeth.

The rider was approaching rapidly, and there was no mistaking that erect posture. It was Montgomery himself. Another horse, riderless, was hard on his heels.

She spun around, her wits suddenly as frozen as her face.

Montgomery himself had come for her.

He was upon her like a gust of wind, a flurry of motion and stomping, steaming muscle as he maneuvered the horses across her path.

As if she'd be so foolish as to run at this point.

When she rose from her curtsy, he was staring down his nose at her from the lofty height of his saddle. That was how his forefathers would have looked on the battlefield, imperious men on mean war-horses, their voice the signal that made soldiers raise their swords and hurtle toward peril and glory. Peril it was for her, no doubt. He was stone faced.

"Good afternoon, Miss Archer." His tone was deceptively idle. "Now, what exactly were you hoping to achieve with this?"

His index finger made a circular motion around her and the snowy path at large.

"I'm following your orders, Your Grace. The road permits travel, so I left your house."

"And as you could have safely assumed, that referred to travel by coach, not on foot."

"I wouldn't dare to make assumptions about your orders, Your Grace."

His jaw tightened. "So had I made my order very, very clear, that it precluded travel on foot, you would have stayed put?"

She could say nothing at all now, or blatantly lie. They both knew she would have taken off regardless.

Montgomery nodded, that tight little nod again, and then he smoothly swung from the saddle. Riding crop in hand, he advanced on her, the snow crunching menacingly under his boots.

Her heels dug in to hold her ground. They were under the open sky now, a more equal stage than his library, but he still looked disconcertingly unassailable in his heavy navy topcoat with the double rows of glaring silver buttons. He hadn't even bothered to secure his horse. It stayed put, the poor beast no doubt long harangued into submission.

Montgomery planted himself a mere foot from her, his eyes piercing bright with annoyance.

"I would never order a woman to walk anywhere," he said, "so mount up, if you please." He pointed the crop at the spare horse.

She eyed the beast. It was the size of a small house and looked nervous; besides, she would not go back with him had he shown up in a plush four-in-hand.

"I will reach Hawthorne in an hour, Your Grace."

"You won't," he said, "but it will be dark, and you will be ill." Said with a certainty as if he weren't just foreseeing but steering the course of nature. "You might also lose a few toes," he added for good measure.

Her feet curled in her boots at his mentioning of toes; botheration, she hardly felt them.

"I appreciate your concern—"

"I will not have a woman come to harm on my land," he said. "Concern plays no part in it."

Of course not. "I have no desire to come to harm, merely to get to Hawthorne."

He gave her a cold, cold look. "You are putting pride above your safety, miss."

Well, there was no arguing with that. She gritted her teeth, struggling to control the unfamiliar urge to snarl.

"Get onto the horse," Montgomery ordered.

"I prefer not to, Your Grace. It's huge."

He slapped his riding crop against his boot, and she had a feeling that he'd quite like to slap something else instead.

"There's an inn in Hawthorne where I plan to stay," she said quickly, "and—"

"And then word gets around that I cast my guests out into the cold?" Montgomery snapped. "Certainly not. You are not even wearing a proper coat."

She looked down at herself. "It's a most regular coat."

"And utterly useless for an eight-mile march in these conditions," he shot back; *ridiculous woman* were the unspoken words. He'd never say it out loud, of course, and he didn't have to. He inflicted enough damage with the contempt coloring his cultured voice.

She considered his wide-shouldered form, clearly superior to hers in weight and strength, and wondered what he would do if she tried to walk around him.

"Very well," he said, and then he did something unexpected. He took off his hat.

"It is not the appropriate setting," he said, "but it appears that we will be here a while."

He tucked the hat under his arm and met her eyes. "Miss, I apologize for handling our last encounter in an overly high-handed manner. Please do me the honor of staying at Claremont until the party concludes tomorrow."

It was very quiet on this windless hill in Wiltshire. She heard the sound of her own breath flowing in and out of her lungs, and the slow thump of her heart as she stared back at him, with his hat so formally held under his arm. His breath, like hers, was a white cloud.

No man had ever given her an apology.

Now that she had one, she found she was uncertain what to do with it.

Montgomery's brow lifted impatiently.

Well. He was a duke, after all, and probably not in the habit of apologizing. Ever.

"Why?" she asked softly. "Why would you invite a woman like me into your home?"

The look he gave her was inscrutable. "I won't have *any* woman come to harm on my estate. And our earlier conversation was based on a misunderstanding. It is clear that my brother is quite safe from you."

She cringed. Had he questioned Peregrin about the nature of their relationship? Or worse, Hattie and Catriona? The questions that would cause—

"No one told me," he said. He wore a new expression, and it took her a moment to class it as *mildly amused*.

"That's reassuring," she said, not sounding assured at all.

His lips twitched. "It was plain deductive reasoning, logic, if you will."

"That's a sound method," she acknowledged, wondering where in Hades he was going now.

"You made it perfectly clear that you weren't in the market for a duke," he said. "It follows that my younger brother would be rather out of the question for you."

She blinked. Was he trying to . . . jest with her?

His face gave away nothing, and so, carefully, she said: "But wouldn't that be inductive reasoning, Your Grace?"

He stilled. A glint struck up in the depths of his eyes. "Deductive, I'm sure," he said smoothly.

Deductive, I'm sure. So the premise that a woman would always prefer a duke over any other man was a natural law to him, like the fact that all men were mortal. His arrogance was truly staggering.

"Of course," she muttered.

He smiled at that, just with the corners of his eyes, but it still drew her attention to his mouth. It was an intriguing mouth, upon closer inspection. Enticing, even, well-defined and with a notable softness to his bottom lip when he was of a mind to smile. One might call it a sensual mouth, if one were to think about him in such a way, a promise that this reserved duke knew how to put his lips to use on a woman . . . *This man and I are going to kiss.* The awareness was bright and sudden, a flash at her mind's horizon, a knowing rather than a thought.

Her heart gave a sharp, confused thud.

She glanced away, then back at him. No, this new Montgomery was still there, with his attractive mouth, with intelligent humor simmering in the depth of his eyes.

She knew then that she would never be able to unsee him again.

She gave her head a shake. "I can't return with you," she said, her voice firm, thank God. "I don't know how to ride."

He frowned. "Not at all?"

"Not on a sidesaddle."

Blast. The last thing she wanted was to plant images in his mind of her lifting her skirts and riding astride.

"I see," he said. He clicked his tongue, and his horse stopped nosing at the snow and trotted over, tagging the spare mount along.

Montgomery took the reins in one fist. "You will ride with me," he said.

That was not at all the conclusion she had wanted him to reach. "Is that another jest, Your Grace?"

"I don't jest," he said, sounding faintly appalled.

So she was to sit on the horse with him, clutching him like a damsel in a lurid novel?

Her every feminine instinct cried *no*, and he must have guessed as much, for his expression hardened.

"It seems unsafe," she tried.

"I'm a good horseman," he said, and wedged the crop beneath the stirrup. To clear his hands to lift her, she assumed.

A shiver ran through her, she was not sure whether hot or cold. She could still step around him and continue walking toward the village, as far away from this man as possible.

He shot her a dark look. "Come here."

Unbelievably, she took a step toward him, as if he had tugged at her bodily, and he didn't miss a beat—he took her elbow and turned her, crowding her back against the warm body of the horse. She smelled sweat and leather and wool; the wool had to be him, for he again stood too close, trapping her between the stallion and his chest.

"Near instant compliance, Miss Archer?" he murmured, his gaze intent on her face. "You must be feeling the cold after all."

She stared back into his eyes. She couldn't help it; her gaze became strangely anarchic around him as if it quite forgot that not all gazes were created equal. Perhaps it was the contrasts that drew her in, pale clearness, dark rims; flashes of guarded intensity in cold depths . . . She watched as his attention dropped to her lips.

Her mouth went dry.

His jaw clenched. In an annoyed way.

"Your teeth are chattering," he said. "This is ridiculous."

His hand went to the top button of his coat, a gesture old as instinct, and she froze. So did the duke, his hand suspended in midair. His face was almost comically blank as he looked at her, and she knew his impulse to keep her warm had taken them both by surprise. While he might consider it his duty to keep her from perishing on his land, wrapping her in his coat like a fine lady would go too far. She was not a fine lady. She was not his to protect.

He began working loose his scarf. "Take this." He sounded sterner than ever before. This was a battle she shouldn't pick. She slung the scarf around her neck and tried to ignore the scent of cedar soap and man that wafted from the soft wool.

Montgomery's hands wrapped around her waist with a firm grip; next thing she was perching atop the nervously shifting stallion, half on its neck, half on the saddle, clutching fistfuls of shiny white mane. *Holy Moses.*

And then Montgomery was in the saddle behind her, shockingly close.

"Allow me." He shocked her again by looping an arm around her waist and pulling her snug against his chest. A notably solid chest. Heat shot through her, all the way down into her toes. And that was a feeling she had hoped to never feel again.

Now she felt it everywhere, a warming, a softening of her body in response to the uncompromising masculine strength surrounding her.

She should have walked to the village; it had been such a simple decision.

She'd ignore it, it would be easy to ignore . . .

His left thigh pressed up against hers, and she gasped. "Wait, please."

He reined in the horse. "What is it?"

"Please take me to the village, Your Grace, to the inn. It's a much shorter ride."

He went still for a moment. Then his arm around her tightened. "Too late now."

He spurred the horse into a gallop.

Chapter 9

She smelled of jasmine, sweet and warm like a summer night in Spain. Utterly incongruous with the snow-covered fields flying past, and certainly with the shivering, obstinate creature in his arms. She had marched through the snowdrifts with the determination of a small battalion, and had defied him until her teeth rattled. Her stubborn resistance had left him two options: one, throw her over his shoulder like a barbarian, or two, negotiate. Sebastian's mouth thinned with annoyance. He never negotiated unless the other party had something to offer, and there she had compelled him to present his apology on a hill, and to try a joke to break down her defenses. Even the joke had gone out of control, when she had unexpectedly, cleverly, volleyed it back at him. Trust a bluestocking to know the difference between deductive and inductive logic.

By the time they cantered into the courtyard, it was dark and the lanterns on the palace walls spilled yellow twilight across the cobblestones. His horse chose to be disobedient and veered toward the stables, and he leaned forward to take control of the reins. Miss Archer turned her head, and his nose landed in soft curls and his mouth against one cold ear.

She went stiff.

He straightened. "I beg your pardon."

The iciness of her skin lingered on his lips.

Night would have fallen long before she would have reached Hawthorne. She could have lost her way, and she would have been found in the morning, on one of his fields, a prone, frozen form in a patched-up coat.

An irrationally strong desire to shake her gripped him.

"Your Grace." His groom stood by his left knee, eyeing the woman in Sebastian's arms with blatant astonishment.

"Stevens," he said curtly, "the spare horse."

Miss Archer shifted, the movement pressing her round backside more firmly against his groin. With a silent curse, Sebastian swung from the saddle the moment Stevens was out of the way.

Her face was above him, still and pale as moonlight. He raised his arms to assist her, but she didn't budge, her fists still gripping the horse's mane.

"If you please, miss." Had she fossilized up there? She was suspiciously quiet.

The horse danced sideways, eager to get to the stable. Still she clung on.

He put his hands where her waist would be under layers of clothes, ready to pluck her off, and he heard the faintest of whimpers.

"What now?"

"I'm not sure my legs will carry me," came her voice, annoyed.

It dawned on him that she had probably never been on a horse in full gallop before. He supposed the raw speed of it could be frightening for a novice. His own face was numb from the stiff headwind.

"I assure you I will catch you," he said gruffly.

She all but fell into his arms and clumsily slid along his body, her hands clutching at his shoulders as her feet hit the ground. She blinked up at him, her eyes an undefinable color in the gaslight. He knew for certain, though, that they were green, a surprisingly calm, muted shade like lichen. He had taken a good look earlier.

She strained against him, and he realized his arms were still locked firmly around her. Releasing his hold, he stepped back, a supportive hand below her elbow. "Are you able to stand?"

"Yes, Your Grace."

She seemed rattled. No doubt she was used to standing firmly on her own two feet.

He placed her hand onto his forearm, just in case. Her gloves were worn, and he felt the absurd urge to keep his hand on top of hers until Stevens, slowest groom in Christendom, moved to take over his horse.

He all but dragged her up the main stairs. A small audience awaited them in the bright warmth of the house—Mrs. Beecham hovered, and there at the back of the entrance hall were two young ladies, looking ready to come dashing the moment he was out of the picture.

Miss Archer dropped her hand from his arm, her expression as buttoned-up as her useless coat. It didn't help. She was still beautiful.

He'd noticed her beauty earlier, out on the hill. Even stripped of strategic fineries that would fool a less discerning male eye, even with her nose reddened and her hair windswept, she was beautiful. She had the timeless features that transcended fashion and rank: the graceful neck, the elegant cheekbones, the soft mouth. That mouth. The pink fullness belonged on a courtesan in Brittany, not an Englishwoman, or bluestocking, or country girl . . . He became aware that he was staring, that he was trying to place her in any one of the categories of females he knew, and, amazingly, he could not.

She still wore his scarf, and the monogrammed crest of Montgomery had settled like a badge on the swell of her left breast. A dark, hot emotion surged through him at the sight, incinerating calm and conscious thought. *Possessiveness.* For a moment, it beat through every part of him, a searing want, a near physical pull tugging him toward her.

Christ.

He stepped back.

Lichen-green eyes followed him suspiciously.

"I trust I will see you at dinner, miss." The coolness of his voice turned it into a command, and her mouth gave a mutinous little twitch.

He stalked off, almost tasting the base satisfaction of sinking his teeth into her plush bottom lip.

⁓⁂⁓

An hour later, he was staring at his reflection in the washstand mirror, restored. A bath, a close shave, a valet who knew what he was doing, and from the outside, even he couldn't tell that he had unboarded a ferry in Dover this morning and then chased after an impossibly stubborn female. But there was still a hollowness, an unease in his chest. Perhaps he was beginning to feel his age.

"I heard the young gentlemen are pleased to be dining with you so unexpectedly, Your Grace," Ramsey remarked as he tapped the pin into his cravat.

Sebastian watched his mouth curve into an ironic smile. At least one young gentleman was presently not pleased at the prospect of dining with him. Peregrin aside, he was well aware that while he edified a party, he didn't make it a more pleasant occasion for the people in attendance. When he entered a room, conversations sputtered, laughter became muted, and everything became a little more purposeful. Everyone had something to gain from a duke, and everyone had something to lose. His presence spun a web of caution around people, trapping truths and impulse like a spider's lair with a wayward fly. There came a point in a duke's life when he rarely encountered an honest opinion, where he could be on his way to hell in a handcart and everyone would politely step aside and wish him godspeed.

"Ramsey," he said. The valet had begun dusting off his already pristine dinner jacket sleeve.

"Your Grace?"

"If you were to walk in on me in my study, and you saw me stand-ing amid great chaos, and a pair of legs sticking out from under my desk, what would you do?"

Ramsey went still. Carefully raised his eyes to ascertain his mood, though he'd know by now that he wouldn't see anything Sebastian didn't choose to show. "Why, Your Grace," he then said, "I would fetch a broom."

Indeed he would.

"That will be all, Ramsey."

He had to lead his guests into the dining room and spend the next three hours not strangling his brother.

⚬✦⚬

Peregrin approached the seat next to him much as a well-bred man would approach a whipping post: collected, pale, and rather stiff in the legs. His normally wayward hair was meticulously slicked and parted. But he was evading Sebastian's eyes like a coward. God grant him strength—if he were to fall off his horse tomorrow, eight hun-dred years of Montgomery history would pass into this boy's hands. Castle Montgomery would move out of his family's reach forever. Not strangling Peregrin would take some effort.

Scraping and shuffling ensued as people were being seated; fur-ther down the table there was a subdued commotion as Lord Hamp-shire and Lord Palmer batted their eyes at the men to their left, and James Tomlinson pretended to fan himself. They sat in the seat where a lady would have sat, had someone with half a brain organized the house party. As it was, the elderly aunt of Julien Greenfield and three bluestockings were scattered among thirteen young men. Sebastian wouldn't even try to begin understanding such a thing.

"How refreshing, to have so many young people at one table," Greenfield's aunt said loudly from his right.

"Isn't it just," he replied smoothly.

Peregrin seemed deeply fascinated by his empty plate.

Footmen lined up and lifted silver domes off the first dish, revealing choice pieces of pheasant in a blood-red sauce.

Cutlery clinked; wineglasses reflected the candlelight.

Peregrin still hadn't mustered the courage to look at him. Sebastian glared at his brother's profile, his anger on the tipping point to wrath.

Ever so slowly, Peregrin raised his gaze to him.

A shudder ran through the young man when their gazes locked.

Sebastian gave him a thin smile. "How is the pheasant?"

Peregrin's eyes widened. "It's excellent, thank you." He poked his fork at his food. "I, ah, trust your journey was uneventful, sir?"

"It was," Sebastian said, taking a sip from his water. "It was upon my arrival that things became interesting."

Peregrin swallowed audibly.

The guests had fallen into animated conversation. He could pick out the calm hum of Miss Archer's alto voice from the other end of the table, followed by the too-loud laughter of the eager young men around her. He nearly scoffed. Whatever it was that would truly keep a woman like Miss Archer entertained, none of those boys could provide it.

"I will go to London tomorrow," he said to Peregrin, "and when I'm back on Monday, I shall expect you in my study at six o'clock."

He hadn't thought it possible, but his brother's face turned even whiter.

And just to see what would happen, he picked up his knife and skewered the slab of meat on his plate.

Peregrin's fork clattered onto the table.

Sixteen heads swiveled toward them, as if a shot had been fired.

Chapter 10

Annabelle woke from a soft clanking noise she couldn't place. She was of a mind to ignore it, for the pillow beneath her cheek was incredibly, alluringly soft, a cloud in her arms.

And . . . unfamiliar.

And it was past six o'clock; she felt it in her bones.

She had overslept.

She lurched into a sitting position, and a squeak sounded somewhere in the shadows.

The shapes of the room came into focus: opulent bedposts, high windows, the faint glint of a chandelier . . . she was in the Duke of Montgomery's house, and there was a maid by the fireplace with a poker.

She sagged back into the pillows. There was no fire she needed to tend, no cousin or half a dozen children waiting for their breakfast . . .

She ran a hand over her face. Her forehead was damp. "What time is it?"

"About six thirty, miss," the maid said. "Would you like me to send for some tea?"

How tempting, to have tea in bed. Despite the extra half hour of sleep, her body felt oddly sluggish. But she still had a translation to do before the activities of the day began. She forced a leg out of bed. Her foot was heavy as if filled with lead.

"Will there be any breakfast at the table at this time?" she asked.

The maid's eyes widened when she seemed to piece together her intentions. She had probably never seen a houseguest rise before dawn. Noblemen didn't rise until noon; Annabelle had that on good account.

⁂

The footman marched ahead into the breakfast room, then halted abruptly to click his heels together. "Your Grace, Miss Archer," he announced.

She nearly froze in midstride.

Indeed. There was already someone at the foot of the table. He was concealed by a wide-open newspaper, but there was no mistaking the master of the house.

Naturally, she had to be the guest of the one nobleman in England who didn't rise at noon.

Montgomery's eyes met hers over the rim of the paper, startlingly alert despite the hour, and their impact caused a swift, warm bloom of awareness in her belly. She tightly clasped her hands in front of her.

One of Montgomery's straight brows flicked up. "Miss Archer. Is anything amiss?"

Yes.

He unsettled her.

His damned intelligent eyes and effortless self-assurance impressed upon her, and now her body wasn't able to shake the feel of him. It remembered the strength of his arm around her, the feel of his hard chest against her back, the cool touch of his lips against her ear . . . his scent, so subtle and yet compelling, had clung to her until she had soaked in the bath last night. Her body knew things about him now and was intrigued when it shouldn't be. She did not even like the man.

"I was told I may have breakfast here, Your Grace."

"You may," he said, and she had the impression that he was making a number of quick decisions as he spoke. He put the paper down and gestured to a footman to begin preparing the place to his left.

Her stomach dropped. That was not where she should sit. But he was already folding up the newspaper as if the matter were very much settled.

It was a long walk past empty chairs and yards of table to reach her assigned seat.

Montgomery was watching her with his neutral aristo expression. A diamond pin glinted equally impenetrable against the smooth black silk of his cravat.

"I trust it was not something in your room that had you rising this early?" he asked.

"The room is excellent, Your Grace. I simply don't find that it's that early in the day."

That seemed to spark some interest in his eyes. "Indeed, it isn't."

Unlike her, he probably hadn't had to be trained to rise before dawn. He probably enjoyed such a thing.

The footman who had moved her chair leaned over her shoulder. "Would you like tea or coffee, miss?"

"Tea, please," she said, mindful not to thank him, because one did not say thank you to staff in such a house. He proceeded to ask whether she wanted him to put a plate together for her, and because it would have been awkward to get up again right after sitting down, she said yes. In truth, she wasn't hungry. The maid must have laced in her stomach more tightly than she was accustomed.

Montgomery seemed to have long finished eating. Next to his stack of newspapers was an empty cup. Just why had he ordered her to sit next to him? He had been immersed in his read. But she knew now that he was a dutiful man. Being *polite* was probably as much a duty to him as riding out into the cold to save a willful houseguest from herself. She would have to make a note on his profile sheet, *very polite*. As long as he didn't mistake one for a social climbing tart, of course.

"You are one of Lady Tedbury's activists," he said.

Well. *Does not mince words.*

"Yes, Your Grace."

"Why?"

She could sense interest in him, genuine interest.

Beads of sweat gathered on her back.

She had the ear of their enemy, and she was not in shape. *Calm. Stay calm.*

"I'm a woman," she said. "It is only natural for me to believe in women's rights."

Montgomery gave a surprisingly Gallic, one-shouldered shrug. "Plenty of women don't believe in this kind of women's rights," he said, "and whether the 1870 Property Act is amended or not will not make a difference for you personally."

There it was again, the arrogance. Of course he guessed she didn't have any property to lose to a husband, and thus no voting rights to forfeit. His arrogance was most annoying when it was right on the truth.

She licked her dry lips. "I also believe in Aristotelian ethics," she said, "and Aristotle says that there is greater value in striving for the common good than the individual good."

"But women didn't have the vote in the Greek democracies," he said, a ghost of a smile hovering over his mouth. One could almost think he was enjoying this.

The gleam in his eyes made her reckless. "They forgot to include women's rights in the common good," she said. "An easy mistake; it seems to be forgotten frequently."

He nodded. "But then what do you make of the fact that men without property cannot vote, either?"

He *was* enjoying this. Like a tomcat enjoyed swatting at a mouse before he ate it.

A mallet had begun pounding her temples, turning her skull into a mass of pulsing ache. But they were alone, and she had his ear. She had to try.

"Perhaps there should be more equality for the men as well, Your Grace." That had been the wrong thing to say.

He shook his head. "A socialist as well as a feminist," he said. "Do I need to worry about the corruption of my staff while you are here, Miss Archer? Will I have mutiny on my hands when I return from London tomorrow?"

"I wouldn't dare," she murmured. "There's probably a dungeon under the house."

He contemplated her with a hawklike gaze. "There is," he said, and then, "Are you quite well, miss?"

"I'm fine." Dungeon? There was no denying any longer that she had a wee fever.

The footman reappeared and placed a plate under her nose. Kippers and fried kidneys and a greenish mush. A hot, salty fragrance wafted up, and her stomach roiled.

Montgomery snapped his fingers. "Bring Miss Archer an orange, peeled," he said to no one in particular.

She stared at his hand, gloveless and now idle again on the table. An elegant hand, with long, elegant fingers. It could have belonged to a man who'd mastered a classical instrument. On its pinky, the dark blue sapphire on the ducal signet ring seemed to swallow the light like a tiny ocean.

She felt his eyes on her, felt him noticing that she was noticing him.

"That's the *Manchester Guardian*," she said quickly, nodding at the paper he had put aside.

Montgomery gave her a wry look. "I take it you took me for a *Times* reader."

"The *Morning Post*, actually." A paper even more stuffy than the *Times*. Suffragists read the *Guardian*.

"Right on all accounts," he said, and lifted the copy of the *Guardian* to reveal the *Times*. Then the *Morning Post*.

"That's very thorough, Your Grace."

"Not really. When you want to understand what is happening in the country at large, you read all sides."

She remembered that this was the man the queen had put in charge of leading the Tory party to victory. He would want to know all that was happening in the country, the better to steer it.

Ah, she had sensed it already on Parliament Square when they had locked eyes, had sensed it like any creature recognized one of its kind: Montgomery was a clever, clever man. It was as unsettling as the intimate knowledge that his silky waistcoat concealed a well-muscled body.

She reached for the teacup, and the delicate china rattled and tea sloshed over the rim.

"Apologies," she murmured.

Montgomery's gaze narrowed at her.

A footman swooped, picked up cup and flooded saucer, and carried it off.

She tried to stretch, to get more air into her lungs. It didn't help; a boulder seemed to crush her chest.

"I beg your pardon," she whispered. "I have to excuse myself."

The duke said something, but she couldn't quite make sense of it. Her legs were heavy; she all but struggled to her feet. One step, another step, away from the table . . . her vision dimmed.

Oh, lord no.

A chair scraped across the floor, and she fell headlong into a black tunnel.

⁓⸎⁓

She came to flat on her back, her body buzzing as if swarmed by a million bees. She was on a settee, with her feet propped up and the acrid stench of smelling salts in her nose. Faces were hovering above her. Mrs. Beecham the housekeeper, the butler, and Montgomery.

The duke's expression was grim. "So you were not fine," he said.

She glowered at him, he who had practically compelled her to become ill with his doom-say prophecy on the fields yesterday.

"I'm fine enough, Your Grace."

He went down on one knee beside her, his eyes hard. "You would have cracked your head on the floor had I not caught you."

Damsel on his horse, damsel fainting into his arms. She was gripped by the insane impulse to laugh, and it came out as an awful choking sound. Mrs. Beecham clasped a worried hand over her mouth.

"My physician will be here shortly," Montgomery said.

A doctor? She made to sit up. "I can't—"

His hand closed over her shoulder and pushed her back down, gently but firm.

"She might be delirious," the butler said to Mrs. Beecham, as if she couldn't hear him.

"You don't understand," she said, hating the desperation in her voice. She hadn't been ill since she had been a girl. She couldn't be, there was always something that needed doing. Now it was her coursework . . . her pupils . . .

"Whom may I notify?" Montgomery asked.

The words rolled through her head sluggishly. "Professor Jenkins," she said. "I don't think I'll finish the translation on time."

"Definitely delirious," Mrs. Beecham said, "the poor thing."

"I meant a next of kin, miss," Montgomery said impatiently.

"Oh," she said. "There's no one."

What good would it do to tell Gilbert? She was the one taking care of them; he'd only become flustered. Tears stung hotly in her nose. If she fell behind in her coursework, she'd jeopardize her stipend . . . her future . . . "There's no one," she repeated, "so I can't . . . I can't be ill."

There was a pause.

"I see," Montgomery said. She glanced at him, for his tone had softened suspiciously.

"You will be in good hands here," he said. She realized his hand was still on her shoulder, its weight anchoring her body, which seemed to have turned to hot steam.

"I cannot afford—" *A doctor*, she wanted to say, but he shook his head.

"You will be safe here."

Safe.

A promise of a tall order. But he sounded so calm, there was no question that what he said would be done. That one could safely let him take over for a while. Apparently, one didn't have to like a man to trust him.

Sebastian was pacing in front of Miss Archer's chamber door, frowning at the pocket watch in his hand. By the looks of it, he'd be well on his way to London before Dr. Bärwald arrived, and he'd have to rely on his butler to give all the proper instructions.

She would have fainted and fallen in midwalk, like timber. And the gleam of panic in her eyes just now . . . He would not feel guilty about this. She was a grown woman in possession of all her senses. It had been entirely her decision to take off in freezing temperatures in a threadbare coat.

He slid the watch back into his pocket and turned to Bonville. "Should her condition worsen while I'm in London, have a telegram sent to the Belgravia residence."

The butler's lips pursed in surprise. "Yes, Your Grace."

"And, Bonville?"

The butler stepped closer. "Your Grace?"

"Tell my man to find out about Miss Archer."

Chapter 11

———❧———

Annabelle jerked awake, heart pounding and gasping for breath. It was the old nightmare, the fall from a great height, and just as her every muscle had braced for impact, her eyes slitted open.

The bright light of a winter morning sliced right into her skull.

"Fiddlesticks." Her voice emerged as a croak.

"You're awake." Hattie bounced out of the armchair by the fireplace; Catriona rose with more decorum. The mattress dipped as they both settled on the edge of the bed, their gazes homing in on her.

Annabelle dragged herself into a sitting position and tucked her disheveled braid back behind her ear. "What time is it?" she whispered.

"Nine o'clock," Hattie said, handing her a glass of water. "December sixteenth," she added.

Good gracious. Monday. So she had slept a day and two nights and remembered very little. She took a sip of water.

Hattie made to feel her forehead. "How do you feel?"

Battered. Like a wall had collapsed on her. "A little tired," she said, "thank you."

Both her friends had faint purple crescents beneath their eyes. It must have been their soft fingers that she had felt on her face in her fever dreams. They had kept her cool and hydrated.

Her throat squeezed shut. "I never meant to ruin this house party for you." In fact . . . "Weren't we meant to leave yesterday?"

"You were in no position to travel, so we sent word and stayed," Catriona said. "We will stay for a few more days."

Aghast, she put down the glass. "That's very kind but hardly necessary."

Hattie tutted. "We can hardly leave you here all alone; the duke is practically a bachelor."

Bother, but that was true.

She shifted under the blankets. It was physically uncomfortable, accepting such care lavished upon her person, like wearing an itchy corset. Or perhaps that was the feeling of guilt. She could tell that they were waiting for an explanation for all of this, politely, patiently.

She wondered how sympathetic they'd be if they knew the real reason why she had taken off like a rifle shot.

Ladies, seven years ago, I had a lover. No, not the letter-writing type who steals a kiss or two; the type who rucks up your skirts and takes your innocence, and his father berated me just like the duke did, and so I ran.

"I'm sorry," she said. "As I said in the note—the duke recognized me and it resulted in a misunderstanding. I left too hastily."

"But you see, that's the worrying part," Hattie said. "You are always so thoughtful. We couldn't see you doing anything hasty—unless . . ."

"Unless?"

"Say, was he awfully horrible to you?"

You picked the wrong man . . . your efforts will lead you nowhere . . . She cringed a little just recalling Montgomery's words.

"He was not his charming self," she said.

Hattie pursed her lips. "He has a charming self?"

He didn't.

But then she remembered how he had looked with his hat in his hand there on the hill. *Sincere.* Infinitely more valuable than charming . . .

"His valet delivered this for you," Catriona said, pointing at the nightstand.

There was a stack of books that hadn't been there before.

"There's a note." Hattie handed her the white envelope. "We have been dying to know what it says."

The paper of the note was thick and smooth like pressed silk. The ducal monogram was engraved across the top in golden swirls.

Dear Miss Archer,

His Grace the Duke of Montgomery wishes you a speedy recovery. He puts these books at your disposal: some Voltaire, Rousseau, and Locke, as well as some more lighthearted reading. If you have a specific book in mind, please do not hesitate to ask for it. The library is at your disposal.

Your servant,
Ramsey

Annabelle handed the note to her friends. "He wishes me a speedy recovery," she said, perusing the books. Voltaire, Rousseau, Locke. Notably all of them were philosophers with ideas about democracy. The last book, a hefty tome, she didn't know.

"Dostoyevsky," Catriona said, "a Russian novel recently translated to English. I hear it's all the rage in London."

Annabelle opened to the first page. "*Crime and Punishment*. A shocking tale about a student and the perils of ideological intoxication," she read out. She looked up. "His Grace is sending a message about political activism," she said sourly.

Or was this his idea of a joke? She knew now that a clever sense of humor lurked beneath the cool façade. If it was a joke, it was a strangely private one.

She sank back into the pillows, already exhausted and unsure whether to smile or to frown. She might not exactly like him. But she very, very much wanted to make sense of him.

A tentative rap on the door had Sebastian glancing from his desk at the clock. His brother was punctual to the minute. Regrettable, that Peregrin acted in a disciplined manner only when he felt the noose tightening around his neck. That was about to change.

His brother sidled into the room, his expression somber.

"Sit," Sebastian said.

Peregrin hesitated. "May I offer an apology first?" There were dark smudges under his eyes. He looked as though he hadn't slept a wink.

"You may."

Peregrin let out a shuddering breath. "I regret what I have done," he began. "I just wanted some company before going to Wales. I didn't do it to provoke you for the sake of it; they were supposed to be gone by the time you returned."

And he had done well until that last sentence. A faint pulse began beating in Sebastian's ears. "Surely you must have expected that there would be consequences either way."

Peregrin swallowed. "The truth is, once I thought better of it, I didn't think I could rescind the invitations."

"Sit," Sebastian repeated, and then he said, "That's the issue, isn't it. You get caught in traps of your own making, because you act without considering the consequences." He braced his arms on the desk. "That's the behavior of a child, Peregrin. The world of men does not work that way. There is always a price to pay for your actions, and no one is going to pay it for you."

Peregrin's gaze skittered away. "I know I've earned a punishment for this."

"I'm not going to punish you."

Hazel eyes narrowed at him with suspicion.

"Make no mistake," he said, "you belong in the stocks. But since the corrective effects are obviously lost on you, I don't see the point."

He picked up the paper he had brought back from London. "I met with Admiral Blyton yesterday."

Peregrin went still.

Sebastian slid the form across the desk. "Your acceptance letter to the Royal Navy."

A parade of emotions chased across Peregrin's face: confusion, disbelief, panic. Panic it was. He made to rise, the blood drained from his face. "No."

Sebastian leveled a glare at him. "Sit down. And, yes."

Peregrin gripped the edge of the desk. "I'm not a soldier."

"Obviously," Sebastian said. "If you were, you would know a modicum of discipline and I wouldn't have encountered sixteen uninvited guests in my house."

Peregrin blinked at him as if he were seeing him for the first time. "You would send me to my death because of a party?"

"Your death?" The pulse began to pound in his ears. "Peregrin, this is training, not combat."

"But these ships—they are infested with deadly diseases and rotten food and . . . rats!"

"In the navy with the highest hygiene standards in the world? Nonsense."

"I'd be at sea for weeks, months," Peregrin yelped.

"That has not yet killed a man, either," Sebastian said, feeling entirely unmoved. "You will leave for Plymouth in February. Now sign it."

Peregrin was staring at pen and paper before him as if they were a cup of hemlock.

When he looked up, his lips were trembling. "You . . . you can't make me."

That didn't even merit a response. He could make Peregrin do anything; he could lock him up or toss him out, cut off all his credit, and turn the peers of the realm against him. He could take the last shirt on his back and no one would dare question him about it. Such was the lot of younger sons and brothers.

Sweat gathered on Peregrin's brow. "I could prove myself," he croaked. "Have me run one of the northern estates for a year . . ."

"Sign it."

"Brother, please." The words dropped between them helplessly like birds shot down in flight.

Sebastian stilled.

The fear in his brother's voice felt like a punch to the chest.

His own brother was afraid of him, as if he were some crazed tyrant, demanding unreasonable things.

Abruptly, he came to his feet. Wariness flashed across Peregrin's face, and that only irritated him more. He rounded his desk, only just stopping short of grabbing his brother by the scruff of his neck.

"Stand up."

Peregrin scrambled to his feet, and Sebastian gripped his shoulder and spun him toward the wall.

"Look at this," he said, pointing at the rows of estate paintings. "This is not just about you. We have ten estates in two countries. Our family is one of the oldest in Britain, we are one of the biggest land-holders in England, and if I fell off my horse and broke my neck to-morrow, all of this would be in your hands." He turned his brother to face him. "Unless you are a capable man, our house would bury you like an avalanche, and you won't be the only one going down. Do you think the lives of thousands of staff and tenants are a game? Christ, getting Castle Montgomery back is a mission in its own right, and not a day goes by when I don't detest the fact that our family seat is in the hands of another man."

Peregrin's eyes flashed with the wild, reckless look of a man cornered. "But that *is* it," he said. "I don't want this."

"What was that?"

"I can't, don't you see?" His voice was rising, actually rising. "I can't. I can't be you."

"Keep your voice down," Sebastian said, his own voice having dropped dangerously low.

Peregrin began to squirm in his grip. "You don't care what happens to me; if I weren't your heir, you wouldn't even notice my existence, but I can't be duke."

The revelations fell like blows. Suddenly pieces shifted into place, and things that had long seemed *senseless* began making sense. Icy fury rose in his throat. "Is that what this has been about all along? Your absurd behavior? To demonstrate how unfit you are?"

Peregrin's eyes were glittering hot, his hand clutching at Sebastian's restraining arm. "It's not my place to be duke."

"Hereditary succession says it is, whether you like it or not," Sebastian said coldly.

"You could have sons," Peregrin shot back. "Why don't you? Why do you make me pay for that?"

Suddenly they were toe to toe, his hand a fist in his brother's jacket, and Peregrin's face twisted with fury and disbelief. He still gave like a puppy in his grip.

It halted Sebastian in his tracks like a wall.

God. It shouldn't even have come this far.

He dropped his hand and stepped back, his pulse thrumming in his neck.

Peregrin sagged into himself.

Well, bloody hell. Sebastian straightened his sleeves. He took another backward step, put more distance between them.

His brother's cheeks were burning red, but he had pulled himself together, waiting, watching him defiantly and no doubt feeling sorry for himself.

Not that long ago, the boy had barely come up to his elbow, his hair a mop of fluffy blond curls. Not notice his existence? Sebastian shook his head. He would step in the path of a bullet for his brother, as reflexively as he drew breath.

When he spoke next, his voice was implacable. "In February, you will go to Plymouth. And I will forget the things you said today."

Peregrin's eyes shuttered. He gave a slow nod. "Yes, sir." And he kept nodding as he dropped his gaze and stared at his shoes, and Sebastian understood that it was to force back tears.

He turned to look out the window. Against the black of night, he saw only his own distorted reflection.

"I advise you to see it as an opportunity and not as a punishment," he said. He should probably have said something more, but as usual when tears were involved, no words came to mind. "Sign it. Then you may leave."

∽✺∼

Somewhere in her diary, his former wife said that he had a lump of ice where others had a heart. He was inclined to agree. He turned cold from the inside out when faced with adversity, a reflex, like another man's pulse might speed up in the face of danger. If that was being heartless, so be it. It had advantages that a part of his brain kept cool under all circumstances. Except, apparently, when his brother stabbed into his Achilles' heel with the precision of Paris himself.

You could have sons . . . why don't you?

The hour was nearing midnight now, the fire crackling low on the grate, but his brother's voice still echoed through his study, and it had him reaching for his cigarette case.

He leaned back in his chair and exhaled smoke.

Watched through the wafting gray tendrils, Castle Montgomery appeared to come alive on the dark office wall across. It was always misty around the castle. It was a place of shadows and echoes. It had never felt like a home; now it had long become a ball and chain. But duty was duty. One did not lose an ancestral seat in a card game.

Why don't you?

His brother was an idiot. But he had a point.

He bent and unlocked the bottom drawer of his desk.

There glinted the frilly yellow silk case of the diary. It used to have an ornate little lock that had offered no resistance.

He flipped it open.

The sight of the loops and swirls of girlish penmanship tightened his grip on the book. He had read it only once; still, all the relevant words were etched into his memory. But nearly two years on, they might sound different.

12th January, 1878

M officially proposed today. I knew this day would come, it has long been arranged, but I'm strangely torn. A young lady could hardly aspire to more than becoming a duchess. I do want to be a duchess. Mama and Papa are thrilled, of course. But I can't deny that my heart aches for T. He's so distraught, begged me to elope, even, and swears he shall love me forever . . . it's terribly romantic. If it were not for his title, I certainly should never choose the duke. He isn't romantic at all. He's awfully quiet and severe, and I've never seen him dance. He's by far the least charming gentleman of the ton . . .

Ah well.

Sebastian dumped the diary back into the drawer.

No need to live through it again word by word when the ending was engraved on his mind anyway. Not six months later, she had run away with the young man she thought she loved. And he hadn't seen it coming. Ironic, how he excelled at reading people for his dealings in politics, and hadn't noticed that his own wife had grown bored and resentful, or both, and wouldn't hesitate to set fire to a powder keg. In fairness, understanding a well-bred woman required nothing short of mind-reading. They were, after all, trained to please and endure with a smile.

And all his options for a wife were the same—ladies trained to please and endure. He had to marry a diamond of the first water, even more so now than before the divorce if only to silence his detractors. He'd never really know if the future duchess was only barely suffering him . . .

A soft scratching sound had him glancing at the door. "Enter."

Ramsey moved into the room quietly, a silver tray with a note in hand.

"Your Grace. There was a note for you. I'm afraid the delivery was delayed."

"Who sends it?"

"Miss Archer, Your Grace."

He straightened in his chair. "How is she?"

"Still rather weak, I understand, still feverish."

But able to write, that had to be a good sign. Then again, she had tried to debate politics with him while on the verge of fainting. Stubborn woman.

He opened the envelope. "Has my informant sent anything on her yet?"

"No, Your Grace."

Stubborn, and mysterious.

Her handwriting was not feminine. It was efficient, the hand of a person who wrote a lot, and fast.

Your Grace,

I much appreciate your hospitality and I endeavor to get well as speedily as possible. Thank you for your generous book loan. I am particularly intrigued by the Russian tale on ideological intoxication—a purely incidental choice, I believe?

Sincerely,
A. Archer

Stubborn, mysterious, and witty.

He had sent up books because it was a polite thing to do for a bedridden guest. He had sent those particular books because for some reason, he had known they'd make her think, and her thoughts intrigued him. With her expressive eyes, she was not hard to read, and yet he found her rather unpredictable. Well, one thing was certain—this one would take a man to task if he displeased her. God knew he didn't care for contrariness; his life was presently littered enough with the wreckage of insubordination, but at least she'd make noise before the man in her life crushed her. Did she have a man in her life? She had said she had no one . . .

He realized that he had left his valet hanging, absorbed in his musings about Annabelle Archer.

He tucked her note into his breast pocket. "That will be all, Ramsey."

Chapter 12

The next morning, Sebastian cornered Dr. Bärwald in the hallway outside Miss Archer's bedchamber. The young physician's expression was harried. "But, Your Grace, unless you are a next of kin or the husband, I can't go into detail about her condition."

"She does not have a husband or any next of kin nearby," Sebastian said impatiently. "She is presently my responsibility."

"And with all due respect, Your Grace, she's my patient."

"Which can be changed, easily," Sebastian said, and Bärwald's eyes widened behind his glasses. Sebastian was not normally in the habit of throwing his weight around; certainly he had never done it to Bärwald.

Several seconds ticked past as they stared at each other.

The doctor looked away first. "Very well," he said, his German accent thick. "She is already recovering nicely, they are resilient, country women, yes? But between us, the reason the cold could overpower her so utterly is that she suffers from long-term exhaustion. She displays signs of sleep deprivation and malnourishment."

Sebastian was taken aback. "She does not look it."

"As I said, she's resilient," the doctor said with a shrug, "but for her to truly recover, I recommend she does not travel for another week after her fever has gone."

"That will not be a problem," Sebastian said automatically.

"I'm not so sure about that," Bärwald murmured.

"How so?"

"Because the *Fräulein* objects to the order, Your Grace."

Sebastian felt the unfamiliar urge to roll his eyes. "Yes. The *Fräulein* would do that."

"Modern women," Bärwald said, shaking his head. "Give them a grand education, and next, they think they know better than the doctor ordered."

"Oh, she will follow the orders," Sebastian said, staring at the door to her chamber. Malnourished?

A sour feeling unfurled in his gut. Not on his watch. Until Christmas, she would eat, and whatever her troubles, they would stay outside the gates of Claremont.

⁂

"A week!" Annabelle's indignation flared afresh the moment Catriona and Hattie walked into her chamber after their morning ride. "I'll be here until Christmas."

Hattie settled at the vanity table, examining the wind burn on her cheeks. "I do like the sound of that," she said. "Just think! The duke might invite you to the New Year's party. We could all go to the ball together."

Annabelle was briefly stunned into silence. As she lay propped up against the pillows in the vast bed, her head aching, an upper-class ball was the very last thing on her mind.

"I shall leave when you leave, it's simple," she said.

"No," came the unison reply.

Annabelle glowered at her friends. "*Et tu*, Brutus?"

"Surely Dr. Bärwald only has your best interest in mind," Hattie said gently.

Dr. Bärwald also had no idea about her assignments for Jenkins, her pupils, or that she was expected in Chorleywood. As soon as she could leave the bed, she'd ask Montgomery to get a coach ready for her.

"I've asked Aunty to stay here as a chaperone," Hattie said. "She's glad to do so."

Grand. Annabelle stared up at the velvety bed canopy. She couldn't remember ever having been so dependent on other people's help, and she resented all of it.

Well, perhaps not *all* of it.

There were the books.

And the food. The kitchen was sending up almost more than she could eat. The stew yesterday had been flavorful, with big chunks of chicken in the broth and hot rolls as a side. She had eaten all of those. And there was an exotic selection of fresh fruits on her breakfast tray, oranges and grapes and pears, and she had eaten all of those, too, smothered in thick, golden custard.

Catriona pulled a chair closer to the bed. "Do you want me to read some more from *Crime and Punishment*?"

There was an unwilling sound from the direction of the vanity table. "Can't we ask for something nicer, like Jane Austen?" Hattie said. "I vow, I shall have to draw up a family tree in order to follow this novel. And why does the same character have to be called three completely different names?"

"I doubt the duke stocks women's novels, Hattie," Annabelle said mildly.

"How about Tomlinson's lovely sonnet, then? Could we hear that again?"

Annabelle eyed the pile of well-wishes on her nightstand. In lieu of flowers, the dozen young gentlemen at Claremont had tried to outdo each other with various attempts at poetry in her honor. Peregrin had also sent up a deck of cards one could apparently play alone. She reached for James Tomlinson's sonnet. His iambic pentameters were shaky, but Hattie found that made it all the more charming.

Tomlinson would be on her list of eligible bachelors, if only he had a title.

Montgomery hadn't even replied to her thank-you note. Of course, there was no reason for him to reply at all; still, she kept catching herself listening for the footfall of a servant bearing a silver tray. Indeed, she would leave this bed, and Claremont, as soon as her legs could carry her.

⁓⳿⳾⳿⁓

That night, she slept fretfully, afraid of dreaming about tumbling into a black hole. When she woke, the dark had the soundless, heavy quality of the hours past midnight. And someone had been in her room.

Annabelle turned up the lamp next to the bed with sleepy fingers.

There was a new book on her nightstand, and another fancy card lay on top of it.

She opened the envelope in a deliberate, civilized manner.

The handwriting was different, scratched onto the paper with bold precision.

She rushed through the words.

Miss Archer,

I have been informed that you enjoy Jane Austen's work—

Her head jerked up. *Blast you, Hattie.* What would Montgomery think about such an insatiable and random appetite for reading material?

—and we have several of her novels in the library. I—incidentally— selected a copy of Pride and Prejudice. *Do not hesitate to send for more.*

M.

She gave a bemused laugh. *Pride and Prejudice.* There was no doubt now that they were playing a game. With book titles.

Her fingertip touched the *M.*, scrawled so confidently in black ink. *He's very arrogant, and you don't like his type.*

Something to remember as long as she was trapped in this splendid bubble where food came at the ring of a bell and the libraries had starlit skies.

Still, a restlessness that had been roiling inside her all day seemed to dissipate. Her body stretched out long as soon as she had extinguished the lamp, and she plummeted into sleep like a small child.

⁓⁓

Sebastian's day had been ruthlessly productive since morning. That happened when there were no guests in need of entertaining. He had read the reports on all estates, had decided on a new irrigation method for the northern landholdings, and had finalized the draft for the last leg of the Tory campaign. He would need the queen on his side to push the approach through, because Disraeli would object, but since he had just signed off the bill for the biggest bloody firework show in England, he figured Her Majesty would indulge him.

A scratch at the door, and Ramsey slunk in.

"Your Grace, the organizers for the ball had another suggestion for the décor."

He shot the valet an incredulous look. "I don't have time to approve decorative details."

"Indeed, it is just, with this particular detail—"

"What is it?"

"Reindeer."

"Live reindeer?"

"Yes, Your Grace." Said with a perfectly straight face.

"In the ballroom?"

"Yes. Apparently, they are highly popular with the guests."

He rubbed his temples. "Ramsey, did you think I would approve of a herd of ungulate animals on the parquet to please the masses?"

"No, Your Grace."

"Then feel free to not bother me with it."

"Yes, Your Grace."

Sebastian scanned the neat stacks of paper on his desk. "Has there been any correspondence for me?"

"I delivered all to your desk this morning, as usual," Ramsey replied.

He knew that. There had been a note from Caroline, Lady Ling-ham, asking him to bring Miss Archer along to her annual Christmas dinner on the twenty-fourth. News of his guest had traveled fast and wide, and naturally, Caroline would take note.

"Are you certain there was nothing else in the meantime?"

Ramsey knew better than to look nonplussed at his master's insistence that there be mail. "No, but if you have a specific sender in mind I can make inquiries—"

He shook his head. "No. Tell the groom to get my horse ready."

❧

Annabelle had had the armchair moved to the window. The sun was dissolving into a pink hue on the horizon but it was still light enough to read a letter from Lucie that had arrived during her afternoon nap.

Dear Annabelle,

I am sorry to hear about your illness, unless it was a ploy all along to stay on behind enemy lines, in which case, I salute you for your dedication to our cause.

I have little hope of us converting M.—I recently learned through my more secret sources that the queen promised him his family seat back in case he helps win the election. I think he'll move heaven and earth to keep Disraeli in power. So we have to move fast on other fronts. I heard the suffragist chapter in Manchester is planning a large demonstration on Parliament Square during the Tories' pre-election meeting in January. I am presently coordinating with Millicent Fawcett's chapter in London to join them. I strongly believe we should pull together and mobilize all the scattered suffrage chapters throughout England. Strength is to be had in numbers. It is still a secret, though, so I must ask you to treat this confidentially. As for—

Hoofbeats sounded on the cobblestones below. She lowered the letter into her lap. Gathering up her robe, she leaned forward and peered down into the courtyard. Her heart gave an appalling leap when she saw the white horse prancing past the fountain. Her first instinct was to shrink back, but then again, she couldn't.

The duke's head turned toward her window.

Her heart began to beat like a drum.

Montgomery raised his hand and touched the rim of his hat. Slowly and deliberately enough that it could not be mistaken for anything other than an acknowledgment.

She sank back into her chair.

She hadn't yet thanked him for the latest book. She had begun to give too much thought to the wording, hopelessly gauche. And the deeper truth was, she liked being the one owing the answer. Much more so than waiting for letters from a man who made her heart beat faster.

⁓⁓⁓

The next morning, her fever was gone. Annabelle padded to the windows and pushed the heavy curtains aside. The morning sky was bright blue and spotless as if freshly rinsed. Below in the quad, smatterings of snow sparkled like carelessly scattered diamonds.

Ah, she could almost taste the fresh air.

A quick glance at the mirror said that she looked presentable.

Soaking in the tub the night before had washed away much of her exhaustion, and indulging in rolls and custard for three days had restored a long-lost softness to her face. She secured her hair in a simple bun, brushed her teeth, and splashed herself with the rose-scented water from the washbasin. Chemise, corset—loosely laced— Lady Mabel's gray walking dress, hat. She shrugged into her coat and slipped out the door.

She managed to find her way through the labyrinth of stairs and hallways to the ground floor. There was a vast stone terrace, curving like the prow of a ship, at the back of the house, and one of the glass doors leading outside was already ajar.

She glided into the open, drinking in the clear air as she closed her eyes against the warm glare of the sun. When she opened her eyes, her next breath lodged in her throat.

His back turned, Montgomery stood at the balustrade.

She was still holding her breath.

Even from behind, the duke did not look welcoming, his coat stretched taut across his shoulders, his stance as rigid as the weathered stone statues to his left and right.

It stirred an emotion in her, the way he held himself so still and looked so . . . alone. Perhaps that was why she did not tiptoe back into the house.

And of course, he had sensed that she was there. He did not as much turn as rotate toward her.

Her mouth went dry. When had she begun thinking of him as handsome? Because he was; indeed, he looked as attractively crisp and cool as the winter morning.

His brow promptly creased with disapproval. "Should you be out yet, miss?"

"I'm much improved, Your Grace." She strolled closer. "The fever was gone yesterday."

The view from the balustrade was magnificent, a vast rectangular expanse of symmetrically swirling evergreen hedges, as favored by the old French kings. One would hear the gurgle of fountains from here in summer.

Montgomery was still scrutinizing her.

She met his gaze furtively, the well-mannered way. "I couldn't bear another minute in my room."

His frown deepened. "Is there anything you need?"

"No. You have provided everything and more, thank you. I just cannot stay confined for long."

His lips quirked at that. "No," he said, "I did not think you could."

It was remarkable that he should have formed an opinion about her. Then again, it might not be a flattering opinion. Perhaps he considered an urge for the outdoors a defect in a woman.

"May I ask what brings you to that conclusion, Your Grace?"

"It's the second time I've seen you walk away from a warm place in the space of a few days. That's not a woman who is amenable to confinement."

"I wasn't aware there were women who are amenable to confinement."

That seemed to amuse him. "Most are. Confinement is but the other side of safety. Take the rule of law, or a warm room. Or a husband. Most women desire the safety that comes with this, and accept the confinement."

Safety.

She wanted to be safe. But apparently, not at all costs. She had of course known that about herself already—what rattled her was that he, apparently, knew this about her, too.

"It doesn't mean that women wouldn't prefer freedom," she said.

"Freedom," Montgomery said, testing the word. "Is that what you prefer?"

His face revealed no clue as to why he was asking about her. She had to glance away, because looking into his clever eyes made her feel strange. Strangely overheated, strangely queasy low in her belly.

Mundane gestures became infused with meaning; her senses opened and sharpened, and there was an unnerving awareness of the rapid beat of her heart against her ribs.

She focused on their hands, side by side on the granite banister. Her gloves looked shoddy next to pristine kid leather, and she dropped her hands and folded them in front of her.

"Yes, I prefer freedom," she said. "John Stuart Mill says it is better to have choices even if it complicates matters, that it is better to be a dissatisfied human than a satisfied pig."

Montgomery made a sound that resembled a laugh, choked back just in time. "Compelling," he said. "Are you implying that most of your fellow women aren't fully human?"

"I'm not implying that at all," she said quickly. "I'm well aware that with how things are, the price women pay for independence is often too high."

"Everything always has a price," Montgomery said.

Still not a trace of resentment in his voice over her philosophical foray, no attempt to lecture her on John Stuart Mill. An unexpected thrill of elation licked through her, much as when they had been sparring over voting rights at the breakfast table. There was something to be said about debating with a learned man who had nothing to prove. It took more than an educated woman with opinions to threaten him. And that allowed for an easy, absurdly pleasing intimacy. *He is still the enemy to your cause, you goose.*

Montgomery turned toward the stairs leading down to the French garden. "Come, if you will."

She took a step before it dawned on her that she was about to walk with him. Alone. Instinctively, she cast a look around the terrace for a chaperone. She saw the precise moment when the duke understood her predicament. His face assumed a mildly derisive expression. *Do you think anyone here could stop me or hold me accountable?* said that expression, and there was an annoying, challenging glint in his eyes. Blast her inability to resist a good challenge. To his credit, he didn't gloat when she wordlessly took the arm he offered. He led her down the stairs in silence, then steered her left onto a gravel path.

"What do you think people would do if someone handed them their freedom on a platter tomorrow?" he asked.

They would breathe. "They would go on to find a purposeful life, suited to them."

Montgomery shook his head. "They would be frightened witless. Why do you think some young people rebel until they hit a boundary?"

"To become capable adults with independent minds?"

"Hardly. To get a sense of themselves by way of their limits, to feel assured that there is something to stop them from spiraling into disorientation no matter what they do." He seemed to have someone specific in mind now, for his voice had darkened with some private displeasure.

"Why not just ask the rebel in question about his motivations?" she ventured.

"But that presupposes that what he thinks he wants is actually what he needs." He sounded bemused. Clearly, that wasn't a possibility.

Annabelle peered up at him. The morning light was unforgiving on his face, showing every line. It had to be exhausting, striding through life knowing better what people needed than the people themselves. But that was part of his attraction, was it not? In a world where everyone was swept along in the murky current of circumstances, paddling frantically this way or that, his unapologetic self-assurance loomed like a rock in the rapids. Here was a man who would take charge, and then not bungle it.

Out of nowhere flashed a thought: what would it be like, to be married to such a man?

Free. At the side of a man who took care of things, a woman could be free.

She nearly stumbled on the perfectly even path. What a ridiculous notion—freedom was probably the very last thing a domineering male like Montgomery would offer. With his wealth and position he'd certainly provide more safety than she could wish for, but anyone with an ounce of independent thought would be crushed under his protection. He'd manage her and demand submission, convinced he'd always know best, inside and outside the marriage bed, and no, she really should not have thought of him in bed, performing his marital duties, with his eyes glazed over with lust and his fair hair damp and plastered against his temples . . . A heat wave surged through her veins.

She kept her gaze firmly on the path. His merciless eyes would spot it immediately, that her whole treacherous body had blushed pink.

"So," she muttered, "is it always a matter of being either free or safe, Your Grace?"

"Actually," she heard him say, "I find it is usually a compromise between the two."

They rounded the corner and a flat stone building with a large glass cupola at its center came into view. Long rows of floor-to-ceiling windows brightly reflected the morning light and made her shield her eyes with her hand.

"What is this place?"

"A compromise," Montgomery said, and steered her toward the building. He halted at a side entrance and swung back the door.

The green tangle and pungent warmth of a jungle greeted them. Towering canopies in lush shades of green absorbed the light that slanted through the glass cupola above.

"It's a conservatory," she said softly.

The air clung and throbbed like a physical thing, a blend of rich, damp soil, of overripe fruit and nectar and decay. A flagstone path disappeared into the thicket ahead, enticing her to follow scattered pink and red blossoms like the will-o'-the-wisp. And it was so warm. She *had* been feeling cold.

He must have expected her to refuse to go back inside.

A compromise.

She turned to him, feeling strangely somber. "It's magical."

∼⚭∼

Magical? Such whimsy from a woman who read Thucydides. In Greek. But then he was learning that Miss Archer was many things.

And here he was staring at her face again. He knew he had an exacting eye. He had never been able to not notice the error in a ledger, or that one quavering note in a song. But her features were arranged exactly how some primal aesthetic blueprint in his head envisioned beauty. It made her look oddly familiar, as if he had long known her and now she had walked back into his life. Impossible, that. She might speak and carry herself like landed gentry, but his informant had finally sent his report, which said she had been a maid in her cousin's dilapidated cottage in Kent.

Her green eyes widened. "Is it my imagination, or does the floor feel warm?"

"That would be the underfloor heating."

She made an excited little noise, and it sent a thrill up his spine.

"The building is state-of-the-art," he said, "very functional. It allows crop breeding year round with great efficiency."

Her eyes gleamed with some secret mirth. "Without doubt, Your Grace."

She began meandering along the path looking up and around in wonder, and he followed, strangely mesmerized by the gentle sway of her skirts around her ankles.

"How did you collect all these plants?" she asked.

"The botanist in my employ does. He takes off to a foreign country to acquire them, or he purchases them from other traders here in England."

She touched her fingertip to the delicate pink petals of an oleander blossom. "What a marvelous profession," she said, "to travel all the corners of the world to bring back beautiful things."

The way her face had lit up made it hard to look away from her.

He had no time for indoor walks with her. He presently had a revolt of Tory backbenchers on his hands over his latest campaign proposal and he should be in his study, writing threatening letters. There was no other reason for him to be here than that he wanted to be here, and he didn't even feel inclined to question why a most unsuitable woman—a commoner, a bluestocking, a suffragist—would give him so much pleasure.

"So, to which corner of the world would you travel, miss?"

Her eyes darted to his face, probing the sincerity of his question.

She did not give lightly of herself.

"I should like to go to Persia," she finally said.

Most people would have said Paris. Perhaps Rome. "An ambitious destination."

She shook her head. "I used to dream of owning a Greek galleon. In my mind, I have already sailed the seven seas."

"A Greek galleon?" But of course, she studied the classics. "Did Odysseus inspire you?"

She looked at him from the corner of her eye. "Possibly."

"Why Persia?" he asked, intrigued. "Odysseus never left the Mediterranean Sea."

"Because," she said slowly, "there are theories about how Persia and Greece have influenced each other, in terms of architecture, government, literature . . . but we have few concrete proofs, and either side denies having been influenced by the other. And now my professor is very focused on this area of research."

"Would that be Professor Jenkins?"

"Why, yes! Are you familiar with his work?"

"I've never met the man, but my secretary reads his proposals," he said. "I sponsor some of his expeditions. Perhaps you have heard of the Royal Society."

"But of course. I just wasn't aware that you were a benefactor."

"My family was one of the founding members."

She gave him a thoroughly appreciative look, and he nearly preened. Ridiculous.

"Thanks to you, then, Professor Jenkins will begin a project in the Peloponnese in April," she said.

"To do what?"

"They have located a battleship on the bottom of Pylos Bay, and will lift parts of it to study them."

She had become increasingly animated while talking about it, her body vibrating with suppressed passion, and damned if that didn't affect him, urging his mind down wholly unacademic paths—

"Is he good to you, Jenkins?" he asked, pretending to study one of the thermostats on a tree trunk.

"Oh yes," she said cheerfully. "He works me hard, but he helped me get my place at Oxford. I'm very grateful to him."

For some reason, he didn't like the sound of that overly much. "Helped you how?"

"He was my late father's correspondent," she said. "After my father passed, I sorted his correspondence and found a half-written reply to Jenkins. I finished the letter, and well, he wrote back again. For years."

"And he never expressed reservations about discussing academic matters with a woman?"

He could tell the question annoyed her a little.

"No. My father had taught me well, it turned out. And . . ."

". . . and?"

"It may not have been clear from my signature, A. Archer, that I was, in fact, a woman."

Her raised chin was daring him to take umbrage at her little subterfuge.

He very nearly smiled. "When did you tell him the truth?"

"When I knew I needed his help to secure a place at Oxford. He took no offense, none at all. I'm grateful," she repeated.

She shouldn't have to be grateful. She had proven herself capable; she should have her chance.

The large terrarium by the wall drew her attention entirely for the next minute.

"What are those?" She pointed a slender finger at a neat row of green pods that clung to a branch behind the glass.

"Chrysalides. Butterfly cocoons."

She glanced back at him over her shoulder. "You keep butterflies, Your Grace?"

"They were my brother's idea. After I vetoed his suggestion to introduce a troop of monkeys here."

She laughed. A small burst of genuine laughter, showing pretty teeth and a flash of pink tongue, and it hit his blood dizzying like a gulp of sugar water. Want. He wanted to frame her laughing face in his hands and kiss it, anywhere, forehead, cheeks, nose. He wanted to feel her against his mouth. The hell . . .

She had already turned back to the display, bending forward.

"I think I see a caterpillar," she breathed. "How fascinating."

"Very."

There was a pale inch of skin exposed between her collar and her nape. A stray curl nestled there, wound tight in the damp air. So tempting, to try and wind this silkiness around his finger . . . to touch the delicate softness of her neck with his lips.

Her shoulders went rigid, as if he had said it all out loud, and he realized he had begun to lean over her, hunting for her scent.

Good God.

He straightened, head spinning. The heavy air was clearly muddling his brain.

She turned, a wary expression in her eyes. "I didn't think butterflies thrived in a terrarium."

"They are released when they are ready." His voice was hoarse. "You can open the lid"—he demonstrated it—"and anything with wings can leave."

She didn't smile.

She wasn't an innocent, he understood. He saw the same awareness in her eyes now that she doubtlessly saw in his—that they were
a man and a woman, alone in a secluded place throbbing with heat,
and that some invisible rope kept tugging at him to step into her
space, to slide his fingers into her collar and pull her against him.
And as he watched her, her mouth softened, softened as if it would
welcome . . .

A bird of paradise squawked and flapped and landed on the terrarium with a *thunk*.

She jumped.

"Ah, Peregrin," he said, annoyed. "He feeds them. They think you
will feed them when you stand here."

Two hectic red flags were burning on her cheeks, not the kind of
blush he liked to inspire in a woman. She stepped sideways, straight
out of his reach. He gave the bird an evil stare.

"Your Grace, I had been meaning to discuss my departure with
you."

A bucket of cold water would have had the same effect on his head.

It took him a moment to formulate a response. "I assume you
want to ignore the doctor's orders and leave posthaste."

She nodded.

"You said there was no one to look after you."

"I have relations in Kent, and they are expecting me."

The cousin with the dilapidated house. More sleep deprivation
and malnourishment.

"The doctor was clear," he said. "Seven days. And you are welcome at Claremont."

Determination flickered in her eyes. "Thank you, Your Grace, but
I have matters to attend to."

"Matters more urgent than your health?"

She looked away. "I'm well now."

She wasn't; she was suffering from severe stubbornness.

Sweat slid down his back, because God help him, he stood in a greenhouse in his bloody winter coat.

"You are free to leave anytime," he said, "but have a care for my conscience, since I will be called upon to abet your demise by supplying a coach."

That seemed to give her pause.

Ah. So she had a care for others, if not for herself.

"And your friends," he added. "They were worried about you and it would undo all their good work at your bedside if you relapsed."

The look in her eyes said she knew exactly what he was doing, that it was working, and that she resented him for it. So be it. If she were his, they wouldn't even be having this discussion, she'd be upstairs in bed, snug and warm.

"Well," she said reluctantly, "I suppose it would be more sensible to stay."

Disconcerting, how much he liked hearing that. "Until Christmas."

She gave a hesitant nod. "Until Christmas."

On the way back to the house, she was silent. Her profile was drawn and too pale. The outing had taken its toll on her. What would it take, for her to allow, no, to expect, someone to take care of her? She was twenty-and-five. Too young for the self-possession she displayed. Too old to still be unmarried. But that had to be by choice, unless every man in Kent was deaf and blind. His report said she had disappeared from her father's home for two years and returned only after her father's passing. There was hardly ever a good reason for a young woman to leave home for two years. *What price have you paid for your independence, Annabelle?*

"Would you accompany me on a walk through the stables tomorrow morning?" he asked.

She gave him an opaque look.

"The stables are warm," he said. "And the horses are some of the finest in England."

She was silent for a long moment. "It will depend on the state of my health."

And even more so on the state of her mood, presumably.

He offered her his arm to ascend the steps to the terrace. With some hesitation, she placed her hand on him. What had happened in the greenhouse had unsettled her.

What *had* happened in the greenhouse?

Nothing had happened. *Wanting* was a perfectly normal reaction when a man looked at a beautiful woman, wasn't it?

Chapter 13

It had been an unusually pleasant morning: clear skies and a good yield of birds. Sebastian hadn't expected to get a good shot after spending half the night at his desk outmaneuvering unruly party members. His contentment spiked when he saw a slender figure approaching the stables from the direction of the house.

"You seem improved, miss," he said, greeting her over the whining beagles swarming round his feet.

Her eyes swept first over him, then over Stevens, who was wearing the pheasants they had shot on strings around his neck.

"It occurred to me I owe your horse a treat," she said, and opened her right hand, revealing a small apple in her palm. "For carrying a double burden the other day."

The other day, when he had had to all but drag her back to Claremont. He could almost feel her weight in his arms, the softness of her hair against his face.

"That horse is working with McMahon in the paddock, miss," Stevens said.

Sebastian handed him his rifle. "Meet us at the paddock, then."

Her shoulders relaxed, and he knew he had guessed correctly—she preferred not to be alone with him today. And yet she had come.

They walked the first minute in silence. It was easy, walking with her, as she had naturally fallen into the long stride of a country woman. *Because she is a country woman.* He studied her even profile and wondered how much of her French blood was blue. His report said her maternal ancestors had come over from France with a count during the Terror, and the French had a reputation for fathering bastards on their staff.

"Do you enjoy hunting, Your Grace?" She sounded polite. Conversational.

"Yes," he replied. "It's one of the few pleasures of being a landowner." There. That was almost as if he hadn't been inches from kissing her beautiful neck just yesterday.

"What are the other pleasures of owning land?" she asked, a trace of irony in her voice.

"To put the right management practices into place. To know that the land will yield sustainably and profitably rather than go to waste."

Her gaze locked with his for the first time this morning. "I thought that was the stewards' responsibility."

"They report to me," he said. "Ultimately, the responsibility is mine." For all one hundred twenty thousand acres. The first week after his father's sudden demise, when he had locked himself in the study to scour stacks of ledgers and letters and contracts, he had been at an utter loss as to how his father could have been drinking, gambling, and spending time with his mistress while tens of thousand of acres lay ravaged by poor management. Another week and countless cigarettes later, he had concluded that his father had taken to drink and cards *because* of the estates—coupled with the poor liquidity and a few dismal investment decisions, their houses had become bottomless pits. Across Britain, more land holdings than not had steadily turned into white elephants since the industrial revolution. And he couldn't expect Annabelle Archer, clever as she was, to know such a thing; after all, the aristocracy itself pretended not to know that its names rested on feet of clay.

The paddock was busy; a few of the retired horses were on the far end, grooming each other. His horse was cantering circles on a lunge

line around McMahon, the sunlight gleaming off the powerful muscles working beneath the white coat.

Annabelle curled her hands around the banister, her eyes riveted
on the stallion. "He's magnificent," she said, "so strong, and yet so
graceful."

"He was bred to be so," he said. "The Andalusian horse is a cross
of European warmbloods and the Arabian thoroughbred, the best of
both worlds."

That made her smile, one of those small smiles that left him wondering.

"What's his name?" she asked.

He rattled off the official, very long, very Spanish name that was
recorded on the stallion's papers.

"Goodness," she said, "and what do you call him?"

"I don't," he said, and when he saw her bemused face, he added,
"It's a horse." A man might name a dog, but a horse?

The cogs were still visibly spinning behind her eyes.

"Out with it, miss," he said. "I can tell you have named him already."

She looked back at the horse, shielding her eyes against the glare
of the sun with her hand. "He looks like an Apollo."

The Greek god of light. Why not? It actually suited him.

One of the retired horses came trotting over, his ears twitching
back and forth with interest.

"And who are you?" Annabelle crooned at the animal, and he
couldn't help the stab of awareness that her tone was considerably
warmer now than when she was speaking to him. The gelding nuzzled
at her palm, nostrils flaring as he picked up the scent of the apple.

She glanced up at him, worry creasing her brow. "Why is his coat
so patchy? Is he ill?"

"No. He's old, nearing thirty."

She patted the eager gray muzzle. "Isn't he too frail to work,
then?"

"He's not working anymore, he is retired."

She stilled. "You keep retired horses?"

"Yes."

"Why?"

"Because they served me well and there is no need to turn them into soap before their time."

She was silent for a beat. Then she resumed stroking the horse and murmured something that sounded like "but it would be so much more efficient." The words could have annoyed him, but her tone was as tender as when she had greeted the decrepit horse. Something in his chest responded, a sudden bloom of warmth in the cold. He swallowed. He hadn't drunk in near two decades, but this was not unlike the heated sensation of Scotch burning down his throat. Could one become drunk on the presence of a woman?

She peered up at him from the corner of her eye, and whatever it was in her gaze made his head spin.

Yes. Yes, apparently, one could get drunk on a woman. Damn the obedient Stevens for putting an end to their cozy twosome.

❧

"Annabelle, you must give me your measurements before I leave today," said Hattie.

Annabelle raised her eyes from her correspondence.

The gray light of the afternoon filled the parlor. Hattie was lounging on the settee like an empress, a bowl of grapes on the low-legged table before her.

"And why is that, Miss Greenfield?"

"Because I have a feeling that you will be invited to Montgomery's New Year's Eve party, so you will need a ball gown."

"That's hardly likely."

"You're going to Lady Lingham's Christmas dinner."

"Because I'll still be stuck at Claremont when that takes place."

"Very well. Just imagine another unlikely situation occurs that leads to an invitation to the biggest house party of the year, and you have to decline because you have nothing to wear."

"Imagine I ordered a ball gown and wasn't invited to the party."

Hattie popped another grape into her mouth. "Then you would have a ball gown, which is never, ever a bad thing."

Annabelle sighed. "Catriona, say something."

Catriona, curled up in a large armchair, obligingly looked up from her notebook. "I'd stay away from any ball I could, but since my father insists I go, I'd rather we all go together."

Annabelle narrowed her gaze at her. "You're not helping, dear."

"Celeste has a new emerald silk in store," Hattie said. "My sister told me." She waved at a letter next to the fruit bowl. "You would look splendid in emerald."

Celeste. The Bond Street seamstress who was so famous, she could afford to go simply by *Celeste*, and people like Annabelle only knew her from the high-end fashion magazines Hattie smuggled into their college's common room. *Her silks flow like water . . . her creations do for a lady what a gold setting does for a diamond . . .*

Annabelle glanced down at her letter to Gilbert, where she claimed that she was convalescing in Catriona's Oxford residence at St. John's College. If she announced that she was spending Christmas with the Duke of Montgomery and was discussing silks by Celeste, they'd suspect her mind had derailed after a mere three months in higher education, and she'd be ordered back to Chorleywood quicker than she could say *Merry Christmas*.

She lowered the pen back onto the paper.

"You won't even think about it?" Hattie sounded disappointed.

"I cannot afford a ball gown."

A delicate little pause ensued.

"I was wondering what to get you for Christmas."

She fixed her friend with an incredulous look. "Hattie. I am not your *noble cause*."

At least the girl had the decency to look contrite—for a moment. Then a sly look entered her eyes. "But of course not," she said. "It'll cost you handsomely. Five hours a week sitting as Helen of Troy."

Helen of Troy again?

"Emerald silk," Hattie singsonged, "champagne, waltzing, eligible bachelors. And—"

Annabelle threw up her hands. "All right, all right. You will get my measurements, and Helen of Troy."

Hattie's face lit up like the enormous Christmas tree in Claremont's main sitting room. "Fabulous!"

In the corner, the pendulum clock bonged, once, twice.

"Do excuse me," Hattie said, "Aunty will be waking from her nap."

Catriona looked on in awe as the door fell shut behind their friend. "She has just talked you into sitting for a painting you don't want to sit for in order to get a gown you don't want."

Annabelle gave a shrug. "It is of no consequence. I won't be invited."

"I think Hattie is not entirely wrong," Catriona said, her expression pensive.

Annabelle frowned. "What do you mean?"

"It's just a feeling."

That was suspect. Catriona never just had feelings; there was usually a long list of facts underpinning the things she said.

"What dress are you going to wear for the Christmas dinner?" Catriona asked.

"The light blue damask." It was the finest one she had been given, but she had worn it before, here at Claremont. It had to do.

"I heard that Lady Lingham and the duke . . . have an arrangement," Catriona said.

Oh.

The blush tinging Catriona's cheeks left little doubt over the nature of that arrangement.

Why should this surprise her? Men of Montgomery's standing usually had a mistress tucked away somewhere. But an arrangement with a social equal?

She kept her voice neutral. "What is she like, the countess?"

"She's his neighbor. Older, and widowed," Catriona said. "She might have influence over him, so perhaps we should target ladies like her with our campaign."

"That's a grand idea," Annabelle muttered. She shifted on her chair, her skin itching uncomfortably underneath her walking dress. "You know, that blue gown looks ghastly on me."

Catriona looked confused. "It does?"

"Yes. The color doesn't suit me and it adds bulk in the wrong places."

"Can you add a ribbon?" Catriona tried.

"I could, but it would be like adding a ribbon to a train wreck."

"You're not normally prone to exaggerations," Catriona said slowly. "Is something the matter?"

"No," Annabelle said, tapping her pen on the letter and splattering ink. "I've just remembered that I'm not that old, and I don't recall the last time I have worn a pretty dress."

A lifetime ago, she used to have taste, an interest in braiding ribbons into her hair and matching her earbobs to her eyes. She hadn't taken any joy in that since that summer with William; her looks were an empty promise at best, a liability at worst. And now . . . now she was almost writhing with the need to burst out of this drab gray shell she had cultivated for so long.

But she couldn't. Right now, she was exactly as she had to be to move forward on a respectable, independent path.

She could, however, stay away from Montgomery. Yesterday in the greenhouse, he had wanted to kiss her. She knew the look he had got on his face by the terrarium, the fixed stare, the singular male intent. Such intensity was usually followed by a grab for her person and a slap to the man's face. But Montgomery hadn't made a grab for her. Even more shocking, she was fairly certain she wouldn't have slapped him. No, she had gone back for more of his company this morning. It hadn't helped to learn that he kept his moth-eaten horses, as if a generous, caring heart were beating in his hard chest . . .

She'd find ways to avoid him until the Christmas dinner; no more breakfasting with him, no more letters and walks and intimate talks. What had she been thinking?

⁘

The journey to Lady Lingham's Christmas dinner was awkward. Perhaps for efficiency reasons, Montgomery had all four of them travel in the same carriage—himself, Peregrin, Aunty Greenfield, and her. Aunty kept sagging against her as she slipped in and out of her nap, and the two men opposite looked terribly stern, which was owed only in part to their sharp dark twin topcoats. They seemed right cross with each other, staring determinedly into nothingness, a look that suited Montgomery but not Peregrin. She had spent a lot of hours with the young lord in the past few days, first to avoid the duke, but soon because Peregrin turned out to be exceptionally friendly, quick-witted company. *Higher powers are forcing me to revise Plato's* Republic *during my Christmas break*, he had confessed. *Would you happen to know anything about that particular book?* Tutoring him had been so delightful, it had—briefly—distracted her from her ludicrous attraction to Montgomery.

The attraction was now firmly back in place, yes, she was beyond denying it: she was hopelessly preoccupied with the grim-faced aristocrat across the footwell. Even now, despite his coldly bored expression, his nearness warmed her body like a bonfire right to her core.

She forced her eyes away from him to study her hands in her lap. Still, she saw him, like the glow of a fire spilling into her field of vision. Good lord. Perhaps dining with his *arrangement* would douse the flare of infatuation.

Her stomach gave a queasy twist when Lingham Hall came into

view. Admittedly, the house itself was lovely, a conveniently sized manor with a smooth Georgian sandstone façade. Leafless vines ranked around the pillared entrance, where the butler was already waiting.

The moment they entered the foyer, a tall, slim woman in her early forties strode toward them, her heels click-clacking confidently on the marble floor.

"Montgomery," she exclaimed softly. Her slender hand lingered on his arm just a fraction too long.

Annabelle could not blame her. Montgomery's straight shoulders filled the black evening jacket perfectly, and the pale gray of his waistcoat made his eyes gleam like polished silver. He was a picture of masculine elegance that would compel any woman who was entitled to do so to steal second touches.

"And you must be Miss Archer." The countess's expression was mildly curious. "Poor thing, how ghastly to be taken ill at such a merry time."

Lady Lingham had that look that her father used to describe as "long of face and large of tooth," a look that was considered appealing chiefly because it spoke of centuries of wealth and good breeding. She had also mastered the art of effortless elegance—her sleek gray gown clung to her lithe figure in all the right places and the knot of blond hair atop her head looked deceptively simple. A maid could spend an hour on creating such a knot. It would never work with Annabelle's mass of wavy hair.

When they entered the sitting room, a dozen pairs of eyes shifted to the duke like metal to a magnet. Lady Lingham detached herself from his arm as people began drifting toward them, and then she alarmed Annabelle by taking her elbow as if they were old confidantes. "Take a turn around the room with me, Miss Archer."

Warily, Annabelle fell into step beside her. They were of similar height, but the countess was fine boned like a bird, the touch of her gloved hand hardly registering on her arm. Delicate lines rayed from the corners of her cool blue eyes. Intelligent eyes. Montgomery had not picked a simpering miss for his arrangement, and she wasn't sure whether she found this good or bad.

"Thank you for inviting me tonight, my lady," she said.

Lady Lingham's eyes twinkled. "The pleasure is mine. The neighborhood was abuzz about you." She gave a little laugh. "Oh, no need to look startled. Of course there will be gossip, and all of it too ludicrous to be borne. My lady's maid was adamant that Montgomery was seen with you up on his horse, riding across the fields like a knight in shining armor with his princess."

What?

"Goodness," she managed.

"Precisely," Lady Lingham said, shaking her head, "so do not fret. Everyone knows Montgomery would never contemplate such a display. He tells me you are from a clergy family?"

"Yes, my lady." What else had Montgomery told the countess about her?

"How charming," Lady Lingham said, "and so I have just the table partner for you."

They had reached a slight, dark-haired man who stood by himself next to a large potted plant.

"Miss Archer, meet Peter Humphrys, the curate on my estate."

Peter Humphrys's blush was instant and fierce when he bowed far too low. "What a pleasure, Miss Archer," he exclaimed. "This splendid evening has just become even more splendid." He promptly followed them around the room for the remaining introductions to Lady Lingham's other neighbors.

There was the Earl of Marsden, a heavyset older nobleman with florid cheeks who looked straight through her. His wife kept touching her bony fingers to the egg-sized ruby pendant that looked too heavy for her thin neck. A Viscount Easton, who had brought his adolescent son and daughter, and an elderly couple, the Richmonds, whose two daughters gave Annabelle's blue dress a sweeping glance of pity.

Matters did not improve in the dining hall. She was seated at the nether end of the table across from the young Easton siblings. Montgomery was at the other end, the guest of honor to Lady Lingham's right. His blond hair flashed in the periphery of Annabelle's vision whenever he attentively leaned closer to the countess.

Peter Humphrys lifted the metal cup next to his wineglass to his nose and inhaled. "Mint julep," he announced, and happily smacked his lips. "Careful, miss. This cocktail contains a hearty dash of bourbon."

She picked up her cup. It was cold to the touch and the contents smelled like peppermint.

At the far end of the table, Lady Lingham's tinkling laugh said the countess was having a fabulous time. They looked good together, she and Montgomery. Toothy or not, she was the female to his male, equally austere, refined, inscrutable; they were the Adam and Eve of the aristocracy.

Annabelle's hesitant nip of mint julep quickly turned into a hearty sip. Icy sweetness trickled down her throat, treacherous because she couldn't taste even a trace of liqueur. *Perfect.*

"Do the flora of Wiltshire differ much from what you observe in Kent?" asked Peter Humphrys.

"I'm not sure. I find they are both equally snowed under at present, Mr. Humphrys."

He gave a startled grunt. Eyebrows rose in their direction. The Easton girl smirked. Annabelle drained her mint julep cup and gestured to a footman for a refill.

The curate leaned closer as if to impart secrets. "There is a lovely copse next to the vicarage," he said. "In spring, I often observe the great spotted woodpecker there, the *Dendrocopos major.*"

She stretched her lips into a smile.

"Do you like birds, Miss Archer?" He sounded hopeful.

"I adore them. Woodpeckers especially."

If she were a normal woman, she'd throw her cap for the clergyman. Eligible bachelors—meaning kind, employed, unencumbered by a wife—were a rare commodity. But she had indulged in a summer of passion, and it had left her changed. In the words of Sappho, *Eros shook my mind, like a mountain wind falling on oak trees.* She had eaten the apple; she could not return to humility. Desire had ruined Peter Humphrys for her.

Elsewhere at the table, polite and meaningless conversation took an unusual turn.

"Of course they are trying to get women the vote," Lord Marsden said. "They know only idiots vote for them. Mark me, should women get the vote, the Liberals will never leave power."

His wife's thin hand crept across the table toward his sleeve on a mission to placate. Marsden ignored it. "Idiots," he repeated.

"Careful, Tuppy," said Lady Lingham from her end of the table, "there are quite a few perfectly witty women present tonight."

Tuppy, Lord Marsden, waved a plump hand. "You know how I mean it, Countess."

The women at the table exchanged discreet glances, uncertain how Lord Marsden had meant it.

"Miss Archer here studies at Oxford," Lady Lingham said. "Now, what do you make of that?"

Annabelle's head turned to her sharply.

The countess was smiling. Not unfriendly, a little intrigued. For an aristo, everything could be a game.

Marsden squinted at Annabelle. "Is that so."

The faint thud of her pulse started up in her ears. "Yes, my lord."

From the corner of her eye, she saw Montgomery put down his cutlery.

"And what is the use of such a tremendous overeducation?" Marsden probed.

All other conversations had petered out and the collective attention shifted onto her, hot and exposing like a spotlight. Heat crept up her neck.

"I believe a higher education will improve me for whatever I decide to do, my lord."

An ambivalent murmur swept the length of the table. People who had to improve their lot evidently hadn't been blessed with a good station in life.

"And do you aspire to get the vote?" pressed the earl.

The minty drink had congealed to a lump in her throat. Lucie would never forgive her if she alienated several men of influence at once. She'd have a hard time forgiving herself if she made a fool of herself in front of one particular man.

"Yes, I think women should be given the vote."

Marsden triumphantly glared around the table.

"Why not give everyone who actually grasps politics the vote and exclude the rest, man or woman," Lady Lingham suggested amicably.

Marsden scoffed. "But by her very nature, a female is unable to grasp politics, or any issue of the kind."

"By her very nature?" Lady Lingham sounded notably less amicable.

"Oh, yes." The earl turned back to Annabelle. "Have you read the article recently published by the Marchioness of Hampshire? On the matter of the female brain?"

"I'm afraid not."

"Lady Hampshire is formidable," Lady Marsden said.

Everyone nodded.

"Now, miss, listen closely," Marsden said. "Lady Hampshire advises against women taking up higher education, the vote, political roles. Science has shown that the female brain is not only smaller than a man's, it is also wound up differently." His hands made a rolling, winding motion. "So even if you, Miss Archer, read all the same books and heard all the same speeches as a man, your brain would never produce the same sound analysis. You enter the same input into your brain, but something gets lost in its twists and turns, so you get a different output, a diminished output."

He looked at her expectantly.

"That sounds disconcerting," she allowed.

"Well indeed," he said impatiently, "so why not follow Lady Hampshire's advice? Keep yourself content in your femininity instead of confused?"

She could hardly dismiss the judgment of the *formidable* Lady Hampshire in front of this audience, and Marsden knew it. His eyes held glints of smugness and victory.

It must have been that, and the hearty dash of bourbon, that made her say: "Because, my lord, if the marchioness believes that the female brain is incapable of forming a sound analysis on political issues, why should anyone trust her analysis on women in politics?"

Silence filled the dining room.

Then a coughing noise erupted from Peregrin, and he quickly raised his napkin to his mouth, his eyes watering with suppressed glee.

"Why, Miss Archer," Lord Easton said slowly, "you should take up law. You would give my old solicitor Beadle a good run for his money."

"Hear, hear," Richmond said, "she's much easier on the eye than Beadle, too."

More than a few people chuckled, and Marsden turned red in the face. "The spread of rampant liberalism is no laughing matter," he barked.

"Rampant liberalism was not your problem here, Marsden."

The duke had said so little all evening, the sudden sound of his voice had the effect of a thunderbolt.

All heads swiveled toward his end of the table.

Montgomery was stone faced.

Marsden looked a little uncertain. "Then what would you call it, Duke?"

Montgomery picked up his glass. "It is called logic," he said, and raised the glass toward Annabelle in a small but unmistaken salute.

Warmth flowed through her. The look in his eyes had briefly taken her breath away, a bright amalgam of anger and . . . admiration?

Everyone else was looking at her warily now. Everyone except Lady Lingham. Her expression was pensive.

"Now there's a toast we can all agree on," the countess said blithely and raised her glass. "To logic."

When the dinner finished and the party was ushered back to the sitting room, Peter was stitched to her side, explaining things about birds in wrongly pronounced Latin, and she was almost grateful for it as it allowed her to appear in deep conversation rather than acknowledge Lord Marsden, who tried murdering her with dark stares. Neither Montgomery nor the countess was anywhere in sight.

She spotted a door to the terrace that was ajar, and the moment the sourish Richmond daughters approached the curate, she seized her chance and dove headlong into the dark.

The hum of inane chatter was immediately muffled.

Cold, clean air had never felt so good. Greedily she sucked deep breaths of it into her lungs.

And stilled.

Someone else was out here, a man, his face tilted up to the dark sky.

She recognized Peregrin's lanky form against the torchlight before he turned.

"Miss Archer." He politely stubbed out his cigarette.

"Lord Devereux." She came to stand beside him and looked up at the stars. "Were you looking for something in particular up there?"

"The North Star. Did you know seamen have used it for orientation for thousands of years?"

"Yes, since the Phoenicians."

He chuckled. "Have you by any chance missed that class at finishing school where they teach you to feign delightful ignorance in the presence of a man?"

"I'm afraid so." She had never been near a finishing school.

"Marsden sure noticed," Peregrin said. His gaze turned speculative. "I don't think he'll recover anytime soon from my brother's very public dressing-down."

She was eager to change the topic. "Are you looking forward to the fireworks?"

Peregrin stiffened. "I won't be here for the party."

"I'm sorry to hear that," she said, and she was. He had been kind to her at Claremont, not just perfunctorily polite. Just yesterday he had taken the time to show her the first English edition of *The Odyssey* in Montgomery's library, and had been thoroughly amused at her excitement. Now he seemed as downcast as in the carriage earlier.

"I've never seen fireworks," she tried.

His frown deepened. "Never?" As he mulled it over, her bare arms snared his attention. "I'll have someone fetch your coat," he said.

"It's on its way," came a smooth voice from the dark.

They both started.

How long had Montgomery been standing there in the shadows?

In the flickering light, it was impossible to gauge his mood as he strolled closer.

Was he cross with her because of Lord Marsden?

"Montgomery," Peregrin said. "I shall leave Miss Archer in your hands, then." He nodded at Annabelle. "Miss."

He ambled back into the house, and Montgomery stared after him as if he were of a mind to order him back. Instead, he said: "Are you hiding out here, miss?"

She cringed. "I'd call it a strategic evasion."

He made a soft noise, a huff, a scoff?

"Thank you," she began, "thank you for . . ." Protecting me?

Because that was what he had done with his little intervention, from his own peers, no less.

"It's not worth mentioning," he said.

"You repeatedly implied that I had a problem with authority," she said lightly. "I'm beginning to agree with you."

Montgomery leaned back against the balustrade. "A problem with authority, or with stupidity?"

"I beg your pardon?"

"The argument put forward tonight had a blatant logical flaw. I imagine the temptation to point it out was overwhelming."

She gave a baffled laugh. "Indeed it was."

For a moment, they were looking at each other, and his lips were twitching as if trying not to smile. That was when she noticed that she was smiling rather widely at him.

She turned away to the dark gardens below the terrace. "Isn't the whole point of an authority figure that he can't be challenged, no matter what?"

"No," he said, "first, Marsden is not your commander in chief. And second, a leader who doesn't know what he is doing will eventually face mutiny."

"Are you making a case for leadership based on merit, Your Grace?" It came out decidedly more sarcastic than she had intended, to him who was placed at the helm of the ship thanks to his birthright alone.

He was quiet for a long moment, and she realized that she was taking something out on him that had nothing to do with him: frustration over Marsden, the Marchioness of Hampshire, and, possibly, his liaison. And he let her, like a big cat would let a kitten claw at it.

"Tell me," he said, "how frustrating is it to be surrounded by people considered your betters when they don't hold a candle to your abilities?"

She stared into the dark, briefly lost for words.

How? How did he know these things about her?

And why did him *knowing* urge her to spill more secrets to him? To tell him that it was like a slow drip of poison, this daily flattering and placating of men for a modicum of autonomy; that she sometimes worried it would one day harden both her heart and her face?

She shook her head. "It is how it is, Your Grace. I have always struggled with just following my betters. I suppose it's a defect in me."

"A defect," he repeated. "You know, the most important lesson I learned during my time at Sandhurst was on leadership. People have many motivations to follow someone, but a soldier will only ever follow a man for two reasons: his competency, and his integrity."

It was not really a surprise to hear he had been at Sandhurst rather than Oxford or Cambridge—enough aristocratic families sent their sons to the renowned military academy, and truth be told, military suited Montgomery.

"I believe that," she said, "but I'm not a soldier."

"Perhaps you are. At heart."

Now she looked at him. What a whimsical thing to say for a man like him. Her, a soldier. But oh, it resonated, it plucked at something deep inside her chest. It almost *hurt*. "A soldier must be discerning as his very life depends on his leader's competency," she murmured.

He gave a shrug. "As a woman's life depends on the competency of the men in her life."

"You will find it can be the other way around," she said dryly, thinking of Gilbert, unable to make the money last until the end of the month, or her father, forgetting to eat because he was immersed in a book.

"Is that why you have not married? Because the men in Kent are incompetent?"

He tossed it at her casually, as if it weren't a shocking intrusion on her privacy.

She was too stunned to even attempt a reply.

Twin flames were dancing in his eyes, mirroring the flicker of the torches.

"I have spoken out of turn," he said when she remained silent.

Astutely observed, Your Grace, you have. Somehow she didn't think it had been an accident. Very few things he did or said seemed to be accidental.

"I don't wish to marry," she said. "My reasons are my own."

The door behind her creaked, and a footman appeared with her coat.

She huddled into the protective shell, grateful for the interruption because now they were just silent together, her and Montgomery, pretending to study the night sky.

"Why did you put stars on the library ceiling?" she asked.

"The ceiling was my father's idea," he said. "He had a liking for that sort of thing."

"For astronomy?"

She could feel rather than see his wry smile.

"No," he said, "for costly, whimsical things."

She might have quite liked the late duke. "Why the winter sky, though?"

Montgomery went quiet, in a way that said she had touched on something intimate.

"Because I was born in winter," he finally said. "It depicts the sky over Montgomery Castle on the night of my birth."

Something in his voice forbade a reply. Perhaps he liked it as little as she did, revealing private pieces of himself. And yet, he just had. *A piece for a piece.* He was a fair man, after all.

"Have you really never seen fireworks?" he asked.

"No. They are rather thin on the ground in the Kentish country-side."

"Then stay for the house party," he said, "if you forgive the rather spontaneous nature of the invitation."

For a second time in the space of a few minutes, he shocked her. Her thoughts swarmed like bees; it was a ludicrous proposition, she should not even consider it. And how would she pay Gilbert if she did not work for yet another week? The dresses, perhaps; she could sell these ill-fitting, good-quality dresses to seamstresses . . .

The door the footman had closed swung open, flooding the terrace with laughter from the sitting room. Lady Lingham's long shadow fell between them. "There you are," she said, sounding pleased. "Duke, I must steal Miss Archer away from you. I'm having all the ladies taste the first batch of Lingham sherry."

       ✑

As the carriage jostled back to Claremont, Annabelle's eyelids were drooping, deliciously heavy from Lingham sherry and too much mint julep. She had to send a note to Hattie tomorrow morning. She needed a dress, because *holy Moses*, she was going to a ball.

Montgomery's face was as dark and brooding as on the ride to the manor, or possibly darker. Why had he invited her to the party? Why was his grimness so appealing? Her imagination drifted, pretending that they were alone in the carriage, in a different life, where she could lean across the footwell and kiss his stern mouth, gently, persistently, offering feminine warmth until his lips softened against hers and the tension left his shoulders. It had been a lifetime since she had kissed a man, but she remembered the joys of it so well when she looked at him . . . the slick brush of a tongue, the feel of hard, eager planes of muscle against her palms, her blood turning sweet and heavy like molasses . . .

He turned his head toward her as if she had whispered his name.

She smiled at him drowsily.

His eyes darkened like the skies before a storm. The sudden, heated intensity transfixed her, pulled at her, and she was falling,

falling forward into the depths of him as he threw the gates wide open for a beat. She heard a soft gasp and realized it had come from her own lips. There it was, the fire she had sensed behind the ice, smoldering at a thousand degrees hotter than leaping flames. Oh, they had it wrong, the people who called him cool and aloof. He was a man who did not do things by halves, and he knew. So he leashed himself. Untether him, and he would burn as hotly as he was cold, and the dark force of her own passion would crash against his like a wave against a rock rather than pull him under.

He is my match.

The thought hit like a splash of cold water.

It was one thing to dream. But the connection between him and her didn't feel like a dream anymore. It felt real. And that could not be.

She shivered.

On the bench across, Montgomery had clenched his hands to fists by his sides.

⁓◈⁓

She was swaying on her feet with fatigue when she reached her room at Claremont. It took a moment to register the large rectangular parcel on the end of her bed.

She drew closer.

It was wrapped in green paper, tied with a red satin bow. She couldn't remember the last time she had been given a present, but that was her name on the tag affixed to the ribbon.

She untied the bow with clumsy fingers.

The smell of new wool rose from the box when she lifted the lid.

It was a coat. Hunter green, with generous fur trimmings on cuffs and collar.

She looked at it stupidly for a moment. Then she reached for the little note.

Dear Miss Archer,

Claremont servant staff wishes you a merry Christmas and a pros-
perous New Year.

Your servant,
Ramsey

She slid her arms into the coat, and it enveloped her like a downy blanket. She turned back and forth in front of the vanity table mirror. Perfection. A classic, timeless cut rather than the current fashion. Rabbit fur, not mink, but excellently made, promising to keep her warm, quite possibly, forever.

Someone had really thought this through.

She sank onto the bed.

The staff had been unwaveringly polite to her, but why would they make such a gesture?

It was Montgomery who scowled every time he saw her coat. But he would have violated all the rules of propriety by giving her such a gift directly, making it impossible for her to accept.

She ran her fingers over one soft fur cuff.

This went beyond politeness. Which raised the question: what did Montgomery want?

Chapter 14

A few days earlier, after the greenhouse, it had seemed perfectly reasonable to order her a coat—hers was useless, and he was in a position to fix that, so he had. He quickened his pace, his boot heels pounding the stable's flagstone floor. He had been deluding himself; he'd known it the moment he had wanted to take Marsden outside last night. The truth was, he wanted Annabelle Archer, commoner, bluestocking, and suffragist, in his bed, under him, with a carnal urgency he hadn't felt since . . . he couldn't remember.

He rounded the corner to the horse stall and stopped dead, for there she stood as if he had conjured her up. The morning light from the window behind her cast a fiery halo around her hair, and she looked tall and radiant in a hunter-green coat.

A tide of primal satisfaction filled his chest. He liked seeing her wear something he had picked, and he hadn't been sure she would. Sure enough, she was observing him warily.

Apollo whinnied, shrill and unabashed in a bid for his attention.

"Shh." He placed a hand on the horse's nose without taking his eyes off her.

Only when her expression turned bemused did he realize he had not yet said a word.

"Good morning, miss."

She curtsied. "Merry Christmas, Your Grace."

"Ah. Yes." Very eloquent, that. He cleared his throat. "What brings you to the stable this early?"

Somehow, they had drifted closer together, and he could smell her now, her warm floral essence that edged out dust and leather and horse. His blood began to buzz like last night in the carriage, when her sleepy smile had gone straight to his cock . . . when he had nearly made a grab for her like a Neanderthal.

She took a small step back. "I received a Christmas gift from the staff." She gestured over the coat.

"I see," he said. "It suits you."

She clasped her hands before her primly, but there was a heat in the depths of her eyes that warmed him all over.

"Would you please thank them on my behalf," she said. "It's too generous. It's exactly what I need."

He could give her so much more.

Except, he couldn't.

It went against the very nature of his being to not go after what he wanted, but this was different. She was vastly below his station, and a guest under his roof. Manners, if not honor, demanded that he not bother her with his attentions, for how could she possibly refuse him if she wished?

A good thing their time alone together was at an end. He had filled the next two days with appointments in the city to avoid the last-minute madness leading up to the house party, which had been a reasonable plan before she had walked into his life.

"I'm going to London today," he said, and she blinked at the sudden coolness of his voice. "And I had a missive from Lady Lingham. She suggests you take Mr. Peter Humphrys as your escort for the ball."

The warmth he had been basking in faded from her eyes. "That's very considerate of her ladyship, Your Grace," she said. "I'm indeed in need of an escort."

He stared after her as she left, unable to shake the impression that he had offended her in some way.

⁕

"You said *emerald green*." Annabelle's gaze flashed between Hattie and the open dress box on her bed.

"I know," Hattie said, "but isn't this much more exciting?"

"It's . . ." She didn't even know what this color was. *Garish pink* did not quite describe it.

"It's magenta," Hattie supplied. "It's very modern."

She breathed slowly through her nose. She'd stand out like a peacock tonight; there was no chance in Hades that she'd find another dress on time. House party guests had begun arriving shortly after breakfast; there was an endless stream of carriages pulling up below her windows. She could either wear magenta or not go to the ball at all.

"You dislike it." Hattie sounded small.

"I'm sure you meant well."

"Oh. Oh, no. You really are cross." Hattie's face flamed hot red like a torch. "I didn't mean—it's just that everyone with green eyes will wear emerald tonight, when magenta is the perfect foil for your coloring, a complementary color contrast if you will. And you always wear such dreary things . . . Oh dear, that came out wrong. I just . . . I couldn't help it. I heard myself say, 'I'll take the magenta.'"

Annabelle lifted the dress. A gauzy petticoat appeared beneath, then a pair of white midlength gloves. Two smaller boxes still sat unopened on the counterpane. The first contained an exquisitely embroidered velvet choker, the second a set of earrings, large pearl drops affixed to square, rose-colored stones.

"Those will be on loan," Hattie said quickly, "for I know you wouldn't accept those, right?"

"Right," Annabelle said, exasperation grappling with a strange tightness in her chest. Hattie had put a lot of thought into this ensemble. How could she explain that this would make her look like an impostor? Like a vicar's daughter playing lady for a night?

She considered the dress. It seemed less bright now, but it looked awfully narrow, a princess sheath cut she'd only ever seen in magazine clippings in the college's common room.

"This requires a . . . a corset that goes down to midthigh, doesn't it?"

Hattie's eyes widened at the mentioning of unmentionables. "It does. Why?"

Annabelle looked at her with comical despair. "Mine finishes at the waist." The type that had gone out of fashion years ago and posed no problem with her dated dresses.

Hattie wrung her hands. "Borrow one of mine?"

"But you are much shorter than I."

"And if we asked—"

"I can hardly ask random ladies to borrow their . . . under-garments," Annabelle hissed. They were both red in the face now.

"Blast." Hattie slumped onto the bed. "I've really made a mess of it, haven't I? And here I thought at least one of us would look stunning tonight."

Annabelle sat down next to her. "Whatever do you mean?"

Her friend smoothed a hand over the magenta silk. "I'm going to look hideous. Mama picks my dresses, and she is clueless. I'll be wearing pastel, with not a hint of cleavage in sight."

A reluctant grin tugged at the corner of Annabelle's mouth. "And so you planned to dress vicariously through me."

Hattie gave a sulky shrug.

Annabelle took her hand and gave it a squeeze. "You put a very . . . complete outfit together for me, and I thank you for that, truly."

Hattie hesitantly squeezed back. "But what about the, eh, under-clothes?" she whispered.

She'd do what she usually did. "I will have to be practical about it."

That meant hoping her natural shape would fill the dress, and, Lord help her, possibly not wearing any drawers in case they would bunch and show through the clinging fabric . . .

Catriona burst through the doors, looking around wildly. "Have you seen my glasses?"

"Catriona," Hattie exclaimed, "you look diffcrent."

Catriona turned her head in her direction and blinked. Her face looked startlingly bare and unlike the Catriona they knew. Pretty, though. The spectacles had hidden large Celtic blue eyes fringed with long, black lashes.

"I don't understand," Catriona said. "I'm awfully scatterbrained today."

She swept out of the room again.

Hattie shot Annabelle a meaningful glance. "I think she's nursing a tendre for Peregrin Devereux," she murmured. "I think she took the glasses off to practice looking good at the ball tonight."

Annabelle frowned. "But Lord Devereux left for Wales about an hour ago." She had seen him climb aboard the travel coach looking confusingly stone faced.

His brother, however, had not yet returned to Claremont.

A frisson of anticipation traveled up her spine.

"Ye gods, please let that dress fit," she said, and abruptly came to her feet.

⁂

Claremont's reception room was abuzz with the chatter of a few hundred people ready to revel and dance. Jewels and champagne flutes shone softly in the muted light. A far cry from a country dance, this, a veritable sea of unfamiliar pale faces. Glances strayed her way, raking over her like fingers. "Look. It's Celeste," a lady said. "No, I am certain the gown is all Celeste . . . but who is she?"

I'm the woman who wears a Celeste sans undergarments.

The gown's silky skirt had been too filmy for drawers; it clung like a skin to the thin underskirt. The feeling of nakedness was compounded by the snug, low-cut bodice that presented the tops of her breasts with rather dramatic effect. And apart from the lace trimmings on the flounces of the small train, there were no adornments to attract attention away from, well, her. The woman in the mirror had looked like a wealthy, fashionable stranger. Like she had every right to attend an illustrious ball. Peter, her escort, had turned the color of a beetroot once she had descended the grand staircase.

"Annabelle." Hattie emerged from the crowd on the arm of a handsome young gentleman with chestnut hair. She left his side and rushed toward her.

"How stunning you look," she exclaimed, pressing a hand to her heart. "Oh my. Zachary," she said, turning back to her escort, "isn't she stunning? I'm awfully envious. Annabelle, may I present my brother, Zachary Greenfield."

The young man's brown eyes twinkled as he sketched a bow. "Miss Archer. You are as striking as a lotus flower and as graceful as a willow reed."

The moment he and Peter began exchanging opinions on the brandy, Hattie linked her arm through Annabelle's and pulled her aside.

"I told you," she muttered, gesturing over her own dress. The cascade of bows and flounces swamped her pleasantly plump figure, their color somewhere between beige and yellow. "Apricot," she groaned, "and these frothy layers—I look like a rice pudding."

"You look lovely," Annabelle lied.

Hattie gave her a speaking glance. "I'm sure my brother paid his friends to fill my dance card."

At least Hattie *had* a dance card. She'd be watching people dance tonight. No nobleman could ask her for a turn without causing talk, and Peter had informed her that as a man of the church, he didn't dance, and he had stammered but stood firm when she had tried to bargain for at least a quadrille. So she would stay planted on a chair like a magenta wallflower all evening.

Peter sidled up to her, offering his arm. "Shall we traverse to the ballroom, Miss Archer? I hear live reindeer are part of the decoration."

The melodies of Vivaldi's *Winter* drifted through the wide open wing doors. The ballroom beyond glittered cool and bright like an ice palace—crystal chandeliers floated below the wintry blue ceiling, sparking stars and rainbows. Silvery glints struck from the champagne chillers and tiered platters on the refreshment tables. A profusion of snowy white orchids cascaded down from the upper balconies.

The only thing that held her attention was the man greeting his guests by the entrance.

Her pulse sped up. An exquisite tension tightened her body all over.

God, but Montgomery was achingly handsome. His lean frame and austere face were perfect for the sharp, elegant lines of the black-and-white evening attire.

When it was her turn to greet him, Montgomery did a double take. For a beat, he was as still as the ice sculptures lining the walls. But she had seen his gaze dip and graze over the swells of her breasts, a reflex against which he seemed as helpless as the next man.

Faint color began tingeing his cheekbones. "Miss Archer." His voice was clipped.

"Your Grace."

He was already turning to her escort. "Mr. Humphrys. Welcome to Claremont."

Dismissed.

It stung.

For a moment, she walked on Peter's arm blindly, feeling foolish. What had she expected? That words like *graceful willow reed* would pass Montgomery's lips? Actually, yes. Apparently, she had begun thinking of him purely as a man with whom she shared a connection, and was hoping for affirmation. She blew out a breath. Gallic pride? Gallic delusions!

She stiffly lowered herself onto the velvet chair near the far wall where she'd be stationed for the night. Peter remained standing, craning his neck around the ballroom.

"I believe the reindeer were a rumor," she snipped.

He blinked. "Of course." He gave a little laugh. "I mean, it would have been quite outrageous, wouldn't it, and impractical . . ."

She bit her lip. It was ill done of her to take her strange mood out on the man who was nothing but kind. Unlike Montgomery, who blew hot and cold. He was presently conversing with a grand older lady and a pretty girl in white, who was glancing up at him shyly now and again.

"The Countess of Wareham," Peter muttered, following the direction of her gaze, "they say her daughter, Lady Sophie, is one of the potential candidates for the new duchess."

Her throat constricted unpleasantly. "The new duchess?"

Peter looked back down at her. "The duke will remarry next year. May I bring you a sandwich?"

"Yes, please," she murmured. She did not feel even the hint of an appetite.

⁓ ✤ ⁓

The dance floor was soon busy with whirling couples who turned the air thick with an amalgam of perfumes and sweat. Hattie's yellow-beige dress flashed in the crowd as Tomlinson spun her round in a quadrille. Peter Humphrys was lecturing her on red deer native to Wiltshire.

It was still two hours until midnight.

"Would you like another sweetmeat?" Peter's eyes were on her, always on her.

"No, thank you."

"Another sandwich, then?"

"No, thanks, the last one was quite filling."

Montgomery wasn't dancing. He was at the edge of the ballroom, hands clasped behind his back, talking to guests, too many of them women with debutante daughters in tow or men who looked eager to talk politics.

Another dance ended, and Hattie approached, her red hair frizzy. She was vigorously fanning her gleaming throat.

Peter swooped. "May I bring you ladies some refreshments?"

"Some of the pink champagne, please," Annabelle said quickly.

The pink champagne bowl was on the other end of the ballroom.

"Your wish is my command," the curate exclaimed, and flung himself into the milling crowd.

Hattie promptly took Annabelle's arm.

"I have to tell you, Tomlinson has been most attentive," she murmured. "In fact"—she meaningfully waggled her tawny eyebrows—"he has mentioned taking some fresh air on the terrace."

"Do not go onto the terrace with him." The words were out before Annabelle could take the sharpness out of her voice.

Hattie's face fell.

"Just . . . don't," Annabelle repeated, softer now.

"But it's in full view of the ballroom."

"Even worse. Do you want to marry him?"

Hattie flinched. "Marry? Why, no. He's not titled." She surreptitiously eyed the young man, who was presently thumping Lord Palmer's back and braying with laughter. "And he's not exactly a Gabriel," she conceded.

"Then you really do not want to be caught in a compromising position in full view of the ton."

"But—"

"No terrace. No alcoves. No dark, empty hallways," Annabelle said. "Forgive me for sounding like a governess," she added, attempting to make light of things.

"You do sound rather like Miss Mayer right now," Hattie said, sounding like a very lovely, very rich girl who was pondering whether to take advice from a woman about two dozen steps below in social rank.

It stabbed like a little dagger between Annabelle's ribs. "I'd rather you not get hurt," she said softly.

Tomlinson had sensed that he was an object of discussion; he half turned and raised his champagne flute to them. With his shiny eyes and fluffy hair, he looked as threatening as a poodle pup.

He was still a man.

"Hattie," Annabelle said. "Men . . . they sometimes do outrageous things when they find themselves alone with a lady."

Hattie frowned. "My dear, I might not be as clever as you are in managing the gentlemen, but I assure you I know how to fend off an admirer."

"And what if you don't want to fend him off?"

Hattie's eyes widened. "Are you implying I'd . . . let him?"

"No, no, not like that," Annabelle said hastily, "but there are some gentlemen who will promise anything, and I mean anything, and unless you are perfidious yourself, it's very hard to see him for what he is."

Hattie's mouth relaxed into a small smile. "But he can promise whatever he likes, can he not? As long as he doesn't try to, well, you know"—she lowered her voice to a whisper—"kiss me."

"And what if he kisses you and you like it so much that you forget all about fending him off, and when you come to, you realize he has maneuvered you behind a yew hedge."

"A . . . yew hedge?"

Annabelle flushed. "Any hedge."

Hattie's eyes had grown soft and dreamy rather than appalled. "To be kissed like that," she sighed. "Oh, just once in her life every woman should be kissed in such a way that she forgets herself." She ducked closer, her voice curious. "How do you know these things, Annabelle?"

Oh, hell's bells.

Lord Palmer saved her from speaking a grave lie by strolling over to fetch Hattie for the next dance.

Peter had not yet returned. Rather than sit back down, Annabelle took a couple of steps to loosen her legs . . . and found herself face to face with Lady Lingham.

The countess looked comely in icy blue silk with matching fan and earbobs. She was still squarely overshadowed by the young gentleman by her side. Lord. He was one of the most beautiful men she had ever seen—imposingly tall, but neither bulky nor lanky, just right, as if he had been made with ideal proportions in mind. Gleaming auburn hair fell in soft waves around his high-cut cheekbones and perfectly angled jaw. A face suitable for any one of the archangels. His loud pink waistcoat said he was anything but a heavenly creature. It was, in fact, a magenta-colored waistcoat.

She must have stared at the man a moment too long, for his amber eyes shifted to her and promptly began to smolder. Her belly clenched with unease. She knew a predator when she saw one.

"Miss Archer."

To her dismay, Lady Lingham's fan was beckoning.

She approached the pair reluctantly.

The countess appraised her with a deliberate glance, her mouth smiling as if she were greeting a long-lost friend. "Miss Archer. How splendid you look tonight," she said. "It's a Celeste, is it not?"

"Yes, my lady."

"Consider yourself fortunate," said Lady Lingham. "Her designs are unforgiving." She pointed her fan at her stunning companion. "Miss Archer, allow me to introduce Lord Tristan Ballentine. Lord Tristan, it's a pleasure to present Miss Archer."

Lord Ballentine dipped his head. A diamond stud winked at Annabelle from in his right ear.

"Lord Tristan has just returned from a ghastly little war in the colonies," Lady Lingham said. "He received the Victoria Cross for outstanding bravery on the battlefield a few days ago."

"You are humbling me, my lady," Ballentine said, not sounding humbled at all. His eyes were busy examining Annabelle's cleavage. "How come I have never made your acquaintance before, miss? I'm usually familiar with all the great beauties of the ball."

Lady Lingham pursed her fine lips. "Miss Archer is from the country."

He looked up and raised a brow. "The country? Whereabouts?"

"Kent, my lord," Annabelle said.

"Lovely," he said blandly. "Will you do me the honor of the next dance, and tell me all about that quaint place?"

That was the last thing she wanted. He couldn't be much older than her, but there was a depraved edge to his mouth that only came with a life of utter dissolution.

"I'm afraid I have a touch of a headache."

His mouth quirked. "From not dancing a single dance yet?"

That left her speechless. A gentleman wouldn't press a woman, lady or not. He'd certainly not lead on that he had been watching her. Then again, he didn't seem to stand on protocol—he had an *earring*.

"I'm a rather clumsy dancer," she said. "I fear partnering with me would endanger your feet."

"Beautiful women usually endanger a man one way or another," he said. "I tend to find it worth the trouble."

"How valiant. I can see how the Victoria Cross has come to pass."

That had been a mistake. Ballentine's lips pulled into a slow smile, the way a superior fighter might smile just before he picked up a gauntlet. "Indeed," he drawled, "I cannot help it, the valiance. It's my family motto, you see—*Cum Vigor et Valor.*"

No doubt he thought he was outrageously charming, and to someone other than her, he might be.

He presented his arm.

She glared at it. She could not refuse now without causing a scene.

"Oh, do us all a favor and dance with the man, child," Lady Ling-ham tutted. "Ballentine never takes no for an answer and we will be bantering coyly until the morning hours if you don't take a turn with him."

Perhaps there was a section in *Debrett's Etiquette Manual* on how to fend off a joint attack by a countess and a viscount. If there was, she hadn't read it.

Slowly, she placed her hand on Ballentine.

Lady Lingham smiled and tapped the scoundrel's shoulder with her fan. "Do behave yourself."

The first notes of the music already filled the air.

A waltz.

She promptly forgot her displeasure and felt a sting of panic. She had not waltzed in over seven years.

A big, warm hand settled on her waist.

"Eyes on me, darling." Ballentine's silky voice came from high above and she tipped back her head to face him. He really was absurdly tall.

And then her heart stumbled over itself.

Over Ballentine's right shoulder, her gaze locked with Mont-gomery's.

He stood right above her on the second floor at the balcony rail-ings, his eyes blazing slits of silver.

She yanked her gaze away, fixing it on Lord Ballentine's tanned throat. It was a very fine throat, but it managed to hold her attention for all of three seconds, and then she glanced back.

Montgomery was gone.

The music picked up, and Lord Ballentine swept her into the first turn. Her worries about having forgotten all the steps quickly proved needless—the viscount could have partnered a sack of flour and made it look good. He led her with a firm hand, a languid grace in his movements that was unusual in a man of his size.

"Is it true, then," he asked, "you have no idea who I am? No rumors have blackened your opinion of me beforehand?" He was watching her with lion eyes.

How long was a waltz? Surely she could handle him for a couple of minutes.

"I know that you have received our highest military honor, and who would find a fault with that?"

The corner of his mouth kicked up. "Are you awfully impressed?"

"Of course," she said. "What woman is not impressed by a brave man in uniform?"

"Ah yes, the uniform. Alas, that bright red does not suit my coloring in the slightest."

He winked at her.

Almost against her will, she was intrigued by his outrageous vanity.

"The war—was it the Zulu invasion?" she asked.

His shoulder tensed beneath her palm. "No," he said. "Afghanistan."

Oh. "I hear it was devastating," she said earnestly.

"It's always devastating in Afghanistan," he said, "but it is rare to find a woman interested in politics." His expression had turned polite, so polite it was almost blank. Admittedly, he was right to block that avenue of conversation. War was a most unsuitable subject for small talk.

"Perhaps you should have been warned of *my* reputation, my lord," she said.

That rekindled the spark in his eyes. "Now you tell me. What danger am I in, miss?"

"I'm a bluestocking," she said. "I study at Oxford and I read all the pages of a newspaper. Especially the pages on politics."

His gaze darkened and in the next turn, he pulled her closer, and she could smell sandalwood and tobacco on him. "Careful," he murmured, his voice impossibly low, "some men consider intelligence in a woman a rather potent aphrodisiac."

He'd probably consider it an aphrodisiac if a woman was looking his way and breathing. She strained slightly against his hold, and mercifully, he gave an inch.

"If you are at Oxford, you know Lady Lucie," he said.

Surprise almost made her misstep. "She's a friend, my lord."

An odd expression crossed his handsome face. "How wonderful," he said. "Does she still have her cat?"

"Her . . . cat?"

"Yes, Boudicca. A fierce, clever little thing, much like its owner."

She hadn't known Lucie had a cat, so how did he know?

She realized then that the music had ceased and that he was still holding her hand.

She gave a light tug.

Ballentine placed her hand onto his arm. "Where may I escort you, miss? I'd suggest the terrace."

"I'd rather sit down again." She scanned the ballroom from the corner of her eyes. Where was safe, manageable Peter?

"Come now," Ballentine said, perusing her face with his half-lidded gaze, "we both know you are utterly wasted as a wallflower."

He began to walk unerringly toward the terrace doors, and she had to follow.

"My lord," she said tightly, but he only grinned.

Ballentine never takes no for an answer.

Panic raced down her spine, and her heart began to drum. She would have to cause a scene. She would have to dig in her heels and it would cause a scene, but she couldn't end up alone with this randy giant . . .

There was a movement in the crowd, and her head turned inexorably, like a compass needle turning north.

Montgomery was scything across the dance floor toward them, his cold bright eyes trained on Lord Ballentine like a marksman aiming a rifle. Ballentine's arm turned rigid beneath her hand, his body immediately responding to the threat.

When the duke reached them, the air around him was snapping with barely checked tension.

"Miss Archer," he said, his eyes remaining on Lord Ballentine.

"Your Grace?"

"Ballentine."

Ballentine bobbed his head. "Duke."

Montgomery offered his arm to her, still staring at the young viscount. "Allow me."

Ballentine didn't miss a beat; he did not quite fling her hand away, but he released her speedily and bowed. "Miss, it was an honor." He turned to Montgomery and nodded. "Duke."

"Ballentine."

Annabelle stared at Lord Ballentine's retreating back, then at her hand, now curled over Montgomery's forearm. He had rescued her in the middle of the ballroom.

She did not dare to look at him. She felt the tightly coiled tension in his muscles through layers of silk and wool, felt the eyes of a hundred people on her. Her skin was burning hot. Would that the floor opened and swallowed her now.

The merry tunes of another quadrille picked up, and Montgomery led her away from the dance floor as the *stomp stomp stomp* of the dancers' feet echoed the frenetic pulse of her blood.

Chapter 15

The reception room was a blur, and then the cacophony of voices and music faded and cool air touched her heated face. Montgomery was still staring ahead as he walked, displeasure swirling around him like steam.

"I advise you to stay away from Ballentine," he said.

"I had no intention of keeping him close, Your Grace."

"You danced with him."

"Because he and Lady—"

She bit her lip. She didn't have to explain herself; she was her own woman.

"The next time he comes for you," he said, "turn him away. His company is a risk for you."

She dropped her hand from his arm, her throat tight with frustration. "Then perhaps Your Grace should take the matter up with Lord Ballentine."

He stopped in his tracks and manners, Hades take them, forced her to face him.

An angry heat filled his gaze. "I just did," he said, "take it up with Ballentine, though given the way you look tonight, he might yet forget all about his self-preservation."

She raised her chin. "What is wrong with how I look?"

His gaze dragged over her bare throat, and something dark flashed in his eyes. "Wrong?" he echoed.

She glared at him, almost willing him to say something awful.

"Hell," he said softly, "you aren't playing coy, are you?"

"I—"

"You are the most alluring woman in the ballroom tonight, and obviously unprotected"—he cut her off—"flirt with the worst libertine of London, and every man here regards you as available."

Flirt?

She had never liked him less than in this moment. "Please do not trouble yourself on my behalf," she said. "I'm perfectly capable of taking care of myself."

His brows lowered. "Now that is where we disagree."

He was walking her backward, and the light dimmed and the walls were closing in.

She sobered in a blink.

She was in an alcove. With a man looming over her. The music of the ballroom hummed faintly from a hundred miles away.

Botheration.

She had been so focused on squabbling with him, she had followed him here trustingly like a calf to market. Because this was Montgomery. He was dutiful, and sincere . . .

He was still a man.

And he was close, so close she could smell the clean, soapy scent on his neck.

Instinctively, she stepped back.

Her bare shoulders bumped against cool plaster.

She swallowed, her throat working audibly in the silence.

She had not seen the predator in him. Until now. Now she could almost *taste* his intent . . .

It took him one step to close the distance between them.

She raised her hands.

They landed flat on a solid chest.

"Your Grace—"

He braced his forearms to either side of her head against the wall.

"Enough," he murmured, "enough."

He lowered his head, and she felt his lips, smooth and silken, against the side of her neck.

Was that a kiss?

She stared over his shoulder unseeing as the heat of his skin touched her throat.

This man and I are going to kiss.

She had known, hadn't she?

She had been aware of him since she had first seen him, aloof and commanding on Parliament Square, and this . . . this was the natural conclusion.

They seemed suspended in time, cheek to cheek, his scent in her nose, as he held himself still and waited, waited for something . . .

Her hand curled into the lapel of his jacket.

He pulled back, took one hard look at her face, and then his mouth was on hers. His fingers thrust into the soft hair at her nape, the warm pressure of his lips parted hers, and his tongue delved in, slick and demanding.

Liquid heat poured through her.

She was being kissed by Montgomery.

And she was pressing closer, tasting him, letting him in.

He wasn't aloof now. A tug angled her head back, and the kiss became voluptuous; soft, urgent strokes of his tongue against hers, firm, knowing lips guiding hers . . . She sagged against him and his arms tightened around her, and the feel of his controlled strength brought all her sensitive places pulsing to life. She moaned softly into his mouth, and she heard his breathing fracture. His hands began coasting over her bare arms, the tender sides of her breasts, the dip of her waist . . . palmed her hips . . . clasping, kneading . . . he froze. His fingertips dug searchingly into the tops of her thighs. Lord. *No corset there, no drawers.*

She tore her lips from his. "I didn't—"

He made a gruff sound in his throat. His hands clamped over her bottom and hitched her up against him, and she felt him between her legs, hot and heavily aroused. Her thoughts shattered. She arched against him on instinct, needing to offer her softness to his hardness.

His head tipped back and he groaned, low like a man in pain, urging all that was female in her to both torment and soothe him with her body, her hands, her mouth . . .

He released her and eased back.

No. She followed him, chasing the intimate friction.

His hands wrapped around hers and flattened them against his chest. "Annabelle." His voice was hoarse.

No.

She hadn't thought she'd ever know reckless, ecstatic desire again, and now he had filled her to the brim with it. She wanted him inside her, and that feeling could not end, not yet.

She rose to her toes to fasten her mouth to his again, but he turned his head, and her kiss landed on his jaw. A gentle rejection, but a rejection still.

Her heart seemed to plummet down into her stomach.

"Annabelle."

She didn't dare face him. But she felt the wild thud of his heart beneath her trapped hand. His breathing came in gulps. So did hers.

Sweat cooled on her skin.

From afar, she could again hear fragments of the music.

Holy hell.

She had tried to climb Montgomery like a cat.

She took a step back. "I . . ." Her voice was thready. "I don't normally . . ."

"Shh." He leaned his warm forehead against hers. "I forgot myself."

He hadn't. If it weren't for his self-control, where would this have gone? There was no curtain. She was not even wearing under-garments . . . What must he be thinking?

He turned her around.

His hands gave her shoulders a reassuring squeeze. "Don't move."

She heard his knees crack softly, and she understood that the duke was picking up scattered hairpins from the floor, and then he set about reassembling her coiffure. With astonishing alacrity, too. He knew a thing or two about women's hair. He certainly knew a thing or two about seduction; she would have let him have his way with her in an alcove, where anyone could have walked past.

His fingers slid around her neck, his thumbs stroking lightly over her spine.

"I can hear you thinking," he murmured. "Your word, that you will not go haring off into the night now."

She huffed.

"Your word, Annabelle." His voice was low and insistent.

She gave an indignant nod.

"Good." He pressed a kiss to her nape, soft and quick. "Tomorrow, we will talk." He gave her a gentle push. "Now go."

She left the alcove on unsteady legs, blindly following the sound of the music. The feel of his mouth on her nape lingered, sizzling like a branding . . . Someone touched her arm, and she flinched.

"Annabelle." Catriona was staring back at her.

"There you are," she said, wincing at the unnatural pitch in her voice. "Where were you?"

"Your hair is mussed," Catriona said.

Her hand went to the back of her head. "Oh. It must have come loose while I was . . . dancing."

Catriona's eyes were concealed, behind her glasses. So she had found them. Still, she looked alien.

It's me.

Her mouth was tingling violently from Montgomery's kisses.

Next time she saw him, she would remember how he felt and tasted. This knowledge threw the rest of the world off center.

"You danced?" asked Catriona.

"Lord Ballentine asked me for a waltz."

Her friend's brow furrowed. "He's a rake," she said. "Did he behave?"

"Like a rake."

So had she. She had moaned and rubbed herself against Montgomery's impressive erection, oh God, his erection—

"Will you help me fix my hair?" she asked, suddenly desperate to not go back into the ballroom, to sit on a chair and pretend nothing had happened.

Catriona slid her arm through hers. "Of course. The powder room is this way."

Sebastian absently offered matches to the Marquess of Whitmore, who had come to join him on the balcony to discuss the election campaign. He hesitated before putting the matches away. While he craved a cigarette himself, he wanted to savor the taste of Annabelle more.

She was back on the chair by the wall. Her glossy hair was tousled, and her cheeks and throat were flushed pink. She looked like a woman who had been debauched in an alcove, and the fact that other men could see her like this urged him to prowl circles around her like a primitive creature.

She had awakened that creature. It had begun to stir when he had galloped across the fields with her delectable backside bumping against his crotch, and it had finally snapped its leash when she had faced down Marsden with nothing but her rapier-sharp mind. Strange thoughts had begun invading his head, and stranger feelings still were now roiling in his chest. Last year, when the Earl of Bevington had fallen from grace by marrying an opera singer, he had cut all contact with the man. Bevington had to be mad to sacrifice everything that mattered over an unsuitable woman: his standing in society, his political career, the respect of his half-grown children. The man now vegetated in a dump in Verona with the singer wife. And just now, in the alcove, with Annabelle's soft curves and lips pressing against him, feeling her need . . . for a few mad seconds, he had understood why some men did it, risked everything.

The unlit cigarette between his fingers was trembling slightly.

He had nearly lost control—*over a kiss.*

Was that how disaster had begun for Bevington?

"Lovely creature." Whitmore was leaning over the banister. For the past few minutes, the marquess's lecherous stare had followed Annabelle around like a dog after a juicy bone.

"Good Gad," Whitmore muttered, "behold those tits."

The banister near cracked in Sebastian's grip. He must not hit the man. He was an important political ally. "You are speaking about a lady."

"Oh, I heard she's just a country girl," Whitmore said, oblivious of the imminent danger to his jaw. "Though it is a pity when a prime piece like that happens to be a pleb, is it not? Look at that poise—just think, the same girl would have been a diamond of the first water, had someone slapped a title on her father in time."

"What a sentimental notion," Sebastian said. The words emerged cold and flat.

"I'm not complaining," Whitmore said, his belly quivering with a silent chuckle. "Who is her protector, do you know?"

Everything inside Sebastian went quiet. Like the quiet after a shot had been fired, when the birds had stopped singing and the wind held its breath.

He took the matches from his chest pocket and lit the cigarette.

"You are not going to be her protector, Whitmore."

The older man gave a little start.

Older, younger, fellow duke or prince. He would have said it to any one of them, Sebastian realized. It was almost as if the words had said themselves.

"I, ah, did not realize that was the way of things," Whitmore said.

"There is nothing to realize."

Whitmore held up a pacifying hand. "Of course, of course, and I wouldn't fancy trespassing on ducal property. That's not what a clever chap does now, is it."

He watched the marquess retreat, his muscles still taut with tension. Whitmore wouldn't be the only man present who was laboring under misapprehensions where Annabelle was concerned. From his vantage point, he could see them circling her, restrained only by a flimsy fence of etiquette. But they would make inquiries. She might have callers all the way to Oxford.

The cigarette snapped between his fingers. Manners and honor be damned. He could not do what Bevington had done, but he could take the next best option.

He gestured for a footman, and one promptly detached from the shadows.

"A pen, and a card," Sebastian said.

He had the card delivered to her room while she was chatting with Greenfield's daughter and studiously avoiding his eyes.

Annabelle,

Meet me at the entrance of the evergreen maze at 2 pm.

Yrs,
M.

Chapter 16

"A Mendelssohn matinée the day after a ball," Julien Greenfield grumbled to his wife. "Only a sadist would devise such a program."

It was one o'clock and groups of lords and ladies were trailing toward Claremont's music room, all in various stages of fatigue. The ball had concluded around three in the morning after the consumption of copious amounts of champagne, cognac, and cigars. By the time the last couples had limped off the dance floor, the flower decorations had wilted and conversations had become slurred and inane.

Sebastian moved among his guests like a panther among sheep. He was wired, filled with an impatience he only knew before important negotiations, during that precarious stretch before he was finally in the arena doing battle.

"Montgomery." Caroline moved away from a trio of ladies and fell into step beside him, and he reflexively offered her his arm.

"My lady. You had a good morning?"

"Quite," she said, "but I'm of a mind to be cross with you. How do you do it? You are the only one to not look even remotely shattered this morning."

Because I never sleep much anyway.

He glanced down at her upturned face. As usual, she was immaculately made up, but because he could never overlook a detail even if he tried he did notice the bags beneath her eyes.

He knew that if he were to meet her gaze directly, he'd see the question she'd never ask him: *Why did you not come to my room last night?*

He stared straight ahead.

God knew he needed a woman; unspent desire was crawling beneath his skin like a swarm of mad ants, and Caroline was everything he had come to appreciate—mature, sophisticated, and not shy to express her likes and dislikes. Dealings with her resulted in mutual satisfaction instead of drama.

He also knew that taking her to bed a hundred times would not make his frustration go away. No, this went deeper than the natural urge for release, and relief was hopelessly pegged to one green-eyed bluestocking.

She had not replied to his message. And he had not seen her at breakfast.

He prowled through the doors of the music room and methodically scanned the rows of plush chairs.

At last he caught the familiar glint of mahogany hair.

His palms turned hot and damp.

His heart began battering against his ribs as if he had run up a few flights of stairs.

He stood, stupefied. How could this happen to him? He was nearly thirty-and-six.

Annabelle looked up from her lap, and her clear green gaze hit him in the chest like a physical object, hurled with force.

He swallowed. Oh, it was most definitely happening to him.

He felt Caroline's gaze on him, vaguely expectant, and he realized his abrupt stopping had caused a pileup behind him. He smoothly fell into step again and steered toward his chair in the front row near the piano.

Annabelle was seated at the very back, next to a baroness he knew loosely. Neither woman probably spoke a word of German. He should have had a translation of the songs printed for his guests. It suddenly seemed very important that she *liked* the songs.

Caroline took the seat beside him, wrapping him in her powdery fragrance.

He resisted the urge to turn his head to glance back.

A rare flash of anger crackled through him. He had found half of society's social conventions and rituals void of reason from the moment he had been old enough to use his own brain. He mastered them, of course, but rarely had he felt these petty constraints chafing as much as he did now, where he could not sit next to the woman he wanted in his own music room. And all around him, people were scraping the chairs and dragging their heels over the polished wooden floor, coughing and wheezing and just plainly incapable of sitting still.

Finally, the pianist and the singers appeared, a soprano and a mezzo-soprano called the Divine Duo.

The noise died down. His irritation remained. The duo, their ridiculous name notwithstanding, was excellent, their voices rising and falling seemingly effortless, carrying the gamut of human emotions from melancholy to joy and back, and yet his mind refused to take flight with the melodies. Instead, he was starkly aware of the clock above the fireplace behind the pianist and of Annabelle some fifteen rows behind him.

He glanced at the clock a total of four times.

At a quarter to two, the last song finished.

At thirteen minutes to, the applause had ceased and everyone was making for the exit.

The progress to the door was slow, encumbered by guests wanting a word, a moment of his time, and the moments added up. Then he was stopped dead by the protruding bosom of the Marchioness of Hampshire. As he dutifully exchanged pleasantries, Annabelle was being herded right past him by the flow of people.

She did not spare him a glance.

"Did you enjoy the concert, dear?" the marchioness loudly asked Caroline, who was still by his side.

"Quite," the countess replied, "to think that something so sweet would come from the pen of a staid and stoic German."

Sweet?

Sebastian realized he was frowning down at her.

She raised her thin brows questioningly.

"I suppose," he said slowly, "that they have feelings, too. The Germans."

Her eyes took on a slightly bewildered expression. Then she gave a small apologetic shrug.

When he looked up again, Annabelle had disappeared.

He was running late. He was never late, and he had to force himself to maintain a dignified pace as he approached the maze. Relief crashed through him when the entrance came into view. She was waiting for him next to a limestone lion in her new coat and the same hat she always wore, a brown, nondescript thing that he'd quite like to see her replace with a dozen new ones.

"Miss Archer." He lifted his top hat.

She curtsied. Her cheeks were flushed, but that could well be the cold.

He offered his arm. "Would you accompany me on a walk?"

"Your Grace—"

"Montgomery," he said.

She arched a brow. "Your Grace?"

He arched a brow right back at her. "I believe we can safely suspend that formality in light of the circumstances."

There was a hitch in her breathing.

He wondered if she was going to play coy and deny the circumstances. Not a chance. He could still feel the soft, round contours of her body imprinted on his palms, urging him to fill his hands with her again, and he would, soon.

Finally, she took his proffered arm.

For a long moment, the only sound between them was the crunch of icy gravel beneath their feet as he led her into the maze.

Absurd.

He had talked his country out of a trade war with the Ottoman Empire. Now he didn't know where to begin.

"Did you play here as a boy?"

She was gazing up at him, a tentative playfulness in her tone that was new, and it took him a moment to reply. "No. I never did."

She looked bemused. "How does one keep a boy away from a maze for even a day?"

By locking him up with a pile of books and duties.

His mother, cold and unflappable as she had presented herself to the world, had been quietly terrified by her husband's antics. She had been determined that her son would be much different.

"What do you think of Mendelssohn?" he said instead.

That elicited a small smile. "I confess *sweet* isn't the word I'd use to describe him."

"Well, good," he said, "for he really is not."

"I didn't understand a word, but the music was so . . . moving. It was as though someone had reached into my chest and—" She interrupted herself, suddenly aware of her glowing enthusiasm.

"And what?" he coaxed as he steered her onto a side path, moving them deeper into the maze. Whenever her passion rose to the surface, he felt an elemental jolt of response in his body. Maddening. She made him forget who he was, left him only the base needs and cravings that seemed to come with being a man. And he seemed unwilling to stop the indulgence.

"Melancholic," she said softly, "that's the word I'd use to describe him."

Melancholic was precisely the word.

Holy God but he wanted to be inside this woman.

"The last song," she said, "it sounded so wistful, it almost made me sad. What is it about?"

He nodded. "*Auf Flügeln des Gesanges*. It is about a man taking his sweetheart on a flight of fancy."

Her hand flexed on his forearm, holding on more tightly. "What does it say?"

Her skirts brushed his leg with every step now. If he were to turn his head, pull her closer just an inch, he would smell the warm scent of her hair.

He shook his head, trying to unearth his German amid his swimming senses. "'On wings of song, my love, I carry you away,'" he said, "'away to the fields of the Ganges, where I know the most beautiful place—'" Now he stopped himself. Reciting romantic lines?

"How does it end?" she whispered.

Her eyes were a hundred miles deep. A man might never come up again once he took the plunge.

Damn it all.

"They make love under a tree," he said.

He felt rather than heard her gasp.

He rounded a corner and pulled her against him in one movement. He saw her eyes widen when he lowered his head, and then he kissed her.

Soft.

Her lips were indescribably soft, petal soft, and for a blink he didn't move, didn't breathe, only savored the velvety warmth against his mouth. And at last he exhaled. And it seemed that he had been holding this breath since yesterday, when he had last held her in his arms.

He inhaled deeply, jasmine and sweet woman.

The sun was bright and hot on his closed eyelids.

Somewhere, a robin sang.

He ran the tip of his tongue over her plush bottom lip.

She made a tiny noise in her throat, and his eyes slitted open.

Her eyes were closed, her lashes quivering like crescent fans against her cheeks.

His heart swelled in his chest, so fast, so violently, it ached. He pressed his mouth back to hers, and she opened for him, gave him access to the drugging heat that had had him aching half the night. He angled her head back to taste her more deeply, and she let him, shyly stroked her tongue against his, and his cock grew heavy. With a silent curse, he stilled again. He had meant to make it up to her, the frustrated claiming in the alcove. He carefully loosened his grip and molded her body against his with a tenderness that he had not afforded last night. But the feel of her against him . . . their fit was so, so good. Her teeth scraped against his bottom lip, and he groaned. Without breaking the kiss, he wrestled a hand from its glove and cupped the delicate curve of her jaw in his palm. The cool, satiny feel of her skin against his fingers sent another searing rush of pleasure through him. He wanted to ease her onto the ground and straddle her . . . undo all the hooks and buttons down her front, then strip away the more intimate laces. He'd touch every soft and giving inch of her with his hands and tongue, the pale fullness of her breasts, the sweet nip of her waist, the tender place between her legs . . . That especially. He would lick and kiss her there until she was writhing against his mouth.

He felt a resistance in her, and he realized that he had arched her back over his arm, and he was moving his hips against hers.

He tore his mouth off hers.

She blinked at him with a heavy-lidded gaze, her curls dislodged by his roaming hands. He noted his glove, flung carelessly into the snow.

"Annabelle," he murmured.

At that, she smiled faintly. "Montgomery."

He liked hearing his name like this, soft and husky. His hand went to cradle her face again, his thumb dragging over her bottom lip, and she pushed into his caress and pressed a kiss to the pad of his thumb, as if it were the most natural thing in the world. As if they'd done it hundreds of times before and would do it a thousand more.

Part of him recoiled with a sense of alarm.

He dropped his hand.

He picked up his glove and began to pace.

⁂

She watched him as if in a dream, his hands, one bare, one gloved, clasped behind his back. The world was unnaturally bright around her, the greens and whites glaring beneath a sharp blue sky. She wasn't feeling quite steady, and her hands were yearning to reach for him again. His strong shoulders seemed their rightful place now.

She hadn't slept. She had replayed their encounter in the alcove, over and over, recalled every sound and touch, and she had resolved to not follow his invitation and to stay away from him. She might as well have decided to stop breathing; one look at him across the music room, and her feet had carried her to the entrance of the maze at two o'clock sharp.

Montgomery turned back to her, his face determined. "Annabelle. I'm aware that we have not been acquainted for long, if one merely counts the days. And yet . . . surely you must know . . . how much you occupy my thoughts." He shook his head, and in an afterthought, he took off his hat and dragged a hand through his hair, leaving the short locks in disarray.

"I could in fact say that I desire your company all the time, and I have reason to hope that you return a measure of these feelings." He stepped closer and took her hand, his usually calculating eyes soft and warm like smoke.

Her heart gave a violent thud. Where was he going with this?

"Annabelle, I would like—"

He raised his head like a predator catching scent.

Now she heard it, too—rapid footsteps scattering gravel.

Montgomery's brows lowered ominously as he stepped away from her.

"Your Grace!" Ramsey burst into the alley; he was red-faced, his breath coming in gulps. His usually immaculately parted brown hair all but stood on edge.

Goose bumps spread over Annabelle's neck.

"This better be of importance, Ramsey." Montgomery's voice was cold enough to freeze the poor valet into next winter.

The man flinched. "I believe so, Your Grace." His eyes darted nervously between the duke and Annabelle.

She tugged her shawl closer around her shoulders. "I'll return to the house," she said, suddenly aware of her disheveled appearance. She didn't wait for Montgomery's dismissal, but rounded the hedge onto the main path quickly.

She still heard Ramsey's voice, carrying clearly in the quiet afternoon air. "Your Grace. Your brother, Lord Devereux—he's gone."

Chapter 17

⸺⸙⸺

Utter silence followed Ramsey's announcement. Sebastian's mind was a blank, the words floating through his head incomprehensibly. Then they sharpened and came down like a blade.

"An abduction?"

"Unlikely," Ramsey said quickly. "Apparently, his lordship left a note."

He was already on the main path.

Annabelle had turned back, her eyes large in her pale face.

"You heard?" he asked, not slowing down.

"Yes," she said, "I could not help overhearing it."

Well. Ramsey had announced everything loudly enough.

"Come."

He was vaguely aware that both Annabelle and Ramsey were forced into a run to keep up with him. He managed to slow down for her, but his mind was already racing ahead. "Where is his protection officer?"

"I had him wait at the ground-floor study, Your Grace," Ramsey panted.

Groups and couples were milling on the terrace and the garden that came into view. Heads were turning toward him, expectations reaching out to him like tentacles.

He changed course toward the servant entrance at the east wing.

"What other information do you have?"

"None, Your Grace," Ramsey said. "I came to find you as quickly as possible."

"You did well," Sebastian said, all but shouldering his way through the back door into a dimly lit corridor. Two maids froze on the spot, their eyes widening beneath their white caps as if they'd seen a ghost when he strode past.

There wouldn't be a note from Peregrin had anything happened to him. *Unless it was a ploy.* He forced that thought aside until he reached his study. A tall, burly man hovered by the door, his bowler hat in his fist by his side. Craig Fergusson. The man had been in his employ for a decade. He had one task—to guard his brother, discreetly and effectively. He suppressed the urge to grab Fergusson by the throat to shake an answer out of him right here in the hallway.

Ramsey lunged ahead to push open the door, and everyone filed into the study.

Sebastian rounded on the protection officer. "What happened?" he snarled.

Fergusson gulped. "Last night, we stayed over at the hotel in Carmarthen—"

"Yes?"

"And this morning, when I was waiting for his lordship and his valet in the hallway to come down to the breakfast room, I became suspicious because the young lord always likes to eat plenty, but the train was about to leave. So I got a feeling and went to investigate. I found the valet in the antechamber, knocked out clean by some laudanum—"

"Knocked out?" Sebastian interrupted, every hair on his body standing on end.

"Yes, Your Grace," Fergusson said. "I only got the man to wake with some good slaps. He's still groggy. He said Lord Devereux had asked him to share some wine the night before, and then he quickly fell asleep and heard nothing."

Disbelief momentarily eclipsed alarm. "He thinks my brother drugged him?"

Fergusson shifted uncomfortably. "It appears so, Your Grace."

Peregrin's valet had been with the family for twenty-five years; he had been Sebastian's valet before he had given him to Peregrin, to make sure his brother was surrounded only by the most trustworthy people. That man was probably not part of a ploy.

"I understand there is a note," he said.

Fergusson nodded as he fingered an envelope from his satchel. "He left this on his bed."

Sebastian snatched the letter from the man's hand.

The thick paper was from his own stationery. He broke the seal and tore the envelope open with his fingers. Two lines, in Peregrin's loopy handwriting.

Sir,

In regards to the Royal Navy, I have given it due consideration, and I simply cannot do it.

Respectfully,
P.

I simply cannot do it.

Very likely not abducted, then.

Sebastian briefly closed his eyes. His heart began to beat again, a hard tattoo against the wall of his chest. *Not abducted. Not hurt.* But the truth was that the little runt had bailed on him.

He very carefully placed the letter onto the desk. "Any indication where he is now?"

Fergusson shook his head. "No one's seen him. Several trains and plenty of coaches are leaving from the train station from six o'clock in the morning. I brought every schedule."

Sebastian ignored the papers Fergusson laid out on his desk; he already knew that there were several routes to coastal towns, and at least one train stopped at Plymouth. Ferries were leaving from there. His brother could well be on his way to France. And his protection officer was presently here at Claremont.

An emotion moved through him, almost too strong to be contained.

He went behind his desk, whipped out a sheet of paper, and began jotting down instructions.

"Get the coach ready," he said to Ramsey as he was writing, "and send a cable to Edward Bryson that I will see him this evening."

"The h-head of Scotland Yard, Your Grace?"

Sebastian looked up sharply. "Is there another Edward Bryson who could be relevant to this situation?"

Ramsey turned crimson. "No, Your Grace."

"After you have wired him, inform the town house. Fergusson, be ready to leave in twenty minutes. We are going to London."

Ramsey and Fergusson bowed and hastily headed for the door.

Annabelle made to follow them, and Sebastian put down the pen. "You stay, miss," he said. "If you please," he added in a softer tone when he saw her stiffen.

She turned. Her eyes were wary. Did he look as crazed as he felt?

"Stay," he repeated.

She nodded, her expression still reserved. He didn't want her reserved. He rounded the desk, his impulse to go to her, but then he veered toward the row of windows. He could not put into words what he wanted or needed from her right now; he could hardly set her down on his desk and pull up her skirts . . . abruptly, he turned to the view over the fields. With a certain indifference, he noted the tightness in his chest, the difficulty in drawing a deep breath. That was a low point in a man's life, when his own brother betrayed him.

"I trust you won't say a word about this to anyone," he said without turning.

"Of course not," he heard her say. Her voice was so soothing, a balm on his raw temper. Damnation, had his mooning over her allowed his brother to scheme his escape under his very nose? He glared at the barren planes of his land, disgusted with himself.

⁓⸜⸝⁓

Annabelle couldn't blame the two grown men for scrambling from the study like chastised schoolboys. Montgomery's anger was terrifying, the kind that sucked the very air from a room. Luckily, she was inured, having had some experiences of her own with forceful emotions. But it hurt to see him like this, every line of his body so rigid he might crack. At some point, he had put his glove back on, and the hand that had caressed her face so tenderly in the garden was now a fist by his side, and the sight of that angry fist made her heart, withered and dusty as it had been for years, unfurl and overflow for him.

She approached slowly.

"Have you known my brother much?" he said to the window. "Have you any inkling as to where he would hide awhile?"

"Hide?" Another step. "No. And we were never close enough for him to confide in me."

She was near enough to touch him now. She hesitated. This was audacious, but very necessary.

She slid her arms around his waist.

He felt hard and unyielding, like a block of granite in her arms that radiated furious heat. When he made no move to rebuff her, she leaned her cheek into the space between his shoulder blades.

He turned and stared down at her, a bit like a lion would stare at a lamb that had foolishly wandered into his cave, deciding whether to devour her flat-out or to roar and chase her off. She burrowed closer, pressed her face against his chest right where his heart was beating, and wondered if he'd take a bite out of her.

Finally, finally, he wrapped her in his arms, taking what meager comfort she offered.

She gave a relieved sigh.

He tucked her head under his chin. "He has run away," he said gruffly.

"I'm sorry," she murmured.

His hands began smoothing circles up and down her back. "He drugged his valet."

"It sounds like it, yes."

She had done right to not offer him platitudes. His chest expanded and fell, and she felt the slow ease of some of the tension in his muscles.

"He has a discipline problem," he said. "I enlisted him in the Royal Navy, and this is his answer."

Oh. That was remarkably bad. As remarkable as the fact that he was sharing it with her.

The clock began to bong; surely the twenty minutes were up soon, but Montgomery made no sign of releasing her. When she looked up, he was focused on something on the wall behind her, and she turned in his arms. Rows of paintings depicting stately homes and castles covered the wall to the right of the door. A lone painting hung to the left. It showed a sheer cliff with a castle, the ancient, drafty kind with walls six feet deep.

"Is that your castle?"

"Yes. Castle Montgomery." His voice was thick, and the tension returned to his body.

She leaned into him, and he locked his forearms beneath her breasts and pulled her snug against him.

"Managing nearly a dozen estates presents little challenge compared to the proper management of one brother," he said. He gave her a light squeeze. "What do you make of that with your fine mind, Miss Archer?"

She smiled wryly. "I suppose human relationships require a different approach. A brother is not so easily put into a ledger."

"Ah, but he is," he said. "I know exactly how much he costs me."

"In coin, yes. But when do emotions ever add up neatly?"

He paused. "Emotions," he said. He released her and stepped away, the sudden absence of his warm body leaving her disoriented.

"I must go." He started for the desk. "I must find him as soon as possible."

"Is there a chance that he will come back on his own?"

He shot her a sardonic glance. "Of course not." He began sliding the train schedules the protection officer had left into a satchel. "He knows he is in for it if he were to show his face here now."

The threat thrumming in his calm voice was unmistakable, and she knew instinctively that speaking up for Peregrin now would push him too far. He believed that competent men had their orders followed, and here his own brother had gone into hiding rather than obey. What a terrible blow to his pride. Most other men would have struck the protection officer, or at least shifted the blame.

"You will find him," she said quietly.

Many messages could be transported with this.

I trust in you.

I'm on your side.

I hate that you are upset.

And all the implications that came with that.

He seemed to hear them all, for he stopped packing and looked up. Their gazes locked across the Persian rug, and his expression softened, perhaps because her face showed everything, that she felt him hurting, that her chest was aching in a strange way because she wasn't sure when she would see him next.

With two long strides, he closed the distance between them. His hand curled around her nape, its grip both gentle and possessive, and for one brief moment, his attention was on her as if she were the one and only thing on his mind.

"I will come back to you," he said. He kissed her hard on the mouth, then more softly on the forehead, and all but bundled her out the door.

⁓⸙⁓

The logs in the fireplace popped and released a burst of sparks before collapsing on the grate with a hiss. Indeed. She had retreated to the blue parlor with Hattie and Catriona for an evening of reading and sketching, but the book in her hands was hardly more than camouflage. In the lazy silence, her mind strayed back to Montgomery's kisses again and again, as if the coaxing pressure of his mouth against her own had become her new center of gravity that compelled all her thoughts to revolve around him.

She shuddered. It was precariously close to her feelings of that fateful summer years ago, that breathless, reckless, dizzying yearning for the whirl of passion itself, the desire to pit herself with all she had against a masculine force and to surrender in a glorious blaze . . . Of course, she knew better now than the girl she once was. Yes, she could take a few sips of pleasure instead of headlong drowning in it.

He hadn't returned today. Tomorrow was her last day at Claremont. Would he find his brother?

"Who is in line for the dukedom after Peregrin Devereux?" she asked.

Hattie slowly looked up from her sketch pad. "What makes you ask such a thing?"

"Well, we have been here for weeks," she said, "and the duke's profile is still incomplete. We're behind with the entire campaign."

"I'm not sure about the line of inheritance, nor how we could exploit it for our cause," Hattie said. "Catriona?"

For once, Catriona had to give a clueless shrug. "He will get his direct heir soon enough," she said. "Everyone says he will remarry next year."

An ugly emotion twisted in Annabelle's belly. *Jealousy.*

How juvenile. Of course he would marry. One of the pretty debutantes who had drifted through his wintery ballroom, white and silent like snowflakes.

She came to her feet and paced toward the dying fire.

"I confess I'm glad that he would never contemplate a bride from a merchant family," Hattie said, "else Mama would try to arrange a match with one of my pretty sisters." She shuddered visibly. "I pity the future duchess. Do you think she will be a tragic figure, a Georgiana of Devonshire? What if she only produces girls? Imagine, to be the first Montgomery duchess in eight hundred years to not produce a son. Will he divorce her, too, I wonder?"

"Luckily, we have progressed since Georgian times," Annabelle said irritably, "and if a woman must serve as a man's broodmare, I imagine there are men much worse than the duke."

"Broodmare?" Hattie clicked her tongue. "Methinks you have been spending too much time with dear Lucie. Speaking of which, what do you think of her idea to join forces with Millicent Fawcett for a demonstration on Parliament Square?"

"Hush," Catriona said, "someone might hear."

"But what do you think?" Hattie whispered loudly.

"It will be trouble," Catriona replied.

"Indeed," Hattie agreed gleefully, "so much trouble."

Chapter 18

⸙

The next morning, the noise of trumpets and kettledrums blasted the breakfast room, infusing everyone with patriotic enthusiasm except, it seemed, the small group of suffragists and Aunty Greenfield.

"What is this dreadful noise, dear?" the elderly lady bellowed at Catriona.

"The music for tonight," Catriona replied at the same penetrating volume. "They are setting up the orchestra below the terrace."

"I see," Aunty said, unimpressed. "I daresay they don't play like they used to play." She cast a disapproving glance around the table and it promptly snagged on Annabelle. "You are pale, child. Goodness, are you feeling unwell again?"

Annabelle gave her an unconvincing smile. "No, ma'am, I'm fine."

"Good," Aunty Greenfield said, "you should be. At your age, your health should still be quite robust."

At her age, she should be wiser than to moon over a duke who hadn't returned.

Catriona folded up her napkin. "I'm going to watch the experts prepare the fireworks."

Annabelle was on her feet. "I'll come with you." Fresh air was exactly what she needed.

The fireworks were being set up on the other end of the French garden. The thin layer of snow had receded overnight, revealing the smooth white gravel covering the paths and the intricate stone carvings on the dry fountains and weathering Greek marbles. It would be so lovely to see the gardens in summer, with the trees in all their lush green glory and a warm breeze rustling through.

"This is such a beautiful place," she murmured.

"It is," Catriona said, her eyes on the wooden structure ahead that was growing steadily under the workmen's hands. "But have you seen those snow globes with tiny castles inside?"

"Eh. Yes?"

"That's Claremont."

"I'm not sure I follow."

"It is in a bubble. It isn't real. Not for us."

"And Oxford is? The town is unchanged since the crusades." She found herself strangely aggravated by the discussion.

Catriona looped an arm through hers. "Never mind. I just mean to say that Oxford is a good place for us."

"Of course it is," she murmured.

❧

An hour before midnight, a rumor circulated that the lord of the manor had returned, and yet he still shone with his absence. The house party guests gathered in the reception room for drinks and snacks and gossip.

". . . rockets were imported directly from China . . ." someone said.

". . . the last duke had hired a contortionist, not sure whether it was male or female . . ."

". . . and then Lady Swindon's hat went up in flames."

When the large pendulum clock struck eleven thirty, Lady Lingham, who seemed to stand in as hostess, ordered everyone to move to the terrace. Annabelle drifted along, the stream of people carrying her to the ballroom where the doors to the terrace were flung open wide. There should have been a dark, forbidding figure on the upper balconies.

But there wasn't.

How could he not attend his own New Year's Eve party?

"Annabelle!" Hattie was weaving her way toward her. "Come! I have reserved you a seat with us."

She was tugged along onto the terrace.

The chatter and laughter of a few hundred inebriated aristocrats engulfed her, leaving her briefly disoriented. The terrace and the French garden had turned into a fairground. Rows of floating red paper lanterns threw flickering shadows; fragments of music drifted up from the depths of the garden.

He was not here, she felt it in her bones.

It was for the best. It was madness, this urge to be near him.

A group of children flitted between her and Hattie, and her hand slipped from her friend's grasp.

Before she could catch up, she was stopped in her tracks by an apple hovering before her, ruby red and glossy in its sugary coat.

"A candied apple, milady?"

The vendor towered over her on stilts, his long, striped trouser legs billowing. His wide smile was painted on.

"Annabelle." Hattie's voice reached from a few paces ahead.

She didn't move.

Madness or not, she had to say good-bye, and not when they were leaving tomorrow, terribly formal in the courtyard. In truth, she did not want to say good-bye to him at all.

She turned on her heels.

Not sensible of her at all.

She moved faster, dodging animated guests streaming toward her.

In the ballroom, the throng of people moving through had thinned. She paused under the grand chandelier, pondering, then took a course back to the great entrance hall.

The long hand of the clock stood at twenty minutes to midnight.

And then she knew where she had to go. She turned toward the west wing.

She hurried along dimly lit corridors on soundless tiptoes like a thief. She arrived at the door to his study panting; a breathless moment of hesitation, and then she rapped against the dark wood.

Silence.

Her hand hovered over the door handle.

She quickly, quickly, pressed down and—found that the door was locked.

Her heart sank.

She moved on, using paintings and potted plants as markers to find her way back to the music room. She opened the ornate double door and stuck her head through the gap. Yawning emptiness. The piano looked alien and abandoned in a shaft of moonlight.

A wave of panic welled from her stomach. Had he returned at all?

She dashed through another corridor, and another, until all sense of direction was lost and her corset was biting into her flesh. She had to pause and hold on to a banister, her chest heaving.

Reason, see reason.

Claremont had three floors and two hundred rooms; she could never search them all.

Damnation. She had been so good, so sensible.

How could she have allowed Montgomery to turn her into a panting madwoman haunting his castle?

How could she not?

She had evidently sleepwalked through her days in Kent. Oxford had revived her mind. Montgomery had shocked the whole of her back to life; he hadn't even tried, he had been cool reserve and bluntness and before she knew it he had snuck under her skin. Now she didn't know how to dislodge him again. Did not quite want to, either. It felt too good to be alive. It felt too good to be *seen*. His kisses had lifted a loneliness off her she hadn't even known she carried.

She forced another breath into her lungs. The skin on her back was sticky and beginning to cool.

One last attempt, and then she'd return to the terrace.

Up, up, up a flight of stairs, down another corridor, past a startled maid . . .

He stood near the door to the winter-sky library with Bonville the butler.

She came to an abrupt halt, her head swimming.

Montgomery turned toward her, and the moment their eyes locked, tension crackled up and down the length of the corridor.

He must have said something to Bonville, for the butler melted into the shadows.

A rushing noise was in her ears as she approached. She should have laid out the words, the purpose, for this beforehand. She hadn't; her body had been driven to find him like an animal was driven to find water after a spell of sweltering heat. Now that he was here in the flesh, watching her, the urge faded into a dizzying sensation, a shyness. She hadn't expected to feel shy.

By the time she reached him, meeting his eyes was a little difficult.

He looked taller than she remembered. He felt different, too; there was a raw, glinting edge just beneath his quiet surface.

His fingertips glanced over her cheek, and the contact shimmied through her whole body. His caress traveled along the soft curve of her jaw to the side of her neck, where her pulse fluttered and her skin was damp.

"You ran." There was a rasp to his voice.

She swallowed, and he stroked lightly over her jugular, as if to settle her right where she couldn't hide her agitation. It worked. Gradually, her limbs loosened, and a heavy warmth sank into her limbs under the steady up-and-down glide of his fingers.

"Your brother," she whispered, "have you found him?"

His hand slid from her neck to her shoulder as his other hand reached for the door behind him, and he pulled her with him into the dark silence of the library. He backed her against the door, then she heard the key twist in the lock.

A pang of trepidation rippled through her. The nearness of his body felt as impelling as if he were pinning her to the door with his weight.

He leaned closer. "Tell me why you ran."

His breath brushed over her lips, and her chin tilted up, seeking the full pressure of his soft mouth against hers.

"Tell me," he repeated.

"You said you'd come back."

He shook his head. "I need to hear you say it."

Against the spill of moonlight through the window behind him the outline of his shoulders was rigid, and his hands were clenched by his sides as if he were checking himself with some difficulty.

It dawned on her then that most men in his position would simply take what they wanted, and didn't she know it. She had forgotten all about it around him. But there was no doubt that right now, Montgomery wanted her badly. The tension humming in his muscles reverberated through her own body, and she could smell the salty note of an aroused male on him. If she stroked her hand over the front of his trousers, she'd find him hard. But the choice was hers.

A twinge of pleasure and pain throbbed in her chest.

Beautiful, wondrous man.

He had to know that alone in the dark, they were equals in their longing.

She slipped her hand beneath his coat.

He froze. Under the warm silk of his waistcoat, bands of muscle contracted, and the hardness against her knuckles left her reeling. She watched as her hand flattened against him . . . glided over the silver chain of his pocket watch to his ribs, then up the firm, tapered shape of his torso. So sleek, yet solid, so many strengths contained in one man . . . Slowly, her hand slid down again, down, down over his tense abdomen, over the outside of his trousers.

Montgomery seemed to have stopped breathing. His throat worked as he swallowed, as she hovered, hesitated . . . gently, gently, she pressed her palm against him. She gasped, unprepared for the jolt of pleasure that shot through her at the feel of him. Her fingers curved around him, and the soft grunt this drew from Montgomery set her blood on fire. The mighty man sounded . . . helpless. She caressed him again, inflamed by feeling him heat and twitch, by the rustle of fine wool against her palm.

With a groan, Montgomery clamped his hand over hers, and then her wrist was pinned against the smooth wood of the door and his lips were on hers. At the first taste, things turned fast and mindless. His free hand clutched her waist, hers roamed over his back, his nape, the slippery silk of his hair as his demanding mouth urged her from one kiss into the next. Reality dissolved into shadows and heat, the firm, soft urgency of a man's kiss, the thick ridge of his desire.

A draft of cool air brushed the back of her knees. She blinked down and found her skirt wadding around her waist, and a hard male thigh invaded between hers. She moaned at the sudden pressure against her softest place.

"Yes," he murmured, his fingers digging into the curve of her hip. Her uncorseted hip—he groaned into her mouth at the feel of it. His hand on her hip was guiding her in small, rhythmic thrusts against his thigh, and heat bloomed from the friction between her legs. She made an agitated sound. "Please, I can't . . ."

He made a soothing noise and palmed her thigh, up and over her backside, finding the slit in her drawers from behind, and *help*, he was touching her. He was touching her *there*, with slick, knowing fingertips . . . It had only been minutes since the corridor; how could it come to this within minutes? *Because they had been needing it for weeks.* He stroked harder, and she melted around him as bliss curled through her, curled her toes . . . A finger slid inside her, and her spine arched as she gave a little cry.

They weren't equal in this at all—he was leading her headlong into frantic oblivion.

Trapped between his thigh and his sliding fingers, devastating pleasure gathered and knotted, and she gripped his arm to stay him, but his muscles flexed so wonderfully as he was pleasuring her, steadily, relentlessly, the tension burst in a white-hot blaze, pulsing in her lips, her toes, her fingertips. Her next cry was muffled against his shoulder, Montgomery's other hand clasping the back of her head.

She clung to him, her knees like water, the sound of her breathing a roar in her ears.

The fine wool of his coat was rough against her cheek.

He withdrew from her gently.

Behind closed eyelids, white dots flashed and faded like stars.

The haze cleared when his foot pushed at her instep. He was widening her stance, making a space for himself. His hand moved between them, and she knew then that he was working on the fastenings of his trousers.

He wanted her. Right here, standing up against the door.

Her fingers clenched in his shirt. "I . . . I don't . . ."

Oh, she did. And then she didn't. She couldn't. This hadn't been the plan—there had been no plan.

His hand stilled. "You wish to stop?" He sounded fairly calm, for a man aching to take his pleasure.

Help. She had recklessly unleashed him, and now female instincts battled, the urge to assuage his need, and deeper fears, and then, the obvious—to not look like a complete trollop.

"I can't," she whispered, the beginnings of a panic washing over her. "Not . . . like this."

Not up against a door. Not in any location, had she been thinking at all.

Montgomery's chest tensed beneath her palms. "Of course," he murmured. "Tomorrow."

"Tomorrow?" A frisson of foreboding raised the hair on her nape.

"I will have put everything in writing, whatever your terms," he said. "You have my word."

Terms?

He made to kiss her again. Something in her expression stopped him. He eased back, adjusting the front of his trousers, his lips twisting with discomfort. "Well, I won't get a hold of my solicitor now," he said.

Her blood ran cold. So she had understood him right. He thought she wanted to negotiate an arrangement.

"You thought I meant to negotiate an arrangement," she said out loud.

He frowned at the flat tone of her voice. "You did not?"

He was still breathing hard. He looked oddly boyish, with his cravat rumpled and his hair mussed from her greedy hands, and God knew what she looked like.

Who would try to talk terms on the brink of lovemaking, when a man was half crazed and prone to promise anything? A calculating courtesan, that's who.

Nausea welled in her stomach.

"And you'd sign *whatever* my terms?" she heard herself say. "How about a yacht, Your Grace?"

He tilted his head. "If you need one."

She gave a small, ugly laugh.

He had not seen her at all.

Never mind their talks and walks and breathless kisses, all along, he had clearly never stopped thinking of her as a woman who'd bargain her favors for money. He'd have hardly propositioned a respectable woman for a knee-trembler in his library in the first place.

She smoothed her hands over her skirts. "I told you that I wasn't in the market for such a thing."

There was a pause. When he spoke next, his voice was cool. "What do you want, Annabelle?"

You.

At some point, she must have begun feeling, wanting, impossible things. "I don't want to be your mistress."

His eyes raked over her, his incredulity palpable, and she knew what he saw, a disheveled female who had brazenly put her hand on his cock.

Her heart crumpled. She felt naked, and utterly foolish.

She was as deluded and impulsive at twenty-and-five as when she'd been a girl.

She turned abruptly and felt for the key in the door lock.

A beat later, he was behind her, his hand staying her frantic efforts.

"Annabelle."

She shook her head.

"I feel I have offended you, which was never my intention," he said.

"Please," she said, "I gave you the wrong impression, which I regret. But I won't be your mistress. I won't."

He hesitated, for two heartbeats, perhaps three. Then his hand fell away and he stepped back, taking the warmth of his body with him. "As you wish."

His tone was formal. Impersonal, even. Not unlike how he had sounded during their very first meeting in this library.

She unlocked the door and hurried into the night. From afar, she heard the pops and explosions of yet another firework display she didn't see.

Chapter 19

Dawn had barely dragged itself over the horizon, but the coach to his weekly London appointment was ready for departure.

Sebastian halted in the entrance hall halfway to the doors. "Bonville," he barked.

The man seemed to materialize from thin air. "Your Grace?"

"Something is wrong with the lighting."

The butler cast a quick assessing glance around, at the plaster work above, the chandelier, the French seating arrangement before the fireplace, and a touch of panic rose in his eyes. Clearly, Bonville did not find anything wrong with the lighting situation.

"The lamps," Sebastian said impatiently, starting for the entrance again. "They seem to have dimmed. I reckon the circuit has been overburdened during the house party."

Granted. It was a subtle thing, but it made the house feel unacceptably dull.

Bonville was all business now. "I will have the gas specialists called in to examine the pipes and every single bulb, Your Grace."

Sebastian gave a curt nod.

The footmen swung open the double doors for him, and a blast of cold morning air made his eyes water. He briskly stamped down the slippery stairs to the carriage. The light cover of snow that had made Claremont look pristine and enchanted had turned into sludge during the past couple of days. Not that it mattered. The weather was always the same in his study.

London was slowly but steadily soaked by gray drizzle. By the time he entered Buckingham Palace, his leather shoes were glistening wet despite the black umbrella hovering above him.

He did not expect a warm welcome in the royal apartment today. Neither the queen nor Disraeli would be keen on his latest recommendations. He'd push his strategy through regardless. He just *knew* when a plan was right, like his farmers had a sixth sense for how the weather would change. What niggled at the back of his mind as he took his seat was whether Victoria already knew that his heir presumptive had absconded. That would open a can of worms he'd prefer to keep firmly closed.

The queen and the prime minister sat in their usual spots, she in her thronelike armchair by the window, he right next to the fireplace, as if he suffered from a perpetual chill. Sebastian's briefing was laid out neatly on the low table.

The queen's eyes were as opaque as her onyx earbobs. "I was very pleased to hear that your New Year's Eve party was a success," she said.

He blinked at the unexpected sting between his ribs. He'd forever associate that party with personal rejection.

"I'm glad it lived up to expectations, ma'am."

"I had no doubt it would." Her gaze slid away from him to the briefing before her. "We were, however, surprised by your suggestions for the campaign. Indulging the farmers, Montgomery?"

"You once described them as the backbone of Britain, ma'am," he said smoothly.

The queen pursed her lips, deciding whether she liked having her own words played back to her like that.

"Farmers are not our clientele," Disraeli said. His white hair stood on end at the back of his head, as if he'd taken a nap in his wing chair and not yet fixed himself. "Local soil is not the running ticket of the Tories. Besides, the Liberals firmly have their claws in them already."

"They are easy prey for Gladstone because they still hold a grudge against you over the corn laws," Sebastian said. "Enough of them could be turned if given a few concessions."

Disraeli was gripped by a coughing fit; he coughed until his eyes bulged and watered. "But how many farmers are there?" he asked when he had caught his breath.

"Around three thousand."

"Not a number that will make or break our victory, surely? Even if they had the vote."

Sebastian resisted the urge to rub a hand over his face. How this man had managed to weasel his way into a position of leadership and into the queen's good graces continued to astound him.

"Give each of these three thousand farmers a few partners in trade they can infect with their outrage in the pub every Friday, and we have the tens of thousands of outraged tradesmen who are bound to influence their constituencies," he said. "The Liberal party is still very effectively blaming the economic downturn on the Tories, and they are blaming us daily, in town halls and market squares all over Britain."

Disraeli's lips twisted as if he were trying to rid himself of a bad taste in his mouth. "You were there when I wrote the Tory manifesto. We stand for expanding the empire, endless horizons. Glory. Greatness. That is what uplifts people, even the most lowly man. Uplift the empire and farmers will follow you gladly."

Sebastian's smile was entirely void of humor. "And I give every man credit who prefers starving for glory over feeding his family," he said, "but the current polls are what they are and they demand a change in tactics."

One did not even have to read four newspapers every morning to know this, or have a spy planted among the opposition. He, like every man of his class, had tenants. Unlike his peers, he saw their toils; he found them reflected in his own balance sheets when a harvest was bad or imported grain was sold too cheaply. It was all there if one cared to look. And he had looked hard in the past five days; every moment he hadn't spent speaking to Scotland Yard, he had buried himself in paperwork and figure columns and reports. Of course, facts hardly convinced people whose emotions wanted it to be otherwise; a pity, for he found he was surprisingly unwilling to indulge petty sentiments today.

The silence in the royal apartment thickened. Disraeli shifted in his chair until the queen produced a displeased little sigh. "Very well," she said. "While three thousand men are not a problem, tens of thousands could well be. Beaconsfield, we suggest you do as the duke recommends. As long as it can be done discreetly."

⁓ঙ৯⁓

What a curious thing power was, Sebastian thought when he was back on the train. The one person in Britain who could effectively tell him what to do barely reached his chest. And it was he who had given her much of that power, because he valued his mission and he needed her to achieve it. It was a worthy mission, of course. The men who had come before him had, save a few shameful exceptions, guarded and improved their dynasty for hundreds of years.

Still, as the sooty fog and grime of London faded into the distance behind him like a bad dream, he wondered where the line was between being a servant and a prisoner to a cause.

The train screeched to a halt at the next station.

"Oxford," a member of staff announced below his coach window. "Ladies and gentlemen, please alight here for Oxford."

Christ. The urge to scan the platform for the familiar glint of mahogany hair was absurdly overwhelming. He stared straight ahead, making Ramsey squirm in his corner across.

She had been gone for five days. He had caught up with an impressive stack of paperwork since, and he had quickly found several reasons why it was a good thing that Annabelle Archer had walked back out of his life.

It grated, of course, that he was not sure what had caused her to refuse him. He didn't like unfinished business. And as the days passed, he was thinking of her more, not less. He caught himself looking for her in the stables. Had stared like a fool at the armchair where he had first found her. He woke hard and aching every morning, and couldn't get relief from his own hand because in the end, he didn't find release until he made it about her—her soft mouth, her soft moans, the sweet hot welcome of her body . . . hell no, the last thing he needed was to link Annabelle Archer ever more closely to his desires.

A shudder ran through the coach as the train prepared to leave.

A visceral urge to jump into action shot through Sebastian's limbs.

I could have her.

He could get off the train. He could find her, take her, drag her back to his bedroom, and keep her until she haunted him no longer. His ancestors wouldn't have hesitated to do exactly that. Even today men like him could get away with unspeakable things . . .

With a huff, the train detached from the platform.

He exhaled a shuddering breath. Cold sweat had broken over his forehead, and for a moment, he sat in awe at his own dark impulses.

There were more civilized options to woo her—writing a letter, calling on her.

He would do nothing.

He had been an inch from taking her against the library door, like a drunk using a wench behind a tavern. He had never treated a woman thus before. But the truth was, a shocking emotion had held him in its clutches that night—to be inside her, or die.

No one should have that much power over him.

He opened his eyes to the empty winter landscape rushing past. The horizon was fading into a sickly yellow hue.

He allowed his mind to return to Oxford one more time, pictured her with her head bent over a book, her hair curling against her soft nape and her clever mind whirring. A bittersweet pull made his chest contract. He supposed that was how it felt to miss someone.

⚬⊱⊰⚬

It was a grave, grave offense to be late for a tutorial. Annabelle's boot heels were hammering a wild staccato on the flagstone floors of St. John's, and she all but skittered to a halt in front of Jenkins's heavy office door, her breath coming in unrefined gulps.

Her life had become all about running from place to place. Between her assignments, the suffragists, tutoring poorly paying pupils, and making true on her promise to pose as Helen of Troy, the calm and poise she had once tried to cultivate lay hopelessly in tatters.

She was still panting when the door swung open and Professor Jenkins's lanky form towered on the threshold.

Her stomach lurched.

"Miss Archer," he said mildly, "I thought I had heard someone galloping down the cloisters."

"Professor, I'm so—"

"These flagstones are uneven. If you tripped and cracked your head, now that would be a real shame." He stepped aside. "Do come in." His brows lowered darkly. "Your chaperone is already here."

Jenkins's study smelled like old paper and had the hushed feeling of a cathedral. The vaulted ceiling was higher than the room was wide, and dust danced in the shafts of light from the windows. Bookshelves sagged under the weight of leather-bound tomes and curious, random artifacts from the Mediterranean, most of which were cracked or chipped. A desk claimed the center of the room, a wooden bulwark with high piling stacks of papers on the left and a strategically placed bust of Julius Caesar to the right. Strategically placed because the emperor's sightless marble eyes were leveled squarely at whichever student took his seat opposite Jenkins. And today, blast it, Cae-

sar nearly made her trip over her own feet, because with his sharp
nose and imperious frown, he bore an uncanny resemblance to a
certain duke.

Annabelle lowered her heavy satchel to the ground next to the
chair, trying to breathe quietly.

"Good evening, Mrs. Forsyth."

The chaperone peered down her nose at her, a remarkable feat
considering she was already seated. With much grumbling, Jenkins
had squeezed an armchair into the remaining space near the fireplace. A noiseless embroidery frame balanced on her knees.

"You look flushed," she observed. "It does not become you."

"The color of her complexion is her prerogative entirely," Jenkins
said as he moved behind his desk. "I am, however, taking issue with
the alertness of her brain."

Annabelle sank into her seat. That sounded ominous.

Jenkins pulled a slim file from one of the paper stacks and slapped
it onto the desk, an academic throwing down the gauntlet. "Your
essay was a surprise."

"Oh," Annabelle said weakly.

"It wasn't entirely appalling," Jenkins continued, "but it was notably below your usual standards. Granted, your usual standards are
exceptional; in fact, your previous essay was excellent. But I prefer to
eradicate the rot before it eats away."

"Rot," Annabelle echoed. The man didn't mince his words with
the fair sex. On a better day, she would have appreciated it. But her
heart was still thudding in her ears. Beads of sweat trickled between
her breasts. Her chemise would turn clammy and itchy before this
was over.

"Much as it pains me, *rot* is an adequate term in this case," Jenkins said. "Your wording lacks precision in places; I'd go as far as
to say it was blurry. Your conclusions? Solid, but not particularly
original."

Mrs. Forsyth had gone notably still in her armchair.

Annabelle breathed deep.

It quelled the wave of nausea rising from her stomach.

Jenkins took off his glasses, unleashing the full force of his disapproving eyes. "I got the impression that your thoughts were slurred. So I must ask—was this just a miss, or do you partake in spirits?"

She took a moment to form a reply. "Are you asking whether I . . . drink?"

"I am," Jenkins said, his fingers now drumming on the desk. "Morning, or evening?"

She almost laughed. The world expert on the Peloponnesian Wars thought she was writing her papers intoxicated. That was of course a common enough behavior among the male students, but it hardly softened the blow. If she now lost her mental faculties, what did she have left?

"No, sir," she said, "I do not drink."

"Hm."

She could tell he was unconvinced.

Briefly, she was tempted to tell him the much more simple truth behind her rotting standards.

She had written the excellent essay in Claremont, where she had evidently soared happily on wings of great delusion. But ever since her return, she had gone tired and hungry. Selling Mabel's dresses had given her enough coin to pay Gilbert for January, but sitting for Hattie's portrait meant fewer hours working for money. It meant fewer pennies, and less food.

She could hardly admit any of that to him.

"I will pay close attention to the next piece, Professor."

As if on cue, her stomach growled loudly. Mortified, she clasped a hand over her belly.

Jenkins frowned. "Did you know the brain requires nourishment? Eating feeds the mind as well as the body."

"I appreciate the advice, Professor."

"I myself tend to forget it," he said, "but you must be disciplined about it."

"Certainly, Professor."

She felt the weight of his stare on her midriff and realized that she was still clutching her belly.

And then she noticed a dawning understanding in Jenkins's eyes.

She bristled. Letting a man know she was in dire straits could only lead to worse situations.

Jenkins pushed away from the desk and wandered toward the nearest bookshelf, his slender fingers skating over leather-bound spines. "You are familiar with the expedition I'm planning to Pylos Bay in April?"

"Yes."

He turned and looked at her poignantly. "I'm in need of an assistant to prepare the excursion."

There was a disapproving little huff from the direction of Mrs. Forsyth.

Annabelle blinked.

"Miss Archer?" He mouthed her name carefully, as if addressing a person hard of hearing. "What say you? Is that a position you would find interesting? It would cover a range of tasks: letter writing, coordinating the logistics—an utter nightmare, I grant you, since Mediterranean people are involved, chaotic lot—but also translations and archive work."

Her hands curled around the chair's armrests. She couldn't imagine a better position if she tried, but why ask her? He must have more qualified candidates to pick from.

"I believe it's a very interesting position, sir."

"Well, of course it is," he said. "That leaves the matter of compensation—how much do you think your work would cost the faculty?"

Her thoughts fell over each other. Instinct urged her to set the sum low, to make sure that he would hire her. But if she worked for Jenkins, there wouldn't be time for anything else, and Gilbert would still demand his two pounds in full every month.

"Two pounds a month," she said.

Jenkins tilted his head. "Reasonable. So that's settled."

He wandered back to the desk, pulled open a drawer, and picked something up.

"Excuse me for a couple of minutes," he said.

He strode toward the door, but in passing he put something in front of her.

An apple. A bit shriveled from hibernating in a dark basement since autumn; still, her mouth began to water, and she could practically taste the tart, crisp flavor.

The thud of the heavy door falling shut sounded behind her. It wasn't a stretch to assume that Jenkins was giving her some privacy to eat.

"Be careful, gal," came Mrs. Forsyth's quiet voice.

Annabelle turned on her chair. "It's just an apple," she said.

Caesar was staring at her, too, his stony countenance radiating disapproval.

Her stomach cramped, from an emotion much more powerful than hunger.

To defy, or to cry. She kept her eyes on the emperor as she reached for the apple and sank her teeth into it.

Chapter 20

The Scottish chapters have agreed to come down to London for the demonstration."

Save the sound of rain tapping softly against the windows, a cautious silence greeted Lucie's announcement. The suffragists had gathered in Hattie's plush sitting room. The embers were fading on the grate and steam rose from a dozen dainty cups. It wasn't an atmosphere that lent itself to discussing illicit demonstrations.

"Well, that's exciting," Hattie finally said.

Lucie shot her a wry glance.

Catriona took off her glasses. "Do you think it will make a difference, Lucie?"

"With the other chapters we have mobilized, we currently have around fifteen hundred women marching on Westminster during a Tory pre-election meeting," Lucie said. "So yes, I believe we are going to be in every newspaper of the country."

"But the northern chapters held such events before," Catriona said. "It only seems to agitate people."

Lucie threw up her hands. "Well, sitting prettily certainly doesn't seem to make a difference at all. If it did, why do we still turn into property the day a man puts his ring on our finger? I say let us try making noise for a change."

There was a rustle of silk as the ladies shifted in their seats. *Mak-*

ing noise sounded ominous when, from the cradle, one had been taught to be quiet.

"Now," Lucie continued, "on to the next point. I have taken the liberty to set up your schedules for the personal petitioning sessions with our MPs."

She pulled out a slim file from her ever-present leather satchel and began distributing sheets.

Annabelle's stomach gave a queasy twist when Lucie halted before her.

"Annabelle. I have reassigned the Duke of Montgomery to you."

Every hair on Annabelle's body stood on end. "But you said I was only to research him."

"Indeed, but that was before he took a shine to you."

She froze. "Whatever do you mean?"

"I understand he invited you on walks, to a Christmas dinner, and to his house party," Lucie enumerated on dainty fingers. "You clearly must have had his ear, so you are our best woman for the task."

Well. There was no arguing with that logic.

Her heart thrummed unsteadily against her ribs. It had been ten days since she left Claremont, and yet the mention of his name still put her on shaky ground.

"If I didn't manage to convince him then, I won't convince him now," she said.

"Did you clearly ask him to please draw up the amendment, and he clearly said no?"

Now would be a good moment to lie. "Our discussions were not that concrete, but I gathered—"

"Then we should try," Lucie said, and pushed the sheet into her hand. "Nothing wagered, nothing gained. When I set up the appointment with his secretary, I still thought Lady Mabel would go, but I doubt he'll mind the change of plans."

The sheet showed an address, and a date—a chamber in the House of Lords, the day after tomorrow.

Something inside Annabelle's chest did a slow, agonizing somer-sault. "I can't."

Lucie frowned. "Why?"

"I have two essays due."

Lucie gave her an incredulous look. "We have been working toward this for months. It was your idea to include him, and he is one of the most important figures in our plan. How can *essays* be an obstacle now?"

A terse silence settled over the room. Hattie looked mildly confused. Catriona studied something on the rug.

Oh, how she wanted to spill the whole tale about Montgomery to her friends right here. Of course, they'd quickly become her *former* friends if she did that.

"I'll do it," she muttered.

Lucie's frown eased.

"I'll do it," she repeated. "It will be fine."

⌒ɘ⌒

On the day of reckoning, the sun had finally conquered the low-hanging clouds that had darkened the sky for the past week. The bright rays were like a warm, reassuring touch on Annabelle's face as she made her way to the platform. She would handle this encounter. She had perfected feigning indifference over the years; she might, in fact, feel wholly indifferent in truth. She'd be polite, of course; she'd—she bumped into something soft and expensively scented.

"I beg your pardon," she said reflexively.

A young lady glared back at her. Her mink coat shimmered like an opal in the sun, and the open front revealed a cascade of priceless blond lace.

With an audible huff, the lady turned and gave her the cold shoulder.

Annabelle bit her lip. She wore her old coat and looked every inch the underclass. She would have liked to wear her new coat, but he'd

probably see that as an offer. God only knew why she was still holding on to the garment; selling it would make her solvent for two
months at least.

The wooden benches in her coach were already crowded, and she
had to wiggle her hips into the narrow space between the wall and a
sturdy matron who had a large, erratically moving hemp bag on her
lap. Her odor crept into Annabelle's nose: wool grease, smoke, and,
more faintly, manure.

She held her breath. It was the smell of life in Chorleywood, and
apparently, she was no longer immune to it. Next to her, the hemp
bag began to cluck.

I could travel first class. She could have a lace-trimmed dress and a
fur coat. She could probably purchase a whole new wardrobe every
season with Montgomery's money, and a few houses, too. She'd never
have to worry about being fed and clothed ever again. All she had to
do was open her legs for him.

Heat licked through her, flames of anger, shame, desire. Chiefly,
desire. Because apparently, her treacherous body didn't care that she
could not like the duke anymore. It wanted what it wanted, and it
seemed it wanted her flat on her back with her ankles locked behind
Montgomery's hips as he . . . she nearly gave herself a slap. The
woman with the bag gave her a suspicious side-eye.

And still the soft heat lingered in all her private places.

That was why they called it temptation—it never presented itself
as something ugly, or tepid, or harmless; no, it came in the guise of
glorious feelings and a sense of utter *rightness*, even when it was
wrong. That was why one needed principles. Regrettable, that her
grasp on them was so shaky when it counted.

⁓⤬⁓

When she entered his office, Montgomery nearly shot out of his
chair. It could have been amusing, but seeing his familiar form was
like a physical blow to her chest. Certainly, she felt winded.

"Miss Archer. Do come in."

His voice washed over her, cool and smooth like spring water.

Her mouth was suddenly parched. "Your Grace. I'm aware you expected Lady Mabel, so I hope you have no objections that I have come in her place."

"None at all," he said wryly.

An elderly secretary appeared from nowhere to help her out of her coat.

Despite her sturdy, high-necked dress, she felt exposed. Montgomery was watching her with his hawk eyes, and his gaze darkened as he took in the return of the hollows beneath her cheekbones.

He stepped around the imposing desk. "Leave us, Carson."

That was her moment to protest, but the secretary bowed and scurried toward the exit rather swiftly.

Then it was just the two of them.

Montgomery strolled closer. He was, as usual, exquisitely dressed, his charcoal-gray suit and waistcoat emphasizing the crisp whiteness of his shirt and his fair hair. No, he hadn't lost an ounce of his attractiveness.

Her innards twisted into a hot ball of dread.

"Thank you for taking the time to meet with the National Society for Women's Suffrage, Your Grace," she said.

He halted, processing all the messages she had just conveyed. Then he gestured at the chair opposite his desk. "It's my duty to receive petitioners. Please, have a seat."

She sat and busied herself with taking her pen and her tiny notebook from the reticule in her lap. When she finally looked at him, his eyes were oddly soft.

It should have warned her.

"I will not come out in favor of the amendment," he said.

She blinked as if he had flicked something at her face. "You won't?"

Of all the scenarios she had anticipated, this one had not occurred to her.

He shook his head.

"But . . . whyever did you agree to meet us?"

The corners of his mouth lifted, and all at once she realized that she had stopped Your Gracing him, that she was questioning him, something a random petitioner would never dare. Oh, blast him.

"I won't support it," he said, "but I can give you the names of MPs you should focus on. And I can advise you on how to improve your campaign in general."

She tried gathering her scattered wits. "You won't vote in our favor, but you are willing to help?"

"I am not against your proposal on principle, Annabelle."

A monstrous thought crossed her mind. "Is it . . . Is this personal?"

A small pause ensued. "You think I hold a grudge because you rejected my offer."

She could only nod.

He scrubbed his hand over his face. "Do you genuinely think that? That would hardly be flattering to either of us."

"I don't know what to think anymore."

"It is not in my interest to officially support the issue at this point in time," he said, and she could *feel* that this was his final word on the matter.

A lump of bone-deep frustration blocked her throat. Why did this feel like a personal betrayal?

She came to her feet, making him stand also.

"This is regrettable," she said, and, pettily, she added, "I thought you were a fair man."

His face went blank. "I am," he said coolly.

"Perhaps you can explain it to me, then," she said, "how is it fair that my utterly inept cousin is in command of me, for no reason other than that he's a man and I'm a woman? How is it fair that I master Latin and Greek as well as any man at Oxford, yet I am taught over a baker's shop? How is it fair that a man can tell me my brain was wired wrong, when his main achievement in life seems to be his birth into a life of privilege? And why do I have to beg a man to please make it his *interest* that I, too, may vote on the laws that govern my life every day?"

Her voice had turned hectic and sharp, and she was clutching her pen in her fist like a dagger, but she had somehow become incensed beyond caution, her blood a dull roar in her ears. Montgomery was watching her blatantly unfazed, and that made her want to pick up his shiny paperweight and hurl it against the wall, just to hear something crash.

"Oh no, you won't," he said, and moved with surprising speed; before she blinked, he was in front of her, crowding her back against his desk.

She glared up at him. His nearness should have irritated her, but this close, she could smell him, his scent familiar and exhilarating, and she wavered. Anguish began creeping into the cracks of her anger.

Her hand with the pen fell useless to her side.

Montgomery made a soothing sound. "That is better," he said.

"What is?" she said warily.

He took a small step back. "You speaking your mind," he said, "instead of maintaining that pretense."

"I assure you, it was not a pretense," she said stiffly.

"Don't try to manage me like a fool," he shot back.

"I—" She closed her mouth again.

He was right. She had not been honest with him.

If only he knew that until today, she had felt more like herself in his presence, had been more true in her actions around him than with any other man.

She became aware of how close he still stood, how his chest rose and fell with every breath he took. How awfully right it felt to be close. How right it would feel to just bury her face against his competent shoulder and feel his arms around her.

"I believe we are finished here," she said.

"You and I should talk," he replied.

"Perhaps you would be so kind to set out your recommendations for us in a letter," she said, and squeezed past him to reach her reticule.

"Annabelle." His hand closed over hers, warm and certain.

She glanced up and met his eyes, clear and deep like a glacial lake, and God help her she wanted to fall in and sink to the bottom.

She swallowed. "There's nothing to say about you and me, Your Grace."

"That is what I thought," he said, "but then you unexpectedly showed up in my office."

Her heart began beating unpleasantly fast again. "I was sent here in an official capacity."

"You could have declined."

"I assure you, I tried."

"Who would know if you hadn't followed through with the meeting," he challenged, "had you gone to a café instead of coming here?"

"Are you suggesting I should have lied to my friends?" she asked, incredulous, and damned if she hadn't considered doing exactly that. Somehow, she had still ended up in his office. "Lies have a tendency of getting exposed," she informed him.

Annoyance and amusement warred behind his eyes, and the fact that it showed so plainly meant that he wasn't half as unmoved as his calm voice made him out to be.

She realized he was still holding her hand. His thumb had begun stroking back and forth over her palm, the friction creating a warm, tingling sensation that made her head swim.

And of course, he noticed. His eyes heated. "Annabelle," he said softly. "How have you been?"

She pulled her hand away, grasping for the tattered remnants of her resolve to be *indifferent*.

"I'm well, thank you." She began stowing her notebook and her pen in her reticule.

"Good," she heard him say. "I admit, I am not. You are constantly on my mind."

Her gaze flew to his face.

There was his sincerity again, etched in every feature.

She hadn't expected him to speak about feelings. She hadn't been sure he had any feelings.

Her throat tightened with an overwhelming emotion. Of course she'd known, somewhere deep down. She'd been lying to herself. It had been easier to ignore the whole sorry affair as long as she could pretend he cared nothing for her. Now he was taking even that away from her.

"Such sentiments pass," she said tightly.

He tilted his head. "Perhaps. But unlikely. Once in place, my inclinations are rather persistent."

Indeed, they would be. He did nothing half-measure, so the object of his *inclination* had better be prepared for a long and thorough stint of his attention.

Her shoulders sagged. "How could you," she said. "How could you believe that I . . ." Her voice frayed. The scorching, frantic intimacy they had shared in his library flashed before her eyes and derailed anything she had ever learned about rhetoric.

"How could I believe what," he coaxed gently.

"In the library. How could you think that I would negotiate *terms*," she said, "and at such a moment."

Understanding dawned in his eyes, surprisingly slowly for a man known as one of the country's sharpest strategists.

"I see," he said. "The timing did take me by surprise, but it was never a question that we would talk terms, Annabelle. A man takes care of the woman in his life."

His *life*. Not his *bed*. She was trained to pay attention to the choice and nuances of words for her academic work, and this was a glaring, significant choice of one word over the other.

She felt hot and weak, too weak to move away when he raised his hand to her face. His fingertip stroked lightly over her bottom lip, and the tender contact unleashed a shower of sparks through her body.

Unthinking, she turned away and started toward the nearest window.

His study was on an upper floor, granting him an unobstructed view of Westminster Abbey. The steep spires and turrets were pointing like arrows toward the clear sky.

Footfalls approached and he halted next to her, his hands clasped behind his back, and so they stood side by side, wordlessly, acutely aware of the air pulsing heavily between them. On the street below, people carried on with their lives, a soundless teeming like ants across a forest floor.

"Were you married in the abbey?" she asked.

"No." There was a sarcastic smile in his voice. "But they will bury me there."

Her head jerked toward him. Lit by the pale winter sun, his strong profile looked vital, if not indestructible. The idea of him cold and white in a crypt, his perceptive eyes forever closed, squeezed her throat like a fist. For a beat, the world careened around her in complete silence, as if she'd gone deaf.

She wrapped her arms around herself.

He turned to her, forever sensing her shifts in mood. Surely he knew that she was still wholly in his thrall. Possibly for years to come.

"All right," she said quietly. "How would it work? Us."

His eyes narrowed. "How would you want it to work?" he finally said, his calm tone not fooling her for a moment. His body was tense as a panther's coiling to pounce.

She gave a sullen shrug. "I wouldn't know. I have no experiences with that sort of *business*."

"Neither do I," he said evenly. "Either way, the rules are for us to make."

She gave him a skeptical look. "You haven't kept a mistress before?"

"Once. A long time ago."

Well. He did have his other *arrangements*, a certain countess for one.

He had stealthily moved in on her. She slipped out of his reach and began to pace on the rug in the center of the room.

"These are the things I do know," she said. "If I were to accept your offer, I would lose all my friends. No decent woman would be seen with me." His jaw tensed, and she continued quickly: "Second, I would lose my place at Oxford, and Oxford was my father's lifelong dream. And third, once you tire of me, with my friends gone, who would keep me company? Other fallen women and the next man with deep pockets?"

His pupils flared. "Other men be damned," he said, and stepped forward, "and I'm not going to tire of you."

"How can you say that with certainty? Men often *do* tire of their companions, and walk away without as much as a backward glance."

He halted. "Is that what you are afraid of," he said, "that I will abandon you?"

"I'm not afraid," she protested. "I'm not afraid. I just stand to lose a lot."

He didn't reply. Because he couldn't deny any of what she had said, and, worse, because he had no solutions to offer. She had expected this, but it was undeniably disappointing.

"And what about the things you would gain," he said, "all the things I can give you?"

She would have to be a fool to not have considered it. With him in control, survival was certain. The worries that followed her everywhere, unshakable like shadows, the constant scouring for opportunities to keep herself warm and fed and safe—everything that drove her mind in circles at night—Montgomery could take away with the stroke of a pen. And none of that tempted her half as much as the prospect of being with him. Within weeks he had gone from a stranger to someone whose presence she craved; she wanted to fall asleep in his arms with his scent in her nose. She wanted to be the keeper of his worries and joys until his hair had turned white and they were old.

But what he offered was built on sand.

The sin of it all aside, outside the walls of her fancy house she would become invisible. Montgomery would become her world, and he'd own her body and soul. She'd spend her days waiting for him, alone in an empty house, and the gaps between his visits might grow longer, and longer . . .

Unbelievably, her heart still dithered. And so she said something she would have liked to forget completely: "What about your wife?"

His body went rigid. "What about her?"

She had to shove the words out of her mouth. "Everyone expects you to take a new wife within the year."

His face shuttered. "It would have nothing to do with us."

"How would it be?" she pressed. "Would you come to me although you have been with your duchess? Go back to her after you have shared my bed?"

"That would be inevitable," he said, a cruel note entering his voice. Never say he'd try charm and deception to get what he wanted; if only he did, it would be easier to give him up.

"And if your wife objected?"

"She would not, as you well know," he said.

Yes, she knew. Wives of men like him had to turn a blind eye.

The mere thought of him sharing himself intimately with another woman tore through her gut like a clawed, snarling beast. "What if it caused her great unhappiness?" she whispered.

Montgomery gave a bitter laugh. "Touché, my sweet. I cannot

possibly win with that question, as any answer would make me either a liar or a careless bastard of a husband, and I doubt you'd respect either type of man."

Oh, if only he didn't know her so well. "This is not a game to be won."

"Well, it certainly seems like a tremendous defeat to let you go," he said, his eyes glittering with barely checked frustration.

Don't let me go.

He would, though, and it felt like a free fall. Grasping blindly, she said: "If I were a highborn lady—"

"But you are not"—he cut her off—"you are not, just as I am not a headmaster or a man of trade."

And if she needed any proof of that, she'd only have to look out the window, where eight hundred years ago in the abbey, Montgomery's distant relative William the Conqueror had been crowned king.

The finality of that rose like a wall between them. And she couldn't bear to look at him a moment longer. She moved to the desk to finally pick up her reticule.

Montgomery helped her into her coat. He politely opened the door and stood aside.

She only had to make it into a hackney, and there she could crumple . . .

She was almost past him when he stayed her with his hand at her elbow.

"I know you are planning a march on Parliament Square."

Her gaze flew to his face. Perfectly unreadable.

"Will you hinder us?" she asked after a pause.

"No. But others might."

She nodded. "Thank you."

His hand dropped from her arm. *This was the last time he will ever touch me*, she thought.

"If we were of equal station," he said softly, "I would have proposed to you when we took our walk in the maze."

Oh.

The magnitude of this was too enormous to sink in, with her standing on a doorstep, about to walk away. She felt strangely suspended in time, her breathing turned shaky. "I wish you would not have told me this." Because she could never, ever be anyone other than plain Miss Annabelle Archer, and now she'd forever know how dearly that had cost her.

His eyes had the brittle shine of crystal. "If you were to take only one piece of my advice, call off the march," he said. "It will only cause you trouble."

Her smile was steely. "Perhaps this is not a question of staying out of trouble, Your Grace. Perhaps this is about deciding on which side of history you want to be."

Chapter 21

A letter from the Greek excavation team in Messenia had arrived in Jenkins's office, and from the lengthy, convoluted paragraphs, Annabelle was able to deduce a number of books and tools Jenkins should pack for his excursion. She had spent the past half hour tiptoeing up and down the ladder to locate said books and equipment on the shelves while her mind had ventured a few thousand miles south. Spring came to Greece early. Right now, the skies over the sea would be cloudless, and the air would soon smell of rosemary and thyme.

> *On wings of song,*
> *My love, I carry you away,*
> *Away to the fields of the Ganges,*
> *Where I know the most beautiful place . . .*

"Do you like Mendelssohn, Miss Archer?"

She glanced over her shoulder, one foot on the bottom rung of the ladder. Jenkins was looking at her quizzically from behind his desk, the tip of his pen still on the paper.

"My apologies, Professor. I had not realized I was humming out loud."

He noticed the growing ink blotch on his article and muttered a profanity under his breath. "Don't apologize," he said. "It's no trouble."

That niggled. The clicking sound of knitting needles turned him rabid. Surely, humming *would* trouble him.

"So, do you?" he prompted.

"Yes. I like Mendelssohn."

He nodded. "Very thorough people, the Germans, very precise. Did you know the same precision that makes a good engineer also makes a good composer?"

"No, but I can imagine." Though how the sum of precision could generate magic was beyond her.

Jenkins returned his attention to his paper. "Professor Campbell, his daughter, and I are going to a concert in the Royal Albert Hall this Friday," he said. "A duo will sing a selection of Mendelssohn songs."

Well, that had her struggle for her next breath. "That sounds lovely."

"You are friends with Campbell's daughter, are you not?" Jenkins said as his pen scratched onward.

"I am, sir."

She soon gave up waiting for any further elaborations. Jenkins tended to sink back into his vast inner world and forget all about her very existence.

❧

The next morning, a small envelope was waiting for her in her pigeonhole.

Miss Archer,

Would you do me the honor of accompanying our party to the Divine Duo in the Royal Albert Hall this coming Friday? If it is acceptable,

I shall arrange for you to travel to London together with Lady Catriona.

C. Jenkins

Annabelle pensively ran her thumb over the card. It was neither satin-smooth nor embossed with gilded letters. But she had not spoken to Catriona much ever since their return from Claremont, and it could be interesting to see Christopher Jenkins outside his natural habitat. And, frankly, to put it in Hattie's words—she deserved some amusement.

~⁓∞⁓~

After ten years as the head of Scotland Yard, Sir Edward Bryson had plumbed the bleakest depths of the human soul, and he'd readily describe himself as a hardened man.

The unblinking stare of the Duke of Montgomery still filled him with an urge to writhe and explain himself. "We may not have found him yet, but we have narrowed the area down to middle England with great certainty, Your Grace."

Sebastian knew he was making the man uncomfortable. He wanted to make him uncomfortable. He was spending a hundred pounds a week on this mission, and for all he knew, his brother could be dead. Kidnapped, or stuck in a bog, or clubbed over his blond head and robbed.

He took a deep, deliberate breath to ease the pressure in his chest. "What makes you certain, Bryson?"

"The men stationed in the ports on the south coast report no movement," Bryson said quickly, "and we have men monitoring all major roads and guest houses to the north—"

Sebastian held up a hand. "I'm aware of that," he said, "but how can you look me in the eye and tell me that you know with *great certainty* the whereabouts of a lone man in a country the size of Britain? The possibilities are endless."

Bryson's thin face tensed. "With all due respect, Your Grace, even if a young gentleman wears a disguise, he usually still sticks out like a sore thumb because of how he acts and speaks. And runaway noblemen inevitably stay on roads and seek the convenience of guest houses. It simply doesn't occur to them to venture into the forests, build a shelter with their bare hands, and live off the land."

Sebastian leaned forward in his chair. "So your investigation is based on the assumption that my brother is a milksop."

Bryson frowned. "It is based on experience. The possibilities may be endless, but the mind is limited. People hardly ever contemplate options outside of what they know."

Sebastian sat brooding at his desk long after Edward Bryson had left.

He finally made his way to his dressing room, where Ramsey had prepared his evening clothes.

A lost brother. An unwilling lover. A meddling queen. Any one of the three dilemmas would drive a man to drink. And since he didn't drink, and since he was in London, he had decided to go out.

An hour later, he strode out the side door where his carriage was waiting to take him to the Royal Concert Hall.

⚬⚬⚬

The concert hall looked exactly as it always had—the stage below to the right of his ducal box, the four chandeliers, the ever-dusty red velvet drapes. And yet it was all completely wrong, because three boxes down toward the stage sat Annabelle.

She had been leaning over the banister, taking in the atrium with serious, wondering eyes. And when her gaze had finally met his, she had gone tense and motionless like a doe in front of his rifle.

He had not given her a nod, for if he had, it would be in the papers the next day.

He was still staring. She was not supposed to be here. The reality of Annabelle in his evening program was as bizarre as seeing two moons in the sky.

Frustration crackled through him. Was this how it was going to be—she would reject him, and he would try to move on, only for her to reappear again and again like some exotic malady?

Caroline, Lady Lingham, placed the tip of her fan onto his forearm.

"How curious," she said. "I believe that is your charming country girl, there in the box of Wester Ross."

He'd be damned if he'd take that bait. "How perceptive of you," he said, "but it is hardly curious. Miss Archer is friends with Wester Ross's daughter. As you can see they are seated next to each other."

And he was ridiculously unable to look away from her. She wore a dress he did not recognize, something low-cut that revealed more than a hint of her milky-white cleavage.

He was about to force himself to pay attention to Caroline when a tall, lanky fellow appeared in Wester Ross's box. He bent over Annabelle with easy familiarity to hand her a glass of wine. And Annabelle smiled up at him as if he had presented her with the Holy Grail.

Sebastian's body went rigid at the unexpected bite of pain.

His eyes narrowed.

The man wore round glasses and a shoddy tweed coat; clearly he was the cerebral kind. Annabelle's smile seemed to encourage him to keep hovering over her, no doubt sneaking glances down her bodice, and when he finally sat, the bastard stuck his head close to hers under the pretense of pointing out things around the theater . . .

"Well, well," Caroline said, her soft voice intrigued. "She may be friends with Lady Catriona, but it seems she's here as the companion of this fellow from the Royal Society. What's his name? Jenkins, I believe."

Annabelle kept her eyes on the stage, but the music reached her as a meaningless hum. She was more than aware of Montgomery's eyes burning a hole between her bare shoulder blades.

She should have expected him to be here. Fine. Perhaps a part of her *had* expected him to be here. A part of her seemed to be *waiting* for him all the time these days. Perhaps that had been her real reason for spending a night painstakingly altering an old dress into a fashionable one. What she had not expected was that he would attend with the coolly attractive Lady Lingham by his side.

She curled her trembling fingers around the stem of her wineglass.

If we were of equal station, I would have proposed to you. She should treasure the sentiment and gracefully move on from things that could not be changed. Instead, his words haunted and angered her in turn. There had been no need to add tragedy to an already difficult situation.

On the stage below, the duo warbled on and on. Jenkins leaned closer now and again, murmuring something clever about the performance, and she remembered to nod when he did. Until the opening notes of "On Wings of Song" pierced her chest like a barrage of arrows.

She rose, her breathing coming in shallow gasps.

Campbell and Jenkins also came to their feet.

"Are you not well?" Jenkins asked softly as he took in her expression with a frown.

She shook her head. "I shall be back in a few minutes."

Jenkins placed a protective hand on her elbow. "I will accompany you."

"No, please," she whispered. "I shall only be a moment, right outside the box."

The professor relented. He pulled back the heavy drapes for her, and she hurried through the dark vestibule into the hallway.

She sagged back against the wall, her chest rising and falling hard. Air. She needed fresh air. The hallway came to a dead end to her right, but to her left, it followed the curve of the atrium to the main staircase.

She had not gone far when a man detached from one of the box entries and stepped into her path.

Her heart leapt against her ribs. "Montgomery."

He had never looked less like a knight in shining armor; his eyes glittered as coldly as the sapphire on his finger.

"Do me the honor," he said, and then his hand was on her back and she was deftly maneuvered through a door. They were in a dimly lit antechamber, its windows staring into the black of night.

She spun around to face him. "What is the meaning of this?" Her voice emerged low and tense. If they were found here alone together, she'd be ruined.

Montgomery leaned back against the door and surveyed her with hooded eyes. "What is he to you?"

Confusion creased her brow. "Who?"

"Your companion. The professor."

She gasped. "I don't believe I owe you an explanation."

"He touched you," he said, and he reached for her to idly brush two gloved fingers over her elbow.

The contact rushed over her skin like wildfire, hot and uncontrolled.

She all but jumped back. "You have no claim on me, Your Grace."

Something savage flickered in his eyes, as if he were of a mind to lay his claim on her right there and then. "But he does?" he demanded instead.

Unbelievable! And then she nearly choked on her tart reply when she deciphered the dark expression on his face.

"My goodness," she breathed. "You are jealous."

Montgomery blinked. "It appears that I am, yes," he said. His mouth twisted with slight disgust.

"But that's absurd," she said. "You are here with Lady Lingham."

His brows lowered. "And that is relevant how?"

"I know you are—I know that she's your . . . arrangement."

He pounced, and his hands clamped around her shoulders.

"She's not my anything," he snarled, "not since I met you. And you seem to think that this is going according to some plan—it isn't, none of this."

He spun her round and she was pinned flush against the door, trapped between oak wood and one incensed aristocrat. Out of the two, the oak would yield more easily.

"Your Grace—"

He thrust his face so close, their noses were an inch from touching. Fire and ice warred in the depths of his eyes.

"Do you think I planned it?" he said through his teeth. "Do you think I planned being mastered by my *feelings*?"

"I—"

His fingers closed around her nape and his lips slammed down on hers.

The kiss was rough, but it was frustration, not aggression she sensed in his hands, in the silky push of his tongue, the angry heat of his mouth, and in seconds, she was furious and desperate. Her hands pushed at his chest, futilely, because he was unyielding like a wall and her mouth was hungrily returning his kisses, matching every pull and slide and nip of his lips until a dull ache stirred between her thighs.

She jerked her head back and glared at him. "Am I in danger of being ravished against a door again, Your Grace?"

The primitive emotion burning in his gaze said it was an imminent possibility.

He dragged his thumb over her damp bottom lip. "Do you let him kiss you?"

She pushed his hand away. "Please don't. Jenkins is an honorable man. He appreciates me for my mind."

He gave an aggravating laugh. "If you think so. But know that I appreciate you for a lot more than that."

"Truly?" she snapped. "I didn't think you appreciated me much at all, given that you thought I'd gladly agree to be your whore."

He reared back as if she had slapped him. "I did no such thing."

His eyes had the bewildered look of a man genuinely affronted.

She threw up her hands. "Well, where I come from, that's what they call a woman who makes free with her body for coin."

"That is not how it is between us."

"And pray, what exactly is the difference?"

His face had gone stark white. "You would be with me for me," he said hoarsely, "not for my money."

The hint of a plea beneath his imperious voice knocked the belligerence right out of her. For a long moment, they stared at each other, taking stock of the wounds inflicted.

They both had drawn blood.

She slumped back against the door.

"Even if I had no care for my own reputation," she said, "in the arrangement you propose, any child we had would be a bastard."

The mention of children seemed to take him by surprise. Of course. They never thought of that as a consequence of their pleasure.

"A ducal bastard leads a better life than the vast majority of the British population," he said.

"In terms of worldly goods, yes. But one day, they would understand my role. And that they'd always come second to your other children."

He gritted his teeth. "What do you expect from me, Annabelle? A bloody proposal?"

A proposal.

Marriage. To Sebastian.

The words reverberated through her very essence, raised a chorus of hungry whispers. She silenced them with a tiny shake of her head.

"I'm not expecting anything."

He began to pace. "I can give you everything, everything except that, and you know it. My name has survived one scandal; it will hardly survive another. It would ruin my brother. It would taint my children. I would lose my allies. My standing, the Montgomery name—what sort of man would I be? I'd be no better than my father, at the mercy of his passions and whims." He rounded on her, his body vibrating with tension. "Is that what you want? Would you have me change my place in history to prove how much I want you?"

The room seemed to close in on her: walls, ceiling, the floor, contorting.

She closed her eyes, trying to slow the flurry of words in her head. "This madness between us, it must stop," she managed.

Silence.

"It's not madness," he ground out, "it's . . ."

His face was grim. She watched him struggle, grasping for the right words. Naming it would make no difference. His name would always be more important to him.

"Whatever it is," she said, "it will pass, if only you leave me alone."

Chapter 22

The morning of the march on Parliament, Lucie gathered the suffragists at Oxford Station. A cold breeze swept over the platform and shrouded them in the suffocating plumes of black smoke that rose from the waiting train.

"Now, I cannot repeat this often enough," Lucie said. "Much as it pains me, this must be an utterly peaceful demonstration, so no chanting, no accidental or purposeful obstruction of the entries to Parliament. No petitioning of passersby."

Annabelle had informed Lucie that Montgomery was aware of their plans. Of course, Lucie had decided to go ahead. She seemed in an excellent mood this morning; the gleam in her gray eyes was positively rapacious. *Ideological intoxication.* Annabelle gave herself a mental shake. The sooner she stopped seeing and hearing Montgomery everywhere, the better.

"How about the banner?" asked Lady Mabel.

Lucie nodded. "It is being stowed in the luggage coach as we speak."

"I hope so," Lady Mabel said. "I've spent hours trying to space the letters evenly."

"Should've used some math to do it," muttered Catriona at Annabelle's shoulder. Annabelle eyed her with surprise. It was very unlike Catriona to make biting remarks. Perhaps she was nervous, considering what lay ahead. Annabelle certainly missed Hattie's unwavering cheerfulness, but everyone except Hattie had agreed that it would be best for her to stay in Oxford. No one wanted to bring the wrath of the mighty Julien Greenfield down onto their cause in case something went wrong.

Nothing will go wrong.

The train emitted a deafening whistle.

"Do you all have your sashes?" Lucie said. "I have some spare ones, just in case." She patted her satchel, which hung heavy on her hip. No one stepped forward. The threat of a public dressing-down by Lady Lucie had seen everyone pack their sashes most diligently.

They split up as Annabelle made her way to third class. Ahead of her, a hooded figure in a voluminous gray cloak was moving slowly, causing a pileup of disgruntled passengers in her wake. At the train doors, the person stopped altogether and seemed to study the coach hesitantly.

Shoving and grumbling ensued.

"Apologies," came a female voice from the depths of the cloak.

Impossible! With a few determined strides, Annabelle pushed past the woman and peered at her face.

"Hattie!"

"Hush," Hattie said, glancing around nervously.

Annabelle pulled her aside. "What on earth are you doing here?"

"I'm going to London."

Annabelle was aghast. "You can't."

"But I'm perfectly camouflaged, see?" She pointed at the woolen monstrosity that shrouded her.

"Camouflaged? Hattie, this cloak went out of fashion about five hundred years ago. You couldn't look more conspicuous if you tried."

Mutiny flared in Hattie's eyes. "I'm going to London."

"But what if someone recognized you? Your father would be furious; it would get us all into trouble."

"This is my cause as much as yours. I have been to every meeting, I have done my research. I don't want to stay behind like a namby-pamby prince while my friends are at the front."

Goodness. "We all know you want to be there," Annabelle said. "No one will hold it against you if you stay here."

Hattie shook her head. "I have already escaped Mr. Graves. I can't get the man in trouble for nothing."

"Who is Mr. Graves?"

"My protection officer."

Annabelle fell silent. She had never noticed a protection officer trailing Hattie.

Her friend gave a cynical little smile. "He is trained to be invisible. Would you feel comfortable walking anywhere with me if a grim man with a pistol were breathing down your neck? Well, I always know he's there, whether I see him or not."

Taking Hattie to London was wrong; Annabelle knew it with the finely honed instincts of someone who had long had to watch out for herself.

A whistle rang, and station staff were waving at them, urging them to climb aboard.

"Fine," she muttered, "just stay close. And don't turn your back on the men or you'll get groped or pinched."

"Groped and pinched?" Hattie looked at her blankly.

Annabelle gave her a speaking glance. "You're not in first class anymore."

⁂

The Marquess of Hartford, present owner of Sebastian's family seat, was a slow man, his pace impeded by his gout, and it lengthened each corridor of Parliament by a mile. They crept toward the chamber in unsociable silence, perfectly acceptable considering that a mutual dislike was the only thing they had in common.

"Gentlemen, you have to see this." The Earl of Rochester stood at one of the hallway windows, his gaze riveted on something on the streets below.

Sebastian's pulse sped up. He could guess what had attracted Rochester's attention. Still, it hadn't prepared him for the picture of the rapidly gathering crowd on the square below. Streams of women were converging from all directions, their green sashes glinting in the sunlight.

"I say," Hartford said, "so the rumors were true." He chuckled. "This should be entertaining."

"It's thousands of them," Rochester said. His profile was rigid with disapproval.

"No matter," Hartford said, "the police will soon put an end to it."

"It has to be quashed hard and fast, else we can expect a circus like that every week. They should call in stewards for reinforcing the police."

Sebastian looked at Rochester sharply. "Stewards are not trained for handling this."

Hartford ran the tip of his tongue over his bottom lip. "If these women behaved in the first place, they'd have nothing to fear, would they?"

Sebastian gave him a cold stare. "Assembling in a public place is the right of every British citizen."

"For something like this?" Rochester said. "Only if they have been granted a permit."

"They have a permit," Sebastian said.

"That's impossible." Hartford sounded annoyed. "On what grounds? Any council would have denied it; they endanger the peace of the public."

"It appears the council had no such concerns."

Rochester and Hartford frowned but did not question him. He was known to know things they didn't.

On the square, the women linked arms, forming human chains as if safety could be had in numbers.

Was she down there?

Probably. When had Annabelle ever heeded his advice not to do something?

"Unnatural creatures," Rochester muttered under his breath. He was usually a bone-dry man, but now his face was pinched with some ugly emotion.

Sebastian had known it for a while now, but it had never been so glaringly obvious that his party, the party of rational interests, was not rational at all. There were Disraeli's visions of an endless empire, of people wanting glory over bread. Rochester and Hartford, ready to see women harmed for their ideas. At the end of the day, their party was steered by emotions as much as the socialist who wanted to crush the aristocracy. It made him feel as though his skin were too tight for his body, and he shifted on his feet, not unlike Apollo when he was ready to bolt.

Rochester pulled out his pocket watch. "Montgomery. You are to open the floor in three minutes' time."

Sebastian resisted the reflex to scan the square once more. Annabelle was not his responsibility. She had made it very clear that she didn't want to be his responsibility. Besides. He had an election to win.

Parliament Square reminded Annabelle of a beehive—purposeful and abuzz with busy females. The weather was on their side; the sun stood high in the sky and had lifted the usual blanket of wintry fog. Their banner would be well visible from hundreds of yards away.

Lucie pushed past her, a steep frown between her slender brows. "More have come than expected," she said. "I'd say a thousand more."

That would explain why there was hardly space to turn around. "Is that a problem?"

The lines between Lucie's brows did not ease. "No," she said. "As long as everyone stays civil and calm. Everyone, stay civil and calm."

"Lucie . . ."

"I have to give the command for the banner," Lucie said, and vanished.

A minute later, the banner rose above their hats in all its twenty-foot-long glory, drawing a chorus of aahs. *Amend the Married Women's Property Act Now*, it demanded in tall letters. No man glancing down into the square from the windows of Westminster could overlook it.

"Oh, that is lovely," Hattie murmured.

Annabelle nodded, a tight feeling in her chest. The emotions of the women around her were filtering through her like sun rays through water, spiking her pulse and warming her inside and out. Was that why people did it, joining causes?

Big Ben struck a quarter past the hour. Spectators had begun lining the pavement, but if they expected a performance, they would be disappointed. The plan was to be seen, not heard.

At half past the hour, a sudden wave of alertness rippled through the crowd. Warily, Annabelle glanced around. Being taller, she spotted them quickly—a united front of hats with glinting spikes was moving in from the left. A thrill of alarm shot up her spine. The hats belonged to the London Metropolitan Police.

"What is it?" Hattie asked, craning her neck.

"The police."

"Oh, lord." Hattie's complexion turned white as chalk.

Annabelle squeezed her shoulder and realized her friend was trembling. "We will be fine," she said. "I suppose the crowd is just too large."

Hattie frantically shook her head. "My father . . . if he finds out . . . and that I ran from Mr. Graves . . ."

"Perhaps take off your sash," Annabelle said calmly, "and try to look cheerful."

Looking terrified, Hattie yanked the sash over her head and made to stuff it into her cloak pocket.

"No," Annabelle said, "give it to me. They mustn't find it on you."

The officers had split up and were filtering swiftly through the crowd. They seemed to be trying to break the mass of demonstrators into smaller groups to herd them from the square.

A gray-haired officer with a drooping mustache stopped in front of them. A younger officer was following him, and his oily dark eyes immediately set Annabelle on edge.

"Please follow me, miss," the older officer said to her. "Ladies, move along."

Hattie clutched her arm. "What if they take our details?" she whispered.

"They have no reason to do so," Annabelle murmured, but Hattie's breathing was coming in alarming little gasps. "Can you get rid of the cloak? Then break away when we pass the pavement. Pretend you are a bystander."

Hattie slid the conspicuous cloak off her shoulders as she walked, revealing a plain brown servant uniform that hugged her voluptuous figure far too tightly. Somewhere, a kitchen maid was missing a dress.

"Why, you're a bonnie wench, aren't you?" The silken voice raised the hair on Annabelle's nape. Oily Eyes had caught up with them, and his gaze was roaming freely over Hattie as he strolled alongside her. "What's your name, luv?"

Annabelle's heart began to pound. That sort of man needed to be managed very, very carefully. Hattie, of course, did what any well-bred lady would do—she turned up her nose and ignored him.

The officer's expression turned oddly flat. "Oi," he snarled, "I'm talking to you."

Annabelle's gaze jerked to the older officer. He was walking farther ahead, possibly oblivious of what was unfolding behind his back.

"You," the officer said, "yes, I'm talking to you."

Hattie kept quiet. Annabelle's thoughts were racing.

"Uppity bitch," the man muttered, and Hattie gasped. The officer's arm had snaked around her waist, hauling Hattie close.

Annabelle didn't think. She simply stepped into their path. "Sir, don't do this." Her own voice sounded through a distant roar in her ears.

The officer halted, surprise in his eyes. Then his gaze traveled over her, slow and slimy like a slug. "Well, who have we here."

"Sir—"

"Keep walking like a good girl," he said. "We are occupied." Without taking his eyes off her, he slid his hand on Hattie's middle up and clamped it over her breast.

Hattie's face froze in shock, sickly pale.

The man's lips stretched into a smile.

A red tide of rage ripped through Annabelle and shot her right fist straight at the man's grin.

A crunch, a howl, as both his hands flew up to his nose.

"Run," Annabelle said to Hattie, "run, run." She gave her friend a shove.

Over his hands clutching his nose, the officer's eyes fixed on her, glittering with fury.

Holy hell. She must have given him a proper jab.

Now she felt the pain ringing in her knuckles.

A whistle shrieked, and she was gripped from behind as Oily Eyes lunged at her. *No.* She kicked at him, and her sturdy boot met his knee. His leg buckled. "Damn you!"

She was yanked around and shaken; violence pulsed around her as her body twisted in panic. Fabric ripped, and she stumbled, her knees connecting hard with the cobblestones. She caught a glimpse of her hat, crushed into the dirt beneath the boots stomping around her.

This was not a game. She had hurt one of them.

Her arms were twisted behind her back as she was dragged back upright.

Her impulse was to writhe and claw like a cat in a trap.

But the dull ache in her knees cut through the haze in her head. No matter what, they would win. So she went limp.

⁓⁓

They bundled her into a nearby police cart and slammed the door shut.

She sat up, pushed her hair back from her face, and cast a wild glance around.

Pale faces stared back at her. Women. Three of them, seated on the benches along the walls.

She struggled to her feet and winced as her knees protested against holding her up.

"Here, sit down, luv." One of the women, hardly older than herself, patted the edge of the wooden bench to her left.

Annabelle sank onto the seat, trying to control the tremor in her limbs. The enraged, nasal voice of the officer she had punched was still blaring through the carriage walls.

"What is happening?" she asked, sounding dazed to her own ears.

Before anyone could reply, the carriage door swung open again and an officer climbed aboard.

Thank God, not the one she had hit.

The cart lurched into motion, nearly toppling her off the bench again.

"Sir," she said hoarsely, "where are you taking us?"

The young officer avoided her eyes. "Please, no talking, miss."

She stared at him, and he stared just as stubbornly ahead.

"They're taking us to prison, luv," said the woman next to her.

Prison?

"I must ask you to be quiet," said the officer, more sharply now, and he placed his truncheon across his knees. On the bench across, a small blond woman in a crumpled green sash began to sob.

Barely fifteen minutes later, the cart halted in front of an imposing building. The iron letters above the entrance gate told Annabelle exactly where she was: Millbank Penitentiary.

⁓≈⁓

They were made to wait for an hour in a musty antechamber. At the sound of a bell, she was marched into a musty office. The clerk at the desk did not as much as glance at her when she took her seat. His eyes were on the voluminous ledger before him, his pen at the ready.

With a flat voice, he asked for her name and place of residence, and told her to turn in her reticule.

Then he moved the ledger toward her.

Next to her name, it said *Obstruction and assault on a public servant.*

Annabelle scrawled a shaky signature. "Sir. What is going to happen now?"

The man didn't even look up, only reached for the bell on his desk.

"Sir," she said pleadingly. He glanced at her then, and then he squinted, as if he had unexpectedly looked into bright light. His hand lowered back onto the desk.

"Well, miss," he said, "you'll know more tomorrow."

Panic rose like bile in her throat. "I'm to stay here overnight?"

"A normal procedure, miss. Unless someone fetches you beforehand and posts bail."

"Bail," she whispered. She had no money to post bail. No one even knew where she was.

The clerk picked up the bell.

She leaned toward him imploringly. "Sir, could you have a message sent for me?"

He hesitated, then shook his head regretfully. "I'm afraid not to-day, miss."

"Please, one message. To Lady Catriona Campbell."

"A lady?" The sympathy faded from his eyes and was replaced with suspicion.

Of course. She didn't look as though ladies would keep her company. She had lost her hat; the buttons of her coat had been torn off; her bodice, too, was missing buttons; and God knew what her hair looked like. If she bandied the name of the Earl of Wester Ross himself around, they might send her straight to Bedlam.

She sank back into the chair. "Never mind."

❧

She was reunited with the women from the cart in a cell. There was a single window high in the wall, a wooden stool, and a narrow cot on the left. The fetid stench of filth and desperation welled from the cracks in the old floorboards.

The woman with the northern accent who had offered her a seat in the cart flung herself onto the dirty cot. The blond girl timidly sat down beside her and clutched her arms around her slim frame. "Why are we here?" she whimpered.

"Me?" The northerner stretched her legs. "Obstructing an officer in his attempt to pinch me breasts."

The girl still standing next to Annabelle cackled. "Yous are riskin' Millbank o'er a li'l slap an' tickle?" she said. The heavy Cockney made Annabelle look at her properly for the first time.

Hard eyes glared back at her from a hard face.

"What are ye looking at," the girl snarled.

"You're not a suffragist," Annabelle said.

The girl's expression turned derisive. "Nah. Me, I was picking pockets there, they say." She sniggered. "Had nuthin' on me, thank the Lord, or else—" She drew a finger across her scrawny neck.

Annabelle sagged against the wall and slowly slid to the floor.

She was in prison. Sharing a cell with real criminals.

But she had made a police officer bleed, so that probably made her a criminal, too.

The room began to spin.

She'd be prosecuted. She'd be imprisoned. She'd lose her place at Oxford . . . her life had just been blown off a cliff, and her stomach lurched as if she were falling.

She pressed her forehead against her knees. Cold seeped into her back from the naked stone wall. There were other aches: in her breasts, her wrists, her scalp, her knees, everywhere she had been grabbed or pulled.

The man's leering grin flashed before her eyes, and a shiver of disgust racked her. He had looked so *pleased*, knowing that he could hurt and humiliate Hattie, and that there was nothing they could do.

She flexed her sore fingers. She had done something. Even Aunt May wouldn't have gone so far as to say her impulsiveness would land her in prison one day.

Time crept, thickening the shadows in the cell into murky darkness. Every quarter of an hour, the chime of Big Ben came through the windowpane.

Sometime after seven, the cell door swung back and a prison guard appeared.

"Anne Hartly."

The northern suffragist girl rose from the cot. "Sir?"

"Your brother is here."

"About time," muttered Anne Hartly. "Good luck," she said over her shoulder, all but stumbling over the hem of her narrow skirts as she hurried out the door.

The pickpocket hadn't even raised her head. The blond suffragist was staring at the door, her eyes shining in the dark. "I got no one," she said. "I got no one to come for me anytime soon." There was a tinny note of hysterics in her voice. "I got no one," she repeated, and began rocking back and forth and the cot began to creak.

"Oi. Shut it," the Cockney girl said.

The girl whimpered, but the creaking continued.

Annabelle dragged herself to her feet. She settled in the vacated spot next to the rocking girl and wordlessly put her arm around her shoulders. The lass slumped against her and cried like a child.

It was approaching ten o'clock when the heavy footfall of a guard approached again.

"Miss Annabelle Archer. Please follow me."

Her knees cracked when she stood. The girl, Maggie, reached for her hand and gave it a feeble squeeze. Resignation had set in a while ago.

She followed the guard on stiff legs, squinting into the bright light of the corridor.

It had to be Professor Campbell, Earl of Wester Ross. Or it was an interrogation.

Please let it be the earl.

They scaled a long flight of stairs that had her knees aching by the time they reached the top.

The guard halted in front of a solid black door. The director's office, said the brass sign below the window in the door. A man was inside, standing with his back turned.

As if through fog, she saw the glint of white-blond hair.

Chapter 23

⸙

The prison director's office was an oppressive room, with a low ceiling, dark wall panels, and the dusty smell of old carpets thickening the air.

And Montgomery was here.

Her whole body had turned weak as water. She wanted to fall into his arms, close her eyes, and let him carry her away. Anywhere.

Belatedly, she remembered to curtsy. "Your Grace."

His expression was strangely blank. His pale eyes traveled over her muddied skirts, the missing buttons . . . She felt herself flush. Self-consciously, she smoothed a hand over her hair.

He reached her with two long strides, bringing with him the smell of rain and damp wool. His gaze searched her face methodically. "Are you hurt?"

The quiet question did what prison had not managed—tears began burning in her nose. She blinked them back rapidly. "I'm fine."

Montgomery's attention shifted to the guard behind her, his eyes growing cold like a frozen sea.

"Show me where she was kept."

A confounded silence filled the office.

"Now."

"Of course, Your Grace," the guard stammered. "Follow me, please, Your Grace."

She stared after Montgomery's retreating back, willing herself to remain calm, calm . . . She startled when someone touched her elbow.

"Ramsey."

The valet was looking down at her with warm brown eyes. "Miss Archer. It is a pleasure to see you again." He cast a disapproving glance around. "Albeit under rather unorthodox circumstances." He guided her to a chair by the wall. "Allow me."

She sank onto the hardwood seat. Beneath her skirts, her knees were shaking.

"How did he know I was here?" she asked.

Ramsey nodded. "First, let me apologize for the delay. The meeting in Westminster went into overtime, naturally. When His Grace made to leave, three young ladies were lying in wait for him and informed him that you had been apprehended by the London Metropolitan Police. It then took a while to locate the correct, erm, facility."

Her mind was whirling. Ramsey's answer raised more questions than it resolved. Why had her friends gone to Montgomery of all people? And, more significantly, why had he come?

Ramsey obviously misinterpreted her troubled silence. "It is all over now, miss," he soothed. "The director of this . . . place . . . should be here any minute and then we can draw a line under all this unpleasantness."

Indeed, the prison director arrived before Montgomery returned, looking like a man who had hastily dragged his clothes back on when he had already been settled comfortably by the hearth. He was accompanied by the clerk who had made her sign the ledger, who, judging by his rain-soaked hat, had been sent out to fetch him.

When Montgomery strode back into the office a few minutes later, his eyes were unnaturally bright, and a muscle was ticking faintly in his left cheek.

The prison director quickly moved behind his vast desk.

"The cells here fall short of any standards set by the Home Office," Montgomery said without preamble. "Too filthy, too cold, and unacceptably overcrowded."

The director tugged at his cravat. "Regrettably, there has been a shortage of—"

"And on what grounds was she being held?" Montgomery demanded. "Their demonstration had been granted a permit."

Had they?

The prison director leafed jerkily through the ledger. "Indeed, they had a permit," he said. "It seems the offenders, I mean, ladies, were held for obstruction and assault." He looked up uncertainly. "Miss Archer here, ah, bloodied a police officer's nose."

There was a brief, incredulous pause.

"A misunderstanding, obviously," Montgomery said silkily.

The prison director nodded. "Obviously, Your Grace."

"Hence, her record should be expunged and the sheriff informed that her case has been dropped."

"Certainly, sir."

Sebastian motioned for Ramsey without taking his eyes off the prison director. "How much is the bail?"

The director looked surprised; he evidently had expected the duke to simply take his prisoner and walk out again. "The bail is at fifty pounds, Your Grace."

Annabelle bit back a gasp. That was a staggering amount of money. She felt ill as she watched Ramsey pull a checkbook from his inner coat pocket.

Montgomery signed the check on the director's desk and wordlessly turned to leave.

Ramsey offered her his arm, but her feet were rooted to the spot.

"Miss?" Ramsey coaxed.

Montgomery turned back, his eyes impatient. His expression turned quizzical when she walked over to him and rose to her toes to whisper into his ear. She didn't want to be this close to him, she probably reeked of prison, but . . . "There's another suffragist in the cell," she said softly, "Maggie. She has no one to fetch her, and she's terrified."

Montgomery pulled back and gave her a long, unreadable stare.

Then he held a hand out to Ramsey, who promptly pulled out the checkbook again.

It was potently silent in the office when the duke signed a second check for fifty pounds and ordered Maggie's release come morning.

Annabelle's cheeks were burning up. She thought of the Cockney woman, and the impulse to help her, too, wrestled with common sense. Montgomery put an end to her quandary by firmly placing her hand on his arm and marching her from the office.

An unmarked carriage was waiting for them at a back entrance in the pouring rain.

Ramsey tossed the drenched driver a coin. "To Thirty-seven Belgrave Square."

As the carriage swayed through the night, they sat in silence. With the light and shadow of the passing streetlights playing over his face, Montgomery looked alien, like a stranger, and it made her feel lost.

She had just cost him a hundred pounds, and she wasn't even his mistress. He had searched the prisons of London to find her after she had told him to stay away. And he was a straightlaced man, so it must have gone against his grain to free her by throwing his weight around. *Thank you* seemed laughably inadequate for what he had just done.

"Where are we going?" she finally asked.

"Apologies," he said, "I thought you knew. My residence in Belgravia."

He wasn't looking at her. Save for searching her face for signs of mistreatment, he had not looked at her much at all tonight. The realization settled like a boulder on her chest.

"Unless you would prefer to stay at Claridge's," he said when she didn't reply.

"The hotel?" Even she had heard of that illustrious place.

He nodded. "You could use my rooms there. Transport to the train station could be arranged easily tomorrow."

He sounded so polite. Impersonally polite. It wasn't just because Ramsey was with them. She could sense the distance between them, the weakness of their connection, as if he had neatly clipped the invisible rope that had tugged them toward each other almost from the start. He obviously still felt protective of her, but it was clear he did not want to feel that way. Well. He was only doing what she had asked him to do: staying away from her. It should have made her feel relieved. Instead, the boulder on her chest was slowly crushing her very lungs.

"I'm perfectly fine with Belgrave Square, Your Grace."

❧

Montgomery's white, stucco-fronted town house rose four stories high and overlooked the now-dark park across the street. Four white pillars framed the main entrance. From prison to London's wealthiest neighborhood in the space of an hour proved a little overwhelming; Annabelle moved up the steps like an old woman on Ramsey's arm. She vaguely registered a chandelier and a wide oak staircase while footmen took gloves and coats and hats.

Montgomery was speaking to a female servant whose crisp dress and demeanor signaled that she was the housekeeper. Finally, he turned to Annabelle, the aloof expression on his face unchanged.

"Millie will show you to your chamber," he said, nodding at a young maid hovering by the housekeeper's side. "Do not hesitate to have a bath, or to order up a tray."

A bath. Food. Heaven.

She would have traded all of it gladly for an ounce of warmth in his voice.

A hint of golden stubble glinted on his jawline. He must have risen and shaved early, and now it was approaching midnight. He'd had another long day, and it showed in the stubble, and the harshness of the lines around his beautiful mouth. At the end of the day, he was a mortal man.

She tried to breathe through the building pressure in her chest. She had never wanted anything more than to bury her face against his shoulder, because mortal or not, he still looked as though the whole world could lean on him awhile. And he could need some tenderness in return.

Her scrutiny did not escape his notice. A flicker sparked in the depths of his eyes, and his stoic expression cracked. For a moment, it looked as though he was going to touch her, but his right hand just clenched and unclenched by his side.

"Good night, Miss Archer," he said.

⁓ ∞ ⁓

"Would you like me to draw you a bath, miss, while I prepare the room?" Millie asked.

The room looked perfectly prepared to Annabelle. The cool elegance of ice-blue wood paneling and a high stucco ceiling was tempered by lush dark velvet drapes and the warmth of the roaring fire on the grate.

"A bath would be lovely," she said. Anything to wash off the degradation of Millbank.

The bathroom was elaborate: white tiles from floor to ceiling, glinting taps, and a large, oval copper tub. Glass jars with cakes of finely milled soap and pink crystal bottles with lavender essence and rose oil lined the shelves.

Millie turned the taps open. Steam rose as hot white jets gushed into the tub. She left when Annabelle undressed, and she bustled back into the room with an armful of crisp white towels, a nightgown, and a white silk robe. She placed the items on a chair by the bath and disappeared in a rustle of starched skirts.

Her entire body sighed when she sank into the hot, lavender-

scented water. Her head lolled back against the rim. How lovely to
feel weightless for a change. She was almost too entranced to reach
for a bar of soap. The lather was silky soft and luxurious like cream.
The gentle friction of the sponge over her limbs drew a prickling heat
to the surface of her skin. It was the same feverish feeling that had
seen her flying through Claremont at midnight, searching for Montgomery as if he were the antidote to some fatal malaise. But back
then she had wanted a last kiss, a last good-bye. Now she knew what
a ludicrous plan that had been. Every kiss they shared had just whet-
ted her appetite for more of his kisses. Quite possibly, no amount of
kisses, no amount of time, would ever be enough before it would feel
right to say good-bye to him.

The sponge brushed against her knuckles, still pink and sore from
punching a man. She winced. She had come close, so close to losing
her future today. Then Montgomery had walked in and freed her as
easily as one would open the cage door for a captive bird. And just
as any rational man would after setting a wild creature free, he would
leave the creature to its own devices.

It hurt.

Whichever route they took, it would end in hurt.

As it was, the thought of never feeling his soft mouth against her
own hurt the most.

She carefully set down the sponge on the rim of the bath.

He had given her back her tomorrow.

She could give them tonight.

Steam swirled off her body when she rose from the tub, and she
swayed, feeling light-headed. She toweled herself off and massaged
some of the rose oil into her still-damp skin; she unpinned her hair
and combed her fingers through the wavy strands until they gleamed.
She slipped into the white silk robe.

Back in her room, she gave the bell pull a tug.

Her heart was beating a hard, slow rhythm by the time Millie
appeared on the doorstep.

"Take me to His Grace, please."

The maid's eyes swept furtively over her flimsy attire. "His Grace will be in his private chambers at this time, miss."

The servants would talk. It mattered not.

She moved toward the door on bare feet. "I know."

Chapter 24

Sebastian was sprawled in his armchair, his hair still curling from his bath, and he was increasingly keen on the idea to go to his club for a round of midnight fencing. The bath had not worked. The book in his hand did not work. Angry, unspent desire was still pulsing through his veins, an aggression without a target. Oh, but he had a target all right. One glance at her, bedraggled and dirty as she was, and he wanted her. Wanted to protect, possess, to *be* with her. And short of bullying her into it, he could do exactly nothing.

The logs in the fire popped so softly, so domestically, it stoked his resentment.

To think this would become one of his greatest challenges yet: to do nothing.

There was little joy in honor tonight.

A light knock on the door jolted him from his brooding. No one came to his chambers at this time of the night. He made to rise to investigate when the doorknob turned.

Somehow, he knew it would be her. He was still unprepared when she appeared.

For a beat, his mind was a blank.

Her hair was down, gleaming, glorious hair, streaming to her waist in mahogany rivers. And she was as good as naked.

Heat swept over him from head to toe.

A filmy white robe clung to her curves as she drifted toward him. Bare feet slipped from beneath the hem, achingly vulnerable pale feet . . .

He felt himself swell and stiffen with arousal. With some difficulty, he dragged his gaze back up to her face.

"Annabelle." His voice emerged roughly. "Is something the matter?"

She stepped between his knees and her scent curled around him. He actually felt weak, smelling her again.

"I'm afraid so," she said.

Every muscle in his body locked when she gently took the book from his hand and lowered herself onto his thigh.

"What is it?" he asked thickly. The soft, feminine weight in his lap had him almost painfully hard.

"I missed you," she murmured.

Her eyes were on his throat, his shoulders, his chest, taking a primal inventory, and her fingertips began skating over the V of bare skin exposed by his loosely fastened robe.

His hands circled her upper arms in an unconsciously rough grip, crushing warm silk between his fingers. "If you are here out of gratitude—"

Her eyes widened. "No," she said, "no."

Her gaze slid down his torso to the bulge at the front of his robe, and he bit back a groan. She may as well have placed her hand on him.

She glanced up, a pink flush tingeing her cheekbones. "I want you, Montgomery."

I want you, Montgomery.

His grip on her relented, and she twisted closer and kissed him on the mouth.

"How I missed you," she whispered against his lips.

She slipped from his lap to kneel between his thighs. His breathing turned shallow when her slender fingers began working on the knot of his belt. He clasped her chin and made her look him in the eye. "I cannot offer you any more than I have."

Her gaze narrowed slightly. "I know."

She spread his robe open.

For a long moment, there was only the sound of ragged breathing and crackling fire.

When she looked back at him, her eyes glittered with emotion.

She leaned in and touched her lips to his chest, drawing a guttural sound from his throat, and she dragged her open mouth down, down, down the tight planes of his stomach . . . His right hand curved around the back of her head of its own volition.

She hovered, her warm breath rushing softly over his aching cock.

"Annabelle—"

She closed her mouth over him.

His body bowed up as pleasure hit him like a whip. "God."

Wet, soft heat and tenderness. Bliss. He groaned, his fingers flexing in her hair. He would have never asked this of her, but God knew he had imagined it. The dark fantasies paled against the sensations that engulfed him now, streaking like fire through his veins at every touch of her tongue.

She began sliding her mouth up and down his length, and sweat broke over his skin; he could already feel the pressure building at the base of his spine. With herculean effort, he pulled back and came to his feet and scooped her up into his arms.

⁘

Montgomery's gaze was fixed on the large bed that dominated the room, and she clung to him, discomfited and thrilled at being carried off like the prize of a conquest. He set her down onto the edge of the mattress with greatest care, but his eyes burned with the scorching blue hue of the center of a flame.

She shivered. So that was what it was like to have all his intensity focused on her. Time and conscious thought went up in sparks, leaving only now, him, her, and the need to be close.

He cupped her face in both hands, his thumbs stroking at the corners of her mouth.

"How I want you," he said, and leaned down and kissed her.

He took it deep on the first stroke, his lips demanding, guiding, giving. He kissed like a man who knew he would not have to stop. He wouldn't have to stop. A vision of his strong body covering hers pulsed through her in a lazy, molten wave, leaving her boneless and breathless.

When he broke the kiss, she was panting and on her back, her legs still lolling over the side of the bed. Her robe had been undone and spread open. Montgomery was looming over her, his eyes savoring and lingering on all the delicate places that most intrigued a man.

She should have clamored to cover her modesty. Alas, there was so little moral fiber in her, hopeless, and so she tipped up her chin and showed him her throat.

The smile vanished from Montgomery's face. He stepped back and his robe slid to the floor with a soft swish.

She swallowed. He could have seduced her with his body alone, all vital confidence and well-honed muscular grace. His skin was fair, the light mat of hair on his chest a sandy color, like the trail running down his flat abdomen to the most male part of him. He was beautiful there, too, heavily erect and straining with want . . .

He inhaled sharply, and her attention snapped to his face. He was homing in on her knees, his eyes narrowed to slits.

"Oh," she said, "it's nothing."

His hands were already on her, gently angling her leg so he could examine the plum-sized bruises on her skin.

"Who did this to you?"

"No one . . . I fell when they took me," she added when he looked up and she met his feral expression.

She shuddered, strangely more aroused than before.

She extended a hand toward him. "Please," she whispered, "come to me."

His gaze traveled over her bare body, sprawled on the bed, and as she had hoped, it distracted him enough for the bloodlust in his eyes to fade.

He sank to his knees. When he brushed a kiss onto her shin right below the bruise, it felt different. His kisses had been charged with desire, the need to possess. This was soft as the touch of a feather. Revering. As if she were precious and made of glass. Another kiss on her thigh, and his fingers stroked the sensitive skin at the back of her knees. The sensation flowed over her warm and sweet like syrup. A flash of tongue on the inside of her thigh, gentle sucks, a light nip of teeth, and she shifted restlessly on the sheets. A warm hand palmed up her other leg, to the junction of her thighs, and there his fingers splayed and anchored her . . . until his thumb moved over her. She jerked. He did it again, a knowing flick, and her lips parted on a silent moan. Heat welled everywhere he touched with his clever fingers, his silky mouth. He kissed her between her legs, his tongue on her warm and fluid, and she was lost, lost to him. He licked and caressed her deeper into oblivion until her hands clenched in the bedsheets and she arched against him with a cry.

She was still limp and pulsing when he rose over her and braced his elbows on either side of her head. The hot, hard nudge at her entrance sent a jolt through the daze.

She flattened a hand against his chest. "Please."

He made a strangled sound, his handsome features stretched taut with the effort to stop.

She said it quickly. "Please don't get me with child."

An unintelligible emotion passed over his face. Then he gave a nod.

She gasped when he pushed forward. It had been too long, and he was big, and there was the instinctive trill of feminine apprehension right on the brink of letting someone in.

He sensed her struggle beneath him, and his movements gentled, became endlessly tender and slow.

"Don't, my love," he murmured, "just let me come to you . . . yes . . ."

His body belied his even voice. Beneath her palms, the muscles in his back were trembling.

It was that, or the husky murmur of his voice near her ear, or the soft scrape of his cheek against hers, but something in her gave, and she watched his eyes glaze over as he sank into her.

He filled her utterly, body and mind, and he planted himself deeper until she had no more to give. Her gaze was riveted on his face, taut with a primal tension, until the feel of his thrusts dissolved any boundaries, left no beginning or end between them. She felt him shudder and wrench away from her just as she peaked again.

His head dropped to the crook of her neck and he slumped against her.

Her hand curled over his damp nape.

He rolled off her and lay like a dead man.

She watched as he crossed the room to the corner with the pitcher and basin and washed, then returned to the bed with a damp cloth. She should feel embarrassed at seeing him wander around stark naked. Most definitely at him carefully wiping her down. But she must have lost the last of her inhibitions somewhere between his chamber door and his armchair.

She placed her hand on her belly, where he had spent himself earlier.

He had kept his word. He had protected her. Wild horses wouldn't have pulled her from the path to ecstasy on which he had set her with his talented mouth, so she had a good idea of what it had cost him to hold on to his wits. Wonderful, trustworthy man.

The mattress dipped when he stretched himself out by her side again.

Raised on his elbow, his chin in his palm, he studied her with half-lidded eyes. He looked different. Younger. She couldn't stop her hand from drifting up to trace the curve of his bottom lip with her fingertip. His mouth, too, looked different, soft and full. This was intimacy, knowing he could look this way. Very few people would ever see him like this, Montgomery the man, not the duke. How she wished he were only a man.

He captured her inquisitive hand and began toying with her fingers. Too late, she remembered to pull back. He wouldn't let her. "You always try to hide your hands," he said. "Why?"

She sighed. "They are not nice."

He gently pried her fist back open. "What makes you say so?"

"The ink stains," she muttered.

He kissed them. "Hardly blemishes."

"And I have calluses," she said, all at once strangely driven to point out her flaws to him.

"So do I," he said.

Her gaze flew to his in surprise.

He spread the fingers of his right hand wide and pointed at a small bump near the top of his middle finger. "From holding the pen." He placed her finger between his middle and ring finger. "From holding the reins."

Watching their fingers stroke and entwine triggered a longing pull low in her belly again. She was greedy all right, especially where he was concerned.

"What about this?" She touched a hard spot in his palm.

"That is from the mallet."

"The mallet?"

"Yes. A big hammer for driving fence posts into the ground."

"And do you do that often, Your Grace, drive fence posts into the ground?"

The corners of his mouth twitched. "Often enough. Working on the land takes my mind off things."

"That explains these," she murmured, and traced her fingers over the curve of his biceps. It hardened reflexively under her perusal. She smiled, also because she was now entitled to touch him like this.

"Did you really give a man a nosebleed?" he asked. He had turned her hand over and studied the pink knuckles.

The smile faded from her lips. "Yes."

She could feel the languor leaving his body.

"Why?" he asked.

"I suppose because the village lads I ran with as a girl didn't teach me how to slap like a lady."

He leaned over her, not a trace of humor in his eyes. "What did he do?"

She evaded his gaze. "He was . . . hurting a friend."

Montgomery's face set in harsh, unforgiving lines. "I see."

"I won't object if you dismantle the entire London Metropolitan Police," she said softly, "but could it perhaps wait until tomorrow?"

Only when she dragged a wanton foot up his calf did his frown ease.

"Minx," he muttered. He raised her hand to his lips and pressed a kiss to her palm, then carefully returned it to her. "This is a very capable hand," he said. "Don't ever hide it."

She made a fist, to keep his kiss. How could she ever have thought of him as cold and severe—he could be that, but she also couldn't feel more charmed and cherished if she tried.

And yet. There were a few heartless things he had done that were facts, and not just opinions.

"Montgomery. May I ask you something?"

"Sebastian."

"I beg your pardon?"

"Call me Sebastian."

She hesitated. "Why?"

"It is my name."

She knew. Sebastian Alexander Charles Avery, to be precise, followed by a lengthy array of grander and lesser titles. She had memorized it when she had first spied on him in the *Annals of the Aristocracy*. She was also fairly certain that only his oldest friends, and perhaps his wife, would ever call a man of his station by his Christian name.

"I'm afraid I don't know you well enough for that," she said.

An ironic smile curved his lips. "I have just been inside you. And I intend to do it again in about fifteen minutes' time."

She could feel her face turn rosy. "That's different."

"Hardly," he said. "Indulge me. Then ask."

She sighed. "Sebastian."

His lashes lowered and he made a noise that sounded suspiciously like a purr.

"Sebastian," she said huskily, just to see what he would do.

His eyes slitted open. "Am I amusing you?"

She giggled, she who never giggled. He slowly smiled back, crinkling the corners of his eyes and showing straight white teeth. Ah, but a smiling Sebastian was a devastating sight.

She almost regretted having to ask.

"Sebastian. Why did you divorce your wife?"

Chapter 25

There was a clock in his bedchamber. She could hear it now, loudly and clearly tick-tocking away another minute of uncomfortable silence as Sebastian lay still as stone. Sharing his bed evidently did not entitle her to ask nosy questions.

"I hadn't much choice in the matter," he finally said. He was staring up at the bed canopy, looking thoughtful rather than annoyed. "Six months into our marriage, she ran away with another man. A baronet's youngest son, of the estate that bordered her father's. It turned out she had fancied herself in love with him since childhood. I found them in an inn on the way to France."

Oh.

"That's dreadful," she finally said.

He gave a shrug. "It is what it is."

But the images came with startling clarity, of Sebastian taking a pair of creaky stairs, a distressed innkeeper hard on his heels . . . of him bursting into a dimly lit room to the shrieks of the terrified lovers . . .

"Why did you not . . ." Her throat became strangely tight.

Strong hands locked around her waist, and he pulled her on top of him. Her thoughts scattered at the feel of his hard, warm body beneath her. But his expression was pensive and wry; clearly lovemaking wasn't on his mind.

"Why did I not shoot them when I found them?" he suggested. She gave a tiny nod.

"Because it would not have been worth it, neither in this life nor the next."

Oh, Sebastian. What did it take, to make him lose his head?

Her face warmed. Well, she now knew *one* thing that made him lose his head.

"Most men would not have thought that far," she said. "Most wouldn't have thought at all."

He stroked her flanks, his palms pressing deliberately as if to draw comfort from the soft feel of her.

"I stood there at the foot of the bed, and they stared back at me with a look in their eyes that said they fully expected me to shoot them," he said. "But in that moment, I felt nothing. Nothing at all. So I could weigh my options. I had them apprehended. I made it a condition that she move to Italy not to return. But I didn't lay a finger on either of them. She always felt I had a heart of ice, and lucky for her, she was right."

"No," she said, "I cannot believe that about your heart. She sounds like a—a rather disloyal person."

His roaming hands began to brazenly fondle her bottom.

"How fiercely you come to my rescue," he murmured. "She was disloyal, yes, but most of all, she was an overemotional girl, and I should never have married her."

"You must have loved her very much to propose," she said, resenting how hollow she felt at the thought.

He shook his head. "I married her because my father had sold her father one of our estates, and the man knew how to play his hand. He wanted a duchess for a daughter, and I needed a wife, so acquiring one with my rather expensive estate thrown in as a dowry seemed efficient."

"Oh."

"A strategic move, but it backfired."

How calculating he made it sound. But that was how his class used marriage, didn't they? To secure alliances that brought more of the same: money, power, land. For pleasure or love, a man might keep a mistress.

"I thought taking lovers was commonplace?"

His gaze darkened. "Not until there is an heir. Any boy child she would have conceived while married to me would have officially been mine, but short of incarcerating her in her chambers, there was no way I could have guaranteed that my heir would be my son. She had already proven that she was willing to risk everything. Besides . . ."

He fell into a brooding silence, but his body had gone tense beneath hers. She brushed her lips against his throat. When that didn't help, she used her tongue.

He gave a soft grunt, and his member stirred against her belly. There was a responding flutter between her legs, and she sat up, straddling him, shifting aimlessly until he stayed her with a firm grip on her hips.

His cheeks were flushed as he stared up at her. "I didn't see it. She either loathed me enough to risk everything to get away, or loved the boy more than anything. Either way, I had not expected it to happen."

She was tempted to tell him that most husbands did not have to expect that their wives would run away to France, but there was more to it, wasn't there.

She slid her palms over his hands on her hips and entwined her fingers with his.

"How do you ever trust anyone?" she whispered.

He moved unexpectedly, and she was on her back and he on top of her. She gave a startled wiggle. And found she could not move. The hard ridge of his arousal was pressing demandingly between her thighs, and her knees came up to cradle him on their own volition. She groaned. Yes, no morals or modesty when it came to him, none.

His eyes lit with a knowing gleam. "I pick my confidants carefully," he said, "and when they look me in the eye, and are hopelessly incapable of keeping an opinion to themselves, I find myself inclined to give them the benefit of the doubt."

She gave a laugh. "Don't ever let it be known. Your life would become infinitely more difficult."

The sudden intensity in his stare should have alarmed her.

She only felt a powerful throb of anticipation.

He flipped her onto her belly.

His hand brushed the tangle of her hair over her shoulder and his tongue was hot against the side of her throat. There was hunger in his kisses, in his exploration of downy skin and sensitive places that came throbbing to life again. She arched her back, enthralled by the feel of firm muscle and crisp chest hair against her shoulders.

"I like hearing you laugh," he murmured between nips. "It's a beautiful sound."

"Better than Mendelssohn?"

She gasped when he bit down on the curve of her neck, lightly enough, mind.

"Yes," he said, "better."

His hands slipped between the mattress and the silky weight of her breasts, and the caress of his palms against the excited pink tips tore a surprised moan from her lips. He knew things about her body she hadn't known, and the more he showed her, the more she could give over, until she was nothing but sensation, until . . . his thighs pressed against hers from behind, spreading her open to fit himself against her.

She stilled when his intention sank in.

His voice was dark and smooth like midnight silk against her ear. "Will you have me like this?"

She swallowed.

His mouth was so soft, so eager, against the curve of her jaw, nipping gently, grazing her tender skin with golden stubble.

"Yes," she whispered. Yes and yes and yes.

She'd be saying yes to everything soon, so deeply was he already under her skin.

There was no struggle this time, only a smooth, hot glide, the relief to be joined to him again. She buried her flaming face against the cool sheets when he hitched her hips a little higher. Her fingers helplessly curled into the mattress.

Plato was wrong. It wasn't a satire, the missing half of a soul. The sense of completeness as Sebastian filled her was frightfully, joyfully real. So right, so real, it should never end. But again he nudged her steadily onward with the slide of his thrusts, with his fingers sliding over the slickness between her legs, until she was dissolving to the distant echo of her own cries. In the thick of her pleasure, there was a pang of regret when he pulled away rather than finding completion inside her.

❦

They lay in a graceless tangle of limbs, him on his back, her tucked against his side with one lethargic leg flung over his thighs. Her cheek rested on his chest. His delicious scent seemed to concentrate there. *It's the hair*, she thought, sifting her fingers through it. *How clever of men to have a little pelt to trap their fragrance exactly where they want a woman's head.*

He was trailing lazy fingers up her nape, scraping gentle fingertips against her scalp, and she wanted to purr like a contented cat. Sure, morning would arrive in a few hours. But she hadn't felt this fulfilled in years, if ever—a deep, quiet calm, as if a constantly niggling question had finally been answered and now everything had slotted into place. She might regret it later, her failure at resisting temptation once again. But not now.

She splayed her fingers over his chest, right where his heart was beating an even rhythm.

"What I did earlier," she said. "When I came to you . . ."

He tipped up her chin with his thumb. "Yes?"

This was more embarrassing than she had expected. "When you were in the armchair," she said.

"Ah," he said, and his eyes heated. "That."

"Yes," she said, "I've never . . . what I mean is, I've only ever read about it before. Accidentally."

"Accidentally," he echoed, one brow arching.

"Yes. Sometimes one accidentally stumbles upon . . . depictions . . . in ancient Greek documents. Or on Greek vases."

"I consider myself indebted to Greek pottery, then," he murmured, his gaze dropping to her mouth.

And, incredibly, she knew she would have him again this moment, if he wanted to.

He gathered the wayward locks of her hair in one hand behind her head.

"Who was he?" he asked softly.

Her heart stuttered to a halt. She had not expected him to broach that subject. Ever.

Her throat squeezed shut. She had probably opened that avenue of discussion just now, with her inane desire to convince him that she was not overly experienced.

But tell him about William?

It made her feel ill.

She sensed that he was waiting, and the longer she said nothing, the more she felt like a shrew, after all he had told her about his duchess. But he was asking to see the ugliest parts of her, while she was still naked and sore from allowing him in. Her meager defenses would not stand his contempt tonight.

"He doesn't matter," she managed.

His fingers began manipulating her shoulders, and she realized her body had gone rigid as a board.

"He does not matter," he said quietly, "unless you need me to put something right for you."

"What do you mean?"

His eyes were unfathomable. "You're experienced, but neither married nor widowed. Someone didn't do right by you."

No, he hadn't done right by her, but she understood that wasn't what Sebastian was asking.

"I did what I did because I wanted it," she said.

His body relaxed against hers.

So he had braced for the worst.

She wondered what he would have done. She remembered his murderous expression when he had seen the bruises on her knees. It was a distinct possibility that he would have gone and destroyed the man.

"I was seventeen when I met him," she said. "Since my father was the vicar, he was sometimes invited to a dinner or a dance at the estate that owned our parish, and he would take me along. One summer, the lord of the manor had a houseguest. William. He was one-and-twenty, and the second son of a viscount."

"A nobleman," Sebastian said softly.

"Yes. He was dashing. Cultured voice. Green velvet coat, and a front lock like Byron."

Sebastian scoffed.

"Indeed. He charmed me on the spot," she said. "He asked me to dance, and I was enamored with his urbane sophistication and his front lock at the end of the second reel."

"He seduced you," Sebastian said grimly.

"I made it shockingly easy for him," she said. "He was unlike any of the young men I had ever encountered. He dazzled. He asked my opinion on literature and politics, which made me feel terribly important. You see, the village was a very small place, and after Mama's passing, my father never went to a town again, but I hadn't grasped how restless that had made me until I met William. Something in me just . . . burst."

"A London lothario with his eye on debauching a vicar's daughter? You stood little chance at seventeen, sweeting."

"But I knew it was wrong," she said. "Every girl knows it's wrong."

"And he knew it was wrong," he replied. "Did he offer for you?"

She gave a hollow laugh. "He certainly said everything that made it sound like it. Asked me to elope to America with him, where he wanted to make his own fortune, away from his father. Well, he did go to America when autumn came. He didn't even leave me a letter."

There was a small, terse pause.

"You loved him," he said, and his voice was cold enough to make her shiver.

"I thought I did," she said. "He had wooed me wonderfully."

He had said that he loved her. It had thrilled her so to hear it, but she'd waited to say it back and when she finally had, it had felt sacred, an oath whispered into his ear as he lay on her, damp and panting. A week and a few couplings later, he had walked out of her life.

She cringed. It had taken days for it to dawn on her that it hadn't been a mistake, that he had left Kent, had left her, without as much as a good-bye. She had been nothing but a pleasant footnote in a rich man's summer.

"What happened then?" Sebastian sounded suspicious.

She closed her eyes. "The worst."

"Word got out?"

She looked at him bleakly. "I found I was increasing."

He turned ghostly pale. "Where," he asked, "where is the child?"

She shook her head. "It never came to be. I lost it soon after my father sent me to Yorkshire, to his aunt. Aunt May." And Aunt May had implied she ought to be glad to have lost the babe. She should have. Instead, she had already come to love the little one. But her body had failed them . . . she had failed everyone.

Sebastian's lips moved against her hair, and she realized she was clinging to him, trembling uncontrollably, unable to stop the words from pouring out.

"My father first dragged me all the way to London after I finally confessed. He was convinced the viscount would force William to do right by me. Of course, his lordship said that I was a strumpet who had tried and failed to hook a rich lordling, and that he had no use for a peasant grandchild."

There was a pause. When Sebastian spoke again, his voice was dangerously soft. "Will you tell me his name?"

By Hades, no. "He said what most men in his position would have said."

"Not most—" Sebastian began, and then he fell abruptly silent. "Damn," he said, "I believe I accused you of something along those lines when we first met at Claremont."

"You did."

He exhaled sharply. "That explains it. You know, I had the impression you wanted to slap me. I thought you must be utterly mad."

"Oh, I was mad. I felt as though I stood in his lordship's study all over again."

He sat up and stared down at her. "Tell me his name."

"I'd rather not. He was horrid, but he was not the one who destroyed my life. I did."

"Destroyed?" He frowned. "You are anything but. I've never known a woman as valiant as you."

She blinked rapidly at the velvet canopy. "I wasn't the only one affected. My father . . . the look in his eyes when I told him—"

It was as though she had switched off the light in him, whatever had remained after her mother's death anyway.

"I don't think he forgave me before he died," she said hoarsely. "We were informed after it had happened; the coroner said it was sudden, that it was his heart. But, Sebastian, he was never good at taking care of himself; he needed me for that. He probably hadn't even noticed he was unwell, and had I been there . . ."

"No," Sebastian said, and then she was in his arms, surrounded by heat, and strength, and certainty. "He was a grown man," she heard him say. "You made your choices; he made his. Don't take on other people's crosses. The only person you can control is yourself."

"But I didn't," she whispered against his chest, "I didn't control myself."

And she had lost, how she had lost. Her virtue, on a dusty stable floor. Her babe, her father's respect, and then, after laying her father to rest, there had been the news that Aunt May, tough northerner though she was, had succumbed to her perpetual cough. And yet once again, she now found herself naked in the arms of a nobleman.

She strained against Sebastian's arms, and he let her up.

"I was foolish and impulsive," she said. "I'm surprised to find you of all people so forgiving about it."

He was silent for a long moment. "It's not my forgiveness you need," he said, "nor mine to give."

He drew back the counterpane and tugged the covers loose.

She let him arrange her as he wished, her back to his chest, his nose against her nape, both his arms and the blanket snug around her. Trapping her well and truly. She was beyond caring; exhaustion was drawing her under like quicksand, and her eyelids drooped.

His lips brushed against her ear. "These wild depths in you, they call to me," he murmured.

His arm around her waist grew heavy, and she knew he had fallen asleep. Like a man who hadn't slept in nearly a full day, and had loved a woman twice in a row.

Behind her closed eyes, her mind spun in lazy circles, round and round.

The night had not turned out as she had expected. Lovers were expected to bring each other a pleasant time, but she had also nearly brought him her tears. And he had listened graciously, as a friend would, and there hadn't been a hint of judgment in his eyes.

Then again. Since he wanted her as his mistress, her lack of virtue played into his hands very conveniently, didn't it? She frowned, willing the nasty little voice to go away. But would he have ever asked an innocent to become his paramour? No. On a profound level, she knew that his sense of honor would forbid that. And would he accept a bride from his own class who had had a lover before? Again, no.

His arms tightened around her in his sleep, as if he sensed her turmoil even then.

She might have cried, if she weren't so tired. She belonged here, right here wrapped in these strong, nonjudgmental, protective arms, and she wasn't sure where to begin again without him.

Chapter 26

———❦———

Sebastian woke with a deliciously sleepy woman sprawled over his chest. The warm strands of her hair fanned over his throat and torso like a silken net. For a heartbeat, he only held her.

It was impossible not to touch her. His hands began to glide over the graceful lines and curves of her body, stroking slowly, reveling in the velvety feel of her against his palms. In the smoky light of dawn, her smooth pale skin shimmered like a pearl.

With a soft rustle, he drew back the sheets and nudged her onto her back.

She made a tiny, unwilling sound, a drowsy attempt to burrow back into the shelter of his body.

A gentleman would let her sleep. But there was nothing tempered, nothing civil in his response to the sight of her in his bed, trusting and naked and soft. Only the urge to feel the tender, willing clasp of her body around him, to see her eyes swimming with the pleasure he gave her.

He moved between her legs and scattered kisses across her collarbone, her neck, her sleep-flushed cheeks.

She stirred beneath him, her lashes quivering as she emerged from her dreams.

He kissed them, too.

When he drew back, her eyes were open, the green depths hazy. He was smiling down at her like a besotted fool as he watched her memories of the night return.

A shadow passed over her face.

He paused. Was she too sore for more of his attentions? But she was already shifting to accommodate him, and the silky brush of her thighs against his hips swept any conscious thoughts from his mind. Her nails bit into the balls of his shoulders, telling him she didn't want him gentle; she was urging him on with small scratches and throaty moans until his own groans and the sound of bodies coming together in a frantic mating filled his bedchamber.

❦

He sprawled back against the bed's headboard, blissfully spent, with Annabelle nestled in the crook of his arm. Her fingers drew circles on his chest. He could feel her breath flow over his cooling skin in gentle puffs. How strange, how marvelous, that he should hold a whole armful of bliss, when he had never set out to pursue it. This sort of happiness was not for men like him, or so he had thought.

He kissed the top of her head. "I will buy you a yacht," he said.

Her hand on his chest stilled.

"I admit it's not a Greek galleon," he continued, "but we could sail to Persia. And I'll buy you a house near Belgrave Square."

He'd do it tomorrow, buying her house. With her nearby, he'd be able to kiss her soft mouth before setting out in the mornings. He'd come home to her after a long day in Parliament and take her to bed.

Annabelle was silent.

"My love?"

More silence. It was beginning to sound meaningful.

He cupped her chin and made her face him, and the look in her eyes took him aback. Weary and miserable. As if all at once the fractured night and a dozen regrets had caught up with her.

"I have not pleased you," he said slowly.

"No," she said, "that's not it." She sat up and took the sheet with her, clutching it to her chest.

A shard of ice slid down his spine. "Then what is it?"

She lowered her lashes.

"Look at me," he ground out.

She obeyed, and he could see the delicate muscles working in her throat as she was trying to hold his gaze. A horrible sinking feeling gripped him as his mind raced, enumerating the facts. She was naked and in his bed. Just ten minutes ago, she had been gasping in his arms with pleasure. She obviously wanted him.

And yet she was retreating, raising up a wall around her with the sole purpose of shutting him out. It set his every predatory instinct on fire.

"Why did you come to me last night?" he asked.

Another nervous glance. "I did not come to you for a business transaction."

"Why," he repeated, "did you come to me?"

Her shoulders drooped. "I wanted you," she murmured. "I wanted you."

"And that has now changed?"

She shook her head, her eyes turning oddly shiny. Good God. Was she about to cry?

"Annabelle . . ."

"I will always want you, Sebastian," she said. "How could I not?"

The words should have elated him, but there was an awful ring of finality to them. Like the singing of a blade as it came down. And pretending it wasn't happening had never stopped a fatal blow.

"You are not going to stay, are you," he asked flatly.

She bit her lip. "I can't. I told you so before."

"You came to me," he said. "You came to me and I told you I cannot offer you more."

"You did, yes. But neither can I."

He gave a soft, derisive laugh. "Indeed you did not say you would agree to my terms. I assumed. I made an assumption. Naturally, the result is a misunderstanding."

"I never meant—"

He held up his hand. "You can't leave. Not after this."

She looked at him beseechingly, and it made him want to give her a shake. "How can you even contemplate it?" he said. "It is extraordinary between us, and you know it."

"Yes," she said, "but it hasn't changed anything, has it?"

It had changed everything. He knew with certainty now that they wouldn't be done for a long, long time.

"Don't," he said hoarsely, "don't throw away what we have just because you cannot have everything."

Her gaze strayed furtively to the door. She was preparing to flee.

An emotion spread in his chest, black and heavy like oil. He had felt it once before, years ago in his late father's study when it had first dawned on him that he was on the brink of losing everything.

"Annabelle." It came out raspy.

Her lips quivered; he could feel the cracks running through her defenses, and still she was holding herself together at the seams with her damned stubbornness. Damn her, damn her will, her pride, her self-possession. Everything that made her his match now turned against him.

"I'm in love with you, Annabelle." The words tumbled out of his mouth. Not how he would have chosen to say them for the very first time.

She froze. An emotion akin to panic flashed across her face, and her hands twisting the coverlet turned white.

The heavy silence stretched between them until it became answer enough.

Something tore inside his chest, something vital, and briefly, he wondered if a man could die from it. The pain all but took his breath away.

What a way to find out he did have a heart.

He rose from the bed and picked up his robe, still pooled on the floor where he had dropped it last night. He shrugged into the garment and meticulously tied the belt as he kept his back to her.

"Sebastian." Her voice was hanging by a thread.

He turned.

Her eyes looked huge in her pale face.

"I have been used and discarded once before," she said, "and some days . . . some days I still feel utterly disposable. I cannot go through it again."

His hands clamped around her arms. "But I give you my word. I will give it to you in writing that you will lack for nothing. I will care for you as if you were my wife."

She gave a small shake. "I believe you. But I'm afraid that it would not feel that way to me."

It was unfathomable that she wouldn't have him, that he would not get what he wanted most because of a hurt he had not even caused.

"You must know that you want too much," he said through his teeth.

Her gaze skittered away. "Yes," she whispered. "I always did."

He released her, his hands clenching into fists by his sides.

He could chain her to his bed.

It would not give him what he wanted.

He bent and brushed his lips against her forehead. Her skin was clammy and cold.

"I shall be in my study," he said, "but anything pertaining to your departure can also be arranged with my housekeeper."

He walked out without a backward glance.

Chapter 27

"Your eyes are not quite right today."

Hattie's aggrieved voice cut through the haze of her brooding. Her nose filled with the acrid smell of turpentine, and she saw that the shadows across the studio floor had lengthened. They had to be close to the end of their session. Their last session for Helen of Troy.

"I'm sorry," she said. "What can I do?"

Hattie lowered the paintbrush. She hesitated. "They have no spark," she finally said.

It wouldn't take an artist's eye to know something was wrong. If eyes were the window to the soul, hers would look empty and distracted today, and for many days to come. Days? Try months, perhaps years.

She took a shaky breath. "I'm afraid I don't know how to change that."

"No, no." Hattie put the brush down and wiped her hands on her color-stained apron. "We will finish it tomorrow. We should have canceled the session today; it's too soon after that awful day." Her brown eyes filled with sudden tears. "I still cannot believe that you ended up in prison because of me; you were so brave and I can't say how sorry—"

"Please," Annabelle said. "I wasn't brave, I just reacted. It was nothing."

"Nothing?" Hattie looked comically outraged. "You near felled that horrid man, with a single punch! I should have painted you as Athena, the goddess of war, taking down men with her bare hands."

Annabelle gave her a tired smile. Athena was also the goddess of wisdom, and she, Annabelle, was far, far, far from wise.

I'm in love with you, Annabelle. His voice had haunted her since the morning she had left London. She had an inkling what it would have cost a man as buttoned-up as Sebastian to lay himself bare, and she had met his intimate revelation with silence. She had been rendered mute, realizing what a colossal mistake she had made to go to his bed. There was no doubt in Sebastian's mind that he was in love with her. He had proven it, too. He must have obtained a permit for the suffragist demonstration, for none of the secretaries had done it. He had put his reputation on the line to free her from prison, and had expected nothing in return. And now she had hurt him deeply. *I didn't know.* How could she have imagined that she held such power over him?

"Now you look positively grim," Hattie said.

"Because I'm stiff. May I move?"

"Goodness, yes, move," Hattie said, her hands making a shooing motion. "Would you like to take a look at yourself?"

Annabelle flexed her arms. "Will that not bring me bad luck, to look at it before it's finished?"

"No," Hattie said. "Painters say that to keep difficult clients from studying their own portrait every hour. You have been exemplary. Behold thyself."

Annabelle picked her way around tightly crammed easels and marble busts, careful to not jostle anything with her skirts.

When she joined Hattie in front of the tall canvas, she was dumbstruck. It was like staring into an enchanted mirror—the woman in the painting reflected her physical features with impressive accuracy, but Hattie's paintbrush had drawn everything to the surface she usually labored to keep hidden.

"That is how you see me?" she asked, aghast.

Hattie untied her apron. "I think it is what you could be," she said, "if you dared. It's certainly how I'd want to be."

"Like . . . this?"

"For once in my life? Yes. Wait until it is finished; I promise it will sparkle."

"More sparkle?" Annabelle said feebly.

"Oh yes," Hattie said. "Trust me, it needs sparkle to shine in Julien Greenfield's sitting room. He's agreed to have the grand reveal during his investment summit in a few days' time."

A shudder ran through Annabelle at the thought of scores of men seeing her like this. It was just as well that she didn't move in those circles.

Hattie's studio at the Ruskin School of Drawing was barely a mile from the Randolph Hotel, so they decided to take a little walk. Mrs. Forsyth and Hattie's protection officer trailed behind as they made their way up High Street. The air was unusually sultry for a winter day, and Oxford's spires and sandstone turrets stood out against a quietly darkening sky. Gratitude welled in Annabelle's chest as she drank in the familiar honey-colored college walls and gray lead roofs. She had come so, so close to losing her place here.

"Hattie," she said, careful to keep her voice low, "whose idea was it exactly, to go to the duke of all people to free me?"

When she had arrived at Oxford yesterday, she had been in a daze, and her friends had talked over each other in their excitement while she had said very little, chiefly to keep the lies regarding her whereabouts to a minimum.

"It was Catriona's idea," Hattie said. "Since Professor Campbell was on his way to Cambridge, she suggested we should go to the duke."

"But why?"

"It's Catriona," Hattie said with a shrug. "Her mind works in mysterious ways. She was quite adamant about it, actually, and rightly so. As a gentleman of your acquaintance, he was obliged to come to your aid. I admit I was skeptical at first, but he didn't hesitate for even a moment." Her face assumed a gossipy expression. "I heard this morning that he bailed out a dozen more suffragists. Did you know that?"

Something inside Annabelle went cold. "A dozen?" she said. "But that's nonsense. Who told you that?"

Hattie frowned. "Lady Mabel. I don't know how she knows; I suppose one of the other women must have said something to someone. A good rumor always finds its way." Her face turned serious. "Annabelle, I know I said it before, but truly, I would have gone to my father to beg for him to help us, had the Montgomery plan failed."

"I know, dear," Annabelle said absently. Talk here in Oxford about Millbank and Sebastian's involvement in the matter was a rather alarming development.

A mighty rumble rolled across the horizon and reverberated through her bones.

Hattie squeaked. "Quick. It will start pouring in a minute." She began to hurry ahead, fleeing the first splats of rain like a disgruntled cat.

∼✦∼

It took barely forty-eight hours for the rumor to spawn consequences. Annabelle had a dark sense of foreboding the moment she found the nondescript envelope in her pigeonhole.

Miss Elizabeth Wordsworth, the warden herself, was summoning her to her office.

The note slipped from her nerveless fingers. The last time she had been in the warden's office, it had been for her personal welcome talk to the college. Her heart had thundered with excitement at the prospect of beginning her new life. Now her pulse was pounding with fear.

"I shall come straight to the point," Miss Wordsworth said as soon as Annabelle had taken her seat. The warden's intelligent face wore a grave expression. "I have been informed that a student from Lady Margaret Hall was apprehended by police at a suffrage demonstration on Parliament Square last Friday. Is this true?"

I am going to be expelled.

The study began to spin before her eyes. She could only nod.

Miss Wordsworth's clear gaze assessed her with a measure of concern. "Were you treated well?"

"Well enough, miss."

"I'm relieved to hear it," Miss Wordsworth said. "Nevertheless, the matter is highly unfortunate. As you are aware, women in higher education already encounter opposition at every turn. Your comportment always reflects on women in higher education and our institution as a whole."

"Yes, miss."

"Scandal is ammunition for the opposition," Miss Wordsworth continued, "which is why I had explicitly advised you to honor the trust we put in you despite your political stipend."

Annabelle heard the warden as if from a distance. "I'm going to be expelled," she said.

Miss Wordsworth's face softened for a moment. "No. But you are rusticated with immediate effect."

Annabelle gave a choked little laugh. Rusticated. Literally, it meant to go and reside in the country. Such a quaint term to describe the end of her dreams. Even if this was but a temporary expulsion, she had no country manor to which she could retreat.

As of now, she had nothing.

She kept her back ramrod straight. As if that could keep everything else from imploding in on itself. "Is it possible to say when I could be reinstated?"

Miss Wordsworth shook her head. "We will initiate an investigation. It normally concludes in favor of the student around the time the rumor has been forgotten."

Annabelle knew enough about rumors to know that this would not be forgotten for years. She had been arrested and imprisoned, with no name to shield her.

She didn't know how she made her way back to her room, made it up the narrow, creaking steps.

For a long minute, she stood in the door and looked at the tiny chamber. The narrow bed, the narrow desk, the small wardrobe that was just big enough to hold her few clothes. For four months, she'd had a room of her own. It was unfathomable that it should come to an end.

⤙⤙∂≈⤚⤚

Through the bars of rain streaking across the window of his landau, Sebastian could make out the gray shape of Buckingham Palace and found the sight tired him profoundly. When this election was over and he had recovered his brother, he would go on a holiday. Somewhere solitary and warm. Greece. Hell no. Not Greece.

He could tell that the queen was not amused the moment he set foot in her apartment. Her compact form looked tense like a trap ready to spring; she was, in fact, brimming with an antagonism that was a little puzzling in its severity.

"First the farmers and the corn laws," she said, casting his latest paper a withering glance, "and again you insist that Beaconsfield speak more in public—in town halls! Why, you will be wanting to give workingmen the vote next."

"You will find no such proposition in my concept, ma'am."

"Not in those words, no," she said acerbically, "but close enough. Town halls! Besides, Beaconsfield's constitution will not allow for the fiendish schedule you suggest."

"Then I labored under the misapprehension," Sebastian said, "that since he is running for the position of prime minister, he would be able to engage with his constituents."

He knew the moment the words had left his mouth that they had been decidedly too sarcastic in tone. He was taken aback. His control had slipped, in a strategy meeting with the queen no less. She seemed equally surprised. Her eyes had widened; now they had narrowed to cool slits.

"Given what is at stake, for the country and for yourself, I would have thought you had an interest in winning this election," she said.

He exhaled slowly. "I do. This is the best strategy for winning it."

"It might well win the election," she conceded, "but it is not how the party must win."

"Ma'am, I don't follow."

"Well, there is little use in a victory for the Tory party, is there, if de facto, they are not the Tory party anymore."

He would never understand it, the desire to turn a straight path to victory into a serpentine one.

The queen rose, and so he rose also, and she began to pace with angry, jerky little steps.

"I thought of you as highly principled," she said, "and now I find you are putting outcome above principles. Oh, we cannot abide an opportunist."

Sebastian's fist clenched behind his back. "And yet none of my suggestions run counter to my principles."

She stopped dead. She rotated toward him slowly, the effect of which would have terrified a lesser man. "Then it is worse than we thought," she said coldly. "You, Montgomery, are a liberal."

She might as well have called him a traitor. They regarded each other across the room, warily taking measure of each other as new cards were being dealt.

When the queen spoke again, her tone was flat. "The day you had your first audience with me, a duke at nineteen and with the eyes of a man much older, I saw something in you. In truth, you reminded me of Albert. He was quiet, too. He had an unshakable moral code, and he preferred deeds over words, qualities that are very rare in a man these days, and which I favor greatly. Say, have you never wondered why you experienced so little inconvenience after your divorce?"

Sebastian bent his head. "I always knew that you helped shield my reputation, for which I'm ever grateful."

She scoffed. "We couldn't tolerate the ruination of an exceptional man by a wicked, foolish girl. And yet we hear you lent support to suffragists last week. Wicked, foolish creatures. And all of them bolstering Gladstone."

Ah well. Well well well. That explained Her Majesty's chagrin, but who, he wondered, who could have pushed the matter all the way to Buckingham Palace, and so quickly? He realized then that the small pause had told the queen all she needed to know. Her face was pinched and furious. He really was slipping.

"My involvement was private, not a political matter," he said.

She gave him an icy glare. "And far be it from us to concern ourselves with our subjects' private matters. We do not, especially not when they are a personal disappointment to us."

She reached for her bell.

"Ma'am, these women were treated like criminals and kept in conditions entirely unsuited for females."

She looked at him as though she did not know him at all. "Do you propose we encourage their agenda? You of all people should know what happens when you let a woman run loose—she knows no moderation. The female heart is a violent creature. We advise you to think wisely from now on where your loyalties lie, Montgomery, what kind of world it is you want. If the esteem of your queen is no motivation for you, at least have a care for your ancestral seat."

The cold tinny sound of the bell rung out. He was dismissed. He had been warned off, and insulted.

What troubled him most was that he didn't truly seem to care.

"Rusticated?" Hattie sounded thunderstruck.

Lucie and Catriona seemed lost for words entirely. The tiny sandwiches on the tiered platters before them were forgotten, as was the bottle of champagne Hattie had ordered to her apartment to celebrate the completion of Helen of Troy last night.

"Yes," Annabelle said, "but they'll reinstate me soon."

She had moved out of Lady Margaret Hall this morning, and her trunks had already been deposited in a tiny lodger's room in Mrs. Forsyth's two-down, one-up in Jericho.

"This is ridiculous," Hattie stormed, "and it's all my fault. Stay with me here; Aunty will be happy to have you around."

"We have a guest room," Catriona said. "Father probably won't even notice your presence."

"I have a cot we could put into my sitting room," Lucie offered.

"Please," Annabelle said, "that's very generous of you, but don't you see? If I am sent down because I'm a blight on the college, I can hardly be seen associating with any of you."

"That's true," Lucie said crisply, "which is why you should stay with me. I have no reputation to lose."

Catriona and Hattie had fallen quiet.

The lavish room felt stuffy and constricting.

She came to her feet. "Lucie, I know you think you're a black sheep, but do you really want to attract such negative publicity for your cause?"

Lucie's delicate face set in determined lines. "You can hardly expect me to just turn my back on you. You wouldn't have been imprisoned if it weren't for the cause, which I obliged you to support, so I'm responsible for this. Stay on in Oxford. Stay with me. We will weather this together."

These crumbs of hope were almost worse than a clean slate of desolation.

"Lucie, the Oxford suffragists are all ladies of quality. If word about me gets out to their fathers, you will have a problem."

An angry furrow formed between Lucie's brows. "Leaving a comrade behind would be terrible for troop morale. This could have happened to anyone."

No. No lady of quality would have thrown a punch.

"We aren't soldiers," Annabelle said. "We don't take arrows for our comrades. We are women, and they measure us by the pristine condition of our dresses and reputation, not our bravery. Trust me, upholding troop morale will be easier for you when I'm gone."

She left her friends in stunned silence and walked right out of the Randolph Hotel into the cold of a drab morning. She pushed on across St. Giles to the arched wing doors of St. John's, where she had one thing left to do.

Jenkins was ensconced behind his desk, elbow-deep in a stack of papers. His hair stuck up on the left side of his head, as if he had tried to forcibly tug one of his brilliant thoughts from the depths of his mind. The sight of organized chaos in his study was so heartbreakingly familiar that it took every ounce of her strength to not begin to cry.

"Miss Archer." Jenkins took off his glasses and blinked. That, too, was a gesture she found saddeningly familiar.

"I did not realize I had called for your assistance today."

"May I come in, Professor?"

"Please do."

Only when she had taken her seat did he glance back at the nowclosed door, frowning. "Where is that noisy chaperone of yours?"

"I'm afraid I have to resign from my assistant position," she said.

Jenkins's features sharpened, and she knew he had left Greek antiquity behind and was present. In as few words as possible, she told him about her circumstances, save the part about Sebastian.

"That is a conundrum," Jenkins said when she had finished. "A foolish circus, but hard to rectify under the circumstances."

She gave a nod, feeling a last spark of hope extinguish.

Jenkins put his glasses back on and leaned back in his chair. "Well, I can't let you go. Your work is too good."

She gave him a watery smile. "Thank you," she said. "I shall miss my work here very much."

He was quiet for a moment. "Do you wish to continue working as my assistant?"

"Yes." She said it without hesitation. Oh, if only there were a way. The mere thought of slinking back to the bleakness of Chorleywood made her want to howl.

"And would you like to stay in Oxford?" Jenkins asked. "It could become quite unpleasant for you for a while."

"It is my greatest wish to stay," she said. "I just don't have an option to do so."

"You do," Jenkins said. "You could marry me."

Chapter 28

Marry me. Marry him? Marry Jenkins?

"I seem to have rendered you speechless," Jenkins remarked. "I suppose the correct way of saying it is 'Miss Archer, would you honor me with your hand in marriage?'" He tilted his head expectantly.

"This . . . comes as a bit of a surprise," she said weakly.

"Does it really?" he asked, bemused. "The possibility must have crossed your mind at some point."

Much as she cared for him, it hadn't crossed her mind. He was of course a brilliant man, and an eligible bachelor, too, not too old and with nice teeth and a good set of shoulders. But normally, a courting phase preceded a proposal.

Then again, he had taken her to a concert. He bickered at her in old Latin twice a week and he fed her apples. Indeed, his proposal had probably been a perfectly foregone conclusion to any bystander. How had she *not* expected it?

"I have contemplated proposing to you for a while," he said. "I want to take you on the excursion to the Peloponnese, and this would be the most expedient way of doing it."

"Expedient," she echoed.

He nodded. "Imagine the breach of propriety otherwise. And no chance in Hades would I take your Mrs. Forsyth along."

"Professor . . ."

"Please," he interjected, "hear me out. Miss, you are a rare find for a man like me. People are either intellectually capable or agreeable. They are hardly ever both. You are. You are the best assistant I've ever had. Furthermore, like myself, you don't seem keen on children, when most women are. I'm aware my standards are unorthodox, which, I assure you, is the sole reason for my bachelorhood; I am otherwise perfectly capable of providing for a wife. And my name would shield you from this nonsense that is presently making life difficult for you; in fact, you could continue with your work as if nothing had happened."

He looked at her now with an expression she had never seen on his face before. *Hopeful.*

She tried to imagine him as her husband, because she liked him and her future was hanging by a thread and both rash decisions and dithering could prove catastrophic at this point.

He was a good man, and he cared about her well-being. His looks, scent, and dress sense were perfectly agreeable, and she expected he had a housekeeper to do the housework, so she would have her head and hands free for assisting him. He was also not an easy man—he was wholly cerebral and irritable, and he'd spend most of his life in his books, but given that she was used to that, she'd deal with it well.

But could she imagine him coming home, and loosening his cravat, and sliding his shirt off his shoulders, and have him cover her with his bare body—

She felt herself flush. "You . . . you mentioned not wanting any children," she said.

Jenkins sat up straighter, sensing they were moving into a negotiation. "I don't mind them as a concept. But for us, well, they would be beside the point, would they not?"

"Most people would argue that the point of marriage is children."

Jenkins made a face. "Most people are bleating fools. My wife would have to understand and assist my work. I am my work. And if you were a man, you'd already be making a name for yourself in our field, given how good you are, but the moment you began to breed, you would become utterly addlebrained, all your razor-sharp thinking blunted by the relentless demands of squalling brats. You would lose a few teeth, too; trust me, I have seen all of it happen to each of my six sisters."

She should take offense. In the history of marriage proposals, this had to be the most shockingly unromantic one ever uttered. But then, as a near-felon, she was not much of a catch, and it was still more respectable than her other offer, the one for the position as a kept woman.

Her silence seemed to make Jenkins nervous. He fiddled with his pen. "Have I perhaps drawn the wrong conclusion?" he asked. "Since you seemed to be a spinster by choice, I didn't think a family was your priority."

She had to force herself to look him in the eye. "I just wondered whether you are proposing a marriage in name only."

To his credit, he did not reply at once but seemed to weigh the question with the consideration it was due. "Is that what you would prefer?" he finally said. His eyes were unreadable behind his reflecting glasses, but his shoulders appeared tense.

Yes would have been the obvious answer to his question. Then again, on paper, he was more than what she could have ever hoped for: an academic, comfortable, and free to ignore the more petty social mores under the guise of brilliant eccentricity. Most important, she liked him. Liked, not loved. He'd never have the power to crush her heart. But if she refused him the marriage bed, would he respect her decision without growing surly over time?

"I would like some time to consider the proposal," she heard herself say. "A week. If that is agreeable to you."

Jenkins nodded after a brief pause. "A week. Perfectly agreeable."

A week. A week to consider an alternative to going back to Gilbert's house. To tell him that studying had been too much of a challenge for her female brain after all, and that she'd gladly be an unpaid drudge for the rest of her days, with no certain future. Perhaps it wouldn't even come to the workhouse. Perhaps she'd end up in Bedlam, muttering to herself that she'd had dukes and Oxford dons vying for her attention in days gone by.

She left the office, thinking she should have just said yes.

A duke had no business attending an investment summit. Glances followed Sebastian around Greenfield's town house, and he knew he would have raised less gossip trawling a low-class bordello. But men like Julien Greenfield wouldn't pass insider information on to Sebastian's investment manager, nor over a discreet dinner; officially grace my home, and receive first-class intelligence in return, that was the deal. Even business was never to be had without the politics, certainly not without the petty power plays.

Greenfield plucked two brandy tumblers from a tray floating past. "I suggest we proceed to the sitting room; these chaps are really keen to make your personal acquaintance," he said, handing one glass to Sebastian and wrapping his plump hand around the other.

Sebastian carried his untouched drink down the corridor, listening to Greenfield's assessment of the diamond mine of which Sebastian planned to become a shareholder. The two South African business partners in Greenfield's sitting room could potentially add a million pounds to his accounts, depending on how trustworthy he found them.

His first impression was promising: firm handshakes, good eye contact. The younger of the two had started out as a mining engineer, so he knew the business inside out and his description of the current project status matched the information Sebastian's man had compiled on the duo.

Disaster struck when he caught a familiar figure from the corner of his eye.

The businessman's speech turned into meaningless noise.

Annabelle.

There on an easel, guarded by a footman, was a life-sized, breathtaking, glowing version of Annabelle.

Her green eyes stared back at him heavy-lidded with some private triumph. Her shoulders were thrown back, her hair whipping about her like the flame of a torch in a storm. From below the hem of her clinging white gown peeked a familiar pale foot.

A giant fist seemed to squeeze the air from his lungs.

Hell. He was in a peculiar sort of hell, where all paths always circled back to the same thing.

He drew closer to the painting as if in a dream, his gaze riveted on her face.

He had stroked these proud cheekbones; he had kissed the fine nose. He had felt this lush mouth on his cock.

Two men were at her feet, bare-chested and on their knees, one dark, one fair, their heads tilted back to glower at her with a rather too-familiar expression of awe and resentment and longing.

Helen of Troy, not as a prize, but as a vindicated puppet master.

"I see you're admiring my daughter's handiwork," Greenfield remarked.

Sebastian grunted.

"Extraordinary, isn't she?" Greenfield tipped his glass toward Annabelle. "Before my own daughter nagged me into letting her go up to Oxford, I was convinced all bluestockings sported beards and warts. Imagine my surprise when she introduced this young woman to us at your New Year's Eve ball. I stood happily corrected."

"I'd stand happily," the engineer said. "I'd launch a thousand ships for that."

"I say, she'd launch me," drawled the older one, and they all sniggered.

"How much," Sebastian said, his voice edged with such menace that the sniggering stopped abruptly. "How much for this?"

Greenfield's bushy brows flew up. "Now, I don't think it is considered for sale—"

"Come now, Greenfield," Sebastian said, "everything has a price."

The banker sobered. This language, he understood. "It is certainly negotiable," he said. "I'm sure Harriet could be moved to part with it for ample compensation."

"Excellent," said Sebastian. He knocked back the brandy in one gulp and set his tumbler down hard on a sideboard. "Have it wrapped and sent to my house in Wiltshire. Good afternoon, gentlemen."

He stalked from the house, leaving a trail of worried and bemused people in his wake who had accidentally been hit by his black stare. A murmur rose: *Did you see the aloof Duke of Montgomery storming out of Greenfield's place, looking dark and mercurial like Vulcan himself?*

Meanwhile, the ducal landau was on course to Victoria Station at breakneck speed.

⁂

The back garden of Claremont smelled of mud and dead leaves.

"Your Grace!" Stevens looked pleasantly surprised to see Sebastian striding toward the stables in the fading evening light.

"Prepare my horse," said Sebastian. "Only him. I'm going alone."

Stevens's eyes widened as he registered his employer's mood, and a short time later, he led a saddled and haltered Apollo from the stable. The stallion released an accusing whinny when it spotted Sebastian, and he absently scrubbed the soft nose that was thrust at his chest.

"He missed his master," Stevens supplied. "Bit McMahon on the behind the other day."

Sebastian frowned. "Have you moved him at all?"

"Not too much, no. The weather was naught but rain for the past few days; fields are soft as mush. He might be a wee bit skittish, Your Grace."

He contained Apollo on the ride down the drive. Tightly coiled tension vibrated in the animal's muscle and sinew, a spring ready, oh so ready to be launched. One slight tap of his heels, an inch of give in the reins, and they would take off unstoppably like a shot.

He had avoided his country home lately, because everything in Claremont reminded him of her. The harder he tried to keep control, to keep the thoughts and emotions firmly buried, the more anarchical it all became, as if a lifetime of leashed passion had broken free and was coming for him with vengeance, as if he had only been spared the lunacy of love before because he had been destined to be brought down by this particular woman.

In another life, he would have made her his wife. She'd already be his wife.

They emerged from the drive and acres of fields opened to either side of them. The twilight leached the colors from the trees, the soil, the sky. Gray, gray, gray.

Enough, he vowed. *Enough of this.*

He'd leave London and return to Claremont. He'd return everything to normal; he always did.

He leaned forward in the saddle, and a jolt went through Apollo.

They galloped along the path, then veered off onto the field headlong to the distant forest. The wind bit his face like a blade. Cold tears streaked across his cheeks from the corners of his eyes as speed overran his senses, the rapid *thud thud thud*, the whistling in his ears, the landscape rushing at him. The mind became a blank; there was only focus, speed, the cold.

Enough, enough, enough.

He ran Apollo harder, faster, until the forest loomed at the edge of the field like a dark mass.

He pulled in the reins.

Something flashed, pale and low on the ground.

Apollo screamed and twisted sideways.

Instinctively, he threw himself forward, but he felt the horse's rump go down, its hind legs breaking away, a horrible, uncontrolled motion that whipped the powerful body beneath him up, up, and over the tipping point.

They were going to flip.

For a blink, the world froze, clear and sharp like a shard of glass. An expanse of blank sky, a flutter of mane above him.

The horse would crush him.

He yanked his feet from the stirrups but the ground was hurtling toward him at brutal speed. The face he loved most in the world looked back at him before darkness fell like an axe.

Beneath the small desk, Annabelle's feet had turned to lumps of ice in the draft. She should go to bed. It was nearing midnight, and the oil lamp was burning low. But she knew she would not sleep. If she only looked at her surroundings, she could have pretended she was still a student with a bright future ahead; the desk, the rickety chair, the narrow cot were much like her room at Lady Margaret Hall. But that was where the similarities ended. There were no books and folders on the desk. Only a sheet of paper with three lonely lines:

Go back to Chorleywood
Become a governess up north
Marry Jenkins

Her present options to keep a roof over her head all while staying on a morally upright path.

Of course, she had come up to Oxford to avoid any such fate:

Chorleywood, underpaid and vulnerable, or married to a man she didn't love.

Two weeks. Mrs. Forsyth had given her two weeks to find a new occupation. *I'm a chaperone*, she had said pointedly. *I'm to keep women from getting into trouble, not associate with troubled women.*

The future was a black maw, ready to swallow her whole.

She pressed her palms to her face, trying to shut out the ugly faces of her fears leering back at her. "I'm a soldier at heart," she whispered. "I can do this . . ."

A sudden commotion in the hallway downstairs had her sit up straight. Agitated voices clashed as Mrs. Forsyth's Maltese barked hysterically.

Alarmed, she came to her feet. It sounded as though a man was arguing with Mrs. Forsyth.

And then male boots stomped up the stairs, the force of it making the floorboards shiver.

She clutched her nightgown to her chest, reflexively casting her glance around the room for a weapon.

Bam bam bam.

The door shook as it was pounded with a fist.

It did not shock her half as much as the man's voice.

"Annabelle!"

"Sir!" Mrs. Forsyth objected shrilly.

Sebastian. Sebastian was here.

Bam bam bam.

She moved toward the door on unsteady legs.

"Sir, desist," Mrs. Forsyth shrieked, and then Sebastian burst into the room, sending the door flying back against the wall with a bang.

Everything stopped: the noise, time, her heart. The vital urgency radiating from his body had blasted the very air from the room. He stared at her wordlessly, and holy hell, he was pale.

With two long strides, he towered over her and pulled her into his arms.

The wintry cold still clung to his clothes; his thick coat was rough against her face.

She stood motionless in his embrace, hardly daring to trust that he was real. She hadn't expected to see him again, certainly not to ever be in his arms once more.

"My love," he said, his voice a rumble in his chest beneath her ear.

How cruel. Her fourth option, her most desired option, her everything, was right here, when all she was trying to do was the right thing, which was decidedly not option four.

"Miss Archer, who is this—?" Mrs. Forsyth appeared in the door and gave an outraged squawk when she saw the couple embracing. "I object, I most utterly object to this," she cried. "No gentlemen are allowed in the house, I laid out that rule very clearly indeed, why, this is not to be borne—"

Sebastian half turned and slammed the door shut in Mrs. Forsyth's enraged face while keeping one arm tightly around Annabelle.

She disentangled herself from his grip. "What is happening?" she asked, and then, "Oh God, is it your brother? Is he—"

"No," he said. There was a hard, metallic look in his eyes that made her feel entirely off balance.

She took a small step back. "Montgomery, you worry me."

A stern line appeared between his brows. "Don't call me that."

"Very well," she said, and crossed her arms over her chest. "Sebastian. Surely there would be a more appropriate time—"

"I came to ask you to marry me."

She looked at him blankly.

"Marry me," he repeated, taking a step toward her.

She gave an uncertain laugh. "Why would you say such a thing?"

"You laugh," he growled. He grabbed her hand and pressed it to his greatcoat, over his heart. "Put an end to this misery, Annabelle. Marry me."

She tugged, and alarm tingled up her spine when he didn't let go. "What has got into you?"

"I fell off the horse this eve."

Her free hand flew to her mouth. "No."

"There was a pheasant," he said, "a small pheasant, hiding in a furrow. Apollo spooked and slipped. He is fine."

Her gaze darted over him, searching for signs of injury. "What about yourself?"

There was a pause. "I thought I was going to die," he said quietly.

The blood drained from her face as an icy hand reached for her heart.

"As you see, it was not yet my time," he said. "The ground was softened from rain, and my hat took the brunt instead of my head."

The feeling of terror that had kept her frozen to the spot subsided, and she flung her arms around his neck.

"Hush," he said as his arms slid around her protectively, "I'm here now."

She only clutched him harder and tried to burrow into him, wanting to tear the heavy topcoat off him, and all the layers of wool and cotton that kept her from feeling the pulsing warmth and strength of his body.

He pressed his mouth into her hair. "Marry me, Annabelle."

Her head jerked back. "Please. Please, do not say such a thing."

He frowned. "Why? You object to being my mistress. Are you saying you don't want to be my wife, either?"

She tried to push away from him, but he would not let her.

As she stared up into his unnaturally bright eyes, fear gripped her.

"What I want is not the point," she stammered. "I don't want to be your mistress, but I certainly can't be your wife."

He tilted his head. "And why not?"

"You've fallen on your head all right! You know why; it's impossible."

"It isn't, actually. I ask, you say yes. That is all it takes."

That is all it takes.

She felt oddly light-headed. Her most secret, outlandish dreams were a simple syllable away.

"No," she managed to say. "No, I would never ask you to ruin your name, your life for me—"

"You wouldn't ruin my life."

She strained against him, and his arms tightened around her, just short of crushing her.

"No," she said, "please, release me."

He did so with an exasperated huff, and she sprung back as if he were scalding her.

"Hear me out," he said, his hands clenching by his sides. "For years, I worried I would fall off my horse before I had produced an heir. And now it has happened, and I was sure I was going to break my neck, and on my last breath, did I think of Castle Montgomery, or my title, my father, or my heir?"

Again he reached for her, again she evaded, and his face darkened.

"I thought of you, damn it," he said. "I saw your face, as clearly as I see it now as you are standing in front of me, and all I felt was the most profound regret that my time with you had been so very short. My unfinished business here is you and I, Annabelle."

Oh, heaven help her. He was dead serious about this.

Or so he thought.

She forced herself to sound calm. "I am honored," she said, "of course I am. But surely you must know that right now, you are not yourself, not thinking clearly."

In truth, his eyes had never looked more lucid.

She began to shiver. His will was so strong, stronger than hers, and he was offering her her heart's desire. But it would be a disaster.

She turned her back to him, desperate to gather her scattered wits. "What about the scandal it would cause?" she said. "What about your brother? If we married, it would taint him, you said so yourself. Your heirs would be shamed—are these reasons not true anymore?"

"Why don't you let me take care of these things," came his bemused voice. "Your part is simply to say yes."

Say yes. Say yes.

"Tomorrow," she said hoarsely. "Why don't we talk about it tomorrow."

"Turn around and look at me," he said, "and I shall tell you that tomorrow will not make a difference. Nor will next week."

She whirled, his stubborn insistence on the impossible enraging her. "You cannot marry the daughter of a vicar. One day you might wake up and look at the shambles of your life, and nothing I am could ever compensate you for it."

His gaze turned assessing and merciless. "You don't trust me," he said flatly. "You don't trust that I know my own mind."

"You've just looked death in the face. I imagine it skews a man's perspective."

His eyes were hard and gray as granite. "Or it finally puts the perspective right. I am not a fickle boy, Annabelle. Don't punish us both for the boys you have known in the past."

She flinched as the barb hit its mark, ammunition she herself had handed him in confidence. No, she must not think of their time wrapped in each other's arms in his bed, cocooned in intimate bliss . . .

Somewhere, Mrs. Forsyth's dog was barking still, rattled and furious.

She pressed her palms to her pounding temples. "I can't," she whispered. "We can't."

"Annabelle." His voice was ragged. "I didn't know I was looking for you until we met. Had we never crossed paths, I might have lived and died a content and sensible man, but now I know what I can feel, and it cannot be undone, I cannot pretend that what we have is a folly that will fade. I can choose to live with a sense of loss over you until the day I die, or to live with you come what may. These are my choices, a life with you, or an existence without you, and as with all choices, it is a matter of paying a price. I know that what we could have is worth anything."

Every word hit her heart like a knife, rapid, dull impacts that would soon bloom into a sharp pain and bleed her dry. How calm he sounded in his madness, when her own sanity was crumbling rapidly. She could have lost him forever today. Her every instinct urged her to be in his arms and never let him go again.

She struggled to draw her next breath. "We can't."

Her lifeless tone made him pause.

For the first time, she sensed a flicker of uncertainty in him. "You are serious," he said slowly. "You are rejecting my proposal."

"Yes," she said, her throat aching with the effort.

He went stark white. An agonizing feeling came over her, rendering her mute.

Honor would forbid him to break an engagement, even if made under duress. Tomorrow, or next week, he would thank her for not having maneuvered himself into an untenable position, he would.

"You know," he said, almost conversationally, "I'm beginning to think you would refuse to be with me in any capacity. And I think it has nothing to do with your morals, or my reputation, but with your own cowardice."

The words stung her from her paralysis like a slap. "Whatever do you mean?"

"You are afraid. Of a man managing you for a change, and I'm not referring to husbandly rule. In fact, I reckon you could exist quite well under draconian rules, because there is a fortress at your very core no one can breach with force. But I have breached it already; you have given yourself to me. Why not let me make an honest woman out of you now?"

Because I love you more than my own happiness.

Renewed determination was etched in every line of his face, and she understood that as long as he thought she loved him, he would not abandon this insane scheme. He'd sacrifice everything. He'd disgrace himself, become an object of ridicule among his peers, in the press. His home, his political standing would be lost, his ancient family line destroyed. He'd ruin his life's work over a country woman. And inevitably, his infatuation would wane, and he would come to resent her, or worse, himself, for everything he had given up.

She wrapped her arms around her quivering body. "If you must know, I had a much more reasonable offer just this morning."

Firing a pistol at Sebastian would have had the same effect, a flash of surprise, and he went rigid.

When he finally spoke, she hardly recognized his voice. "The professor."

She gave a nod.

"Have you accepted him?"

"I have been rusticated," she said, "and he—"

"Have you accepted him?" he repeated, and the look in his eyes had her touch her throat.

"No," she said softly. Guiltily.

"But you have considered it. By God, you are considering it."

"It would be a suitable match—"

His head tipped back on a harsh laugh. "No, madam, no. If you marry him, it will make you more of a whore than you would have ever been as my mistress."

"Why would you say such a thing?" she choked.

He moved suddenly, circling her like a sinewy predator until he paused right behind her. "Because, my sweet, you do not love him," he murmured, his cool breath moving the downy hair on her nape. "You don't love him, and you would have him for the things he can give you, not because you want him."

She squeezed her eyes shut. "I don't love you, either."

"That is a lie," he breathed. "You should see the look in your eyes after I kiss you."

"Of course you would think so, but any woman would be dazzled by the attentions of a man of your position. But the truth is, it was always about the suffragist cause. It was why I was at Claremont in the first place . . . we spied on you. Every conversation we had was me trying to gain your support for the cause. We even have a file, a profile sheet about you."

She was grabbed and turned around.

His expression was icy. "A file?" he demanded. "What are you saying?"

"The truth," she whispered. "The truth."

His grip on her shoulders tightened. "You are lying. You forget I held you in my arms just a few nights ago. I know you, and I know you are lying."

"Do you?" she said tremulously. "You didn't see the truth about your own wife until she ran off with someone else, and she was in your bed for months."

Before her eyes, his face turned still like a death mask.

He released her abruptly, as if he had noticed that he was holding a toxic thing.

The faint, contemptuous curl of his lip cut her to the bone.

She watched, frozen and mute, as he turned his back to her and walked out.

The sound of the door falling shut behind him never reached her ears. A strange ringing noise filled her head. She sank onto the edge of the bed.

This was the right thing. She couldn't breathe, but it was the right thing. At least this tragedy would not make English history. It would be borne in private, and one day die with her.

She didn't know how much time had passed—a minute? an hour?—when Mrs. Forsyth planted herself before her. The unflappable chaperone was red-faced; she glared down at Annabelle with wrathful eyes. "I said no men," she spat, "and on the first night, you bring a ruffian into my home."

"I'm sorry," Annabelle said tonelessly.

"I'm not a cruel woman," Mrs. Forsyth said, "so you may stay the night. But tomorrow, I expect you to be gone."

Chapter 29

Annabelle stole out of Mrs. Forsyth's front door at dawn, her chest heavy with fatigue. The sting of cold morning air was like a reviving slap to her cheeks, but she was still bleary-eyed by the time she reached the arched entrance door of St. John's lodge.

It had taken a kindly porter with a handcart to get both her trunks from Lady Margaret Hall to Mrs. Forsyth's house last evening, and perhaps there'd be an equally obliging one in St. John's to help her move her belongings again. The porters here knew her from her comings and goings for Christopher Jenkins's tutorials. The question was where to move her trunks. Catriona and her father had an apartment in the college's residential west wing. A fleeting association with Annabelle's luggage probably wouldn't do her friend's reputation any harm, though what story she'd tell about her eviction, she didn't know. The mere thought of spinning yet another half-truth made her feel ill.

The porter's lodge lay abandoned. The quadrangle of the college was preternaturally still, except for a lone student strolling along in the shadows of the arcade opposite.

She hovered on the limestone path. Last night had taken her rudder and her sail, leaving her adrift like flotsam. Turning left to the west wing or back to the lodge was an impossible decision.

The student disappeared through the archway to the next quad. No doubt he was going someplace warm and purposeful.

She turned back to the lodge.

The lights had been lit, and there was movement behind the windows.

She walked back to the door and gave a hesitant knock.

From the corner of her eye, she saw the archway at the end of the limestone path to her right, and she frowned, unable to pinpoint the niggling feeling at the back of her mind.

The door to the lodge creaked open and revealed a stout, white-haired porter. "Good morning, miss," he said. "How may I help you?"

"Good morning. I'm a student at Lady Margaret Hall and I—"

And then she knew. The student. The student in the arcade. His lanky form. The ambling gait.

All the fine hairs rose on her body.

She turned on her heels.

"Miss?" the porter exclaimed.

She was already walking toward the archway, the hasty fall of her footsteps echoing from the surrounding walls. By the time she reached the archway, she had broken into a run. Panting, she looked left, right—and caught the movement of a door to the west wing falling shut.

She dashed.

The door opened to a narrow, poorly lit corridor, musty with the smell of ancient stone walls.

The young man had turned right and was moving quickly toward the door at the end of the corridor.

"Sir!"

He didn't break his stride; if anything, he walked faster.

She started after him. "Sir, a word."

His shoulders went rigid.

Bother. What would she say if he was in fact not who she thought he was?

Still, she was surprisingly unprepared when he turned and she was face to face with Peregrin Devereux.

"Oh, goodness," she exclaimed.

Long, lank hair and a pasty pallor detracted considerably from Peregrin's charms. He looked like a creature that only came out at night.

She rushed to him. "Are you all right?"

"Why, good morning, Miss Archer," he said, politely ignoring the hand she had instinctively put on his arm. She snatched it back. "What an unexpected pleasure," he continued. "What brings you to St. John's at this ungodly hour?"

He stiffened when the door behind him swung open.

Annabelle glanced around him, and her chest flooded with relief when she saw Catriona standing in the doorway. "Catriona," she said, "I was just looking for you."

She made to move toward her friend when she noticed the small basket under her arm.

And her utterly guilty expression.

"Catriona?"

Catriona gave her a weak smile. "Annabelle. And Lord Devereux. What a surprise." She sounded guilty, too, and tried hiding her basket, all shifty.

One could almost hear the sound of Peregrin rolling his eyes.

Annabelle stared from one to the other as memories began to strike: Catriona's blushes whenever Peregrin was near, her effort to go without glasses for the ball at Claremont . . . oh, by the fires of Hades.

Her gaze dropped to the damning basket on Catriona's hip. "This is food, isn't it," she said, "food for Lord Devereux?"

Catriona glanced at Peregrin. Asking for permission, was she?

"Do you know that he has been missing for more than a month?" she demanded. "That Scotland Yard is turning over every stone in England to find him as we speak?"

Peregrin and Catriona gasped in unison.

"So you knew," Annabelle said, incredulous.

"How do you know?" Peregrin demanded.

She whirled on him. "Does your brother know you are here?"

His brows flew up at the Duke of Montgomery being called "his brother."

"Miss—"

"Well? Does he?"

"With all due respect, I'm not certain why you ask."

Because he had just been kissing me when he learned that you were gone. Because I held him and could feel his heart crack inside his chest when his own brother had betrayed him. Because whatever hurts him hurts me.

Hypocrite. She had hurt him most of all last night, when she had mercilessly tossed his love, his proposal, and his trust back at him.

She rose to her toes, right into Peregrin's gaunt, aristocratic face. "How could you?" she said. "He doesn't know whether you are dead or alive."

Peregrin's gaze narrowed slightly. "I apologize, miss," he said. "Again, I'm not quite certain what for exactly, but it was not my intention to agitate you."

Oh, his polite restraint could go rot. "I'll speak frankly, then," she said. "You disappeared. You ran away instead of following perfectly reasonable orders, and while you hide in some cozy nook and leech off a girl's goodwill, your brother hardly sleeps because he's worried sick about you."

Two hectic flags of color burned on Peregrin's cheeks; if she were a man, he'd probably deck her. "For some reason, you know a great deal, miss, I grant you that," he drawled, "but you are wrong about one thing—Montgomery is never, ever worried sick about anything. He has neither the temper nor the heart for it, and should I indeed have elicited emotions of the kind in him, I assure you it has much to do with my position as his heir, and very little to do with myself."

Annabelle's hand flew up. She checked it, just in time, but for a blink both she and Peregrin stared at it, suspended in the air, ready to slap a nobleman's cheek.

As Peregrin's gaze traveled from her hand to her face, a suspicion passed behind his eyes. "Miss?"

"How little you know him," she said softly. "Poor Montgomery, to never be seen for what he is by the very people he loves. He does have a heart, you see, a restrained, honorable heart, but it bruises just like yours and mine, and I wager it is a hundred times more steadfast. He is a rare man, not because he is wealthy, or powerful, but because he says what he means and does what he says. He could be a self-indulgent tyrant, and yet he chooses to work hard to keep everyone's lives running smoothly, thinking of everything so others don't have to. And if you, my lord, had but one honorable bone in your body you would help him carry his infernal load of responsibilities instead of acting like a spoiled brat."

She all but spat the word *brat*.

Peregrin had gone pale beneath his pallor.

"Annabelle." Catriona had wedged herself between them, her up-turned face a blur.

"He does have a heart," Annabelle said, "and I love him."

"Annabelle," Catriona said, "you mustn't—"

"I love him, but I lied to him, and now he will forever think badly of me." There was a break in her voice.

Catriona curled a hand around her shoulder, her large blue eyes soft with compassion. The glimpse of kindness proved too much. For the first time since that fateful summer years ago, Annabelle burst into tears.

⁓⤬⁓

"I love him!"

"She's been like this for the past half hour," Hattie told Lucie in a low voice.

The suffragist leader stood in the door to the Campbells' small sitting room, still in her coat and scarf, tendrils of her pale blond hair slipping from her hastily pinned updo.

Annabelle was curled up in the armchair, her body racked from the force of the sobs wrenching from her throat, as if a lifetime of misery were pouring out of her. Catriona was perched on the chair's armrest, awkwardly patting Annabelle's back.

"Well, hell's bells," said Lucie.

She strode to the cabinet on the wall opposite, her intuition rewarded by the sight of a row of glinting bottles when she opened the doors. She uncorked a brandy bottle and poured two fingers into a small tumbler.

"Drink this," she ordered, thrusting the glass at Annabelle.

Annabelle glanced up at her with red-rimmed eyes. Her fine nose glowed an unbecoming pink.

"Is this liquor?" she sniffled.

"Try it," Lucie said darkly. "I promise it is not half as bad as keeping secrets from your friends and cavorting with the enemy. Montgomery, Annabelle? Of all the men in the kingdom!"

Annabelle stared into the tumbler. "He's not the enemy," she said dully. "He was the one who got the permit for the demonstration. He did us a favor. And I—"

"Love him, yes. So you said." Lucie reached back and dragged a chair closer. "And he got us the permit, you say? Why don't you start at the beginning?"

Annabelle nipped on the brandy and made a face when the liquid numbed her lips. "It hardly matters now, does it?"

"Then why are you carrying on as though the world has ended?" Lucie asked, unwinding her long scarf.

Because it has.

Her heart shriveled and died every time she recalled the look on his face when Sebastian had walked out. As if she were his personal Delilah, his Salome, every treacherous female known to man.

She took a gulp of the brandy. "He must despise me," she croaked.

Lucie's silvery eyes were shooting sparks. "That cad," she growled. "I can't believe he seduced you, and under the protection of his own roof, I presume."

"He didn't seduce me," Annabelle protested. "Well, perhaps a little." She had been quite seduced the moment he'd stood before her, hat in hand, uttering a rare apology on a hill in Wiltshire. "It wasn't his fault."

"Goodness," Lucie said, "of course it is. Remember you are a suffragist; we don't believe the tale of the evil temptress and the hapless man. He knew exactly what he was doing."

Annabelle bristled. "What if I told you that I was quite willing?"

Lucie rolled her eyes. "Annabelle, he may look like a cold fish, but he is ten years older than you. He's a calculating strategist, and gained the queen's favor by making grown men do what he wants them to do. You didn't stand a chance, and he knew it. Be honest— did he say all the right things? Did he make you feel as though you had known each other for years, understood each other without words?"

Oh, had he ever done that. "Yes," she whispered.

Hattie made a soft sound of dismay.

Lucie gave a grave nod. "That's how they do it," she said. "I'm so sorry I sent you to lobby the bastard."

"He proposed to me last night," Annabelle said.

A collective gasp rose around her. It was almost funny, the three identical expressions of openmouthed shock.

"Proposed . . . marriage?" Hattie squeaked. Her eyes were perfectly round.

Annabelle nodded. "He appeared in Mrs. Forsyth's house last night to do it. I . . . I refused. It caused a scene, so Mrs. Forsyth asked me to leave."

Silence. A heavy, roiling silence of disbelief.

"Hell's bells," Lucie muttered, and she rose and walked to the liquor cabinet to pour herself a brandy.

"And you refused?" Hattie asked breathlessly.

Annabelle swallowed. "Yes. I could hardly accept him, could I?"

Three vigorously shaking heads were the swift, unanimous answer.

"I mean, you could," Hattie said, "but it would be the scandal of the decade. No, the century. It would, in fact, become a legend—"

"I know," Annabelle said, interrupting her, "I know. It's why I refused him. Oh." She furiously dabbed her sodden handkerchief at her eyes as tears welled afresh.

"I can't believe he proposed," Hattie said, shaking her head. "Not that you aren't worth proposing to," she added hastily, "but it seems such a mad, wild thing to do for such a cold . . . I mean, clever man."

Annabelle gave her a tired smile. "He quite sensibly asked me to be his mistress first."

Lucie's eyes narrowed dangerously. "On the same night?"

"No," Annabelle said, "at Claremont."

"I'm glad you refused *that* offer," Catriona said. "We could be friends with a scandalous duchess, but hardly with a duke's mistress."

Annabelle placed the empty tumbler on the small side table.

"And now," she asked quietly, "will you be friends with me now?"

Hattie frowned. "Why wouldn't we?"

"Because I punched a man," Annabelle said, "because I was arrested, I've been rusticated, I've been propositioned by a duke, and I've been thrown out of the house by my own chaperone."

Lucie's lips quirked behind her brandy glass. "It sounds to me as though you could use a friend or three right now."

"I'm a walking scandal," Annabelle snapped.

Catriona slipped her arm from Annabelle's shoulders and folded her hands in her lap.

"I saw him kissing you at the ball at Claremont," she said, "and I've been your friend since, have I not?"

Annabelle gaped at her. Well, yes. Catriona had been in the hall-

BRINGING DOWN THE DUKE

way when she had left the alcove. She had pointed out her messy hair . . .

"You kissed? At the ball?" Hattie shrieked.

And it seemed Catriona hadn't even spread the gossip.

"Why are you so kind?" Annabelle demanded. "Why aren't you judging me, or exchanging meaningful glances, or trying to wash your hands of me?"

As every single one of the village girls she had once considered her friends had done after the whispers had started about her and William? As her own father had done?

Lucie sighed. "For being so clever, you aren't very bright sometimes," she said. "Look at us. None of us are how we should be." She pointed at Catriona. "Too clever. They use her papers to go treasure hunting, blissfully unaware that a woman has written their handbooks, and I believe at one point you wore trousers and crawled through some caves in Egypt, didn't you?" Catriona nodded, embarrassed heat climbing up her neck. "Then there's me," Lucie continued. "My family disowned me long before the little incident with the Spanish ambassador and the silver fork. If my aunt hadn't left me a small trust, which she only did to spite my father, I'd be either destitute or a raving madwoman confined to my bedroom, for I can't be what they want me to be. I'm not passive, I can't be quiet, I haven't ever envisioned myself surrounded by a large brood of children and serving my lord husband and master. And Hattie . . ." She frowned. "I don't actually know what your oddity is."

Hattie crossed her arms. "Why would I have to be odd at all?"

Lucie gave her a poignant look. "Why else would a daughter of Julien Greenfield be stuck elbow-deep in paint under a slave driver like Professor Ruskin every week?"

Hattie's ever-smiling mouth flattened into a sullen line.

Even my sisters know how to make profitable investments. I cannot copy a row of figures in the correct order, and if I didn't have the red Greenfield hair, my parents would think I was a changeling. I suspect they think it anyway. I think they'd prefer it, less of an embarrassment, I suppose."

"Nonsense," Annabelle murmured, "you are lovely as you are."

"Aw." Hattie perked up. "How nice of you."

"You see, Annabelle," Lucie said, "I'm not saying you aren't scandalous, but you are not alone."

A weak smile curved Annabelle's lips. "No. It seems as though I'm in good company."

Her breathing was flowing more easily now, as if the vise clamping her chest had been loosened by a notch or two.

"You need a place to stay," Lucie said.

"I do," Annabelle said, balling the handkerchief in her fist.

Lucie looked smug. "You should have just stayed with me when I offered it."

"I suppose I should have, yes."

"Let's get your luggage, then. Unless there are any more secrets you should divulge first."

"Not on my part," Annabelle said, "but come to think of it . . ." She turned to Catriona, and her friend ducked her head. "Why and where on earth did you help hide Lord Devereux?"

Chapter 30

———⟡———

Peregrin Devereux was a mellow young man with a sunny disposition. It took dramatic events to drive him to dramatic actions. Was there anything more dramatic than seeing a lovely woman like Miss Archer in tears? With the sound of her pitiful sobs in his ears, he made his way from Oxford to Wiltshire without tarrying once.

His bravado withered the moment Claremont loomed into view. It was dead and gone by the time he stood before the dark, heavy door to his brother's study. Nausea writhed in his stomach. Nothing good had ever happened to him beyond this door.

He closed his eyes and tried to remember all the reasons why he was here. Then he rapped firmly.

No one answered.

Peregrin frowned. Where else would Montgomery possibly be?

He pushed into the room uninvited.

The study was dim. The heavy curtains had been drawn and no lamp, no fire had been lit, and the stale smell of cold tobacco smoke thickened the air.

"Sir?"

Montgomery's eyes gleamed like polished stones in the shadows. He was sprawled in his chair behind the desk, his head lolling back against the leather upholstery.

Peregrin had been unaware his brother even knew how to sprawl. It shocked him almost as much as the empty bottle of Scotch amid the chaos on the desk. And chaos it was. The usually meticulously aligned stacks of papers had toppled; sheets were strewn across the floor as if they had been scattered by a gust of wind.

"Sir . . ."

The duke's hooded gaze slid over him, and Peregrin's throat squeezed shut. His brother's eyes lacked their usual eviscerating edge, but he could still level a calculating enough stare to make a man squirm.

"So you have returned." Montgomery's voice sounded rough from disuse. Or from draining a bottle of Scotch? There wasn't even a glass. Egads! Had he drunk straight from the bottle's neck?

"You look awful," Montgomery remarked. "I'd offer you a drink but as you can see, the supply has dried up." He eyed the empty bottle before him balefully, then prodded it with a fingertip.

Peregrin's mouth opened and closed without producing a sound, like a puppet that had forgotten the script.

His brother waved at the chair opposite with a dramatic flourish of his hand. "Sit down, halfling."

Warily, Peregrin sank onto the edge of the seat.

"Well," Montgomery drawled, "have you perchance lost your speech along with your loyalty?"

"It's just that I thought you didn't drink."

"I don't," Montgomery said curtly.

"Of course you don't," Peregrin said quickly.

"Precisely," Montgomery slurred.

Peregrin had hardly seen a man more drunk in his life, and as the head of a drinking society, he'd seen his fair share. The duke was completely pissed, and no doubt held upright only by his inhuman discipline.

He didn't know what made him say what he said next: "Is it because Father drowned in a puddle when he was in his cups?"

Montgomery's gaze narrowed. "How did you learn that?"

"The usual way. People whisper. I have ears."

Montgomery was quiet. His sight adjusted to the low light, Peregrin could see his brother's face clearly now and found he wasn't the only one who looked awful. Montgomery's features were lined and harsh with tension, but most alarming was the grim set of his mouth. It was a fatalistic grimness, not his usual determined one that said he was about to embark on a grand mission. No, this was an altogether different level of grim.

Finally, Montgomery moved. He switched on the desk lamp, then rifled through a few hopelessly disarrayed sheets, unearthed a slim silver case, and took out a cigarette. He fumbled with the matches, squinting with concentration until one finally hissed to life. He exhaled a stream of smoke toward the ceiling before he met Peregrin's eyes. "Yes," he said. "I don't drink because Charles Devereux ended his life drunk and facedown in a puddle."

A mighty emotion welled in Peregrin's chest. He had thrown out his question because that was what he did: chancing things, following risky impulses. He hadn't expected to reel in a flat-out admission from his brother. Almost as though they were talking man to man.

"Why was I told he had a riding accident?" he ventured, pushing his luck.

Montgomery rolled the cigarette between his fingers. "To keep the past from haunting you."

"I do not need protecting from ugly truths," Peregrin muttered, trying to not remember Miss Archer's scathing verdict that he was a *spoiled brat*.

"It's not about the truth," Montgomery said. "The stories we hear about our fathers can become like a cage to the mind, dictating to us the things we fear or think we should do. Or they give us excuses to be weak. When a man with thousands of people depending on him drowns in a puddle because he was too drunk to stand, what does it say about him?"

Peregrin thought about that. "That he was terribly unlucky?" he suggested.

Montgomery glared at him. "Possibly that, too," he finally allowed. "Why are you here?"

Just like that, the nausea returned. Fear, guilt, and shame congealed in the pit of his stomach.

"I should have never left."

"Indeed," Montgomery said, carelessly flicking ash from his cigarette onto the rug.

"And I saw my error a while ago, but then I did not dare to return, and the longer I stayed away the more difficult a return seemed to become."

"Quite a conundrum." Montgomery nodded without sympathy.

"But then I came upon Miss Archer today," Peregrin said, "and she seemed . . . in distress . . . over you."

Blimey, he could not remember now why it had seemed a good and righteous idea to go there.

Montgomery was oddly frozen in his chair, a disconcerting flicker in his eyes.

"There is just no escaping her, is there," he muttered, "no having her, no getting away."

"Sir?"

His brother's metallic glare made Peregrin shrink back.

"Have you come to defend her honor?" Montgomery demanded, "or to ask an explanation from me? Bold of you. Mad, even. But then I know what her green eyes can do to a man, so I'm inclined to let this go."

"Thank you," Peregrin stammered. *Her green eyes?*

Montgomery frowned. "I proposed to her," he said. "I proposed and she rejected me, so I do not see how she can be the one in distress."

For a minute, Peregrin was speechless. "You proposed to Miss Archer," he said faintly.

"Yes."

"Proposed . . . marriage."

"Correct."

"Are you . . . sure?"

Montgomery's lips twisted impatiently. "I'm drunk, not demented. I'm certain I uttered the words 'Marry me,' and, paraphrasing, she replied, 'Not a chance in hell.'"

"Good God," Peregrin said, and a long moment later, "Good God."

"She wants to marry an Oxford don instead," Montgomery said grimly.

"You proposed," Peregrin yelped. "Whatever made you do such a thing?"

"I received a blow to the head when I fell off the horse earlier," Montgomery replied, "and it made everything perfectly clear."

Peregrin felt more confused by the moment.

"But I had to propose to the one woman in England who would turn down a dukedom—because she does not love the duke," Montgomery continued. "But then, she doesn't love the Oxford don, either." He stared at Peregrin accusingly. "It makes no sense."

Hell.

Peregrin sagged back in his chair.

His brother had it bad. He was head-over-heels obsessed, and he knew what happened when Montgomery became obsessed: he wouldn't stop until he had whatever he was obsessing about. But a commoner? Impossible! And after what he had witnessed today, Peregrin was cautiously certain that a lack of love hadn't been behind Miss Archer's—very sensible—rejection. On the contrary.

It dawned on him that right now, he might be the one person manning the switch on the tracks of the House of Montgomery. One way lay almighty scandal. The other, the continuation of things as they should be.

Gooseflesh spread down his back.

"I'm sorry," he managed. "I hear such . . . afflictions do pass."

Montgomery nodded. "Of course they do."

And then he did something Peregrin had never imagined he'd see his brother do.

He dropped his head and buried his face in his palms.

And stayed that way.

Oh, bloody hell.

"She may have rejected you because of the dukedom, not despite," Peregrin blurted. There. Let him piece it together himself.

Montgomery lowered his hands. "What do you mean?" There was a quivering spark of hope in his eyes.

Perhaps he wasn't obsessed. Perhaps . . . it was much worse. Perhaps he was in love.

Christ. If this was what love did to the least sentimental man in Britain, Peregrin wanted none of it.

"It's just that I spent more than a month in hiding because I did not feel equipped to inherit one of the largest dukedoms in the country," he said. "I can see why Miss Archer would have reservations about being officially the reason for plunging that dukedom into scandal."

Montgomery made an impatient sound. "She wouldn't be responsible."

"There are people who always feel responsible." Peregrin shrugged. "They can't quite help themselves."

The duke's expression turned suspicious. "When did you become wise?" he asked. "Where were you hiding? Some cloister Scotland Yard overlooked?"

Peregrin grimaced. "Almost. I was in the wine cellar of St. John's."

Montgomery blinked. "You were underground for near six weeks?"

"I'm afraid so."

Montgomery studied him with an unreadable expression. "Tell me," he said softly, "am I such a tyrant that hiding in a cellar is preferable to following my orders?"

Peregrin's eyes widened. "A . . . tyrant? No."

To his surprise, Montgomery seemed to be waiting. Waiting for more.

Since when was he interested in explanations?

"I want to follow your orders," he said slowly, "it's just . . . daunting. When I was a boy, I couldn't wait to grow up and be like you. And then one day I understood that one does not simply become like you." It had been a terrible day, he remembered, fraught with existential angst. "I began to understand the magnitude of what you do, and how effortless you make it look. For a while, I thought you were simply better made than most men, but then I understood that you were that and still working morning till night in all these offices. And it felt like someone was choking me, thinking of myself in an office until sunset every day, with thousands of people relying on me . . . I will always come up short as duke, even if I did my best, while you do everything perfectly."

"Perfectly?" Montgomery echoed. "Ah, Peregrin. The first temptation of its kind, and I fell like a house of cards." He swayed a little in his chair. "And in case it has escaped your notice, I'm roaringly drunk and I've been contemplating various ways to destroy an Oxford University professor."

"I did that every other day, up at Oxford," Peregrin murmured.

"I'm aware," Montgomery said. "I sent you to the Royal Navy for that reason."

Peregrin froze. Was that where they would begin talking about his fate? If he was lucky, he'd only be escorted all the way to Plymouth and be stuck in the Royal Navy for a few years. If he were to get what he deserved, he'd receive the whipping of a lifetime first, not that his brother had ever had him whipped before, but there was always a first. Almost certainly, he'd have his allowance cut forever, or perhaps Montgomery would disown him and never speak to him again . . .

Montgomery fixed him with a remarkably sober stare over his steepled fingers. "You are wondering what is going to happen to you, aren't you?"

Peregrin managed to hold his gaze. "I'm p-prepared for the consequences of my actions."

And then Montgomery said a strange thing: "You know that I care about you, Peregrin, don't you?"

"Eh. Yes, sir?"

The duke sighed. "I'm not sure you do." He scrubbed a hand over his tired face. "She was distressed, you say?"

"Miss Archer? Yes, quite."

"I can see that it may have been a bad proposal," Montgomery muttered, "and I do think she was lying," he added cryptically.

"Did she know you had fallen off your horse when you, eh, proposed?" Peregrin asked, because blimey, he was as curious as he was disturbed by the whole development.

"Yes. Why?"

"Well, I reckon no lady wants a proposal right after a man has hit his head."

Montgomery was quiet. "I may have called her a coward, too," he said.

Peregrin's jaw dropped. "I'm no expert, but that sounds like a terrible wooing strategy."

"And I—God." Montgomery groaned. "I was not quite myself last night. I was . . . too forceful."

Of course he would have been too forceful, Peregrin thought, because that was exactly how Montgomery was: forceful, intense, and a little frightening. He probably didn't even intend to be frightening. He probably couldn't fathom that him always having a plan, and always expecting everyone to function logically, was enough to frighten the average fellow. It wasn't quite normal, to unwaveringly have the eye on a noble aim and to be able to drop emotions that did not suit. But then, perhaps that was what confinement made of a man—after all, no one had shielded Montgomery from the cage their father's death had left behind.

A hollow sensation took hold of Peregrin, as though he were about to plunge headfirst into the river Isis off Magdalen Bridge— you never knew what was lurking in the opaque waters. The point was, Montgomery needed a duchess, a durable, intelligent one he could not accidentally steamroll, one who kept him in a good mood and off Peregrin's back. And while Miss Archer was in many ways not a suitable bride for him, perhaps in the most important ways, she was. She made Montgomery *feel*. One could even speculate that she would make his brother happy.

Montgomery was probably too drunk to remember much come morning. Hopefully, he would remember what he was going to hear next. He took a deep breath. "I think there is something you should know about Miss Archer."

Chapter 31

Lucie lived on Norham Gardens in a narrow slice of a yellow brick house of which Lady Mabel rented the other half. The arrangement satisfied the expectation that unmarried ladies of still marriageable age must not live alone, and Annabelle woke in her creaky cot in the mornings with a sense of relief—there was no master of the house to answer to, no one who expected things to be done this way or that. Had she so desired, she could have morosely sat in the nook of the bay window until noon every day with the comforting weight of Lucie's cat in her lap.

Lucie occupied one of the two rooms on the top floor and her housekeeper the other, and she had repurposed the whole ground level for the cause. There was an ancient printing press in the reception room, and in the drawing room the piano had had to make way for a sewing machine and bales of fabric for banners and sashes. A large cherrywood filing cabinet was stocked with stacks of blank paper, old pamphlets, and a copy of every issue of the *Women's Suffrage Journal* since 1870. The wall around the fireplace was papered with news clippings, some yellowing, some crisp like the *Guardian*'s front-page article on their fateful demonstration. Left of the fireplace, a large potted plant had withered and died, the brown leaves looking ready to crumble to dust at a touch.

"This place has much potential," Hattie said as she waltzed in with Lucie on her heels. "Are you sure you don't—"

"Yes," Lucie snipped, "I'm sure. This is a space for serious work; no feminine touch is required."

Hattie made a pout. "I still don't understand how pretty curtains would interfere with our work."

Annabelle's lips attempted a smile. It was the same debate every time before they settled down to work, and there was something reassuring in these little routines when everything else lay in ruins. All through last week, their quartet had met here in the afternoons and gathered round the oversized desk at the center of the room like surgeons around an operating table. The monthly newsletter needed to be sent out, and Lucie was planning an excursion to the Ladies' Gallery in the House of Lords in a few days' time.

"Oho, what have we here," Hattie exclaimed, and tugged on a magazine that was half hidden under a cluster of empty teacups. "*The Female Citizen*? How scandalous."

"What is so scandalous about it?" Annabelle asked without looking up. She was folding the newsletters Catriona had cut to size and sliding them into envelopes. Hattie was supposed to put the address on the envelopes, but she sank into her chair with her nose buried in the magazine. *The Female Citizen* was printed in bold, scarlet letters across the title page.

"It's a radical pamphlet," Catriona supplied. "It writes about unsavory topics."

"Such as?"

"Cases of domestic dispute," Hattie murmured, absorbed, "and the plight of unfortunate women."

"Prostitutes," Lucie said dryly, and Hattie shot her a scandalized look.

"Either way, it's barely legal," Catriona said. "Don't be caught reading one in public."

"Who's the editor?" Annabelle asked, beginning to copy the addresses from their members list on the envelopes herself.

"No one knows," Catriona said. "The copies just show up in letter boxes or public places. If we knew who it was, we could put a stop to it."

"Why would you want to stop them?"

Catriona swept up the paper clippings and disposed of them in the bin under the desk. "Because they alienate people to the cause."

"*The Woman's Suffrage Journal* is too soft in tone to inspire much change, and *The Female Citizen* is considered too radical to appeal to the masses," Lucie said. "I can reveal that I have been working toward launching a new magazine soon that is going to be right between the two." She looked at Annabelle. "I'll need assistance, in case you are interested."

Annabelle lowered her pen. "To help you launch a journal?"

Lucie nodded. "I won't be able to pay a shilling, certainly not at first, but I could supply free lodgings." She eyed the cot in the corner by the dead plant. "The lodgings are of course a bit rustic."

"They are just fine," Annabelle said quickly. For the time being, the cot was all that stood between her and life at Gilbert's, a life as a wife, or the great unknown.

Her stomach churned with unease. The day after tomorrow, Christopher Jenkins expected an answer to his proposal. Two days. She could hardly insult him by asking for more time, and the truth was, she didn't have more time. With her stipend suspended and her pupils lost, her sources of income had dried up, and she couldn't eat Lucie's food and sleep in her sitting room forever.

A streak of black fur shot across the floorboards and up the outside of Lucie's skirt.

"Heavens, Boudicca," Lucie chided as the cat settled on her shoulder and wound her sleek tail around her mistress's neck like a small fur stole. "You are awfully agitated lately, aren't you?"

"Perhaps having a visitor in her sitting room is upsetting to her," Annabelle murmured.

"Nonsense," Lucie said, and turned her face into Boudicca's soft fur. "She knows you are one of us, don't you, puss-puss."

A memory flashed, of a beautiful young viscount in a magenta waistcoat. She had never asked Lucie how Lord Ballentine knew she had a cat. And thinking of that waltz inevitably made her think of Sebastian, and how he had walked toward her across the dance floor in a way that said he was out for Ballentine's blood . . .

"Annabelle, before I forget, there was mail in your pigeonhole," Hattie said, and opened her reticule. "I took the liberty of picking it up for you."

The hope that Miss Wordsworth had written to inform her of her reinstatement was quickly dashed. Annabelle frowned at the spidery penmanship. "It's from my cousin Gilbert."

Of course. She was late with her payments. Was he sending her reminders already? The temptation to toss the letter into the fire unopened loomed large.

She sliced the envelope open with the scissors.

Annabelle,

Yesterday morning, the most disconcerting news reached us about you. A letter from an anonymous well-wisher arrived at the cottage. The paper and envelope were thick and costly, and the handwriting most elegant, but the message was outrageous—I was kindly advised to "save you from yourself," as they put it, as it seems you have fallen in with the wrong crowd. There is talk about political activism, police involvement, and even prison! Furthermore, the writer is concerned that you are mingling with unmarried gentlemen . . .

"Oh, dear Lord," Annabelle said, and rose to her feet.

"What is it?" Hattie asked.

"He knows." How could he possibly know?

. . . If the stationery weren't so fine, I'd suspect this was an ill-done prank. As things are, I am deeply troubled by these allegations, deeply indeed. I've repeatedly warned you about the perils of higher education. Now it seems you have plunged recklessly into your own demise, and we both know this isn't the first time, is it?

I suspect it's only a matter of time until your depravity will be known in all of Chorleywood, or worse, by the master of the manor, seeing that it has already reached the ears of respectable bystanders. And this after I fed you, housed you, and entrusted you with the care of my five children!

As an upright family man and a representative of the Church of England, I must lead by example and not associate with the disgraced. Thus, I ask you to not return to Chorleywood in the near future.

With great disappointment,
Gilbert

Her hand holding the letter sank to the table. "Well. It seems I can strike going back to my family off the list."

She began wandering aimlessly around the room as her friends were crowding around the letter, and their gasps of outrage were scant comfort.

"A letter," she murmured. "Five years, and he lets me go with a letter."

"How ghastly," Hattie said. "Is he always like this?"

"I think you are well rid of this one," Lucie said, "and certainly you are well rid of Montgomery if that is how he handles a perfectly sensible rejection."

"Montgomery." The words lodged in her throat. "You think . . . he wrote to my cousin?"

"Well, who else?"

Not him. Surely not him. "He'd never do anything so petty."

"Your cousin mentions fine stationery and elegant handwriting," Lucie pointed out.

"I know, I know. But that could have been anyone. Perhaps one of the suffragists."

"Now, why would they do that?"

Annabelle pressed her palms to her temples. "I don't know. How did the whole rumor reach Oxford? Montgomery would hardly incriminate himself, so I believe someone else knows."

"But who," Catriona said, "and who would take the trouble to write to your cousin?"

Not Sebastian. Even if she had mortally offended him, and even though it would be easy for him to locate Gilbert's cottage . . . The air in the sitting room was suddenly thick as soup.

"I'm going for a walk," she muttered, and made for the door, if only to escape the sound of his name.

⁂

When his carriage pulled up in front of the elegant façade of Lingham House, Sebastian wasn't surprised that Caroline was not in the entrance hall to greet him. He had formally announced his visit with a calling card, and so she was just as formally waiting in the reception room. Always perfectly on protocol, Caroline. And perhaps she knew that he would eventually put two and two together and figure out who had betrayed his visit at Millbank and who had brought Her Majesty's indignation down upon him. As if formality would save Caroline from him making his feelings known.

It had taken him a while to identify her, because he had fallen on his head and had lost the woman he loved, but after some discussions with his man, he was certain.

What he did not know was why she had done it.

She observed him over the rim of her teacup from her place on the French settee, her eyes as pleasantly cool and blue as the afternoon sky outside the windows behind her.

He shifted on his chair. Soft ground or not, his legs had only recently endured the crushing weight of a full-grown Andalusian horse.

"I read this morning that Gladstone is advancing in the polls again," Caroline said. "Will you be able to stop him, you think?"

"I would have been," he replied, "if the queen had told Disraeli to do as I say. But she's presently holding a personal grudge against me."

A tiny frown marred her brow. "How unusual. Her Majesty is nothing if not sensible. Surely she would put a Tory victory above any personal sensitivities?"

He gave a shrug. "It appears that she considers that opportunism."

A shadow of regret passed over Caroline's intelligent face.

He'd often thought that he had cause to be grateful to her. After his wife's betrayal, it would have been easy to become bitter, to see a treacherous, overemotional creature in every female he met. Caroline had been the antidote with her collected, rational ways, showing him that no, they were not all the same. Had his mind closed itself up entirely, he could have never loved Annabelle.

"Say, Caroline," he said, "are you still the treasurer for the Ladies' Committee for Prison Reform?"

Her expression remained unchanged. But there was a soft rattle of her teacup against the saucer.

Because she knew that he knew that she was indeed still the treasurer of the committee. And that she had a direct line of communication with Queen Victoria.

There was a resigned look in her eyes when she met his gaze. "I overstepped the mark," she said.

"There is no question that you did," he said coolly. "The question is, why. Why, Caroline? I had an election to win. Why not wait before carrying tales to Her Majesty?"

She carefully set her cup on the table between them. "I was not sure you would win the election without . . ." She bit her lip.

"Without what?"

She released a sigh. "Without an intervention from the only authority you accept. Before matters with Miss Archer became too public. I confess I never expected the queen to react in such a manner."

He gritted his teeth so hard, it took a moment before he could speak. "You had no right."

She folded her hands in her lap, a small, sinewy knot against her blue skirts. "Had word got out that you were jeopardizing your name for a country girl, the opposition would have used it to shoot your credibility to pieces. Had I approached you directly, you would have put me in my place."

"And so you went behind my back," he said, and damned if she didn't display an utter lack of repentance.

"The prison director told his wife," she said. "Apparently, it doesn't happen often that a duke walks into his office at night to personally extract prisoners. His wife unfortunately is a gossip, and before I could blink, every lady on the committee knew that you had freed a number of suffragists and a few thieves, and had threatened to personally shut down Millbank, and no matter how much of that is hogwash, these ladies went home to their husbands, and half of those men are not your friends."

"Do you think I wasn't aware of that risk?"

"Of course you were," she cried. "The very fact that you obviously chose to ignore it is what frightened me. Why not call in a favor and send some other peer to do it for you?"

"Ask another man to jeopardize his reputation on my behalf?" He shook his head. "And I always tend to matters personally when they pertain to the people I love."

Caroline paled. "*Love.* Montgomery, this isn't like you."

"Don't presume to know me," he said softly.

"I know enough," she shot back, the knuckles of her clasped hands bone-white. "I'm keenly aware why you asked me to be your lover. You are reluctant to use courtesans, and your code of honor forbids you to bed your own tenants or staff, or to cuckold men below your station. Likewise, you wouldn't take up with the wives of fellow dukes. I was tailor-made for your needs: a widow, an equal, and in close proximity. Sometimes I wondered how you would have solved this conundrum if our estates didn't share a border."

The slight quiver to her chin was far more revealing than her words.

"Be assured I was fond of you for your own sake," he said. "Other than that, I fail to see the point in your rant."

A humorless smile curved her mouth. "The point is that nothing you do is ever impulsive. And from the start, your actions over Miss Archer defied rules and reason, beginning with you galloping around the county with her on your horse. I didn't believe it until I saw the two of you together. The very way you look at her—"

He cut her off with a dark, dark stare.

She swallowed. "History is riddled with men brought to their knees by a pretty face," she murmured. "I could not just stand by and watch. I couldn't."

"It is remarkable, the things women do to try to save me from myself these days," he said.

A glance at his pocket watch said the fifteen minutes of a social call were over.

On his way to the door, she called out for him. And for old times' sake, he turned back.

She stood, perfectly composed again, like a steely reed at the center of the room.

"She is a lovely young woman, Montgomery. Society will bleed her dry by a thousand cuts if you officially make her your mistress. In such matters, the woman always bears the brunt."

"I'm aware." He nodded. "Good-bye, Caroline."

Chapter 32

A light rain fell over Parliament Square, redolent of spring, of tender greens and wispy white cherry blossoms. New beginnings, Annabelle thought, whether one was ready for them or not. She handed a suffrage leaflet to an elderly earl striding past. She knew him from sight; he might have sat in front of her in Claremont's music room a while back. He took her leaflet with a nod, and she moved on to the next man, slowly working her way to the entrance to the House of Lords. Catriona and Lucie were behind her, catching whichever gentleman had slipped her net. Hattie should be waiting for them now in the Ladies' Gallery, as that was something her father allowed. Luckily, Julien Greenfield had never found out about Hattie having been in the thick of the demonstration a few weeks ago. But the headlines they had made had put the Married Women's Property Act back onto the agenda of Parliament, though Lucie predicted that the peers would spend hours debating an inane import tariff just to avoid ever discussing women's rights, mark her words.

The gallery was surprisingly uncomfortable, considering that some of the peers in the chamber below sometimes had their lady wives watching from here. The ceiling was too low, a grille separated them from the men, and the air was stuffy with the smell of rain-damp hair and fabrics.

"Be glad the old chamber burned down," Lucie murmured when she saw Annabelle tilting her head this way or that to get a clear view through the dizzying pattern of the interstices of the grille. "Women then had to sit in the ventilation shaft to listen in on meetings. I hear it was boiling hot."

"One could almost suspect they don't want women to watch them make laws," Annabelle muttered.

Down in the chamber, the peers began debating the first point on the agenda—a possible half-percent tariff increase on Belgian lace.

The droning speech of one of the lords was disrupted when the door to the chamber creaked open again. Someone was running late.

"His Grace, the Duke of Montgomery," the usher announced.

Annabelle froze in her chair, shock turning her blood to ice.

Of course he would be here. He'd be the last man in England to shirk his political duties.

She didn't dare move, as if catching a glimpse of his blond head would turn her to stone.

She felt Hattie's hand on her arm, the soft pressure helping to quell the chagrin ripping through her.

She had made her choices. Sensible choices.

Perhaps one day, when she was ninety years old, they would feel like good choices.

"My lords," she heard him say, "I request to bring the Married Women's Property Act forward on the agenda."

The sound of his dispassionate voice sent a powerful wave of longing through her. So much so that the meaning of his words didn't register until Lucie muttered a profanity under her breath.

"Request approved," said the Speaker.

"My lords," Sebastian said, "I request permission to speak on the Married Women's Property Act."

A bored "Aye" rose from the benches. "Permission granted," the Speaker said.

Annabelle gripped the edges of her chair. Cold sweat gathered on her forehead. Knowing Sebastian was only a few dozen feet away and feeling all her senses come alive in response was distressing, but witnessing him launch a tirade against women's rights, in front of her friends no less, would be unbearable. She fumbled for her reticule. She had to leave.

"Gentlemen, many of you will remember the speech John Stuart Mill gave on the floor of the House of Commons fourteen years ago," Sebastian said, "the speech where he claimed that there remain no legal slaves in Britain, except for the mistress of every house."

That elicited a few *Boo*s and calls of "Shame!"

A small hand touched her knee as Annabelle made to rise. "Stay," Lucie murmured. "I have a feeling this could become interesting."

Interesting? It was nerve-racking, being forced to endure his presence so soon, when her heart throbbed with the phantom pain of a severed limb . . .

"The problem is," Sebastian went on, "when one compares a married woman's current legal status and the definition of slavery, it requires a great deal of self-delusion to ignore the similarities between the two."

The peers made ambivalent noises.

Annabelle sank back into her chair. What was he saying?

"We try to smooth over these technicalities by investing women with other powers, more informal powers," Sebastian said, "and there is of course the matter of keeping them safe. The world of men is a brutal place. And yet women visit our offices, approach us in the streets, and send us petitions with tens of thousands more signatures every year to ask for more freedom. They feel that their safety comes at the expense of their freedom. And, gentlemen, the trouble with freedom is, it isn't just an empty phrase that serves well in a speech. The desire to be free is an instinct deeply ingrained in every living thing. Trap any wild animal, and it will bite off its own paw to be free again. Capture a man, and breaking free will become his sole mission. The only way to dissuade a creature from striving for its freedom is to break it."

"My goodness," Hattie whispered, her eyes searching Annabelle's uncertainly. "Is he on our side?"

"It appears so," Annabelle mumbled. But why? He had made it perfectly clear that it would harm his interests to do so.

Indeed, a stony silence had fallen over the chamber.

"Britain has avoided the revolutions of France and Germany because here in this chamber, we always knew when we were approaching a tipping point, when it was time to make a concession to the people to keep the peace," Sebastian said. "The suffrage movement is rapidly gathering momentum, and what will we do? Will we strike back harder and harder? I for my part am not prepared to try to break half the population of Britain. I am in fact unprepared to see a single woman harmed because of her desire for some liberty. I therefore propose a bill to amend the Married Women's Property Act of 1870."

The collective gasp in the Ladies' Gallery was drowned out by the shouting on the floor below. Annabelle didn't remember rising, but she stood, her fingers curling over the grille brass work like claws.

Sebastian stood at the opposite end of the chamber, and even from here she could see his contemptuous frown as he surveyed the tumultuous scene before him.

"To any suffragists in the Ladies' Gallery," he said, his voice rising over the noise, "I say—brace yourselves. For many people, your demands amount to a declaration of war on the master of every household. It is a war you will not win in the foreseeable future. But today, you gain another ally for your cause. I hereby resign from my role as election campaign advisor."

"No!" Her outcry echoed through the chamber.

Sebastian's head jerked toward her.

He couldn't possibly see her here, behind the grate, dozens of yards away, and yet he caught her eye.

The world seemed to slow on its axis as their gazes locked.

"No," she whispered.

Sebastian folded up his paper, never taking his eyes off her. "And, gentlemen," he said, "I am leaving the Tory party."

Chaos erupted.

Annabelle turned on her heels.

"Annabelle, wait," Hattie called out, but she was already squeezing through rows of stunned spectators to the exit. She hasted blindly along the corridor, her blood pumping in her ears. What had he done? His life's mission depended on him winning the election.

She skipped down a flight of stairs. A startled footman swung back the heavy entrance door for her, and she bolted into the open. Wet droplets hit her face. The light rain had morphed into a roaring downpour; the skies had turned the color of iron.

"Annabelle."

She heard him clearly over the rain.

How had he caught up so quickly?

Because he is always one step ahead.

And her body was driven to flee, its animal instincts shrieking that he was out to catch her again.

She would not escape him today.

When his hand wrapped around her arm from behind, she whirled. "How could you?" she cried. "How could you do this?"

He was grasping for her flailing hands. "Do what?" he said. "Do what?"

"You quit your party, and your role as advisor?"

"Yes," he said, and made to pull her close, and she twisted out of his hold like an angry cat.

"You have just caused a tremendous scandal for yourself!"

"I have, yes."

He was already drenched, his hair plastered to his brow, the icy blond darkened to silver. Rivulets of water were streaming down his face and dripping into his starched collar. He hadn't even put on his topcoat before coming after her.

"How could you," she said, her voice breaking.

Sebastian's eyes softened. "A very clever woman once told me to think about on which side of history I want to be," he said. "I made my choice today."

"Oh, don't," she said. "I have no part in making you commit this . . . self-sabotage."

He shook his head. "No one can make me do anything. I decide who or what masters me."

"Then why? Why did you decide to ruin yourself?"

Buffeted by the elements, pitching her voice against the roar of rain, she felt like the trapped wild creatures he had mentioned earlier. She noticed her hands were gripping the lapels of his coat.

"I'm not ruined," he said, "but what I have done for far too long is make decisions that satisfied my duty, but not my personal integrity. The two are not always the same, I found."

She should step back. She should let go.

He raised a hand to cover hers, and his energy surged through her like an electric current, and her heart thumped its first beat in a week. She might as well try to let go of a lifeline.

"The queen will be furious," she managed.

He nodded. "She is. I was at the palace before coming here."

"But what about Montgomery Castle?"

His face shuttered. "It's lost," he said softly. *Lost.* She sensed a sadness, resolve, but no regrets.

Had he known she'd be in the gallery today?

Through a veil of rain, she saw a small crowd gathering at a safe distance away. They were causing a scene, standing so close, the duke sopping wet, and she realized she was not wearing her coat, either. Water ran down her back like a river.

"I'm going to France for a while," Sebastian said conversationally.

"To France?"

"Yes. Brittany. I remember it is nice in spring."

So he would be a country, not a county away. Her foolish heart twisted with anguish.

"How about you?" he asked. His hand had wandered up along her arm and slipped around her back. Not much was missing for an embrace. "Have you accepted your professor's proposal?"

"No," she said dully.

His hand urged her a little closer into the shelter of his body. "Why not?" he murmured.

The rain had made his dark lashes spiky. How she wished she could be immune to his unlikely charms.

"Lucie made me an offer," she said, "to help her with a new women's journal."

"And that is why you didn't accept Jenkins?"

"He is a good man. He might not think he needs it, but he should be with a woman who truly loves him."

A faint smile tilted Sebastian's lips. "And you don't truly love him?"

His other hand slid around her waist, and she stood in the circle of his arms, quivering like a doe ready to bolt. Too late.

"No," she whispered. "I don't love him."

His mouth, smiling and damp from the rain, held her transfixed, and remembering how it felt, both firm and soft, made her want to feel him against her lips. It mattered not that half of Westminster was watching now. Nothing mattered but feeling him again, absorbing the tender gleam in his eyes as he looked down at her. God help them, the pull of attraction between them had not eased, and probably never would, and the restlessness never ceased until they were close. Two halves of a soul, reunited, knowing they would be parted again in minutes.

She raised her grave eyes to his.

"I'm in love with you," she said. "I love you so much that I'd rather be on my own than with another."

He gently brushed a sodden curl back behind her ear.

"Come to France with me," he said.

"Please. I don't have the strength today to resist you."

"Then don't," he said. "I understand my eligibility is much diminished. My ancestral seat is lost, I'm persona non grata at court, and there are going to be very unflattering cartoons about me in the press for the next year or so. Also, as a divorcé, I cannot marry you in a church. But all I have left would be yours, Annabelle, if you will have me like this."

Tears filled her eyes. "I'd have you with nothing but the clothes on your back."

He held himself very still. "Is that a yes?"

The sensation of balancing on the edge of an abyss gripped her, and for a moment she couldn't breathe. One word, and she'd take a mighty plunge. She had thought it took all her courage to build a life of her own, and now, swaying on the precipice, she understood she had to be even braver to give herself, heart and soul, into the hands of another and build a life with him.

Sebastian's arms tightened around her ever so slightly, and she gave a strangled laugh. Come what may, this man seemed ready to catch her.

"I don't know how to run a palace," she sniffled.

His hold on her trembled. "You study at the best university in the world," he murmured. "Something tells me you will be a quick study."

"Yes," she whispered.

He swallowed hard. "Yes?"

She framed his face in her hands. "Yes," she said, "my answer is yes. Truth be told, I was close to crawling back to you to be your mistress, because even that began to look better than a life without you."

He pulled her against him and his chest shuddered as he exhaled a long-held breath. "The only mistress you will be is the mistress of our home."

She turned her face into his wet shirt, adding her tears to the rain. He was going to catch the cough because he had run after her without his topcoat. She swore there and then that he would never have to run or ride after her ever again.

"How can you still love me," she said, her voice muffled by his chest, "after all the cruel things I said to you?"

She felt him smile into her hair. "Darling," he said, "I have only just begun to love you."

Chapter 33

April

Beneath the white blaze of the Mediterranean sun, a yacht was rocking gently on the Aegean sea.

Lounging in a nest of silken pillows in the shade of a canopy, her unbound hair playing in the warm breeze, Annabelle found that her eyes were falling shut instead of staying focused on the letter on her knees. After finishing her second term at Oxford, helping Lucie with her acquisition of a new women's journal, getting married, and becoming a scandalous duchess in the space of two months, her body was finally demanding its due. Besides, the new bride of an amorous man was not afforded much sleep after sunset, so Sebastian frequently found her napping on the deck of the *Asteria* during the day ever since they had set sail from Saint-Malo two weeks ago.

She took another sip from her champagne glass, set it back down on the small side table, and selected a new letter from the looming pile of Sebastian's unopened correspondence. Had it not been for her insistence, he would have left the whole stack behind untouched at his chateau in Brittany. He was enjoying his newly found laissez-faire attitude with his typical thoroughness. She had read two ignored letters from the new prime minister, William Gladstone, who tried to woo Sebastian to become a strategic advisor for the Liberal party, and from Lady Lingham, who, keen to make amends, offered to introduce Annabelle into polite society in a while, preferably as some "long-lost French nobility." And this missive, holy hell, was from His Royal Highness, the Prince of Wales. Sent months ago!

A splashing sound had her pulse kick up. She lowered the letter in her lap and watched as Sebastian's head appeared over the yacht's ladder, followed by the sculpted curves of his bare shoulders.

Her face heated. After they had set anchor at the Peloponnesian coast a few days ago, her new husband had taken one look at his swimming costume and had decided to dive into the sea naked as God had made him. And he was so, so well made. Tall and lean and gleaming wet in the sunlight, he was a sleek Poseidon rising from his element. Rivulets of water were streaming down his torso, across defined bands of muscle and slim white hips. He was already half aroused, and now her skin was heating up all over.

His bare feet left wet tracks on the smooth floorboards as he padded toward her. In his right hand, he held a glossy pink seashell.

He placed the shell next to her champagne flute and looked down at her expectantly. Here under the azure Greek skies, his eyes looked almost blue.

She smiled. "I see you come bearing gifts."

"Treasures of the sea for Your Grace," he said absently.

His gaze had homed in on where her silk robe had parted in the front and revealed soft, bare skin.

"You have a letter from the Prince of Wales," she said.

"Bertie? What does he want?"

"Essentially, he says, 'I didn't think you had it in you, old chap. You were so dreadfully stuffy back at Eton. Come hunting with me in autumn.'"

"Hmm," Sebastian said, his eyes glittering as if he were already on the stalk.

She couldn't resist stretching languidly under his perusal.

He pounced and crouched over her, showering her and his correspondence with salty droplets.

She squawked and raised the letters over her head. "You are getting everything wet."

"That is the intention," he murmured, and began scattering kisses down between her breasts, pushing her robe open wide.

Pleasure throbbed through her at the hot, urgent feel of his mouth. She shifted restlessly as he kissed lower. "You, sir, are insatiable."

"Are you complaining, wife?"

He licked around her navel.

"No," she managed.

"No?"

His head lowered, and his tongue flicked softly between her legs.

She moaned. "No. Why, it's my duty to please you."

She felt him smile against her. "That is right." He rose over her, then settled his weight on her fully. "And this pleases me very, very much."

She bit her lip when he pushed into her.

"Very much," he repeated, and his eyes lost focus.

She raised her knees higher, allowing him closer, and he gave an appreciative groan.

He rocked into her and it was not long until their cries mingled and he fell against her, his heart hammering against her breast.

She lay still beneath him as the rush of his breath against her neck slowed. Her fingers stroked aimless patterns on his sun-warmed back. High above, the sails were snapping in the breeze.

She tightened her arms around him.

How she loved him.

She had been worried that the price for being with him would be her hard-won slice of independence, but he had continued to be open to her needs and ideas. He had resigned himself to a two-month engagement to let her finish her term at Oxford after he had managed to have her place reinstated. If he had installed a protection

officer against her objections, she never saw the man. His many letters from Brittany had the brevity and efficiency of estate reports, but
that had made it all the sweeter to finally be in his bed again on their
wedding night, where the intensity of his passion had told her more
than words ever could.

He stirred and raised himself onto his elbows, his light eyes searching. "Are you sure you do not want to sail on to Persia tomorrow?"

She grinned. His hair had half-dried and stuck up rakishly.

She smoothed her hand over the ruffled locks. "I like it here," she
said. "It's lovely, not having to do anything or be anywhere."

"Hm." He turned his cheek into her palm, and she felt the scratchy
beginnings of a beard.

"Also, your brother enjoys meeting us for dinner."

Peregrin was two bays away, helping Professor Jenkins with his
excavation work on the battleship. Unlike Sebastian, who had to stay
in the shade or become pink like a shrimp, Peregrin had turned
bronzed and wheat-blond like a Viking in the sun. Being outdoors,
digging and coordinating, suited him infinitely more than sitting
behind a desk, and Jenkins seemed pleased enough with his unlikely
apprentice. Pleased enough to recover somewhat from losing his pro-
spective assistant bride to a duke.

"How about we stay for another week," Sebastian said as he rolled
off her, "and then sail to Persia."

She was quiet for a moment. "Will you go hunting with Prince
Albert in autumn?" she then asked.

He arched a brow. "Are you asking whether we are going to avoid
England forever? We won't. I believe your next term begins in May."

She frowned. "You think our scandal will have died down by
then?"

He gave a short bark of laughter. "No. Next year, perhaps."

Sebastian surveyed his wife, looking rosy and tousled and pon-
derous, and a surge of love made him mount her again.

Her green eyes gazed back at him with a soft welcome. A smattering of golden freckles had begun forming on her nose. He dipped his head and kissed them.

Their scandal would probably never die down. He had changed his place in history for her.

It was his best decision yet.

Besides. He had a feeling that one day, history would squarely side with them, and he was usually correct about these things.

Author's Note

Oxford University opened its first women's colleges in 1879: Lady Margaret Hall and Somerville College. The universities of Cambridge and London had already been admitting female students for years at that point, but when Emily Davies, founder of the first women's college at Cambridge, had scouted Oxford as a possible location in the 1860s, she found herself dissuaded by a strong "monastic tradition, rowdy undergraduates, a lively interest in gossip, and a large population of prostitutes." Gilbert wasn't wrong when he warned Annabelle that Oxford was a place of great debauchery. Nevertheless, the first female students thrived, though it would take until 1920 before they were allowed to fully matriculate and sit final exams like the male students.

Winning voting rights for women would take equally long: the Married Women's Property Act was amended in 1882, two years after Sebastian's speech in Parliament. The amendment allowed women to hold on to some money and property under certain conditions even after marriage. Yet it would still take another thirty-six years until women were allowed to vote or stand as MPs in the UK, so the work for our heroines had only just begun as the story ends.

Their most powerful opponent to women's suffrage would have been their own queen. Victoria was enraged by the women's rights movement. In 1870, she wrote to Theodore Martin that Lady Amberley, a then-prominent feminist, "ought to be whipped." Woman, the queen feared, "would become the most hateful, heartless, and disgusting of human beings," were she allowed to have the same political and social rights as men. Similarly, Elizabeth Wordsworth, the first warden of Lady Margaret Hall and great-niece of poet William Wordsworth, saw no need for women to have a role in parliamentary politics. Miss Wordsworth would later create another Oxford college for women, St. Hugh's, out of her own pocket to help more women access higher education.

What appears to be a contradiction was the common attitude in the Victorian era: most people who supported better education for women did so because they believed it would make women better at their prescribed roles as mothers, homemakers, and companions to men. The idea that women should be people in their own right regardless of how this added value for others was so radical that suffragists faced opposition at every turn. Still they persisted. As such, women like Annabelle, Lucie, Hattie, and Catriona would have been extraordinary people indeed.

But even women pioneers need a place to call home, someone to hold dear, someone who cherishes them for who they are, so it's been a great pleasure to write their happily-ever-after.

Note: I took some artistic license in regard to Dostoyevsky's *Crime and Punishment*—the book was not translated into English until 1885.

Acknowledgments

To finish a book, you need people who firmly stand between you and the life of a crazed hermit.

Bringing Down the Duke wouldn't have happened without the support of a motley crew, and I'd like to express a heartfelt thank-you to:

Lord Robert, commander of pomodores and Master of Nudging.

Sir Richards III, whose edits were everything. Write your own book already.

Mum, who doggedly believed in the story without ever having been given a single page to read.

Oma, because I love you.

Mo, who slogged through first draft chapters rather than study for the bar exam.

Christian, Sarah, Jemima, and Nils, who showed unflagging enthusiasm where others rolled their eyes.

The British Romantic Novelists' Association, in particular the fabulous New Writers' Scheme, which gave me much-needed deadlines, wine, and words of encouragement.

Last but not least, The Lilac Wine Writers Kate, Marilyn, and Montse, who were there every step of the way from the plotting to the final edits. I'm forever grateful for our awesome team— your feedback, hospitality, and open ears made all the difference.

Special thanks to my brilliant agent, Kevan Lyon, and my wonderful editor, Sarah Blumenstock, for taking a chance on Annabelle and Sebastian.

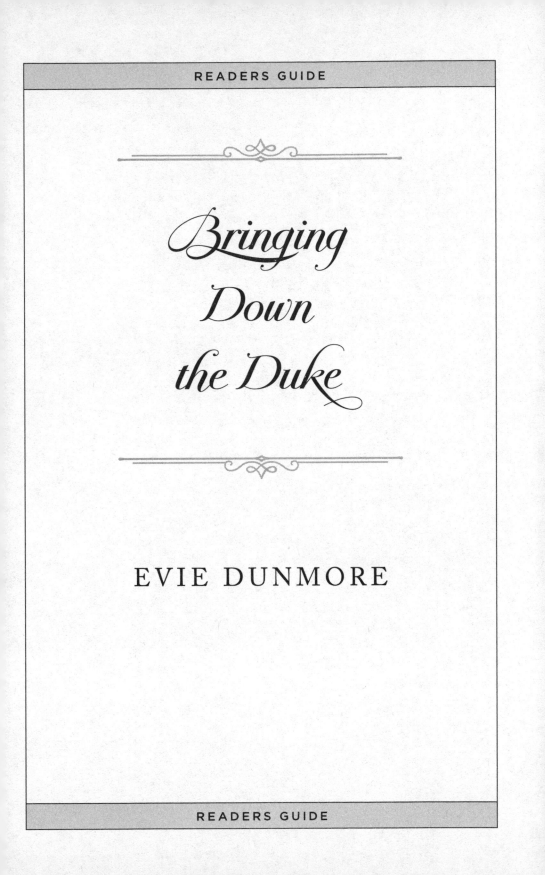

Bringing
Down
the Duke

EVIE DUNMORE

Discussion Questions

1. What obstacles do you think Annabelle and Sebastian will face now that they have finally chosen to be together, considering the opposition their union will encounter in their social circles? How do you envision their first year of marriage?

2. At Lady Lingham's Christmas dinner, Annabelle contemplates how experiencing passion has ruined her for otherwise perfectly eligible men. Is this something you can relate to? How important is passion in a romantic relationship?

3. There are several examples throughout history of British aristocrats who went against protocol and married their commoner mistress, a courtesan, or their favourite actress. Why do you think Sebastian chose Annabelle over his life's work? What consequences do you think he will face?

4. Why do you think Annabelle rejected the position of Sebastian's mistress even though it would have given her the safety net she badly needed? Do you agree or disagree with her choices?

5. When debating the trade-off between freedom and security with Sebastian, Annabelle quotes John Stuart Mill, who says: "It is better to be a human being dissatisfied than a pig satisfied; better to be Socrates dissatisfied than a fool satisfied." What do you think this means? Do you agree or disagree?

6. Annabelle and Sebastian navigate complicated gender and power dynamics as they build their relationship. How would you describe these? How do you think their relationship compares to modern standards?

7. The University of Oxford is an integral part of the book. Why do you think the author chose to set the story there? How does the academic setting impact the story? What does Oxford represent to you?

8. What do you think were the main arguments and worries against women receiving a higher education? How do you see these arguments played out in the book?

9. It is important to Annabelle that she continue her education, even after she marries Sebastian. Is education important to you? Why do you think Annabelle is so determined to receive her Oxford degree?

10. It took British women and their male allies nearly seventy years to achieve the right for women to vote in Parliamentary elections or to run for the office of Member of Parliament. Why do you think the process was so slow? How does it compare to the women's suffrage movement in the United States?

11. Annabelle and her friends organize protests and lobby politicians to fight for their rights. What parallels can you draw to today's political activism? How has political activism changed since then?

12. Both Queen Victoria, the most powerful woman in Europe, and Miss Elizabeth Wordsworth, the first warden of Oxford's first women's college, were against female political activism and women's suffrage. Why do you think such influential and educated women would oppose women's rights? What connections can you draw to present-day politics?

13. In order for the National Society for Women's Suffrage to succeed, they needed to gain the support of influential male figures in the government. What role do men play in modern feminism?

Don't miss Lucie and Tristan's story,
coming Fall 2020 from Berkley!

London, 1880

Had she been born a man, none of this would be happening. She would not be left waiting in this musty antechamber, counting the labored tick-tocks of the pendulum clock. The receptionist wouldn't shoot suspicious glances at her from behind his primly sorted little desk. In fact, she would not be here at all today—Mr. Barnes, editor and current owner of half of London Print, would have signed the contract weeks ago. Instead, he was having her credit and credentials checked and checked again. He had done so very discreetly, of course. But she knew. There were things a woman could do just because she was a woman—such as fainting dead-away over some minor chagrin—and there were things a woman could not do just because she was a woman. And it seemed women did not simply buy a fifty-percent share of a publishing enterprise.

She let her head slump back against the dark wall paneling as far as her hat permitted. Her eyelids were drooping, heavy as lead. It had been another long night away from her bed. But she was close. Barnes had already agreed to the deal, and he was eager to sell quickly because he seemed in some hurry to relocate to India—some trouble with the British treasury, most likely. If she were serious about keeping the place, the side entrance would be the first thing she'd dispose of. From the outside, London Print had an appealing modern look, befitting an established mid-sized English publishing house: a gray granite façade four stories high on one of London's increasingly expensive streets. The interior, however, was as dull as the publisher's editorial choices—desks too small, rooms too dim. And the obligatory side entrance for the only two women working here—one woman, actually, after Mr. Barnes took his typist daughter to India with him—was nothing but a cobwebbed servants' staircase at the back of the house. That entrance would be the first thing to change.

The tinny sound of a bell made her eyes snap open.

The receptionist had come to his feet. "Lady Lucinda, if you please."

Mr. Barnes approached in his usual hasty manner when she entered his office. He hung her tweed jacket onto an overburdened hat rack, then offered her tea as she took her seat at his desk, an offer she declined because she had a train to catch back to Oxford.

More covert glances, this time from the direction of Miss Barnes's desk in the left corner. Unnecessary, really, considering the young woman had seen her in the flesh before. She gave the typist a nod, and Miss Barnes quickly lowered her eyes to her typewriter. Oh, hell's bells. One would think she was a criminal on the loose, not merely a figure in the women's rights movement. Though for most people that amounted to one and the same. Most people gave radicalism a wide berth, lest it might be catching.

Mr. Barnes eyed her warily. "It's the board," he said, "the editorial board is currently trying to understand why you would be interested in taking over magazines such as the *Home Counties Weekly* and the *Discerning Lady's Magazine*."

"Not taking over, but co-owning," Lucie corrected, "and my reasons are the same as before: the magazines have a wide reach within a broad readership, and there is still obvious growth potential. And the fact that you publish the *Pocketful of Poems* line shows that London Print is not afraid to innovate. Everyone with an eye on publishing is interested, Mr. Barnes."

The small format and intelligent marketing of the poetry book had been the one aspect about the publisher that wasn't dusty, a promising silver lining when one secretly plotted to steer the entire enterprise toward the twentieth century. More importantly, there were only two other shareholders, both owning twenty-five percent of London Print each, both living abroad. She'd have as good as nothing standing in the way of her decision making.

"All this is quite true," the director said, "but the board did not know until our last meeting that you were behind the investment consortium."

"I don't see how that changes our deal."

"Well . . . because it is *you*."

"I'm afraid I still don't follow," she said.

Mr. Barnes tugged at his necktie. His bald pate had the telltale shine of nervous perspiration.

Invariably, she had that effect on people—making them nervous. *It's because you always have a plan and a purpose*, Hattie had explained to her. *Perhaps you should smile more to frighten them less.*

Experimentally, she bared her teeth at Mr. Barnes.

He only looked more alarmed.

He took off his small round glasses and made a production of folding them up before finally meeting her eyes. "My lady. Allow me to be frank."

"Please," she said. Frankness was her preferred mode of communication. It was, perhaps regrettably, her only mode.

"You are quite active in politics," Mr. Barnes ventured.

"I'm a leader of the British suffragist movement."

"Indeed. And you must know that as such, you are a controversial figure. In fact, a recent article in the *Times* called you exactly that."

"I believe that article used the words 'nefarious nag' and 'troublesome termagant.'"

"Quite right," Mr. Barnes said awkwardly. "So naturally, the board is wondering why someone with the aim to overturn the present social order would have an interest in owning such wholesome magazines, never mind a line of romantic poetry."

"Why, it almost sounds as though the board fears that I have ulterior motives, Mr. Barnes," she said mildly. "That I am not, in fact, keen on a good business opportunity, but that I shall start a revolution among respectable middle-class women through the *Home Counties Weekly.*"

"Ha ha." Mr. Barnes laughed. Clearly that was precisely what he feared. "Well, no," he then said, "you'd lose readers by the droves."

She gave a grim little nod. "Exactly. We shall leave the revolutionary efforts to *The Female Citizen*, shall we not?"

Mr. Barnes winced at the mention of the radical feminist pamphlet.

He recovered swiftly enough. "Be that as it may, publishing requires a certain passion for the subject matter, an intimate knowledge of the market. These magazines are focused on women's issues, especially the *Discerning Lady.*"

"Which should pose no problem," Lucie said, "considering I'm a woman myself." *Unlike you, Mr Barnes.*

The man looked genuinely confused. "But these magazines focus on healthy feminine qualities and pursuits, such as . . . fashion . . . homemaking . . . a warm, happy family life. Do they not, Beatrix?"

"Why yes, Father," Miss Barnes said at once. Clearly she had hung on every word.

Lucie turned toward her. "Miss Barnes, do you read the *Home Counties Weekly* and the *Discerning Lady's Magazine*?"

"Of course, my lady, every issue."

"And are you married?"

Miss Barnes's apple cheeks flushed a becoming pink. "No, my lady."

"Of course you aren't," Lucie said. "If you were, you would not be allowed to come here every morning to earn your own money by employing your skills at the typewriter. You would be kept at home, entirely dependent upon your husband's wages. And yet"—she turned back to Mr. Barnes—"Miss Barnes is a keen reader of both magazines. Being a single woman apparently does not preclude an interest in *healthy* feminine pursuits."

Now he was clearly at a loss. "But my lady . . . surely you agree that there's a fundamental difference: my daughter would be interested because she has the prospect of *having* all these things in the near future."

Ah.

Whereas she, Lucie, did not have that prospect.

Fashion. A home. A family.

She found her train of thought briefly derailed. Odd, because it shouldn't have been. What Barnes said was only true. She did not possess the attributes that enticed a man, like the softly curving figure and gentle eyes of Miss Barnes; even if she did, she was a political activist, and she was rapidly approaching the age of thirty. She was not just left on the shelf; she *was* the shelf. There wouldn't be a single gentleman in England interested in giving her a warm, happy home. And that was a good thing. She had a printing press in her reception room, and cared for a demanding cat—there was hardly space for a nursery in her house, or her life. And besides, marriage would all but destroy her credibility at this point. Her most prominent campaign was to see the Married Women's Property Act amended. As long as the act was in place and women lost their property and personhood to their husbands upon marriage, she could not marry, even if she wanted to. She did not want to marry. What she wanted was a voice in London Print, and it seemed they were not going to give it to her.

Cold determination gripped her. She hadn't personally cajoled twenty-and-three well-heeled women into investing in this enterprise only to tell them she had failed shortly before the finish line. Was Barnes aware how near deuced impossible it was to find even ten women of means who could spend their money as they wished?

Still, she loathed what she had to say next. Her voice emerged coolly: "The Duchess of Montgomery is a sponsor behind this deal, as you know."

Mr. Barnes gave a startled little leap in his chair. "Indeed."

She gave him a grave stare. "I will call on her in a little while to inform her of our progress. I'm afraid she will be . . . distressed to find her investment was not deemed good enough."

And a distressed duchess meant a displeased duke. A very powerful displeased duke, whose reach extended all the way to India.

Mr. Barnes produced a large white handkerchief from inside his jacket and dabbed at his forehead. "I will present your, erm, arguments to the board," he said. "I am sure this will adequately clarify all their questions."

"You do just that."

"I suggest we meet again in a week."

"I shall see you next Tuesday, then, Mr. Barnes."

∞

Oxford's spires and steeples were blurring into the fading sky when she exited the train station. Normally, the sight of the ancient city she had made her home soothed her. Oxford's timeless golden sandstone structures wore every season well, the wispy pale pink cherry blossoms of spring, the lush greens and cotton ball clouds of summer, crisp blues skies and swirling autumn leaves, the light dusting of snow on gray lead roofs and cupolas in winter. Tonight, the air had the mellow warmth of a dusky evening in May, somewhere between the cooler days of spring and summer.

And yet, some dark emotion was crawling beneath her skin. She tried to evade it by walking the two miles to Norham Gardens at record speed. Still, her body wanted more when she arrived at her doorstep. The muscles in her thighs and calves were fretful, demanding complete exhaustion. She could walk back to St. John's College to see if Catriona was still awake, poring over some ancient script, and tell her about the spineless Mr. Barnes. No. Talking to a friend would not ease her restlessness. In these moments, it would be best to have Thunder nearby. A good long ride would take care of twitchy limbs. But she hadn't seen her horse in nine, ten years, she mused as she wandered through her dim hallway toward her sitting room. Not since her father had declared her persona non grata and she had walked out of Wycliffe Hall. She really should stop using her title; she had been a lady in name only for a long time.

Her lips curved in wry amusement as she surveyed her drawing room when the gaslight had finally guttered to life. The vast, chair-less table in the middle of the room, used for studying maps and preparing suffragist pamphlets, and the sewing machine, now a mere shadow near the wall, its main purpose to make banners and sashes. The newspaper clippings plastered around the cold fireplace. Dozens of letters on her desk, each of them a story of some woman's woes. And there was still the dead plant the size of a man in the left-hand corner. Indeed, every lady worth her salt would abandon this place as fast as her corset allowed.

Small paws drummed on the floorboards as a streak of black fur shot toward her. Boudicca rushed up the outside of her skirt and settled on her left shoulder.

Lucie turned her face into the sleek fur. "Hello, puss."

Boudicca bumped her nose against the top of her head.

"Did you have a fine day?" Lucie cooed.

Another bump, a purr. Satisfied thusly, Boudicca plunged back to the floor and strutted to her corner by the fireplace, her tail with the distinct white tip straight up like an exclamation mark.

Lucie slid her satchel off her shoulder and groaned in half relief, half pain. It was best to not get too comfortable yet. She still had to finish yet another petition letter on the Married Women's Property Act. A tea would be nice, but her housekeeper, Mrs. Heath, had long gone to bed, and she'd probably forget there was water boiling on the stove once she settled down to write. She closed the curtains of the bay window before her desk and lit her writing lamp.

She had just found a comfortable position in her chair when the sound of laughter reached her through the window. She frowned. That high-pitched giggle belonged to Mabel, fellow suffragist and tenant of the adjacent half of the house she rented. And knowing Mabel, there was only one reason why the widow would be tittering like a maiden. Sure enough, there followed the low, seductive hum of a male baritone.

Lucie's fountain pen began scratching over the paper. What Mabel did should not concern her. If brazen enough, a wealthy widow could take liberties with men that no unwed woman would dare, and from what she had had to overhear through the shared bedroom wall, Mabel dared it once in a while. *And why should she not?* After all, most gentlemen took their pleasure whenever an opportunity presented itself . . .

An excited feminine squeak rang through the curtains. She put down her pen. Wealthy widow or not, Mabel was not beyond scandal. Unlike her, Mabel was a student at Oxford, and anything that besmirched her reputation besmirched her fellow female students. The flirtatious pair might be shielded by the large rhododendron bush before her window, but still . . . She rose, rounded her desk, and yanked back the curtains, and movement exploded before her.

She leveled a cool stare at the two shadowy figures that had sprung apart. Faces turned toward her.

Oh. By Hades, no.

The light from her room revealed, unsurprisingly, a disheveled Lady Mabel. But the man . . . there was only one man in England with such masterfully high-cut cheekbones.

Without thinking, she pushed up the window.

"You," she ground out.

Photograph by the author

Debut author **Evie Dunmore** wrote *Bringing Down the Duke*, inspired by the magical scenery of Oxford and her passion for romance, women pioneers, and all things Victorian. In her civilian life, she is a consultant with a M.Sc. in Diplomacy from Oxford. She is a member of the British Romantic Novelists' Association (RNA). Evie lives in Berlin and pours her fascination with nineteenth-century Britain into her writing.

CONNECT ONLINE

eviedunmore.com

f eviedunmoreauthor

🐦 evie_dunmore

📷 evietheauthor